MUMMY'S

Sarah Flint

About *Mummy's Favourite*

He's watching… He's waiting… Who's next?
Buried in a woodland grave are a mother and her child. One is
alive. One is dead.

DC 'Charlie' Stafford is assigned by her boss, DI Geoffrey
Hunter to assist with the missing persons investigation.

As more pairs go missing, the pressure mounts. Leads are going
cold. Suspects are identified but have they got the right person?
Can Charlie stop the sadistic killer whose only wish is to punish
those he deems to have committed a wrong. Or will she herself
unwittingly become a victim.

A gripping, heart-stopping crime thriller, introducing new
series character DC Charlotte 'Charlie' Stafford of London
Metropolitan Police.

To my Mum and Dad, Stan and Sylvia, who died many years ago before I had even attempted story-telling.

They were very much in my mind on the day I received the formal publishing offer for this book. My father would have been 100 years old on that very day in April 2016. It was also the 20th anniversary of my mother passing, joining Dad on his birthday.

I believe it was no coincidence that my hopes should be realised at the same time they were foremost in my thoughts. I wish they were still alive to share my happiness now.

Prologue

It was cold under the floorboards. Cold, sticky and wet. And so very dark. Pitch-black almost. Only the tiniest chink of light. Not enough to give her a clue as to where she was.

Julie Hubbard tried to speak but the thick cloth around her mouth prevented any movement of her dry, cracked lips. Only a thin whimper in the blackness could escape briefly before the sound died in the tiny cavity in which she lay. She moved her tongue and felt the cold liquid fill her mouth. Water. Cool, thirst-quenching, life-prolonging. She gulped it down, moving her tongue again to cover the small tube sticking through the cloth, knowing instinctively that this was her only hope of survival. She didn't dare drink the water too quickly. It had to be rationed, eked out slowly. She didn't know how long she was going to be there. She didn't know anything in fact.

She tried to shift herself carefully. Every muscle hurt. A wad of bedding underneath her body took away some of the cold and discomfort, but her body felt stiff and achy from lying in the same position. Her head pounded in time with her breath, each temple following the same rhythmic pulse. She could barely move her limbs; they were bound together with cord, wrapped around and around and around her wrists and ankles. She could just wriggle her fingers and toes to keep them from getting numb, but that was all. Her fingernails scraped the dirt from the backs of the floor-boards but there was little room to squirm, never mind to bang against the wooden planks. She didn't know where she was but she knew it was remote, away from civilization, away from help. She was on her own. Or was she?

Every sense was heightened now as the muzziness wore off. The air around her was dank, claustrophobic, sweet smelling. It was earthy, musty, but with occasional wafts of cooler, fresher fragrances that slipped in through the gaps. The darkness too was slightly less black and cloying at these tiny spaces. She pushed her body up against the chinks but the boards refused to move, the gaps disappearing into her clothing, a sense of panic overwhelming her at the loss of even these tiny symbols of escape.

She tried to move sideways but the hardness of the impacted earth stopped any further movement. She shifted the other way and her body met something softer. Squirming towards it she managed to twist herself slightly so that her hands touched the softness. She could feel clothing, a belt buckle, flesh. She pulled herself up as close as she could so that she was half facing the form. Her hair slipped across her face into the wetness she had felt earlier. It was sticky and smelt strangely sweet. She wanted to taste it but she daren't. A familiar smell wafted into her nostrils. A smell that she recognized from home, the scent of grown-up children, the scent of boy to man aftershave.

The pounding in her temples grew harder. She strained to see through the pitch-black but there was nothing. From somewhere far away she heard the sound of undergrowth being kicked and stamped upon. The noise was getting louder, joining forces with the noise inside her head, pumping and stamping and pumping. She tried to scream but no sound came out, just the gurgling of the water as it moved down the tube. She swallowed noisily and coughed. Then the pounding was joined by light, streaming all around her, surrounding her as the boards were moved away. She screwed her eyes up as the torchlight bathed her in cold, clammy sweat. Fear, ice-cold and debilitating, stopped her breath as she struggled to make sense of what was happening. She could see nothing but bright light burning into her retinas. Everything behind was shadow. She craned her neck round at the person beside her, wanting to know who they were but fearing the answer. She knew already. She had smelled him. She remembered now. As she opened her eyes, she heard the voice. It was a smiling voice, melancholy, sing-song, pleased with what she was looking at. Laughing at what she was looking at.

And as she recognized the soft curves of her youngest son, Richard's handsome dead face, she saw the vivid red, yawning gash sliced into the soft skin of his neck and the wetness of his blood in her hair and across her shoulders. She heard the voice louder now, mocking her.

'Mummy's favourite. Mummy's favourite.'

Chapter 1

It didn't take long to remove her from the building. Every photo, every item of clothing, every single thing that would remind him of what she looked like, what she sounded like, what she smelled like.

He dropped to the floor and sprayed disinfectant across her favourite spots; the bedside table where she placed her phone, along with the glass of water and the book that she always read at night, when he was trying to sleep. She didn't give a shit about him.

He pulled the sheets back and a waft of her cheap body spray hit his nostrils. How he hated that scent, Impulse, used by her each day, in preference to the expensive perfume he had given her for Christmas. His gift lay disregarded at the back of the dressing table gathering dust, like everything about their relationship. He yanked the sheets off the bed, balling them up and throwing them at the door. The mattress still held traces of her smell. He sprayed it with fabric freshener. He hated her smell.

The clothes and shoes took more space than he'd thought, bin bag after bin bag full of her life's discarded rubbish. He lined the bags up, row upon row, a mountain of her excesses and all at his expense. She had treated him like a mug, just there to pay the bills and deal with her shit. Well now she was gone, and he was glad she wasn't there anymore; glad she was out of his life; glad he would never have to listen to her whining or sarcastic digs.

He ran downstairs and put the bedding into the washing machine, switching it up to the highest temperature setting. If it was ruined it didn't matter. He'd just buy some more. He didn't care if everything about her was destroyed. He just wanted to cleanse the house of every single molecule of the bitch. Filling another bowl with boiling water and bleach he grabbed the mop and started to scrub at the wooden floors, cleaning and exterminating her filth. It didn't matter that it was gone midnight. He would spend all night if necessary. And all the next day. And if she'd chosen to take her favourite little boy, so be it. She reaped what she sowed and she would have to deal with it.

He peered into the bedroom where his other child slept, unaware of the whole situation. His breathing was steady; the duvet pulled back allowing his shoulders and arms to move freely, unfettered by its smothering restraint. A leg stuck out from the side of the bed. A shaft of moonlight shone down on the boy's face, making it appear almost angelic in the darkness of the night. His glance moved from his son's face to a photo on the bedside cabinet next to him. She was in it and he couldn't bear to see her mocking him.

He tiptoed across the room and snatched the photo up, turning it round to stare at her features in the light of the moon. How he hated her.

His son stirred, pulling his leg back under the duvet and turning on to his side away from him. He stared at the photo one last time before pushing it firmly under his arm.

'That bitch ain't never coming back,' he whispered to his son. 'I hope she rots in hell.'

Chapter 2

Charlie Stafford was late. She was always late. Things just happened in front of her. Today she'd helped the ticket collector catch a wayward youth who'd jumped the barriers to escape paying his fare. Last Wednesday it was the pedal cyclist knocked from his bike and on Thursday it had been the old lady crying because she'd lost her purse. Tomorrow it would be something else. However hard she tried to be on time, things just happened!

It had all started on 6th July 2007 when, at the age of twenty, in front of the Commissioner no less, she'd turned up late for her own passing-out parade, having stumbled across two recruits squaring up to each other in one of the site tower blocks. It had been the last ever ceremony to be held in front of the statue of Sir Robert Peel, founder of the Metropolitan police, at Hendon Training school before it closed its doors to new trainees. She hadn't lived it down.

Nine years on and she was still always late. Nothing had changed!

She was either labelled a 'shit magnet' by some of her lazier colleagues or a 'thief-taker' by conscientious officers, jealous of the uncanny way she came across crime and criminals. One thing that was accepted, however, was that you never had a quiet day if you were working with Charlie.

She broke into a slow jog now, her favourite trainers squeaking slightly at the extra pressure. It was Monday and she hated Mondays; Mondays and Wednesdays, but today somehow felt different. She'd been on a course at the end of the previous week. Maybe it was having that extra day off that had made the atmosphere strangely impatient, and maybe, added to the weekend, it was being away for slightly longer? She didn't know what it was but there was something in the air; a new challenge, maybe a new case to pit her wits against.

Lambeth HQ came into sight. She glanced towards its

imposing glass frontage, squinting slightly as the early morning sun reflected against the buildings opposite. It always looked impressive in the mornings, set back a couple of hundred yards from the River Thames on the south side of London; its upper floors looking across towards the Houses of Parliament and Big Ben. It was home to the various squads and departments that serviced the Borough of Lambeth, with its twenty-seven square kilometres of policing challenges: ranging from the London Eye and South Bank in the north, through the clubs and eateries of Vauxhall and Clapham, to the shopping and housing areas of Brixton and Streatham in the south.

She glanced up at the glass trying to identify her office on the fourth floor, before checking her watch. Her team would all be in by now.

Vaulting the cycle railing outside HQ, she stared at her reflection in the glass of the revolving doors, realizing yet again that she'd forgotten to calm the tuft of unruly hair that always presented itself, like the horn of a rhino, at the front of her head. Even short hair managed to defeat her in the mornings. She checked herself critically. Plain, but with potential; or so her mother said. Medium height and athletic, but with a few excess pounds to shed. Skin: clear but rather pasty-looking; time to get out into the countryside for some exercise and adrenalin. As for her clothes; crumpled, with dirty knees and elbows from her tussle with the fare-dodger. All in all, she had to admit that today she did look scruffy, even by her own standards.

Her spirits dipped slightly. Damn, she'd get another dressing-down from her boss, Hunter. Running her hands over her head in a futile attempt to calm the stubborn quiff, she doubted whether, even if she were the commander of Lambeth Borough, he would turn a blind eye to her appearance today.

*

'Ah DC Stafford, you're late again and you look like shit. Glad you could make it though, fresh from your Super Recognizer's course. Where have you been? We've all been waiting for you. Or did you fail to recognize it was 8.30 and not 8 a.m.?'

DI Geoffrey Hunter didn't wait for an answer. 'Right, now we're all here, *at last*. I'll get on.' He accentuated his words and

Charlie felt herself redden at his sarcasm. A bollocking on a Monday morning in front of her colleagues was never the best start to a week.

'Sorry guv,' she tried.

He ignored her. 'We've had a few new reports referred to us over the weekend which I need to assign. One of which has potential.'

Charlie pricked her ears up. There were rarely cases with potential in her department, unless Hunter meant potential for trouble. She worked in the Community Support Unit, a branch of the CID or Criminal Investigation Department, having only acknowledged her ambition to investigate major crime in the last year.

Up until then she had put off becoming a detective, preferring to be out on the streets dealing with crime as it happened, and as it often happened right in front of her she had excelled.

Her first big collar after leaving Hendon to join Charing Cross police station had been a rapist she'd recognized from an e-fit. On little more than a hunch and a similarity to the suspect, she'd found him in possession of duct tape, a knife and keys to a Vauxhall. Having scanned the streets, she'd located his car, and discovered photos and details of a female in a nearby street. Her suspicions aroused, she'd headed straight to the woman's address and kicked the door down only to find her gagged and taped up in her bed, the last victim of a series of horrific attacks perpetrated by the same suspect. The mental anguish of the victim in the case affected Charlie greatly. It was personal. She went out of her way to stay with the woman through every step of the investigation, determined to obtain justice for her. She knew what it was like to be on the receiving end of injustice. It was exactly for this reason she'd joined the police.

She stayed at Charing Cross initially loving the adrenalin of the streets before transferring to Lambeth borough, where she continued to revel in her work. She was rewarded with an advanced pursuit driving course and the newly developed Super Recognizer's course and was head-hunted by some of the specialized CID squads in the Met investigating serious crime and criminals.

After being shot at in a backstreet of Brixton, she'd decided that CID was the place to really make a difference so returned to Hendon Training College; only to find it a shell of its previous self, with many of the buildings and tower blocks empty and derelict.

She'd emerged as a detective constable and found herself immediately posted to the CSU, first stop for all budding CID officers. Nearly six months later she was still there.

The unit had the remit to deal with any allegations involving domestic violence, race, faith, sexual orientation or disability, but as she was just discovering, it was the most risky and politically explosive unit in CID. If you got it wrong here, your career would be ended before it had begun.

'Anything interesting?' Charlie asked.

She hoped it would give her the chance to get out and about and, if she did get out, that Hunter would come with her. He might be her boss but he too liked to be out on the streets and had the reputation for attracting action.

'Like I said,' he looked to be studiously avoiding making eye contact with her. He was obviously keen to make her sweat. 'It has potential. A woman and her son, missing since Friday, reported by her husband today. Nothing too sinister at the moment, although the husband sounds like a nasty bastard. It's being dealt with by the missing persons unit, but they've asked us to take a look, as the couple have a history of domestic violence. The chances are the wife's probably just come to her senses and moved out, but it's raised concerns because they have another son who has been left behind.'

He paused and this time looked directly at her.

'Charlie, I want you to look into what we know about them. How many previous DV reports? When was the first report and the last, and if any include an assault or threat to assault. If there are actual assaults, see if they have escalated in severity. It's strange for a mother to take one son but leave the other, particularly if there is a violent history.'

He ran his gaze up and down her critically, his face puckering up in displeasure.

'Once you've done your research, smarten yourself up and we'll go and pay the husband a visit.'

She nodded, her face glowing red.

'There's an iron in my office. When, and only when I think you're smart enough, we'll head out to his address and speak to him personally. I'm more than happy to get some fresh air and see what he's got to say in person, but only if you look like a professional police officer and not something dragged up from a gutter.'

He gave her the same look as he would give a wilful teenager, but she didn't miss the glint of good humour and the slight shake of his head as he turned heel.

Immediately the door closed behind him, and probably before he was out of carshot, Paul let out a loud snigger.

'Charlotte Stafford. What do you look like?'

'Oy, don't call me Charlotte, only my mother is allowed to call me that. And then only if she is having words with me.'

'I bet you get called Charlotte all the time then!'

The quip caught her off guard just for a second. She remembered the first time anyone had called her Charlie, many years ago on a sandy beach in West Wittering. The name had stuck with her from then on. She swallowed hard and pinned a smile back on her face.

'Maybe,' she said and her colleagues burst into laughter.

She worked with five others: Bet, Paul, Colin, Sabira and Naz, though today Sabira and Naz were on the late shift.

Paul threw an arm around her protectively. 'Well, we all love you,' he paused and squeezed her round the shoulder, 'whatever the nasty man says.'

Charlie laughed. Paul was only joking but she didn't like to hear Hunter called that. The 'nasty man' was actually the man she most respected in her life. She'd never known her real father, and her step-father certainly didn't deserve any respect. Aside from some of the male colleagues she now worked with, there had been few other male influences that had garnered her respect. Out of all her bosses, Hunter was definitely the one she admired the most.

He was Hunter by name and certainly a hunter by nature, though his look was more prey than predator. At thirty years old, he'd had the appearance of an old man, short, chubby, bald and ruddy faced. Now, as a fifty-six-year-old Detective Inspector, his body was at last representative of his age.

Charlie loved the man, not in a romantic way; he was old enough to be her father. But he was everything she aspired to be: a fearless leader, a principled, hard-working officer and a thief-taker second to none; but with the added benefit of being highly organized and always punctual. She knew beneath the stern veneer that he loved her, in his own way, too, although he would never in a million years admit it and treated her more like an errant schoolchild.

Judging by his reaction today, however, she was lucky he had still assigned her to do the enquiries.

Anyway Paul was only teasing. He could be a mischievous bugger sometimes and she knew that he had long ago worked out that she had a soft spot for Hunter. He only had to mention their boss's name to get her blushing.

She put her arm around Paul's waist and squeezed him back. She instinctively recognized a friend, foe or neutral, almost within minutes of a first meeting, and he was definitely a friend. He also had the knack of seeing through her outwardly hard-working, happy, confident exterior to the insecure, vulnerable soul underneath. Not many people could do that; she put on a good act.

He was looking rather bleary-eyed this morning. She'd noticed him while Hunter was speaking, sipping carefully from a steaming mug of black coffee. Paul specialized in the sexual orientation and transgender investigations. He was normally immaculately turned out, his blonde, slightly thinning hair gelled carefully and his beard neatly trimmed. Large diamond earrings glinted in both ears and his tongue sported a gold stud which he clicked against the back of his teeth when he was concentrating. Finishing off his smart, man-about-town image were jeans, stylish shoes and a neatly pressed shirt buttoned up to the collar. Today, though, his usual clipped appearance was more dishevelled than dapper.

Keen to change the subject away from herself she patted him on the back.

'Bit of a heavy weekend eh, Paul?'

He wiped his brow, pulling an expression of mock indignation.

'You can't imagine what happened to me on Saturday night, Charlie. I met the man of my dreams, complete with the most *amazing* nipple rings. Get yourself sorted and I'll fill you in, so to speak.'

Charlie nodded. She took off her jacket, tried and failed to brush the creases out of her shirt and trousers, and ran her fingers through her hair for a third time.

'Right, that's me sorted.'

Bet looked up from her computer terminal and shook her head.

'What are you like, Charlie? Pop into the toilet and wet your hair down then slip my coat on and give me your stuff. I'll run the iron over them. Don't let the boss see you like that again or next time he really will do his pieces. Or worse than that, you'll be grounded.'

She did what she was told straight away. There was no way she wanted to be left in the office, if there was a chance of getting out she wasn't going to argue with Bet either.

Bet was a friend too, almost twice her age and more like a surrogate mother than a colleague. She was the oldest member of the office, early fifties, apple-shaped, thick, greying hair, smoked like a trooper and married four times. There was nothing Bet didn't know about the world of domestic violence, both from work and personal experience. Coppers could be just as volatile as the next man or woman and she'd picked a few bad apples in her time.

Charlie logged on to her computer while Bet busied herself.

She flitted between listening to Paul's exploits and dispensing with easy e-mail queries for the first few minutes, before slipping her freshly pressed clothes back on, shielded behind the coat and the computer screen.

The Monday morning revelations were dying down now. She tapped in the name Hunter had left on her desk and watched the screen start to fill, suddenly desperate to get on with her allotted task. If Hunter saw potential, then it must have potential. And she would be the one to prove he was right.

Chapter 3

Julie Hubbard, forty-two years old, married only the once to Keith, was missing with their son Richard, aged fourteen. Their other son, Ryan, aged fifteen, was still with Keith. Both Julie and Richard were fit and healthy, neither had ever gone missing before and there was no suggestion that either might be mentally unstable, suicidal or had a history of self-harm.

Charlie scanned through the missing person's report. There was a history of domestic violence; she'd check that out shortly. Julie had no recorded convictions, however Keith Hubbard was known for assault, possession of weapons, affray and public order offences. He was certainly a volatile and violent man. Julie may well have just left him. In fact, reading the report, the domestic situation certainly seemed as if it could be the reason for the two disappearances.

Other theories were mooted. Maybe Julie had taken Richard out of school early for some kind of mother/son bonding holiday. It was, after all, only two days before the Easter school holidays. Richard's school was being contacted to confirm whether or not Julie had requested the absence.

Charlie suddenly thought back to her childhood. Her own mother, Meg, had made a point of having individual "special days" with her and her two half-sisters, Lucy and Beth, since that Wednesday many years ago when the family's cosy existence had imploded. She had loved those days, alone with her mother, doing her choice of activity. Somehow those random days out with just Meg took away some of her loneliness; but they could never stop her hating Wednesdays.

The more Charlie thought about the theory of mother/son bonding though, the more she discounted it. It was inconceivable to her that Keith or Ryan, in particular, would not know they had gone away. She remembered the lengths Meg had gone to, to make sure she, Lucy and Beth were all aware of each and every special day. Her mum was always scrupulously fair and had to be seen to be fair. She had no favourites. Both her husbands had let her down but she loved her three daughters equally, irrespective of their fathers' failings. No, there was absolutely no way that her mother would have taken one of them away for a weekend, or even a single day, without first clearing it with the others. It would be unthinkable.

She suddenly felt incredibly sad. She still saw her mother and sisters regularly but they had lost that closeness more recently. Lucy and Beth, the children of Meg's second marriage, were still teenagers and were living at the family home in Surrey, sharing the same likes and dislikes in music, fashion and boys. Charlie had moved out to a rented flat in Clapham, nearer to work, and was living alone. She missed her sisters and her mother. Even though the drive was less than 45 minutes, she sometimes felt they were a million miles away. Especially her mum. She wished they could talk like they'd used to, but since her brother's accident it was just too difficult.

The tannoy sounded and she snapped back to the computer screen, scrolling down to Keith's statement. Initially he thought they might have gone away for the weekend without telling him so he didn't bother to report them missing. Then when they didn't return or contact him he presumed Julie had left him and taken the kid. Things hadn't been too good between them of late. It was bollocks as far as Charlie was concerned. If he hadn't known they were going, he should have reported them missing on the Friday night, or certainly by Saturday morning, when they hadn't turned up. No mother takes one child and leaves the other; unless there was something wrong. Or there was something that Keith wasn't telling them. Everything in the report left unanswered questions. Nothing made sense. There was something amiss and it started with Keith Hubbard.

*

There were three DV reports in total; not as many as other cases she'd dealt with so far, but then, how many more incidents had happened before getting to the point where police were called?

The facts made horrific reading. Bet had given her the statistics when she'd joined their office and she had them stored in her head for easy consumption. Statistically, domestic violence issues affected one in every four women and one in every six men and led on average to two women being murdered every week and thirty men each year. DV allegations accounted for sixteen per cent of all violent reported crime, but were also the crimes most likely to go unreported and the most common crime leading to suicide.

A lot of the time the information she stored was useless, but these facts weren't irrelevant, they were shocking, and perhaps the most shocking of all, that Charlie could not get out of her head, was that on average there were likely to have been thirty-five assaults before a victim called police. Thirty-five! She couldn't believe it when she first heard that particular statistic and it made her job in the unit that much more significant. She could really make a difference to the dozens of women and men living in fear of day-to-day abuse. If only they would let her. She wondered how many assaults Julie had endured before she'd first picked up the phone.

According to the reports, the family lived in a quiet residential area, the sort of street where nobody would guess what went on behind closed curtains and would never dream of asking.

She read the first report. Police had been called to a heated argument between Julie and Keith. It had escalated to the stage where Julie had been pushed around, held against the wall and forced down on to the bed. Nothing sexual had happened, but Richard and Ryan had witnessed the fight. Indeed, it had been Richard who had made the call to police and recounted what he'd seen. It was doubtful Julie would have reported the incident had her son not called it in. Charlie flicked down to the outcome. Nothing much had been done on that occasion. There were no injuries and the two adults had denied anything more than a verbal exchange had occurred. All was calm and they had promised it would remain so. Neither wanted any further action to be taken, but the incident had been recorded and the fact that the boys had witnessed it had brought it to the attention of social services.

The second incident had again been reported by Richard. The details were much the same, except this time the level of violence had escalated somewhat. There was still no hospitalization, but a couple of healthy bruises to Julie's cheek and upper arm bore witness to where she had allegedly been grabbed and pushed back against the bedroom wall. A number of items perched on the top of a chest of drawers had been swept across the room, making the scene appear chaotic, with face creams spilling out over the carpet and pot pourri scattered and trodden into the cream. Keith had found himself in the back of a cramped, smelly police van, but the resulting half-day in a cell failed to dull his desire to resort to force and, even though his timid wife had refused to press charges, it had not opened his eyes to the fact that she was now living in fear.

Worse was to follow, and on the third and final occasion, Julie had ended up in the Accident and Emergency department of their local hospital, having her arm put in plaster where it had been twisted and forced backwards, snapping one of the bones at her wrist. She alluded to having had a fall but refused to make a statement, no doubt fearful of the resulting violence that Keith seemed keen to dole out. Richard had, however, told police what he had seen and this time Keith's stay at the police station lengthened into a trip to the local court-room on a charge of GBH. True to form, Julie refused to testify and the Crown Prosecution Service decided against putting their juvenile son in the witness box to give evidence against his father. The case was dropped and Keith walked free. He attended an anger management course and, on follow-up calls had apparently sworn to the CSU officer that things had been going well.

Judging by the latest development, maybe it hadn't been going as well as he'd claimed.

Charlie checked which member of the office had dealt with the family. It was Colin. His desk was the other side of the room to hers. She got up to speak to him. He was the straight, white, middle-aged male member of their team, similar in age to Bet but as opposite in every other way as was possible. He was divorced and now single, with barely any access to his two children, who had been taken off to Ireland by a vindictive ex-wife years ago. Thin, tight-lipped and sad, he had a dry sense of humour and made it his business to look after the rights of all fathers and their children. He worked tirelessly with social services, going above and beyond what was normally required to ensure each child could know both parents. Charlie fully expected to see him on TV one day, dressed up as Superman swinging from Big Ben. What he didn't know about family law was not worth knowing.

He was poring over his computer screen, his face serious.

'Colin, have you got a minute?'

He looked up and nodded.

'Do you remember dealing with a family called the Hubbards? Quite recently?'

He leant back frowning, before rubbing his chin with thin fingers.

'Yes, I do. It was a couple of months ago.' He scratched his chin again. 'If I remember rightly, Julie Hubbard, the wife, had her wrist broken by her husband. She said she'd tripped and broken it in a fall but then refused to co-operate any further. One of their sons, Richard, said that his father had done it.'

'I think I know who I'd believe.'

He shrugged. 'Everyone thought the same, but what can you do? Richard phoned the police each time. He wanted to give evidence but Julie refused to let him and he did everything his mother asked. With just the one juvenile son as a possible witness, it was pretty much impossible to prove. Why do you ask?'

Charlie thought about what Colin had just said. For a young boy, Richard had certainly been brave, going up against his dad like that. The kid was protecting his mother in whatever way he could. Maybe Keith had started bullying him too because he resented the way he defended his mum. Maybe that was why Julie left and had only taken him. Ryan was certainly less vocal. Maybe Ryan was safe and she'd only had the time and resources to take one? There were too many maybes.

'Because Julie and Richard Hubbard are the mother and son that have gone missing.'

Colin frowned and shook his head.

'Really? Though I have to say I'm not surprised. I always thought there was something strange going on. The boy would plead with his mum to leave his father, but she just wouldn't; it was as if she had another agenda. On the last occasion I saw them, Richard was literally begging her to leave Keith, but she whispered something to him that I couldn't hear and he shut up straight away and seemed happier. I wouldn't be at all surprised if she'd been waiting until the time was right.'

'But why not take the other son, Ryan, too?'

'He kept out of it really. Didn't want to get involved. I think he sided with his father a bit more.'

'So did he have a good relationship with Keith then?'

'He probably had to because he didn't have as close a relationship with his mother as Richard did.'

'So what would be your gut feeling? Do you think Keith Hubbard could be responsible for Julie and Richard's disappearance?'

Colin pursed his lips and looked straight up at Charlie.

'I wouldn't like to say. He is a nasty bastard and could easily have done something, but you know what some women are like. It wouldn't surprise me if Julie Hubbard hadn't been planning this all along.'

Chapter 4

Charlie's brain was in overdrive as she headed along the Albert Embankment towards Vauxhall Bridge.

Hunter sat beside her rubbing his eyes. He always did this when they pulled out of the gloom of the underground car park, as if the light hurt him. He needed glasses really but refused to acknowledge he was getting older and stubbornly refused to wear them.

'Are you all right guv?'

'Fine thanks. Glad to see you've smartened yourself up.' He pulled a large white handkerchief out of his pocket and dabbed at his eyes a minute longer. Charlie watched, slightly intrigued. He was the only person she'd ever known to use a proper handkerchief, apart from her grandfather. He'd even got his initials 'GH' embroidered on the corner, as if to distinguish his from all the hundreds of non-existent identical handkerchiefs he might come across. He pushed it back into his pocket and folded his arms.

'So, you've read the reports. What's your gut telling you?' He always did this too, as if testing her to see if she really did possess the same thought waves as he.

'That something's not right. I know there have been DV issues and Julie had every reason to leave. And I know that Richard is close to her and that Ryan got on with Keith pretty well. So I can see why she might take one son and not the other; but it just doesn't quite add up.'

Her thoughts sometimes came out more garbled than they were in her head.

'I spoke to Colin, who dealt with the family. He said he wouldn't be surprised if Julie had left Keith of her own accord and taken Richard. Keith has given accounts too, which are conflicting. First he said he thought they might have gone away and then he said he thought she'd left him. Whatever his feelings about Julie, I can't see why he didn't report his son missing straight away. Unless he's hiding something?'

She stopped talking as they passed the pale green MI5 building standing stoically on the banks of the Thames and navigated the five lanes of traffic circulating the Vauxhall one-way system. A lorry sounded its hooter, loud and long, as they went under one of the railway arches, the noise making Charlie jump slightly. She wondered for an instant whether it was hooting at her but then realized she didn't care if it was. Her mind was concentrating on that last question.

Her body was driving the car, but her mind was elsewhere. She was aware of Hunter gripping his seat. They hurtled out the other side into South Lambeth Road and the dual carriageway melted into single lane. The traffic slowed to a manageable pace. Hunter relaxed his grip and refolded his arms.

'Sorry about that, like doing a lap of Brands Hatch.'

She adjusted the mirror and caught a glimpse of a white and red Yamaha R1 swinging out to overtake them. It roared past, its rider revving impatiently at the slow-moving traffic. She watched it enviously.

Hunter glanced across.

'Don't even think about it. You'd kill yourself within a month.'

'One day guv, though glad to know you care.'

'I never said that now, did I? Anyway, where were we... you think Keith Hubbard's hiding something?'

'Well, I think the thing that really clinches the fact that something is wrong for me, is that Julie doesn't appear to have said anything to Ryan. She hasn't even left a letter explaining her actions or done anything to let him know that she'll be coming back, that she loves him. No mother could do that to their son, could they? How ever much Julie needed to get away from Keith, you'd think she would find a way to let him know somehow.'

'Unless he's been sworn to secrecy?'

'Possible. Or is too frightened of Keith to say? So...I'm thinking that something must have happened to prevent her from talking to Ryan and, as Keith has been extremely slow in coming forward to report it and given two accounts, I would hazard a guess that he might have something to do with it. I'm looking forward to meeting him.'

She glanced at Hunter from the corner of her eye. A

glimmer of a smile played across his lips.

'I'm looking forward to meeting him too.'

She knew in that moment that she had passed the test.

*

Keith Hubbard was in the garage of his semi when Charlie and Hunter pulled up. As a self-employed builder he'd obviously done well for himself. The house clung to the side of a small hill which ran from the diverse centre of Brixton towards the palatial houses around Dulwich, where Margaret Thatcher had once resided. Charlie watched as he lifted his head slowly from the work-bench in the garage and stared towards their car. The slight roll of his eyes gave away the fact that he recognized immediately they were cops and wasn't too keen to see them. She hopped out of the driver's seat carefully and started up the driveway towards him. Hunter followed suit, a little slower, puffing slightly at the gradient.

Early spring daffodils and tulips lined one side of the driveway, neatly arranged in small clumps of red and yellow, bright against the greens and browns of the ground-cover foliage. A swathe of stocks, tall and leafy, filled in any gaps left in the flower bed; and the grass, although still slightly too long and patchy from the winter rains, was a very healthy dark green. It looked every bit, the typical suburban, middle-classed home.

Keith didn't look up again even when she was level with the front of the garage; a fact that irritated Charlie. He'd seen them parking, so why ignore them now.

She pulled out her warrant card and thrust it towards him.

'Mr Hubbard, can we have a word please about your missing wife and son.'

She watched him carefully as he unfurled himself from his stooped, working position. He was a good six foot two inches tall when he stood straight, with a body that was toned and stocky, no doubt from hours spent lugging heavy tools and equipment around all day. His hair was dark and coarse, with flecks of white at the tips which made it look as if his head had been splashed lightly with a coating of brilliant white gloss paint. He had a full beard, which continued down his neck, colliding with the top of his chest hair, and a moustache that was neither trim nor bushy. His nose was distorted and off-centre, most likely the result of a rugby spat, and his left ear was squashed forward and scarred, almost certainly by the same sport. He looked like a mix of middle-aged hippie and thug.

'I told the other coppers everything I know earlier.'

His voice was gruff and he had an air of arrogance that made Charlie bristle immediately. She disliked him as soon as he opened his mouth, possibly even before he uttered a word.

'Well I'd like you to go through it again with us. After all, I think it's a bit more important than a spot of DIY, don't you?'

She kept her voice strong and controlled, which was more than she felt. His manner unsettled her somehow and her sixth sense was playing games with her mind. She had a bad feeling about the visit. She was glad when Hunter walked up behind her.

'Shall we go in and talk,' he instructed, leaving no space for a quarrel.

Keith sighed out loud and made an exaggerated effort to lay his tools down. Slowly he moved round in front of them, climbing the few steps between a small walled flower bed and the front door, and let them all in.

'Let's make it quick then. It's not DIY. It's my job. I'm having to work from home today and I've got things to do.'

Charlie and Hunter followed him through the front door into the hallway. The house smelt of cleaning products and coffee, as if he'd been waiting for an estate agents' visit. The flooring was a thick mottled oak laminate, more expensive than the norm, and the cream walls were adorned with black and white photographs of Keith and a young boy. There were empty spaces of discoloured paintwork where pictures had been removed. They passed the lounge on their left and she just had time to catch a glimpse of the same child as in the photos, playing computer games on the TV. He glanced round at them but quickly returned to the on screen battle scene.

'Is that Ryan?' she asked, suddenly aware that Keith was staring at her with barely concealed malice.

'Yep that's Ryan. At least Julie didn't take him! That was good of her, wasn't it? Left me one of the kids at least. Very fair. I don't think she liked him very much anyway.' He laughed viciously.

'Why do you say that?'

'Because he wasn't always on her side, like Richard was. Richard was her favourite.'

'I'm sure that wasn't the case?'

'In front of others she tried to make it look as if she treated them both the same, but back here at home it was Richard who was the golden boy. Ryan, poor thing couldn't do anything right. A bit like me. Think he's quite glad she didn't make him go with her actually.'

Charlie paused. She doubted whether Ryan really would want to lose his mother and brother even if, as Keith was suggesting, Julie did favour Richard. There really was something about the man that was ringing alarm bells.

'And you!' Hunter chipped in. 'Are you glad she's gone?'

Keith snorted out loud.

'Couldn't be more pleased. She was a bitch towards me. Didn't say too much out loud but made it quite clear she thought she was better than me. Anyway she's done my job for me now. She's upped and left me everything, silly bitch. I haven't had to do a thing. And now she's gone, she ain't never coming back.'

'But she's only been gone a couple of days,' Charlie looked straight at him. 'How can you be so sure she's not coming back?'

'Coz I just know it, that's all.' He turned away from her.

'Is that why you've removed all the pictures of her and Richard from the wall?'

'Yep, there's gonna be nothing left of her soon. I'm chucking all her stuff out. Clearing the boards. Making way for a new start!'

'So what makes you think she hasn't just gone away for the weekend, like you thought initially?'

He snorted out loud again and turned back round, fixing his gaze straight at her.

'She's gone. I just know it. She's taken a few bits and pissed off. Not a word! Now why would she do that without telling me, unless she had something planned? No lady, she's out of my life!'

Charlie winced at the word lady.

'But you didn't report them missing immediately because you said you thought they'd gone away for the weekend. Now you're saying that right from the start you thought they'd left for good. So why report them missing at all?'

Keith rounded on her, his face reddening with anger.

'Does it matter when I reported them missing or what I thought at the time? The fact is the bitch has gone. I only reported them at all because of the school and her family.'

'The fact is that a fourteen-year-old boy has also disappeared. And even if you're not concerned about that, we are.' She kept her voice even. 'And his father appears to care so little about him that he didn't report him missing for nearly four days! Is there something you know that you're not telling us?'

She felt his eyes boring into hers but didn't flinch away. It was important that this bully knew she wasn't scared of him, even though inwardly she had to admit he unnerved her. The man kept his voice equally calm and measured.

'What are you trying to say? That I somehow got rid of them?'

'I'm not trying to say anything. I'm just asking.'

'Julie left and took Richard with her. That's the end of it.' He broke away from her gaze and crossed the kitchen, turning his back on them and looking out the window on to the back garden.

'Well you don't mind then if we take a look around? We need to satisfy ourselves that they're not still here somewhere. Stranger things have happened.'

She saw his shoulders tense involuntarily. His jaw was set when he turned round again towards them.

'Do whatever you have to, but do it quickly and get out of here.'

Charlie smiled at him briefly. She had won that spat and was now able to have a good look around, but he was not making their life easy. Most people reporting loved ones missing were only too keen to help with everything they could. Clearly his wife did not fall into the category of a 'loved one', but Richard? How could he be so blasé and cold about his son being missing? She turned and walked along the hallway, her gaze falling again on the missing picture frames.

Hunter was following closely behind. At the bottom of the stairs she turned towards him.

'So what do you make of him?'

'Haven't made my mind up yet. If Julie has taken the boy

21

and gone, I must say I wouldn't blame her. If he's got something to do with it, he's putting up a very good smokescreen to make it look like she's walked out on him and he's the wronged party. Whichever it is though, I don't like him.'

'Nor do I, but then he doesn't seem to like me either. The feeling is definitely mutual.'

She climbed the stairs, leaving Hunter to check the ground floor, and moved around the first floor taking in the packed suitcases rammed full of clothing and female cosmetics, the spaces on the walls where more pictures had clearly been removed and the obvious attempt being made to extinguish his wife and child from his life. The main bedroom had no photos of the family, or Julie, no perfume, make-up or beauty products left lying around. Only two pillows rested on top of each other and were placed in the central position at the top of the king-size bed.

Richard's bedroom too was tidy with the bed neatly made and storage boxes containing his belongings stacked along one wall.

Even the bathroom had only male cosmetics, with just two remaining toothbrushes sticking out from a tumbler. It was impossible to tell whether Julie had taken items of importance to her or Richard because everything was now packed away.

More striking though was the cleanliness of the place. Each room had been swept clean, the surfaces bore no dust and even the walls and paintwork looked and smelt freshly washed.

Hubbard must have spent the whole weekend scrubbing the place from top to bottom before reporting them missing.

Charlie was bending down examining a damp patch on the bedroom carpet when he came up behind her.

'Found anything interesting then?' he said loudly, making her jump to her feet with surprise.

'I must say, Mr Hubbard, you seem to have gone to great lengths to remove any signs of your wife and son when they may well come back. Don't you think that's a bit strange?'

'No. I don't think it's a bit strange. In fact, I would find it a bit strange for any man to happily take back a wife that has treated him like shit for years.' His voice dropped in volume so she could barely hear it, accentuating each word slowly. 'Wouldn't you?'

She turned to see where Hunter was but he was still

downstairs and the knowledge sent a ripple of apprehension through her. She caught the smile that appeared across Hubbard's face and knew he sensed her foreboding.

'He's downstairs,' he answered her unspoken question. 'Poking his nose around where it's not wanted.'

She stood up straight and tried to sound calm.

'Well I'm done up here, so I may as well go and join him.'

'You didn't answer my question.' His voice was flat. 'I asked you if you would or wouldn't find it strange that a man should take back a wife that treated him like shit?' She started to walk. 'Well would you?' She got to the bedroom door.

'I would find it stranger for a wife to want to return to a bastard of a husband that beat her up regularly in front of their children.'

She reached the top of the stairs and glanced back to find him right behind her. Gripping the banister, she started to descend.

'I thought you might say that,' he whispered from behind.

She turned, releasing her grip slightly, to see his boot coming towards her. It hit her square on the shoulder, the power propelling her forward.

'Mind how you go now,' the shout rang in her ears as she scrabbled to maintain her grip, before tumbling forward into darkness.

Chapter 5

Julie Hubbard was preparing to die. She had lost the will to fight. In any case, the water that she had eked out so carefully at first was now gone and her captor had not visited for some time to replenish it. She had almost lost track of time completely in the continual darkness. Only the depth of blackness and the dawn chorus of myriad small twittering birds as opposed to the night-time hoots and screeches of owls helped her work out whether it was night or day.

The stench of decomposition was all around her. It clung to every strand of hair and every inch of clothing. It filled her nostrils and made her head scream, knowing that with every breath she took, she inhaled Richard's death. Amongst the deadness though was life, creatures crawling and squirming and feeding on the flesh of her son. She could hear them moving, scratching and scraping at the body, wriggling on to her own face and hands and skin. Sometimes they woke her from intermittent sleep as they moved across her closed eyelids and on to her forehead, into her ears. Sometimes the noise got so loud she wanted to scream to drown it out. Sometimes the knowledge of what was happening deadened her to everything.

She hadn't eaten since she'd been in this pit, she'd had only water and now the tube was dry and stuck to her chapped lips. She couldn't even lick her lips properly anymore because there was so little saliva. The hunger pangs had ceased now as her body had got used to starvation. And she was cold, so cold. Her body was so weak she rarely even attempted to move, save to try to rid her skin of the insects.

She had come to almost look forward to the daily visit from her captor. Not that there had been many visits, but for the first few days at least there had been. She had tried to identify the voice. It was familiar but unrecognizable, as if its owner was trying to alter or muffle it. She thought it was a male voice but wasn't completely sure. The only thing that had kept her going up until now was the fact that the voice was disguised. If she was to be killed, why would they bother? It didn't say much, mainly laughed, mocked, but at least she hadn't been forgotten.

She wondered what on earth she could have done to warrant this torture. For years Keith had beaten her as and when he wanted. She hardly dare disagree with him these days, without fearing retribution. Surely, she deserved a little love and happiness outside her marriage. And nobody knew. They'd been so careful.

The voice made no reference to this. It just kept repeating the same two words, over and over again: *Mummy's favourite, Mummy's favourite, Mummy's favourite.* But how could it be a sin to have a favourite?

Obviously her captor thought it was but how did they know what she felt. Only Keith and Ryan knew really. Maybe a few friends and family suspected; maybe even a few work colleagues or a few random strangers watching her with her boys in the park.

But now she didn't care anymore. She was totally and utterly alone; without contact with anything other than insects. Her mouth was dry. Her body was weak. The person she loved the most lay dead and rotting beside her.

She wanted to die now. She was physically and mentally ready. There was nothing more for her to live for.

Chapter 6

'Charlie, Charlie! It's time for school.'

The same few words kept repeating themselves in Charlie's head over and over again. She hated school. She needed to start making excuses.

She felt a hand resting on hers. It was gripping her fingers, squeezing gently. She squeezed the hand back and blinked carefully. Her mother was staring down at her with a concerned look on her face.

'I can't go to school today, Mum. My head is banging.'

Extricating her hand from her mother's, she realized she was actually telling the truth this time. She felt far too rough today. Her head was pounding and she ached all over.

She opened her eyes again slowly, painfully. They felt stuck shut. Pain throbbed through her head and she winced. Slowly she let her eyes acclimatize to the bright light, concentrating on the shape in front of her that she recognized so well. Meg stood next to her, bent over, encouraging, smiling, her blonde hair flat and lifeless.

She tried to open her lips to speak and realized they were dry and didn't want to move. As if reading her thoughts, her mother carefully drew a small, wet sponge across her mouth.

'In case you're wondering, you're in hospital. You took quite a fall down a flight of stairs. You banged your head.'

'So I don't have to go to school today?'

'No you don't.' Her mother was laughing now; laughing and crying. 'But I knew it would get a reaction.'

Charlie smiled weakly. Her mother was totally right. She hated school. For a time, she'd hated everything and everyone. She'd refused to go each morning and had almost lost her way completely. Only her need for justice had saved her.

'You had severe concussion, Charlie, and five stitches in a head wound.' Meg wiped a tear away with her sleeve and was suddenly serious. 'Thank God you're all right.'

She paused and Charlie knew immediately what her mother was thinking. She could hear it in her struggle to find the right words. *Not again!*

'You've been sedated for two days. They needed you to have plenty of bed rest, but even they weren't expecting you to have this much.'

She was still confused. How could it be that long?

'Do you remember what happened?'

She closed her eyes and felt herself immediately falling into space, her arms flailing, grabbing out, losing grip, tumbling forward.

A door opened in front of her and Hunter walked in.

'I remember falling,' she whispered hoarsely, her mouth still dry, opening her eyes to stop the vision.

'More importantly. Do you remember *why* you fell?' Hunter didn't waste time.

'I think we need to leave that question for a few hours until she's back with us properly, don't you?' a nurse bustled in behind Hunter and was not going to be argued with.

He turned back to Charlie with an expression of irritation and stifled remorse. He wasn't used to being told what to do.

'Ok we'll leave it for now.'

Her mother intervened to lighten the atmosphere. 'Just glad you're back with us.'

'So are we all,' Hunter agreed.

She smiled. That little phrase from him meant more to her than anything.

*

Keith Hubbard lay stretched out on the plain sheet, of the plain mattress, of the prison bed and laughed quietly to himself. The stupid bastards thought they knew how to deal with him, but they didn't. They thought they were better than him, but they weren't. He knew how to deal with them and he knew he would never be convicted.

Not in a million years.

Not when it was one word against the other. And the other just happened to be a mad bitch with concussion.

It was just a matter of waiting until his solicitor got him out, and she would. She was quality. He'd just have to wait for the next bail application to get sprung, on the basis that he had a young son tragically left without a mother or father now. Fatherhood would prove to be his saviour, he was sure.

He just had to wait, which was fine, even if it took a week or so. Waiting was just his thing. He was good at waiting and watching and biding his time. So fucking good it made him laugh out loud.

Chapter 7

'I have to admit, Charlie, we're going to struggle. Today's a formality. He'll almost certainly get bail and I'll be surprised if the Crown Prosecution Service doesn't withdraw the charge completely when it goes to committal in a week or so's time. It's your word against his and your initial statement to me at Hubbard's house is going to be torn to shreds by the defence because of your head injury. Any forensic material found on your clothing from his boot will also be totally discredited due to the fact that you were thrown all over the carpet during the fall and any mud or dirt could just as easily have come from that. Even the full statement you made after coming to is likely to be deemed unreliable due to the concussion. We'll have a job proving he did it.'

Hunter shook his head in frustration.

'I wanted to say I'd seen him push you, but with my eyesight and both Hubbard and his son saying I was downstairs I'd have been done for perjury and that wouldn't have helped your case at all. The boss warned me off.'

He pulled a packet of cigarettes from his pocket and shoved one into the corner of his mouth.

'The bastard! I heard him say "mind how you go". If it does get to court, all the jury will think is that he was trying to warn you to go careful because he was worried you'd trip. Not that he was making a sarcastic comment as he booted you down the stairs.'

Charlie was curled up on the most comfortable sofa in the world, at the family home, with her legs wrapped in a warm fleece. The sofa had been there forever, huge, maroon and all encompassing, present in almost all of her best memories. Meg had refused to let her go back to her own flat, insisting she, Lucy and Beth would look after her the best. She felt sick and her head still ached but the pain-killers were keeping it at bay. She'd worn the doctor down, begging to be released, and had only been discharged on a promise to report straight back to A&E if there was any increase in pain or faintness. Seven to ten days of headaches, nausea and dizziness; bed rest, sofa rest, light exercise and then hopefully back to normal. Luckily Hunter was popping in regularly updating her on her case, and that of Julie and Richard Hubbard but she was still determined to get back as soon as possible. She had a job to do; even more so now she'd remembered exactly what had happened.

She heaved herself up and opened the door to the garden. Hunter lit up, blowing the smoke out in a fresh bout of rage.

'It's fucking bollocks! We can't let the bastard get away with what he's done.' He drew on the cigarette again heavily, before throwing it down and grinding it into the stone slabs with his boot. He shook his head at Charlie. 'And yes! I know I should stop smoking.'

'I didn't say a word.'

'You don't have to. I can see it in your face.'

She raised her hands as if in surrender. He was a great boss and a good man too, but she wished he would quit. He had pretty much stopped; but now and again, when he appeared the most stressed, he would pull a crumpled packet from his pocket and light up. It was the worst possible combination, but it was also the worst possible time to choose to make a comment. She had long since learned to button her lip. She might be young, but she was not stupid.

He was pacing now, back and forth on the patio, his footsteps scuffing a path through the thin layer of green mould that appeared as if by magic on the patio slabs every winter.

She knew all he wanted was to put the bad people away, whether that meant a little embellishment of what he had actually seen or heard, or a little over-dramatization of events. These days the scales of justice were weighted too heavily against the victim. Guilty people were able to manipulate the system to obtain the verdicts they required. Sometimes the scales had to be reset with a little bit of creative thinking by law enforcement officers. She believed exactly the same as he did. She'd already seen enough in her short career to know that he was right and was well-respected for it. She worked the same way.

Her head was pounding again.

'Well let's just wait and see. We both know that the

Magistrates won't have the balls to keep him in custody. That's a given. Let's hope you're wrong when it gets to the committal. Who knows?'

The words were empty. She knew he was right. Keith Hubbard would walk; and there was nothing, absolutely nothing, they could do.

*

Julie Hubbard blinked her eyes open and shut several times to push away the insect that was crawling across her lids. She was covered in bedding, thrown down by her captor on the last visit to keep her from freezing, but the insects still managed to burrow down to skin-level. She could feel them scraping against her, nipping and biting. She lay in her own filth, her clothing damp and putrid. The stench hit her nostrils again and she blew out through her nose to dispel the smell. Opening her mouth, she tried to breathe. The smell wasn't so bad if she breathed through her mouth, but the cloth around her face hindered the air movement and made it harder to suck in enough oxygen. Her lungs and chest were so weak now that she could only manage a short time before having to use her nostrils again. Her lips were dry, with deep cracks from lack of moisture. The water from the tube had run out a long time ago.

The call of a wood pigeon rang out from somewhere outside her prison. It sounded close. She had long since given up the hope of having one last view of normality, of light, colours, nature, people, life. It wasn't going to happen. She knew it now and it ceased to faze her. Her breathing was getting harder as her lungs gave up the fight, panting and gasping for air as her body attempted to move the weight of her ribcage. The sound was loud and welcome in the silence. Her head was going muzzy as her brain starved of oxygen. Everything was starving. Ryan and Richard ran across her eye-line, laughing and shouting in childish exuberance. Her eyes were drawn to Richard, the youngest, the most striking. He turned and smiled towards her and she smiled back and their eyes connected. She couldn't turn away even if she'd wanted. She was looking directly into the darkness of his pupils, being pulled forward into their blackness, but she didn't fight against it. She didn't pull back.

She let go and as she did so she knew she would never open her eyes again.

This time they would be united forever.

*

Keith Hubbard shoved his hands deep into his trouser pockets and grinned with satisfaction. Behind him the brickwork and glass of Camberwell Green Magistrates' Court glinted in the sun-light. The sky was a brilliant blue in the background, though the air still held a slight nip of spring, and the court building cast shadows across the concrete concourse and road in front of it. Traffic nudged forward slowly at the approach to the nearby junction.

He turned at the sound of footsteps behind him and shook hands with the smartly dressed young woman who extended her hand towards him. She was quite a classy bitch, even though she too looked down on him, but then she was allowed to, she was Ms Annabel Leigh-Matthews, his solicitor, no less. He expected her to be better educated and better spoken, even though he still didn't like it; particularly in a woman. But then he couldn't object really, seeing as she'd just sprung him from prison with the promise she would get the charges dropped at the next hearing. And she would, he knew she would.

He watched her every step as she tottered away on her high black court shoes, struggling to juggle the bundles of paperwork as she dug into her shoulder bag for her car key. It was a classy car too, a sleek, red BMW 320i with a personalized number plate that he had already committed to memory. He knew where she worked. He knew her car. It wouldn't be hard to find out where she lived.

He stayed silently observing her as she leaned over the boot, carefully placing the bundles down, unaware of his eyes scanning her every curve. Classy bird with a fit body. Nice.

He caught a glimpse of leg as she climbed into the car and didn't stop surveying her until her car was out of sight.

Then, with a sigh, he turned and started to walk towards the train station. The Easter weekend stretched out in front of him, an extra two days to enjoy his pursuits. Before he went and removed Ryan from his grandparents he would go for a walk. It would be good to get away from the grey buildings of the inner city. He quickened his step at the thought. Yes it would be nice to breathe in the fresh, clean air of his favourite woods, so much nicer than being stuck in the stuffy enclosed space of a prison cell.

Chapter 8

The Imperial War Museum was directly en route to Lambeth HQ, not far from Waterloo and the South Bank. The huge brick-built structure containing memorabilia from wars throughout the ages was crowned with a verdigris-coloured domed roof, and its entrance fronted by six imposing pillars. It was situated in a small park area comprising a Tibetan peace garden and a small cafe. A recent wooden statue, almost like a totem pole, honed from the trunk of a fallen tree stood to the side of the entrance. Charlie had watched its weekly progress, intrigued at its transformation from little more than a stump, to a smooth, stunning sculpture.

It was only just past 7 a.m. but Hubbard's committal was scheduled for the afternoon and she wanted to get back up to speed with what had been happening. She had done the least possible time that the doctors had ordered, and although her head was still sore, there was no lasting damage. Only a small scar remained to remind her how lucky she'd been. It could have been so much worse.

She needed to run. A week and a half sitting at home, eating Easter eggs and with barely any exercise had taken its toll. She felt sluggish and almost as stiff as the trusty trainers she had squeezed her feet into. She jogged over to the front of the building where she always stopped briefly to admire the two huge fifteen inch diameter gun barrels which marked the entrance to the museum.

She stood in front of the guns, staring into their black interiors for what seemed like ages, letting her mind flit between past and present. Every morning she made a point of standing in a quiet spot, in silence for two minutes, eyes closed, allowing her memories free rein. Each time she reopened her eyes, her memories had refuelled her motivation for justice. Beth and Lucy had caught her doing it a few times and teased her for it, but for Charlie it worked. Those memories kept her focussed.

When at last she opened her eyes she realized she wasn't alone. Ben Jacobs was there.

He stood to one side, leaning on a pair of crutches, a money box labelled 'Help for Heroes' hung around his neck. He regularly sat, lost in his thoughts, collecting money outside the museum.

'You're early today,' he waved towards her.

'I could say the same about you.'

'Couldn't sleep.'

She knew better than to question him further. She'd taken him out to breakfast a couple of times in the last six months and listened to his story. Sometimes his recurring nightmares led him to the bottle. Sometimes the need for a new bottle brought him out early from his flat.

Unlike the soldiers who had lost limbs, the injuries Ben had suffered in the latest conflict were not obvious to onlookers. He had post-traumatic stress syndrome and the flashbacks, as vivid as the actual fighting, were repeated constantly in his head.

His body mirrored his mind. Sometimes his tall, lean frame would stand upright, shoulders back, dark hair neatly cut, chin and neck cleanly shaved, clothes fresh and smart, eyes alive and smiling, a lop-sided grin lighting up his handsome features. Other times he was stooped, unkempt and dirty; both frightened and frightening.

Today he looked more dishevelled than usual; his eyes dull through lack of sleep, a plaster cast on his right leg. A can of Special Brew dangled from his hand.

Charlie reached into her pockets and scooped out a handful of loose change, slotting each coin carefully into his tin. He deserved way more than a few pennies. Usually she would make time to chat, but today, even though she felt guilty as hell she knew she had to get on.

She pointed to the crutches.

'What have you been up to then?' She already knew the answer.

He shrugged. 'Too much of this.' He held the can up, before putting it to his lips.

'We'll do breakfast again soon, Ben. I promise.'

'I'll hold you to that, Charlie.'

'Don't worry. It's always my pleasure. Just got a big case to crack first.'

'Well hurry up and crack it quickly. I'm hungry.'

She laughed. 'I'll do my best. Can't have you wasting away.'

He waved as she jogged away. He was a lovely guy. It was such a pity to see him so troubled, but she made a point of never judging him. Who could ever know what he had experienced and was still experiencing now. She would be back as soon as she could.

By the time she'd reached the office both Charlie and her trainers were feeling more like normal, which was more than could be said for her entrance. Bet and Paul were straight on their feet, wrapping arms round her, genuinely pleased at her return. They had both kept in daily contact with her for the week and a half she'd been off.

Naz and Sabira hovered in the background, wanting to show their solidarity but not quite sure what to do. Sabira was an Asian lesbian, two features that didn't sit well together in Indian culture. She helped Paul on the LGBT cases but also worked on the increasing number of faith/honour crimes. She was Paul's opposite: quiet and unobtrusive, patient and tolerant, sensible clothes, sensible shoes, someone who was never going to set the world on fire.

Naz, on the other hand, wanted to set the world on fire but, having had two children with different fathers, was now tied down with childcare issues. The world that she inhabited was much smaller and more contained than she'd ever envisaged. Young, black, feisty and proud of the tattooed cleavage regularly on display, she relied on both her mother and grandmother babysitting to enable her to work during the week and, more importantly, to socialize at the weekends. Charlie loved them both.

Colin remained seated but nodded his agreement with the sentiment.

Bet ambled over to the kettle and started a brew. Almost immediately Paul piped up with his plans for this weekend's escapades. Things were the same as always and she was glad to be back to her usual routine, even though her head was throbbing annoyingly.

She let Paul talk without really listening and instead walked across to Colin who was, as usual, bent over his computer screen. He looked up.

'Didn't expect you back so soon. Sounds like you were lucky from what the boss was saying.'

'Think we were all lucky,' Paul chipped in from across the room. 'Two days concussed in hospital without Charlie saying a word. Must be a record?'

'Two *minutes* of silence from you would be a record,' she responded, to grunts of agreement from the others. Paul laughed and pulled an imaginary zip across his lips.

'Well it's all been happening here while you were off.' Colin turned back to his computer, bringing up the missing person report which had now lengthened to dozens of pages of enquiries. He was never one to indulge in the office banter for any longer than needed.

'Yes, so I hear. Hunter said that the case had been escalated to a major enquiry and that after my assault Hubbard's propensity to violence is being re-examined in minute detail. Can you give me a potted version of what's been done so far? I expect you've been keeping tabs on it, seeing as you knew the family?'

Colin nodded and scrolled down through the pages of enquiries.

'Well, it's as full scale an enquiry as it could be without bodies; not quite a murder investigation as yet, but not far from it. In fact, the Murder Investigation Team is being consulted regularly. Nothing's been heard from them now for two weeks. Let me see. They've been making enquiries with banks, building societies, Equifax and the department dealing with child benefits. They've also sent out port notifications to airports and ferry ports. CCTV is being gone through from all the local shopping areas, railway stations and roads around where they live. Both Julie and Richard's mobile phones were switched off early on the Friday evening they disappeared, so every conceivable check is being made on where and when they were last used, and any contacts.'

'Nothing positive as yet?'

'No. It doesn't look as if there have been any real steps forward. They've got forensics in Hubbard's house at the moment, scouring it with a fine-toothed comb.'

'Well they'll be lucky to find anything. Hubbard had cleaned it all before we even got there.'

'And forensics were there after your GBH.'

'Well, I hope that examination hasn't jeopardized the main one then. He's got to be the number one suspect in their disappearance. If he had a problem with his missus that's bad enough, but if he's done something to his kid...'

'You never really know what goes on within families.' Colin clicked the report shut and leant back. 'You only have to look at the news to see what it does to men when they're threatened with losing access to their kids.'

His voice tailed off as he turned and looked away from her, towards the window. A cloud rolled across the sun almost at the moment he spoke. She followed the shadow as it moved across the windowsill.

'Sorry Colin. I know it's a bit close to home for you. Have you had any more luck getting access recently?'

Colin turned back, his eyes hard. 'It's a work in progress, Charlie. I think I'm beginning to win. The kids are dying to see me these days.'

'Glad to hear it. You could use a bit of luck in your situation.'

'Ah is that DC Stafford's voice I can hear. Good to have you back, though you should have had more time off to recover.'

Charlie looked up recognizing Hunter's voice booming across the office. He looked genuinely pleased to see her, though she knew he didn't mean what he'd just said. He'd barely had a day off sick in all his thirty-seven years.

'Can I have a quick word please?'

She nodded and followed him through to his office, closing the door against the eyes she knew would be following her. The room was only small but it was neat, well ordered and compact. Photos of Hunter's children sat proudly on his desk. He was grooming his son to take over from him when he did eventually retire.

'I'll come straight to the point. The CPS is dropping your case. Have a read of this. I suspected it might happen.'

He passed her a single piece of A4 paper on which a few paragraphs were typed before turning away in obvious frustration. 'We winged it a bit when we sent the original file to them, exaggerated how good we hoped the forensic stuff would be. It's turned out to be pretty useless and totally inconclusive. Now they've got the full file they don't think we've got a hope in hell. Hubbard, as I told you, is already out on bail and the case will almost certainly be dropped this afternoon. I've tried to reason with them, but I haven't really got much of a leg to stand on, to be honest.'

He stopped talking and the silence lengthened as she read the CPS memo, short, succinct and brutal. Unless fresh evidence came to light the case would be dropped. Keith Hubbard would get away with it. Even though she'd expected the news, she still couldn't trust herself to speak. Placing the letter back on Hunter's desk carefully, she got up and walked unsteadily to the door, opening it wide. Half a dozen eyes turned to watch and she couldn't bear the pressure of them. She turned back to see Hunter stand and take a pace towards her. She held out her hand to stop him touching her. She didn't want to cry and any contact was likely to start the tears. He paused.

'If my case is being dropped,' she said, loud enough for the main office to hear. 'There shouldn't be any conflict of interest if I helped out further with the investigation into his missing wife and child? So could I be seconded on to the full investigation team for at least a while? I can't just sit back and do nothing.'

Hunter tilted his head and pursed his lips as he stared back at her, considering the request.

'I think it's probably the least we can do. Though you will have to be careful you act completely professionally and any progress you make doesn't look personal.'

He smiled knowingly at her and she noticed his eyes were glinting dangerously.

'I'll have a word and see if we both can.'

Chapter 9

It wasn't fair that Julie was dead. She was supposed to have lived much longer. He'd wanted to keep her there, slowly dying of starvation. Slowly, so slowly, knowing that her son was dead beside her. She was supposed to have lasted at least a month, even up to six weeks. He'd read all about it:

Most doctors and nutritionists state that the average person can live between four to six weeks without food, but a week is a miracle without water.

It was nothing more than she deserved. The fucking bitch. But she'd died already. Too soon, far too soon. He couldn't believe it had happened and yet it had.

A lot depended on the person's state of mind and willpower as well as their body weight and climate.

But she hadn't been too fat or too skinny and he'd thrown down bedding to keep her from freezing. Maybe she'd deliberately wasted all the water in a bid to die quickly and cheat him of even this pleasure. That must have been it. She'd spat out the water. He hadn't been able to come for a few days but there should have been enough for her to survive until he returned. But the bitch had spat it out just to spite him and now she was dead. They both were. Her and Richard, her spoilt brat of a son, mummy's little favourite blue-eyed boy; the golden child who could do nothing wrong.

He stamped downwards on to her head, pleased at the sight of the dirty footprint he left on her face, down her nose, across her cheeks. She was supposed to be alive, damn it. She was supposed to be staring up at him, pleading for survival, desperate to live. Then she'd know what it was like to be lonely. Then she'd know what it was like to be there, but not to be there; to be unseen, unheard, unwanted, unloved. Just as he had been.

He'd read so much. This time he'd wanted to get it right, to make her pay. To make all the conniving mothers pay for their greedy, selfish needs.

'Fuck.' He screamed the word out loud again and again and again. There was no one there. No one ever was. It had been the perfect place to watch and examine and see.

Immediately after death, the heart stops pumping blood around the body and gravity drags the blood down until it pools in blood vessels in the back of the legs and spine. Cells in the body die as there is no oxygen for them to carry out their normal metabolic functions. Neurons die within minutes. Skin cells can last for days because they are able to perform without oxygen. This is called anaerobic fermentation and lactic acid is a by-product. Lactic acid causes rigor mortis which lasts for about thirty-six hours.

He'd watched as this had begun to happen to Richard. So spoilt, so perfect, but not so fucking perfect now, eh? He'd bent down and poked at the body. The experts were right. It had been stiff and unbending.

Bacterial cells, which normally live in the intestine begin to rapidly multiply and digestive enzymes start digesting the body's own tissues. Assuming the body is untouched, insects arrive to the scene very quickly as they are extremely sensitive to the smell of decomposition. Flies lay eggs in skin openings and in entrances to the body - nose, ears and mouth - and maggots will hatch.

He'd watched this too; down in the pit. He'd watched and enjoyed as the insects had arrived. He'd shone a torch and seen how they crawled all over them both. How she couldn't swat them away. How she'd spat and blown them from her mouth and nose. He'd liked that bit. And then there was the smell:

Gases are released giving the body a terrible smell, and the abdomen fills with liquid. This stinking liquid attracts more flies, beetles and other insects. A body can feel warm to the touch at this point due to all of the insect activity. Exposed parts that haven't yet been consumed start to turn black ten to twenty days after death.

He'd reached down and touched Richard's skin. It was warm and swollen and the smell filled his nostrils and hair. Even hours later he could still smell the stench of death. It had amused him on the packed underground to see other passengers wrinkle up their noses. They must have smelt it too, but they didn't know what it was, like he did. The putrid smell of death. The smell of his justice.

Between twenty to fifty days after death, the body begins to dry out and beetles take over. They can chew through the remaining tendons and ligaments, until all that is left is bone

41

and hair. Between fifty to 365 days after death, moths and bacteria consume the hair. All that is left is bone, which can last indefinitely.

And now he wouldn't get the chance to see if the experts were right. The evil cow had taken away the chance. He had no reason to come back now, unless he just wanted to watch, to continue with the experiment. But it didn't mean the same now because she wouldn't be part of it any longer. Julie Hubbard wouldn't be living his experiment.

He slammed the trap-door back down on the pit. She might have ruined everything this time but now, at least, he would have the chance to start all over again. He would build a new lair nearby and complete the experiment with the next pair.

He grabbed his shovel and started to search for a good location. A shiver of excitement ran through him at the thought. It wouldn't be hard. Women were fickle creatures. They couldn't hide their emotions. He could always recognize a special child.

After all, his own brother had been Mummy's favourite before his untimely death.

Chapter 10

Charlie sat at the back of Court One at Camberwell Green Magistrates' Court quietly waiting. Meg sat next to her, deep in thought. She had insisted on coming, much against Charlie's wishes, but now she was here Charlie was glad. Although there was a huge emotional hole in their relationship, her mother was always there on a practical level. Charlie knew she would fight to the death to protect them all.

The door to the court swung open and Hunter sidled in, dipping his head towards the magistrate and sliding along the wooden bench towards her. She knew that he had believed every single word of what had happened and not just because he had been there. He hadn't witnessed the push, nor had he heard all of the whispered conversation that had led up to the assault. Hunter knew the truth, without having to see it with his own eyes.

There were a few warrant applications to be heard and then they were on.

She looked at the magistrate; the man with the power. He was only a small man with narrow shoulders hidden in a loosely fitted dark grey jacket, set off with a flamboyant bright red dicky bow. His skin was sallow in appearance and he wore dark-rimmed spectacles which he would push up on top of his receding hairline when he wasn't inspecting paperwork. His face wore a kindly expression but this could change in an instant if he didn't get the answer he required. He would be reviewing the evidence in Hubbard's case shortly and Charlie wondered whether he would be looking kindly at Hubbard or her.

Both the prosecution and defence were in place now, seated with piles of paperwork and files in front of them. Ms Annabel Leigh-Matthews looked smug before they'd even started, with a supercilious expression that Charlie immediately wanted to wipe off her face. The prosecution solicitor was still leafing through the file. Knowing the CPS like she did, she guessed it had probably been foisted on him that morning and he was desperately trying to acquaint himself fully with its contents as they waited.

The clerk nodded towards the usher who scurried out of the court obediently. She returned less than a minute later with Hubbard in tow. He was smartly dressed today in suit and tie, the epitome of a good, honest, hard-working family man, and he smiled towards the magistrate as he made his way into the dock. He played the part well. Charlie could barely recognizable him from the man who had snarled his contempt towards her from the top of his stairs.

Within minutes it was clear to Charlie that the fact that her life had been seriously threatened was of no consequence against the rights of Hubbard, as asserted by Ms Annabel Leigh-Matthews. The CPS rep all but withdrew every claim the case had relied on.

As both sides sat to await the verdict, the magistrate stared at the CPS solicitor for what seemed like ages before casting his gaze towards Hubbard, who immediately looked down. The magistrate turned towards Charlie. Their eyes held each other's and she sensed his reluctance and sympathy, and even though she had not been introduced as such, she knew that he had recognized in her the victim. He was clearly on her side but with the absence of the prosecution council producing any credible evidence there was nothing he could do.

He nodded, almost unnoticed, towards Charlie before looking straight at Hubbard.

'In this instance, I, unfortunately, have no option but to accept the assertions made by the defence. Case dismissed.'

He remained staring at Hubbard for several seconds longer and she was glad to see her assailant visibly shrinking under his gaze. Clearly the magistrate had not had the wool pulled over his eyes. He just had no alternative.

Ms Annabel Leigh-Matthews closed her file with a slight flourish and nodded towards the magistrate and then turned and smiled at Hubbard, indicating with her head for him to follow her.

It had taken less than ten minutes for the defence to wipe the floor with the CPS rep.

The prosecution solicitor, under the continued scrutiny of

the magistrate, gathered up his papers, without attempting to sort them out and hurriedly exited the court-room, his head bowed, Charlie thought, in shame. Hadn't it been worth giving the case a run? After all, she was of previous good character and a policewoman. Hubbard had a history of violence, possibly even kidnap and murder. Couldn't he have found a way to bring up Hubbard's "bad character" to substantiate her case? But no, the easy option had been taken and there was no justice. There was never any justice for her family.

The anger was welling up inside her as she filed out of the court to see Hubbard with a grin all over his face as he shook hands with Ms Leigh-Matthews in the corridor outside the court. Now he was out, he was going to make the most of his legal victory. Ms Leigh-Matthews, at least, was trying to play down her pleasure at winning, but she couldn't completely hide the glimmer of satisfaction at another professional triumph, a job well done.

Charlie remained tight-lipped as she and Hunter walked past, her head held high, daring them to challenge the truth. Meg trailed behind.

'Congratulations,' Meg said tightly. 'I can imagine you've made both of your mothers proud today. Be sure the truth will eventually emerge though. Justice will always be done in the end.'

Charlie heard Hubbard laugh, a low mocking laugh that she knew was directed at her.

She caught the look on her mother's face. She had obviously heard it too.

Charlie turned briefly as the pair started to follow them out through the revolving doors into the brightness of the spring sunshine. Rage and injustice was coursing through her now at his laughter. Hunter put a hand on her shoulder and a finger to his lips to silence her.

'You'll come again, you bastard. And next time you won't be laughing,' he murmured towards Hubbard, out of earshot of his solicitor but loud enough for him, Charlie and Meg to hear. He caught Charlie's eye and nodded behind his shoulder.

A couple of smart-suited men she recognized well started to move towards them. They nodded their heads in recognition, before continuing past the three of them towards Hubbard and his solicitor.

And now it was Charlie's turn to laugh as they watched his smug expression turn from victory to shocked surprise and anger, as his arms were roughly twisted behind his back and handcuffs were firmly clamped around his wrists.

'You knew that was going to happen, didn't you guv? Why didn't you tell me?' She could barely contain her delight.

'And miss seeing the look on your face now. Priceless.'

He squeezed her shoulder and winked at Meg. 'Now, get yourself down to Brixton nick. We may have lost this battle but we certainly haven't lost the war.'

Chapter 11

Brixton was the thriving centre of the black community in South London, since immigrants from the Caribbean had arrived in the 1950's. Exotic fruit and vegetable traders, fishmongers, butchers and specialist record shops had set up home there and entertainment establishments such as The Ritzy and the Academy turned Brixton into the iconic cultural centre it now was.

Charlie liked Brixton for its eclectic mix, having worked there for around four years. Her first station at Charing Cross police station had been in the heart of theatre-land and Soho. The buzz of the area, with its hordes of tourists, pushy shoppers and thriving underbelly of thieves, drinkers and pick-pockets, unchanged, in essence, since Dickensian times, had given her an excellent grounding.

Having transferred to the London equivalent of The Bronx, she had equally grown to love the blatancy and variety of the street crime, suburban tensions and gang culture in Brixton.

Brixton police station was situated a short way from the town centre. While Lambeth HQ was the brains of Lambeth Borough, housing many of the squads, Brixton was its heart; housing the busy custody centre.

The building itself had been recently refurbished and now boasted a state-of-the-art custody suite, thirty cells, two detention rooms, two medical rooms, five interview rooms with audio facilities, two with video equipment, and two rooms equipped for taking fingerprints, DNA swabs and photographs. The outside of the building remained the same: a mixture of red brick, most likely from the same batch as all the old police buildings in London, and glass to symbolize the new, modern police service to which they all now belonged. It was a far cry from the old days when prisoners were dragged in off the street to a dirty, cramped charge room, ran, without discussion, by an omnipotent sergeant, and where they would literally be thrown into communal cells, rubbing shoulders with the next prostitute, thief or drug addict.

Charlie pulled into the new multi-storey car park at the rear and swiped her warrant card at the security door. She didn't like the new building. It was big, bright and had no personality. Her head started throbbing immediately she entered the vivid fluorescence of the entrance hall and she decided to get the lift to the canteen, rather than climb the stairs.

Bill Morley was sat at a table in the far corner, heading a group of 'old sweats' lamenting how the job was 'fucked'. It was a regular topic of conversation and one that she imagined he had been discussing almost every day of his thirty years in the job.

'Bill,' she came up behind him, putting an arm around his neck in a gentle lock. 'Nice to hear you. Put a different record on though!' She tightened her grip slightly, before releasing it, tousling what was left of his hair and jumping back a couple of steps to avoid the backhand that was sure to follow.

'Oy!' He turned round and his rather irritated expression changed into a wide grin when he saw her.

'Charlie, are you OK? I heard you got yourself GBH'd the other day. Hope whoever did it is looking at a long stretch.'

She leaned over and gave him a hug. Bill had been one of the senior PCs on her team when she had come to Lambeth and had taken her under his wing. She owed him a lot. 'I'm fine now, thanks Bill. But the bastard just got off.'

'You're joking?' He raised his eyebrows questioningly. 'Don't tell me! The CPS?'

She nodded. They both knew.

'For fuck's sake.'

He pulled a chair up next to the group and indicated for her to join them. 'Well I'm sure there's a few of us here who would like to bump into the bastard in a dark alley, if you know what I mean. Bit of summary justice like in the old days.'

He paused as if to emphasize the point.

'There's no fuckin' respect these days. If anyone laid a finger on one of you girls then, they knew what to expect. And it weren't a pat on the back and a few hours fuckin' community service.'

'Well he's just been nicked again.' She pulled the chair away again. 'For a GBH on his own son. He's downstairs now waiting to be booked in; though I'm not sure the custody officer would approve of your methods. '

'Maybe I'll have a quiet word with him another time then,' Bill promised. And somehow Charlie knew that if Bill Morley ever did get the opportunity, he would make sure she got her justice.

*

Keith Hubbard was pacing around the small metal entrance enclosure in the back yard. He looked like a lion trapped behind a glass partition in the zoo, all menace but no means. Charlie was watching his every movement from the canteen window, when Hunter joined her.

'So, when did you know?'

'Yesterday. Forensics found a few remnants of blood in the bathroom that are a match with Richard. Enough to bring Hubbard in, but not enough to charge. To be honest, the kid could have cut himself anytime. You know what boys are like, always getting into scrapes. It's not much to go on, but it'll piss Hubbard off and it gives us the chance to get his account of their disappearance properly on record, under caution.'

'I wonder if he'll come up with a different explanation this time, or stick to one of his previous ones. That's if he says anything. That smarmy solicitor of his will just advise him to go "No comment" through the whole thing.'

Hunter nodded. 'Yeah I know, but it's worth a try. I think you're going to like this next bit though.' He paused before fixing her with a hard stare. 'I'm going to be conducting the interview and I wondered if you'd like to sit in on it? It's up to you. It might be difficult, and I'll understand if you don't want to, but I'm hoping it will unsettle him if you're there. You know he's a liar, and he knows that you know he's a liar.'

She turned to face him in a shot.

'You bet I do!' She felt the adrenalin surge. 'Wouldn't miss it for the world. He might even be tempted to get a bit cocky and say something damning now that he's got off with nearly killing me, you never know?'

Hunter squeezed her shoulder, the small gesture taking her by surprise. 'Come on then, let's go. Either way, it's a win-win situation for us.'

*

Maybe it was the way Keith Hubbard's mouth fell open with surprise or maybe it was the way Annabel Leigh-Matthews pursed hers in ill-contained anger that tickled Charlie, but whichever it was, the small contingent filing into the interview room now were not amused.

'Do you think this is appropriate?' the solicitor was exclaiming, her eyes flicking between Hunter, arms folded across his chest and Charlie sat demurely and firmly in the seat next to the tape machine.

'I think it's very appropriate,' Hunter replied, making it absolutely clear there was no possibility of a change of heart. 'DC Stafford and I probably have more knowledge of your client than the rest of the station put together and she will be staying here to observe and assist me.'

'But...'

'No buts. There is nowhere in our codes of practice that stipulate you have a say in which police officers are present for an interview and, as I'm sure you are well aware, just as Mr Hubbard Keith is no longer a defendant, so too is DC Stafford here no longer a victim and I, no longer a witness. The CPS saw to that!'

'But my client might not wish...'

'Your client might well not wish to have DC Stafford or myself present or to answer any questions. He may not wish to have been arrested and be waiting for an interview, but he has, and now he and you will just have to get on with it. He's had his rights and entitlements and he's had a full consultation with you, so now...' Hunter shut the door firmly behind them, turning to indicate in which seats he wanted them. 'Shall we get on with it?'

Charlie stifled a grin at his words, delivered as they were, with the appropriate amount of authority and malevolent pleasure. Hunter was not one to be messed with, but the gleam in his eyes said it all. He'd engineered the interview just as carefully as he'd arranged the arrest. Having her in the room was a master stroke. Hubbard clearly hated women and she had

50

previous for getting under his skin. Her presence was sure to antagonize him immensely.

'Well I'd like to register my disapproval of not only you interviewing my client, but also your choice of witnessing officer.' Annabel Leigh-Matthews sounded whiney.

'Disapproval registered. Now shall we get on?' Hunter remarked flippantly.

While Hunter went through the preliminaries, Charlie took the chance to have a good look at Hubbard again. He had been watching the battle between his solicitor and Hunter with amusement. She had seen the smirk widen across his face as Ms Leigh-Matthews had initiated the spat, clearly believing she would get her way, his way, as she always seemed to manage. She was good, Charlie had to admit it, but this time she had met her match and had succeeded in nothing more than *registering her disapproval.* Hubbard had not been pleased to lose. He was clearly used to getting his way too and his smirk transformed into a menacing glare as it became obvious the interview would not be on their terms.

He was leaning back on his chair now, with the front two legs lifted high, swaying back and forth as he breathed. His demeanour was surly and he was unwilling to speak up for the tape, his voice little more than a deep growl. His hair had been cropped short recently, his beard and moustache were gone and all that remained was a shadow of stubble which seemed to grow thicker and darker by the hour. He'd looked well-groomed in court but in the confines of the small room he now looked pure thug, crooked nose, cauliflower ear, his menace highlighted by the scars which now showed through the stubbly covering of hair on his head. Even the smart suit was wasted as the tie and belt were gone and his shirt had been unbuttoned several buttons too low, allowing dark tufts of chest hair to stick out. His arms were folded in front of his body and his legs splayed wide. He was clearly trying to dominate the space. Charlie would have found it funny if it hadn't been Hubbard. As it was she eyed him with a mixture of pure hate and amusement at his bravado.

'You have been arrested today for the suspected GBH of your son Richard Hubbard who is still reported missing. Do you know where he is?'

'If I knew that I wouldn't be here.'

Ms Leigh-Matthews put her hand on his arm and shook her head.

'Sorry, no comment,' He corrected.

He looked up at Hunter and grinned, his eyes taking on an almost manic quality.

'No comment, no comment, no comment. There, that's your next three questions answered.'

Hunter wasn't perturbed, after all they'd been expecting it. He just continued with the same line of questioning, pausing after each enquiry to wait for the same answer. When had he last seen Richard? Had he heard from them at all? Was he aware of them spending any money, or using a credit card? What clothes had they taken?

The same old, same old. Hubbard made it clear he wasn't impressed at being asked the same questions as before, but Hunter pressed on irrespective, determined to get any answer, positive, negative or neutral on tape. It didn't matter that Hubbard wasn't giving anything away. Despite being instructed otherwise, they both knew that members of a jury would subconsciously infer guilt. Surely if he was innocent he would tell the police everything he knew so that they could find his wife and son?

And then Hunter started getting down to the details. Was he aware of Richard having any illnesses, being hospitalized? Did he play sport, do any dangerous activities that could cause injury? If he had injured himself where, when, how? Was he aware of Richard bleeding recently? Some of his blood had been found. Did he know where that could have come from? Had he seen him with any cuts? If he had cut himself, where in the house could the blood have been? Who had cleared it up and when? Had he cleared it up, scrubbed it clean at the time? Or had he cleared it up when he'd scrubbed the house from top to bottom the weekend his wife and son had gone missing? Had he caused the blood, hit him, cut him, hurt him? Maybe it was an accident? Maybe it wasn't? Had Richard been winding him up? Maybe Julie had been goading him and he'd taken it out on Richard? Because he had a history of snapping, didn't he? Hitting Julie? And others?

She was staring at Hubbard intently now, watching for every twitch of his face, every slight flicker of guilt. His practised nonchalance couldn't hide his true emotions. And Hunter was winding him up. There was no doubt about it. His cheeks were taking on a redness that hadn't been there at the beginning of the interview. His hands were twitching, balling into fists randomly as he tried to relax, breathe slowly, keep control. Hunter's craft was stunning. It was like watching the heat gradually being increased under a kettle on a hob, tiny bubbles at first, then larger, still rising in the same place, then increasing in number, size, until the whole surface of the water was alive with frothing, raging water, rising up the sides, ready to explode into the air, a living boiling geyser of hate.

Hadn't he been the one to snap, lash out at Richard? Well hadn't he?

He was twisting and turning now, looking from Hunter to her then back to Hunter. Ms Leigh-Matthews wriggled uncomfortably too, but what could she say? Hunter's voice remained quiet, probing, almost offering him excuses. He could never be accused of bullying him, not when he was so calm and reasoned. She allowed a tiny smile to play on her lips at how good he was. She was learning with every question that came from his lips. He was fucking excellent!

And suddenly the kettle was boiling.

'No comment,' Hubbard screamed, leaping up from his seat and slamming the table with his fists. 'No fucking comment.'

The door to the interview room flew open and two burly policemen stood stock-still taking in the scene. Charlie jumped to her feet as Annabel Leigh-Matthews slid from her chair to the floor in the corner of the room, pressing herself against the wall away from the melee as Hubbard reared up again banging his fists against his temples.

'Why can't you lot leave me alone? Going on and on and on and on. Fuckin' messing with my head, that's all you do.'

The officers were on him now, pushing him backwards away from the desk. Charlie threw her weight hard against him too, pinning him against the wall and pulling his arms round to the rear, before clapping him quickly in handcuffs. He was sweating profusely from the effort of resisting but getting nowhere. She stepped back, satisfied and watched as all the fight came out of him and he started to cry, great shuddering sobs that he couldn't control and that made him curse. He swivelled his head round so that he was staring straight at her, his expression venomous.

'See what you've fucking done to me now, you bitch. See what you've done. You've made me like this. You women, all nice and sweet and friendly at first. Julie did that to me too! Why don't you ask the man that keeps on phoning my house what he knows? Pussy! Never speaks. As soon as he hears me, he hangs up. He must want her or else he would say something. Who knows? She's probably screwing him. I loved her you know, but she's fucked everything up and now I hate her. I hate every bit of her, every memory, every fucking mention of her. She's done this to me. She deserves to rot in hell. You women all deserve to rot in hell.'

His cheeks were wet with tears as he was bundled out of the interview room, back towards the cells.

Annabel Leigh-Matthews looked towards the door before pulling herself up to her feet.

'Sorry I wasn't much help,' she mumbled apologetically.

'Don't worry. You were a great help,' Hunter replied, with a satisfied grin. 'Your advice to say no comment assisted us no end.'

He turned to Charlie and spoke seriously.

'Thank you for your presence too, DC Stafford. I think it's fair to say that after our little chat, Mr Hubbard has given us two very strong reasons why Julie and Richard may have disappeared. He doesn't like women and he has distinct anger management issues.'

Chapter 12

Hunter was chewing on the end of a pen impatiently as Charlie jogged in. He had long since worked his way through every one of his finger-nails and small spots of blood framed each cuticle where he had chewed them too low. He was staring at the phone now.

'Why are they taking so bleedin' long?'

'It is Saturday, guv. We're lucky that anyone's in, especially this early.'

He spat out a piece of misshaped plastic from the pen, cursing as the ink cartridge slid out of the flattened end landing in front of him on the desk. Charlie moved to wipe away a small streak of ink, but he brushed her hand away impatiently, throwing the pen towards the bin and cursing again as it hit the rim and bounced off on to the floor. He looked her up and down frowning.

She went to speak but thought better of it, though she did feel more than a little aggrieved that, having come in especially on the weekend to keep up the momentum of the case, Hunter was clearly taking out his bad mood on her. Her mother had also been on her case, warning her not to overdo things too soon. Charlie was literally saved from saying anything by the bell.

As Hunter answered the phone, his expression turned from irritation to astonishment, to glee.

'You must be joking? Are you sure? Thanks.'

After Hubbard's claim in his interview, checks on his home phone had thrown up one number which had appeared on several occasions since Julie's disappearance. They had been waiting to discover the registered owner of that number and Charlie was now totally mesmerized by Hunter's reaction.

'Bloody hell, this is going to be interesting.' He was grinning from ear to ear. 'It's only come back as registered to His highness, the great Justin Latchmere.'

'What! *The* Justin Latchmere?'

He scribbled down an address.

'Well, there can't be too many Justin Latchmeres living in the most exclusive part of Clapham, can there?'

Justin Latchmere was known to everyone in the CID at Lambeth. He worked as a barrister at their local Crown Court and had done so for years. There were few detectives, solicitors or counsel who had failed to come under his spell. Justin was one of those men whose reputation and presence went before them. He was fifty-five years of age with brilliant white hair, swept back off his face into a tiny ponytail at the back of his head, which caused his wig to bulge slightly. Tall, athletic and charismatic, with a finely honed bone structure that made him appear youthful and boyish, while at the same time endowing him with a look of wisdom and knowledge. Justin had worked for both prosecution and defence in the past before settling into the less morally beneficial but more lucrative role of counsel for the defence. Nobody who had ever come across him at court forgot him.

He oozed charm and agreeability, flirting outrageously with any female he needed to get onside, while being every man's best mate, their right-hand man in times of crisis, until they fell into his trap and made a mistake. That done, his killer instinct kicked in, like a spider approaching its silky target, mercilessly reducing his quarry to a stuttering, stammering wreck in the witness box, and all with a persuasive smile plastered across his charming features. Anybody returning to the office after a particularly sound mauling in court would receive the sympathy of all their compatriots if admitting to having been 'Latchmered'.

Given his reputation for incisive and cut-throat questioning, it was hard to understand how everyone still buzzed round him like bees to a honeypot, but they did. Women fell at his feet and he wasn't adverse, so rumour had it, to the odd dalliance here and there, but none lasted long and none were ever allowed to intrude on the longevity of his marriage to his wife, Dana. She was his rock, as he was happy to admit, and even though his roving eye sometimes got the better of him, he would always return after each conquest to her forgiving arms, cowed and chastened slightly but ready to turn on the charm offensive and win her over. Theirs was a solid marriage, not harmed, it seemed, by a spot of outside activity, so long as it didn't affect the relationship by becoming serious. Charlie suspected that as long as the money was still pouring in, Dana Latchmere would allow her errant husband an awful lot of freedom. Having met Dana several times though, she had to say that she'd found her to be a particularly friendly, unassuming woman who quietly but firmly held the purse strings without giving the impression of doing so.

'I wonder why Justin Latchmere has been phoning Hubbard's address then? Seems very strange.'

'I don't know. Maybe Hubbard had spoken to him about his case and Latchmere was going to be his barrister, should it go to Crown Court.'

'But to call him from his own home address? Why on earth would an experienced barrister do that from his personal phone? He must be off his head to allow someone like Hubbard easy access to his private number.'

Hunter was animated and back to his usual self.

'Right. You have ten minutes to smarten yourself up or I'm going without you. Let's hope our honourable friend can come up with some good answers then. It'll make a change for it to be us asking the questions, rather than the other way round.'

*

The house didn't disappoint.

It was set back from the road with a driveway that ran around the front in a generous gravel horseshoe. Ornate black metal gates which opened on the press of a remote control gave access to cars. Matching gates on either side of the vehicular ones allowed foot visitors to come and go. A variety of trees and shrubs framed the garden and large flower beds bordered the immaculately flat, bright green lawn that surrounded the driveway.

The house was large but not imposing, with a country-cottage look belying the fact that it was set in the sprawling capital of England. A slatted, whitewashed front door with a large round door knocker was the focal point with an open, stone porch giving shelter to visitors. Ivy climbed around the frontage on trellises; controlled, it seemed, by the same hard-working gardener whose attention to detail had created the stunning entrance. Double-glazed sash windows receded into the stone window surrounds and a grey tiled roof sloped downwards to join the stonework at a slightly jaunty angle.

All in all, the house looked expensively rural, like a quintessentially English Cotswold home that had been lifted in its entirety and transported to the leafy suburbs of Clapham, South London.

'Wow, nice gaff,' Hunter remarked with a low whistle as they pulled up outside. 'Bet they've got a housekeeper and a gardener to do the work. I can't imagine Justin or Dana being the sort to get their hands dirty.'

They walked towards the porch with the gravel crunching beneath them. Charlie rapped smartly on the front door. There was no reply so she knocked again. When there was still no answer forthcoming, she bent down and pushed the letterbox open. A waft of expensive furniture polish hit her nostrils as she peered through the small gap, trying to see into the house for any movement. Hunter leant forward and banged on the door once more and Charlie was surprised to see a shadow move across her vision.

She stood up quickly but the door remained shut. Bending down again, she called through the letterbox.

'Who is it?' a woman's voice called back.

'It's DC Charlie Stafford and DI Hunter from Lambeth police. Is that you Dana?'

The door opened and Dana Latchmere stood before them. She was just as stunning as her husband, tall and sleek, with long dark hair curling abundantly around her shoulders. Mid-fifties, but well preserved, with subtle eye make-up which enhanced large brown eyes and skin that was smooth and wrinkle-free, save for a few laughter lines. She wore casual brown trousers, a cream cashmere jumper and a thin, loosely tied neck scarf which blended the two shades together perfectly. A single string of pearls and matching earrings completed the look of simple elegance.

'You'd better come in.'

She pulled the door open allowing the two detectives to enter. As they stepped through into the oak panelled hallway, Charlie didn't miss the troubled glance Dana threw behind them before closing the door quickly.

'Sorry for the delay in answering. Justin's out and I was busy upstairs. Is there something I can do for you?'

'We just need a quick chat with you if that's OK. It won't take long.'

Charlie raised her eyebrows at Hunter as they were shown through to a large, expensively furnished lounge at the rear of the house which looked out on to the back garden, resplendent with a small open-air swimming pool and large patio, housing a covered hot tub. Around the room, gilt-framed photographs showed images of their two children: Gemma astride a horse, rosette in hand, and Aiden standing in the front of a red and white-shirted school rugby team.

'Defence work pays well then?' Hunter commented, with another low whistle. 'It's a shame the Crown Prosecution Service isn't so lucrative. Maybe not so many guilty people would be walking free if we could offer the same rate of pay?'

'Innocent until proven guilty,' Dana winked at them as she pulled out a chair and indicated for them to sit down.

Charlie and Hunter made themselves comfortable. They were seated around one end of a large mahogany table so dark and shiny she could almost see her face reflected in the varnished sheen. She tried to smooth her hair back down. It was doing its own thing again.

Dana leant back and placed her hands on the arms of her seat. Hers was at the head of the table, a position that Charlie noted with a wry smile. Dana was already at an advantage over them, at home, in her environment, while she and Hunter were uncomfortably out of place in this opulence. Charlie leant back in her chair, mirroring Dana, who immediately moved forward.

'So what is it that you need to talk to me about? Has Justin beaten you in court again?'

She smiled a little too sweetly towards them.

'Not for a while, thank goodness!' Charlie kept the mood light-hearted. 'Annabel Leigh-Matthews did though recently. I think she's got Justin as her role model. Mind you,' she leant in conspiratorially, 'it seems like Justin might be trying to poach her client off her now.'

Dana frowned. 'I don't know what you're talking about, sorry.'

'Ms Leigh-Matthews's client had assaulted me.'

'Oh! I'm sorry to hear that. I hope you weren't too badly

injured.'

'She was lucky. Five stitches and severe concussion. If she'd fractured her skull it could have been much worse,' Hunter interrupted. 'He walked away from court a free man due to a technicality.'

Dana said nothing. She wouldn't look directly at Charlie. 'I'm sorry to hear that too.' She paused for what seemed like ages. 'But what's it got to do with Justin?'

'The day I got assaulted I was talking to Ms Leigh-Matthews' client about the fact that he had reported his wife and child missing.'

She paused and watched Dana. Her face was giving nothing away, which was unusual; Dana was normally expressive and animated, but this time her face was a mask, as if desperately trying to stifle her emotions.

'The client was arrested in connection with their disappearance yesterday and it appears that he has been receiving silent calls from your home number. '

Dana stood up slowly, her cheeks pale and walked towards the window.

'But why would Justin be trying to poach another solicitor's client?'

'Maybe he is looking around to try and find a more prominent case that will give him more publicity or notoriety?' Charlie tilted her head.

'Now why would I need that?'

Justin Latchmere strode forward into the room, his voice hard and loud and his expression just as stern. 'I have perfectly enough notoriety, as I'm sure both of you, and the vast majority of police and prosecutors, can verify. Now, perhaps you would tell me why you're disturbing my wife and I on a Saturday morning?'

'Good morning, Mr Latchmere. Well, maybe you can tell me why you have been phoning Keith Hubbard's home address then?' She wasn't going to be stopped.

'What?'

'Calls have been made from this address to his number regularly since his wife went missing.'

'I know nothing...' Justin Latchmere stopped mid-sentence. 'Are you interviewing me, officer?'

'There may be a perfectly reasonable explanation why your

number is on Mr Hubbard's call list. We're just giving you a chance to tell us the reason, at the moment. Then we'll decide whether we need to formally interview you.'

'Well I think you're going to have to wait until then. I'm not going to be tricked into saying anything until I know a little more of what is going on. You say Keith Hubbard's wife has been reported missing?'

'Do you know her?'

He said nothing but Charlie got the distinct impression he did.

'She's been gone now for just over two weeks, with one of her sons. Nothing has been heard from them in that time.'

'And you think I might know something about it?'

'We were wondering what the link with your number was?'

'And you want me to tell you without being cautioned or having any legal representative present?'

'I presume you've got some information to tell us then?' She smiled at his obvious concern. He clearly did know something.

'You can presume nothing of the sort other than I want you to leave now. I will make arrangements to come to the police station with my own solicitor and speak with you.'

Hunter stood up and offered him his hand. 'Well that sounds good to me, Mr Latchmere. We'll be in touch to arrange a date that is suitable for us both.'

Dana moved towards Charlie, her voice almost a whisper. 'Can I speak to you for a minute?'

'I'm sure my wife has nothing further to say. Have you, my love?' Justin shot an icy glare at Dana, before finishing off with the same smile that Charlie recognized from their courtroom encounters, the epitome of good-natured, 'case concluded' charm.

'I'm sure she won't be allowed to speak,' Hunter shook his head at the retreating shape of Dana, her head bowed, 'whether she wants to or not.'

Justin ignored the comment and held out his hand towards Charlie. He was smiling again, the same sickly sweet grin, and it made her feel nauseous. She fixed her face in as professional an expression as she could muster and shrugged towards him.

'We'll be in touch,' she said shortly, ignoring his proffered hand and turning to leave. 'Sooner rather than later.'

Chapter 13

It was nearly ready now. One pit. Two neat woodland coffins, seven feet square and three feet down with a smoothed layer of dirt and leaves across the bottom and a heavy trap-door split in two that opened outwards, allowing him a view into every part of it; perfect. A water tank fitted nicely into the top left-hand corner of the pit with a thin rubber hose at its base allowing the water to empty into the mouth of his captive as they sucked. This time he had fitted a valve at the end of the hose so that the water wouldn't be lost needlessly if his captive chose to spit the tube out and leave the tank to drain. He liked to learn. He wanted the pit to evolve and progress with each pair, to maximize his pleasure. He wanted to see every part of the picture, every inch of their bodies, every minute detail of their agony. He wanted to smell their smell, the sickly odour of their sweat, piss, shit and death. He wanted to touch them now too, to feel the cold, dead lifelessness of the favoured one, how they would gradually stiffen, then relax, bloat and empty. He wanted to touch the bitch more this time, feel the difference between life and death; watch the way she would squirm away from his hands. He liked the thought. He liked the thought a lot. Pain for her, pleasure for him. Captivity for her, release for him, Pain and pleasure, pain and pleasure.

He was nearly there. He started to jog through the trail he knew so well, deeper into the woodland, past the huge oak with the hollow centre and the chestnut with the hole that housed the family of tawny owls. He was so close now. He couldn't wait to see it again, to lie down inside it and smell the fresh, earthy smell of the soil and the leaves.

He passed the previous pit. Even in the last few days, since he'd covered the bodies with soil and sealed them in, the woodland had grown up around them. He missed them. There was no odour of death there anymore. It was sealed below, and as long as it wasn't dug up by some woodland creature, the grave would remain anonymous. He laughed at the thought; their final resting place. What a joke. Resting! Well maybe Richard; he was dead by the time his body hit the soil, but Julie. That was the last thing she had done. She had squirmed, cried, pleaded for help, but there was no one to help her. No one to hear except him and he had not listened, just as his own mother had not listened to him. He had been nothing to her, nothing except the one to blame, the one to do the jobs, the one that was hated and used and abused.

He was there now. He felt the raw excitement building in him. His hands were shaking as he bent down and swept the shrubbery away. Open the lid! And there it was; his own private place, away from everything, away from everyone. His own private domain where he could do what he wanted, watch what he wanted, feel what he wanted.

'Fuck you, bitch.'

His voice was low, guttural, filled with rage. 'Fuck you, fuck you, fuck you.'

Climbing in, he inhaled, letting the dampness of the soil fold itself around him. He pulled the door down over him and exhaled, closing his eyes against the darkness. The space was small but not so small that he couldn't move. Light chinked through the gap between the two doors and he pushed himself away from it, against the side of the pit, as far away from the light as he could get.

The voice was filling his head. He curled his legs up to his chest and clung on to them, pulling them tight into him. His breathing was shallow. He held his breath to stop any tiny noise from coming out, holding himself stiff and tight against the wall, trying not to be heard. And then she was there, laughing at him.

'Come out you little bastard. You think you can hide from me do you? Well I'll show you, you little shit. I'll show you.'

And he was falling, falling out from the cupboard on to the hard floor, while she kicked out at him. Screaming, screaming, and the noise filled his head. He was only five. He remembered his nice teacher at school, how his mummy had spoken to her, told his teacher that he was a naughty boy who needed to be punished. But he wasn't and he had said that he wasn't. His mummy had not been pleased. So he had run away and hidden. But now she was there, dragging him across the floor, kicking

63

him. She was turning him over, slapping him across the face.

'Mummy, please don't. Mummy.'

'Think you can tell your teacher lies, do you?'

He was on his back and she was sitting on him, laughing at him, slapping him.

'I'll show you.'

'Please Mummy. I'm sorry.'

But she wasn't listening. She never listened. She was undoing his clothing, pulling his T-shirt up over his face, unbuttoning his shorts. She was going to hurt him again like she always did. She was going to smack him and smack him until he was bruised and sore, until his bottom hurt to sit on. And he squirmed to get free but he couldn't because Mummy was pinning him down, but she wasn't hurting him this time. She had her hand down his pants and he didn't know what was happening but it didn't feel right and it sort of felt nice but strange. She was laughing as she touched him.

'You want to be a good boy then, do you? Well do you?'

He couldn't see her for the T-shirt across his face but he nodded. He wanted to be a good boy, like Tommy, his brother. He wanted to be good, but he wasn't a good boy. Mummy kept telling him he was naughty. Mummy told everyone he was naughty, but he really wasn't.

Mummy was still laughing as she stroked him and he was afraid to say anything. And then she stopped and grabbed his hand and pushed it down inside her clothing. And she pulled the T-shirt off his face and she was smiling down at him now and he didn't know whether to smile back.

And everything felt strange. His Mummy felt strange and was moving in a strange way, and she wouldn't let him take his hand out. She was pulling and pushing at his hand and smiling, and staring down at him.

'Now who's a good boy then?'

And he was pleased that he was making her smile, pleased that he was being good, even though she was making strange moaning sounds.

Then just as quickly, she stopped moving and stopped smiling and he didn't know what was wrong.

'I'm being a good boy.' He wanted to make her smile again but instead she was frowning. Then she punched him and the blow to his tummy hurt and made him feel sick. He started to cry but that just made Mummy more cross.

'Shut up you little bastard,' she was shouting at him now.

And he looked up and there was Tommy standing at the door, watching. And he didn't know how long Tommy had been watching or what Tommy had seen.

'Tommy,' he called out to his brother. Mummy had turned from him now and was going towards Tommy, scooping him up in her arms and kissing him.

'Hello, my beautiful boy,' she whispered to Tommy and he knew that she would never whisper that to him. Never. And he curled back up into a little ball and started to cry again. And then she was gone and he was all alone.

But that was the start of it. That was the beginning of his special times with Mummy. The times that Tommy didn't know about; the times when Mummy smiled at him. But those were the only times when Mummy smiled at him. Tommy, his older brother, was always her favourite. Tommy, her beautiful boy, her smartest, handsomest, cleverest boy...

He could feel the anger surging again now; the rage was building as he lay in his pit. He loved her but he hated her. He forced himself to think of his mummy smiling as she touched him, smiling as he touched her. Nothing else he had ever done had made her smile. That was why, next time, when he had a different mummy captured he would make her strip off. So he could feel her, make her smile too like his mummy used to every time when she did it to him. He reached down into his underwear and felt his hard-on. It made him angry to feel it because his mummy had gone now and it was supposed to be for her, only her. But it was throbbing now, aching to be touched, and he knew he would be thinking of her again as he grasped it.

The tears were starting again. His mummy had gone. He had seen to that. And all the other women were nothing in comparison. They were all bitches that let him down time and time and time again.

But he would show them. He would show them next time and the time after that. He needed to start the process again soon. He couldn't wait much longer. And he knew who the next woman would be. He knew her favourite. He could see it in the eyes of the rejected one. He could see it in the eyes of the chosen one. Soon they would be his. Soon the bitch would lie where he was lying now knowing her favourite was dead beside her. Soon she would die, slowly and painfully and agonizingly.

He could feel the excitement building at the thought. He could feel the tears streaming down his cheeks. And as he spat out his hatred into the soil of his pit he knew it wouldn't be much longer.

Chapter 15

The evening was closing in as Charlie jogged towards the station.

She heard a shout and saw Hunter pulling up across the road in his Jag, a choice of vehicle that always amused her. He looked so diminutive and out of place in the seat of the sleek, dark green executive car, his tweed peaked cap pulled firmly down over his balding head. He would have suited the Escort RS2 or Cortina Ghia far more, the cars of *The Sweeney*, the age of policing which suited him best.

'Hop in. I'll give you a lift.'

She ran across towards him, immediately tempted to jump in. A lift with Hunter was always guaranteed to be action-packed. Things always happened when they were together. The light on his mobile pulsed on. His wife was calling. He left it to ring.

'Aren't you going to answer it?'

'She'll want to know what time I'll be home.' He smiled a little sheepishly. 'You know Mrs H. Ever since the bloody doctors mentioned high blood pressure she thinks I'm going to drop dead if I'm not home by ten.'

He pulled a packet of fags from his pocket and lit one, blowing the smoke out through the open window.

'I'll be in trouble if she finds out I'm doing this too. She's got a nose like a sniffer dog when it comes to Rothmans. Even if I chewed through a whole packet of extra strong mints she'd still notice it on my breath.'

She grinned back at him. It was her turn to act the adult.

'You know she's doing it for the right reasons though, guv. She's just concerned.'

She'd met Mrs H, as Hunter always referred to her, several times and there was no mistaking the genuine love they had for each other. They were both on their second marriages and she was obviously determined that this one would last as long as humanly possible. Having frog-marched him to the doctors for a check-up the previous year, the ensuing diagnosis of hypertension had shaken her to the core. He'd been warned to lose weight, stop smoking and do more exercise, all of which he was failing to do spectacularly. Tablets were keeping his blood pressure down, but Hunter knew best and she couldn't change him, however hard she tried.

It was just a matter of time before his condition worsened but as he stubbornly refused her request to retire, they had come to a compromise whereby he went along with a little over-protectiveness from Mrs H , in return for remaining in post without too much being said, too often.

'I know she is. Had an earful of her concern several times today.' He grinned and tapped the passenger seat next to him. 'Come on, Charlie, let's go for a spin.'

'Gonna have to turn you down, guv. I've been promising my body a bit of a work-out after all the sitting down I've been doing recently.' She thought about the secret promise she'd made to Mrs H to look after him, last time they'd met. 'Besides you'll only get us both into trouble if I get in the car with you.'

She nodded towards the job radio propped up in the centre consul and the old, ripped grey donkey jacket spread across the rear seat. Charlie had seen him in action many a time on and off duty. He'd slip the radio into his jacket pocket when he was out and about and no one would bat an eyelid at him; he was just an old down-and-out. Little did anyone know, when he came across a crime, he would utilize the radio to call in more troops or, if necessity required, as a very effective weapon.

'Your choice then, but who knows what fun you might be missing.'

He winked and put his foot hard down on the accelerator and she watched as the Jag shot off like a bolt of green laser light, wishing she'd agreed, after all to the ride.

She decided to head along the Thames towards Blackfriars, for a change, mulling over the events of the day. Jogging was the time she thought the most about everything.

The clouds were threatening, rising up in huge towering blocks of darkness rimmed by an edge of light from the failing sun. It had been a strange day, particularly the visit to Dana Latchmere, obviously on edge, and wanting to say more than her domineering husband would allow. Now the evening seemed strangely perturbed too. She passed Lambeth Bridge, turning right towards Westminster Bridge with the Houses of Parliament and Big Ben standing guard. The atmosphere was anxious, the calm before a storm, a few birds flitted around and the water of the river moved silently seawards in small, menacing whirlpools and black eddies. She shuddered at the sight of it. She hated water, the way it stealthily changed its character before you had time to realize; one minute calm and inviting, the next minute full of malevolent fury. She felt her pulse quicken at the thought. For an instant she was being tossed and turned in darkness, fighting to come up for air, thrashing about with every last ounce of energy. The trouble was whenever she did come to the surface she knew the panic would only get worse, a thousand times worse.

A Victorian-style lamp flickered on, reacting to the darkening sky. She stopped underneath it, bathed in a halo of light. She closed her eyes and for two minutes allowed the screaming inside her head to quieten.

When she'd recovered sufficiently, she turned her sight away from the river and started to run again, moving swiftly and noiselessly, save for the soft rhythm of her breath. Past St Thomas's hospital and then she was crossing the road leading to Westminster Bridge, still littered with snapping tourists. Onwards towards the London Eye, illuminated against the darkening back-drop, its pods moving silently on their never-ending, relentless daily loop. The South Bank seemed quieter than normal, the evening's activities confined to hastily booked seats within restaurants, with fewer people than normal wandering the walkways.

She heard a commotion within the confines of the riverside skateboard park and turned to see a figure sprawled on the concrete, with three or four people, silhouetted against the graffiti-covered walls, bending over him. A set of crutches lay at angles to the man on the ground, out of his reach and he was calling out. He sounded slightly drunk, the tempo of his voice rising and falling and his words slurred. His tone resonated more with anger than distress. She decided to keep going. It didn't look to be any more than a drunken accident and there were obviously enough people dealing with him. They didn't need another to further antagonize him.

'Charlie. Help me.'

The words stopped her in her tracks. Spinning round, she stared in the direction the voice came from, and suddenly everything was clicking into place. It was Ben Jacobs lying on the ground, his face turned towards her. One of the supposed Good Samaritans bending over him pulled his hand out of Ben's jacket pocket and punched him square in the face. She heard the thud of bone on bone from where she was and saw Ben's nose explode, blood spurting out on to the pavement.

She reacted instantly as she always did; with no concern for her own safety. Screaming loudly, she ran straight at the group, who turned towards her open-mouthed with surprise, before splitting up and sprinting away in all directions. But not before the man who had punched Ben aimed a well-placed boot into his rib-cage. Ben cried out in pain. The man laughed, and as Charlie neared them, he spat on the ground and shouted.

'This is what he deserves. Help for Heroes? He's no hero. Look at him. He's just a drunk.'

Side-stepping Charlie, he delivered a hard shove at her shoulder, catching her off balance, and darted away across the pavement, before turning the corner and disappearing. She went to go after him, but as Ben let out a long groan, she changed her mind and doubled back to help him instead. She'd got a good look at his attacker's leering face and she knew she wouldn't forget it. She'd rather catch the guy later than go after him now and return to find Ben choked to death on his own blood.

He was in a bad way. His nose was slewed to one side, obviously broken and both eyes were swelling even as she looked. Quickly, she dialled 999 requesting an ambulance and police, before bending down to tend to him. His broken leg stretched out in front of him, the plaster cast cracked and broken, as if it had been stamped on. The other leg was folded underneath him at a strange angle, his shoe lying some distance away. To pick on a war hero was despicable, even more so when they were obviously injured, and even worse when so badly outnumbered.

'Bastards! Didn't even give me a chance,' he groaned, trying to open his swollen eyes. 'If they hadn't gone straight for my bleedin' crutches, I would have beaten the crap out of them all with them.'

He turned away from her and punched the pavement,

before hauling himself on to his elbows, wincing in pain as he did so and upending his 'Help for Heroes' collection box. Nothing came out.

'And they've got the day's takings, the gits.'

She could hardly bear to watch. She wanted to help but didn't want to hurt his already injured pride even more by doing so, but the anger was welling up inside her. Ben Jacobs was an honourable young man, mentally maimed in the name of his country and obviously fighting his own demons. He didn't deserve this. The worse thing was that none of it was his fault; he'd been used by the government and, after a cursory term of recuperation, had been left to fend for himself. With a family who didn't understand mental illness and who had quickly disowned him, he'd ended up using drink as a way of dulling the pain. Now here she was, wanting to help but feeling useless in the knowledge that he wouldn't allow her to.

The sirens of the ambulance were getting closer now. She couldn't help breathing a sigh of relief. She knew the basics of life support and first aid, but she was always relieved when the paramedics arrived to take over the responsibility. She couldn't just leave him though.

Ben was looking towards her as they arrived. She quickly gave them a rundown of what had happened before trying to answer their next question out of his hearing.

'Yes, I think he's had a few. His speech is a little slurry and his breath smells of alcohol.' Ben turned away; he'd obviously heard her. She cursed silently that she hadn't refused to answer the question, or moved further out of earshot. The last thing she wanted was to make Ben feel she was judging him. God only knew what she'd be like if she'd seen the things he had.

Bill Morley strode towards them.

'Well I never, Charlie, I don't see you for ages then I see you twice in two days. You're like a bus. Not that I'm complaining.'

'More like the back of a bus.' She pulled her T-shirt down subconsciously.

Bill ignored the comment, taking his notebook from his pocket. 'So, what's happened?'

She explained again what she had seen as Bill took notes. As an ex-serviceman, she knew exactly what Bill would want to do; it was the same as she wanted. She finished by giving him as full a description of all the suspects as she could remember, concentrating particularly on every little detail of the main attacker.

'I got a good look at him, Bill, and you know what I'm like when I've seen someone.'

'Never forget a face!'

She had a reputation for remembering faces. If anyone wanted to identify a suspect, the first port of call would always be Charlie. Whether it was a photo that needed to be ID'd, a description of a distinctive person, or even an unusual tattoo or feature, she was the one to whom everyone turned. Hence her being nominated by Hunter to attend an independent, external course at the University of Greenwich at their campus in Eltham to test her powers of observation and identification. She'd been required to pick out people in crowds, faces from all angles, in poor visibility, for long periods of time or split seconds. After hours of tests she had emerged with the proud title of being a 'super recognizer'. Having failed at school, any acknowledgement of her worth meant a lot to Charlie, and as this was a talent crucial to her job, she was particularly pleased with the accolade.

'When I get a name for the face I'll let you know, Bill. In the meantime though, a quick sample of the main suspect's spit might be a good back-up. He spat on the ground down there.' She pointed at where the thug had spat at Ben. 'Whichever way is quicker, you can come and help me bring him in when we've got a name.'

'It'll be my pleasure, Charlie.'

'Hopefully we'll be seeing quite a lot of each other in the coming weeks then.' She glanced back at Ben. The paramedics were ready to leave for the hospital. He looked lost, strapped onto the stretcher, clutching the crutches that had now been retrieved, as if expecting another attack.

'I'll go with him.' She couldn't bear to see him on his own. She pulled Bill to one side, out of Ben's earshot. 'At least until his family arrive; if any of them can be bothered to turn out for him.'

Bill looked towards her quizzically.

'They've sort of disowned him since he turned to booze.'

'Bloody disgrace,' Bill shook his head. 'After all he's been through.'

She walked back to the ambulance and climbed in, taking

Ben's hand and squeezing it encouragingly. Bill Morley smiled towards her.

'You're a good kid, you know?'

'Yes she is,' Ben agreed. 'The best.' He pulled her hand up towards his lips and gave it a kiss. She felt her cheeks burning, especially when she saw the conspicuous wink Bill gave her as he shut the ambulance door.

Ben was just a mate. She hadn't given anything more than that a thought. But he was still holding her hand tightly and suddenly she didn't quite know what to do. She was just doing her job, and if that meant making sure he was safe and bringing the scum that had done this to him to justice, well that's what she would do.

Pulling her hand gently away, she tried to busy herself with a pen and paper, aware of his eyes watching her every move.

'Right then, Ben,' she tried to get back to a more formal level. 'Give me a few days and I'll have these bastards locked up. You know I always get my man.'

Chapter 15

Charlie slept in the office that night, curled up in the corner on a pile of bright blue, prisoners' blankets she'd borrowed from custody. It had been her favoured option after finally leaving Ben in the early hours of the morning, having been admitted to a ward for observations. Her family home was too far away and her own flat, although near enough in distance was the last place she wanted to be. It was too quiet. She needed to be around people and noise.

Bet woke her with a cup of tea.

'Charlie, are you OK? The guvnor saw you here and asked me to check on you.'

'I'm fine. Is he in already?' she sat up far too quickly, almost shouting the words.

Bet reached over and pulled the earphones out of her ears. The iPod playing her favourite playlist had long since died.

'Yep he's just been called to a briefing on the Hubbard case. The others have all agreed to come in too, even though it's Sunday. They'll be turning up shortly. You might want to jump in the shower quick before they all arrive.'

She hauled herself up, yawned and brushed some blue fluff off her T-shirt, before glancing at the clock above the door. It was less than four hours since she'd first lain down. She'd jump in the shower, have a quick freshen-up and then start looking through the list of known robbers operating on the South Bank. By the time Hunter was finished at his briefing, hopefully she'd have a name for Ben's assailant. She pushed the blankets into a pile with her foot.

Bet bent down, picking one up to fold.

'They are clean ones, I hope. Or shouldn't I ask?'

Charlie shrugged and headed for the door. 'I guess you shouldn't ask.'

Ten minutes later and she was back sitting at her computer, smelling of tangerine and ylang-ylang, with wet hair, hastily combed into place and wearing clean, although not expertly laundered, clothes, salvaged from the bottom of her locker. The tea had been reheated in the office microwave and as each image flicked on to the screen, she took a sip, shook her head and moved on to the next.

'Oh my God, I ache in every part of my body. In fact, I ache in parts of my body that I didn't realize could ache.' Paul pushed the door open with his foot, hung his jacket on a peg and tucked his shirt back into the rear of his trousers all in one continuous movement, as if still asleep. He looked as if hadn't slept at all. 'I was in Heaven until a few hours ago.'

Heaven was Paul's favourite night-club, situated under the arches at Charing Cross. He loved it as much for the double entendre whenever he said the name, as for the dark, throbbing beat of the house music.

Sabira smiled. 'I've been in heaven too.' She happily tapped a code into her phone and quickly flicked to a photo of a rather butch-looking girl sat astride a shiny black Triumph motorcycle. 'Hot eh? Had my first date with her yesterday evening.' Charlie glanced up from the computer images of a group of recently arrested robbers to look at the photo. None of them were her assailants.

'Nice bike,' she commented.

Naz peered over her shoulder.

'Lucky for some; though not sure she's quite my type.' Naz was clearly not happy. She threw herself down on her chair moodily. 'Well, I've been in hell all weekend. In fact, I'm glad to have got out of the house this morning. Even work is better than being cooped up there. I managed to persuade a friend that I was indispensable at work and had to come in. She's looking after the boys for the day.'

'What's the problem then, Naz?' Bet scooped up the mugs to make a fresh cup for everyone.

'My mum's been away on holiday so I've had the kids all by myself and Nathaniel is being a right little git at the moment. I don't know if it's his age or what? I can't remember the last time I've had to be in on a Friday *and* Saturday night. And I don't want another weekend like it again for a long time. In fact, ever.'

'The joys of motherhood, eh. Good old grandparents.' Bet flicked the switch of the kettle. 'At least we're good for something. Baby-sitting and making tea!'

'You could always send him to me, Naz.' Colin sidled over. 'I'll put him to work digging and wear him out. I've been spending every spare moment putting a new fence up down the back of my garden. The neighbours have got a new bloody dog which keeps knocking holes in the old fence and coming and crapping all over my grass. If it carries on, I'm going to start posting it back through their letter box.'

Hunter came in quietly, standing for a few minutes to listen to the conversation.

'Do you lot ever actually get any work done? Charlie said it was like working in the *Jeremy Kyle* studio and it really is.'

Charlie spun away from some more images on her computer and held her hands up in mock surprise.

'Hold it, guys, before you all accuse me of snitching. I'm allowed to say that because you're always telling me I should be on the programme. *"My colleague gets on better with animals than people! Is there something wrong with her?"*'

'One day you'll make a lovely wife, Charlie,' Paul crowed. 'Just not sure who to?'

'Whoever it ends up as, they'll need a bloody medal to put up with her.'

'And a good deal of stamina,' Bet agreed with Hunter. 'She wears me out just listening to her antics.'

'Yes, I've just been hearing about your heroics last night.'

The others all stopped and looked towards her expectantly. Her cheeks immediately started to burn.

'I'm going to have to escort you to your doorstep from now on, to stop you putting your life at risk.' Hunter shook his head at her, but she knew by his expression that he wasn't cross. He turned back towards the others.

'Apparently, she single-handedly stopped a robbery in progress, chased off the four suspects and then did first aid until the cavalry arrived. She even accompanied the victim to hospital and stayed with him until he was OK. I'm sure she'll tell you all about it when I've left the office.' They all turned towards her expectantly. She looked down at the floor, embarrassed. 'Or maybe you'll have to find out from a different source. Oh, and have you all heard the latest?' He switched back to their upturned faces. 'Charlie and I have Justin Latchmere on the ropes, don't we?'

'I'll be phoning him very soon to arrange for him to come in, guv.' She was glad the subject had changed. 'He's got to explain why his home number is logged for incoming calls to Keith Hubbard, after Julie and her son disappeared.'

On cue, her phone rang. It was the front office clerk. Mr Latchmere was waiting, with his solicitor downstairs for them now. She hung up and looked towards Hunter.

'Talk of the devil. We must have got him worried. Latchmere and his solicitor are waiting for us now.'

'He's so fucking slippery,' Hunter shook his head, obviously annoyed. 'He was supposed to phone to tell us when he was available so we could arrange a time that suits us both. He's trying to get us on the back foot. Charlie, get everything together and check whether there have been any more calls since we last spoke with him. I'll go down and tell him we've got a few things that need to be done first. We'll see him when *we're* good and ready, and not before.'

*

Justin Latchmere looked thoroughly irritated when she and Hunter eventually collected him and his solicitor forty-five minutes later.

'Sorry to have kept you.' Hunter smiled sweetly.

Charlie had used the time to prepare thoroughly, checking the latest call data and compiling a full list of dates and times on which the previous calls had been made.

The solicitor, a portly, bald headed man with thick glasses and an ill-fitting suit, sighed heavily. Latchmere scowled, making a play of checking his large Rolex watch.

'We are busy people, you know, and I don't want to have any more of my weekend wasted than I must.'

'So are we,' Hunter replied evenly. 'And if you'd phoned, as arranged, we would have been ready for you. You should know as well as we do what Saturday nights throw up for us to deal with.'

Latchmere frowned harder but said nothing.

Charlie led them into a small interview room off the front office, barely large enough for the four chairs that were needed and a small table which was clean but showed the results of too many people being left for too long on their own. Several names were scratched on to the table and other names and dates were graffittied on the walls and door with marker pens. Some attempts had been made to remove them, leaving darkened patches on the wall, but on the whole they stayed stubbornly present, making the room look shabby. The table was the standard black top with dark wood edging and none of the chairs matched. Altogether the look was more like a junk room at a charity shop than a cutting-edge service welcome.

The surroundings were not lost on Justin Latchmere whose scowl deepened even further as he surveyed the tiny room.

'We won't keep you too long,' Charlie reassured, inwardly revelling in the man's discomfiture. 'Take a seat.'

They all sat down and she began.

'The reason we've asked you to come in is because it's been brought to our attention that there have been a number of calls made from your home phone to the home of Keith Hubbard and he has complained about them.'

'Yes you've already told me this.'

'Well, as you insist that we do this as a formal interview, I'll caution you that you don't have to say anything unless you wish to do so and anything you say will be written down and may be given in evidence. As I'm sure you know, you're not under arrest, you don't have to stay if you don't wish to, and you're entitled to legal advice, which I can see you have.'

'Yes, I know all this. Can we just get on with it?'

She shuffled her papers slowly and noted down the time before pausing awhile. She'd learnt well from Hunter.

'Have you made these calls, Mr Latchmere?'

'No I haven't.'

'Keith Hubbard seemed to think it was a male making the calls.'

'Well it wasn't me.'

'Are there any other males in your house who could have made the calls?'

'No. Unless Dana lets the gardener in.' He smirked. 'But I don't think so. If you saw the guy...' He left the sentence unfinished. She ignored the insinuation.

'Are there any other people who have access to your home phone?'

'No. Just Dana and I, and the gardener and housekeeper

who work for us, but the housekeeper is definitely female.'

'So, really, you are saying that you are the only male in the household who is likely to use the phone.'

'Yes. And it's not me, so it's a bit of a mystery, isn't it?'

'Do you know Keith Hubbard?'

'No, never met the man; though I have read about his wife and son going missing in the local paper recently.'

'And you've never spoken to him?'

'No.'

'Or tried to speak to him?'

'No.'

'What about his wife? Do you know her?'

'Never met her either.'

'Or their son, Richard.'

'No.'

'Doesn't your son go to the same school as Richard?'

'How would I know? Dana does all the school stuff.'

'They both go to Clapham Boy's Academy.'

'I hardly think they would be best friends. Aiden is in the top set, doing very well for himself. Judging by the sound of this Keith Hubbard, I would hazard a guess that his son is not likely to be quite on the same level, shall we say.' His tone was pompous. He raised his eyebrows at his solicitor. Charlie pressed on.

'But they're at the same school.'

'There are over a thousand boys at that same school. Are you speaking to all their parents too?' He stared directly at her and gave her a small impatient smile.

'No. Only the ones who have been making calls to the Hubbard family home address.'

She smiled back at him, wiping the smug expression from his face immediately.

'So you're saying that you have not made any calls to Keith Hubbard's house, you're probably the only male with access to your home phone, except for possibly the gardener, and you do not know and have never met any of the Hubbard family, either Keith, Julie, Ryan or Richard?'

'Yes that's exactly what I'm saying. Anyway what time are these calls supposed to have been made?'

She read through the list.

'There were fifteen calls in all, over eight days, after Julie and Richard went missing. Some days there was only one call, or no calls at all, on other days there were two or three, spaced out about an hour apart. All the calls were made during the daytime.'

'There you go then,' he sounded triumphant. 'I couldn't have made any of the calls. I would have been at work.'

'And you never pop home?'

'Sometimes I pop in when I'm on my way back from court or meeting clients, but I haven't popped home recently. Certainly not on all those days. You can check my diary.'

'Thank you! I will.'

'Is there anything else because I now wish to leave?' He stood up as if to go.

'No that'll be fine for now. We'll make some further enquiries and speak to Dana about who else has access to your phone.'

'You'll do no such thing without me being there.'

'And why's that?'

'She is my wife. If she really needs to be spoken to, I think I am best placed, as her husband and lawyer, to accompany her, don't you think?'

'I believe that could well be a conflict of interest. Dana is a grown woman and quite capable of making that choice herself, don't *you* think?' she threw the question back at him.

'Well of course.'

'Plus, we still haven't got to the bottom of who is making the calls and you don't seem to be able to help any further.'

He pulled himself up to his full height. 'Well I would suggest that you let me know if and when you choose to speak to my wife.'

'And I would suggest that if that's what you want, you tell her first, because if she's happy to speak to us without you, then that's what we'll be doing.'

*

'Why's he so insistent on being there when we speak to Dana?' Charlie said as she and Hunter walked across the gravelled driveway of the Latchmeres' house. They had decided to get to the bottom of who was making the calls straight away and they certainly weren't going to wait for Justin's permission.

'That's twice he's been touchy about us speaking to her without him being present.'

'That's because he's lying,' Hunter was to the point. 'I was watching him during the interview. You did well by the way. He was trying to intimidate you but you wouldn't let him. He was sweating and fidgety.'

'I saw that too. Continually wiping his hands on his trousers. He knows she's the one making the phone calls. *And* he knows why. The calls were silent. It's only Hubbard's presumption that it was a male making the calls. Latchmere knows it's Dana and that's why he's so nervous about letting us speak to her. We've just got to persuade her to tell us why.'

She stopped and looked up at the windows, checking for any sign of life. 'By the way, guv, thanks for letting me conduct the interview. I'm getting to really enjoy them. I love making guilty people sweat.'

'It's good practice for you and it was a good chance for me to sit back and watch Latchmere properly. He likes to come across as such a professional, when he's in court. You almost forget that he's just a man with normal reactions like any other person. He sweats like you and I, and he shits like you and I. And his shit, definitely does not smell like roses.'

'Speak for yourself, guv. You seem to forget I'm a lady and I neither sweat nor shit.'

Hunter chuckled. 'Then why does what you say regularly have a distinct "air de bullshit"? And anyway, the day you become a lady is the day I retire; should see me going for at least a dozen more years.'

Dana's car was in the driveway as they headed towards the house, a sporty Mercedes convertible with a personalized registration plate. There were several upstairs windows open and the sound of music could be faintly heard. Charlie knocked on the door but there was no immediate response.

'She's definitely in.' She banged on the door again. 'I can hear the radio.'

Charlie wandered off to look through a couple of downstairs windows, before returning to the front door and knocking it hard and continuously.

'Dana, answer the door please. We know you're in there.'

The music had gone off but there was still no answer.

'Dana, we're not going away, so you're better off speaking to us now. We'll be sitting in our car outside waiting. I promise you we'll be here all day if necessary.'

They crunched across the driveway.

'What's the betting Justin will have been summonsed back? Give it fifteen minutes,' Hunter said, checking his watch. 'I'm sure he'll be ecstatic to see us again.'

She had just reached the gate when she heard a voice calling out to them.

Turning, she saw Dana standing in the porch beckoning them over. She appeared anxious, scanning the driveway and bushes as they walked back.

'Come in, quickly,' she said, closing the door hurriedly behind them as they stepped into the hallway.

'Are you OK?' Charlie noted the instant relief as the door was shut.

Dana shook her head. 'No, not really. I wanted to speak to you last time, but Justin told me not to get you lot involved.'

'But we are involved.'

'I know and that's what I want to talk to you about.'

They were shown through to the kitchen this time. It was huge, with perfectly ordered units housing built-in white goods, and spacious granite work surfaces, uncluttered and sparklingly clean. A tray had already been laid out with three cups and saucers, a large china teapot and a plate of assorted biscuits.

'You look like you've been expecting us.' Hunter indicated the tray.

'I have. I knew you'd be round as soon as Justin phoned to tell me not to speak to you without him being here. He's got things to do, but I'm sure he'll be back as quickly as he can.'

'So why didn't you answer the door straight away?' Charlie asked, puzzled.

'Because I had to be sure it was you and I couldn't see you when you were in the porch. It was only when you were looking around that I knew I'd be safe.'

'Safe? From what?'

Dana's expression froze. She looked frightened all of a sudden.

'I think you'd better tell us what's been going on.'

Dana nodded. She looked close to tears.

'I'll start at the beginning,' she busied herself, concentrating on pouring the tea. 'I don't know how much you know or have heard about Justin and me?' She didn't allow them to answer. 'But we have a somewhat open relationship. For years now, in fact most of the time we have been married, he has conducted affairs, "dalliances" as he likes to call them. To start with I hated it, but he always insisted they meant nothing and he loved me. He did try to stop, but he can't help himself. He's a flirtatious man and can be very charming, as I'm sure you've seen?' She looked up and caught Charlie's eye. She nodded.

'Go on.'

'I have learned to accept it. His affairs rarely affect our day-to-day relationship or our family. He is a good husband and father in all other ways. He cares for us, looks after us and provides us with everything we need.'

Charlie bit back the temptation to say 'so I can see', instead smiling her encouragement for Dana to continue.

'Just occasionally these affairs have become more serious. Maybe two or three other women have got too close; I can't have that. This is my life, our life, and I am not going to let some tart that he's picked up come between him and our children.'

She was surprised at the sudden hardness in Dana's voice; Justin's wife obviously had hidden strength.

'I have warned Justin to stop and, where necessary I have warned these women to back down. And so far they always have. And Justin and I have always gone back to our normal life after a short time.'

She stopped to take a sip of tea and pass the biscuits around, as if she was talking about the most ordinary occurrence. They both took one, Hunter nibbling at the edges of his, while Charlie dunked hers into the steaming liquid. Dana pursed her lips slightly with distaste and continued.

'Anyway, this time it's different. Justin seems to have fallen in love, or certainly in lust.'

'With Julie Hubbard?' Charlie was incredulous, but she had to admit the pieces began to fit.

Dana nodded. 'Yes. They met at a school function. Justin is on the board of governors at our son, Aiden's school, and Julie's sons also go there. I don't think the boys really know each other and I'm not really sure exactly *why* Justin and Julie were introduced but they certainly did meet and got to know each other very well, intimately even.'

'I wouldn't have put the pair of them together. You're not exactly in the same social league!'

Dana laughed bitterly. 'Oh Justin likes his bits of rough. I think they amuse him and he can dominate them without too much trouble.'

'Has his *dalliance* with Julie been going on for long?'

'Too long. Several months, if not more. Justin doesn't discuss things, but after seeing the way his behaviour changes over the years when he has his affairs, I recognized the signs: staying out late or overnight, spending money on presents et cetera, et cetera. I told him it had to stop, but so far he hasn't been able to end it. He's hooked. I actually think she's better educated than the others. Maybe she's more of a challenge to him. Justin always likes a challenge, as everyone who comes up against him at court knows.' Dana bit her bottom lip.

'Anyway, I decided to warn Julie off too, hence all the phone calls from here to her home address. It was always her husband who answered the phone though, so I didn't say anything. I wanted to speak to Julie. I didn't realize she and Richard had gone missing until I heard it on the news. It's awful. I wanted to tell you when you were here, but I couldn't admit to what Justin had been doing and the state of our marriage. It's not exactly conventional, is it? And I didn't want to hurt him professionally, you see?'

She looked towards them both. Charlie nodded back at her.

'Then he came home and the rest is history really, isn't it?'

'He told us he had never met Keith or Julie Hubbard when he spoke to us earlier.'

'I know, he told me he'd said that. I don't know why he didn't tell you. It's stupid! As if you're not going to find out. Loads of parents at the school know. As soon as Julie went missing, the game was always going to be up. For every day since she was reported, you lot would be digging deeper. I'm surprised it took this long really.'

'We checked the phone messages at the time and nothing in particular came up,' Hunter explained. 'And Keith Hubbard didn't initially say anything, for some reason. Most of the focus has been on Julie's mobile phone and locating that, rather than the home phone.'

Dana was quiet for several minutes. She got up and went to

the window, staring out at the vast expanse of back lawn.

'Justin rarely uses the home phone. He's got a spare phone that's pay as you go. I think he uses that one for his affairs. I found it once.' She paused, swallowing, as if to catch her breath. 'Justin's going to get into trouble because of all this, isn't he?'

'We will need to speak to him again, yes.' She was already looking forward to the opportunity.

'And all the sordid secrets of our marriage will come out, won't they?'

'Well, we won't let them out on purpose, but it will depend on whether he knows more about Julie and Richard's disappearance than he's letting on. There may be further leads or alibis that we will have to investigate.'

'I don't know what he knows. I hope to God it's not much. I don't know how the children are going to cope. It's going to blow our world apart as it is.'

'We'll be in touch with him very soon.' Charlie got up to leave.

'I'll tell him to expect you, but then I would imagine he's already expecting a call. I don't know what he's playing at.'

They walked towards the front door. When they got there, Dana leant forward and peered through the spyhole.

'I thought you were only supposed to check when you were letting someone in? Not when you're letting someone out?'

'I've had a strange man turning up at my front door. I opened the door the first time and he didn't say a word; just stared at me. It gave me the creeps. He's been round several times since, but I don't open the door.'

'Hence the wait when we've been both times? We knew you were in but you took ages to answer.'

'Yes, sorry. I had to be sure it wasn't him or he wasn't hiding just round the corner.'

'Do you know him?'

'I think I might, but I couldn't say for certain. He does frighten me though.'

'So, who is it then?' Hunter looked impatient.

'Well,' Dana's voice was almost a whisper. She looked towards Charlie, her eyes fearful again. 'I haven't told Justin yet, by the way, because I was hoping the man would just stop without us having to get the police involved, but he hasn't. I didn't really want to have to explain about our situation at a police station, but now you both know, hopefully you might be able to help without it going any further.'

She paused, glancing around the front of the house one last time. 'I'm not positive, because I've only passed him on the very occasional school do and I didn't know who he was then, but I think it's Julie Hubbard's husband, Keith.'

Chapter 16

Annabel Leigh-Matthews couldn't get rid of the feeling that she was being followed. It was only 5.45 p.m. and she had stopped off at the local 24/7 supermarket to buy some essentials on the way home, but now she was on edge. She turned to look down the aisle she had just come from for the fourth time and could see nothing out of the ordinary, but still her heart was pounding faster than usual.

For days now she had been like this and she couldn't quite fathom why. Maybe it was the horror film she had watched with Greg, her husband, the other day that had spooked her? Maybe it was the nature of her job: she had been stalked before on several occasions by over enthusiastic clients. Once, she had even been spied on by another defence brief, anxious to do everything in his power to discover what her client's alibi was. But whatever it was, it had left her with clammy hands and a racing pulse, and she didn't like it.

She breathed in deeply and looked around again. There really was nothing out of the ordinary to prompt the anxiety. It was only a small supermarket, but it was busy, mostly with business-type people nipping in to buy a bottle of Merlot or two to drink before the next day's return to work and the onslaught of the following week's busy work schedule. There were a few frazzled-looking mothers, trying to select healthy cereals for tomorrow's breakfast, while their offspring pulled chocolate-coated cornflakes or equally sugary wheat puffs from the shelves. The only other people were several elderly folk hovering around the reduced shelf for any bargains, thrown in as evening approached and the sell-by dates started to expire.

All in all, nothing and nobody to worry about.

She looked down at the contents of her basket and smiled wryly. Fruit and fibre cereal, a box of non-chocolate-covered muesli bars, fromage frais with pictures of jungle animals on the lids, a carton of stuffed green olives and her own bottle of

Merlot. All the necessities for feeding your children good wholesome food at home and school, with nibbles and a couple of glasses of wine to fend off complete capitulation to motherhood. She herself didn't really bother eating at the end of a busy day. By the time she collected the kids from after-school club and got them home, cobbled together a semi-nutritional evening meal and put them through the bedtime routine, she didn't have the energy to prepare another meal. If Greg wasn't away on business she sometimes had to, but more often than not, he would either turn up with a goody bag of specialities from the local deli or with his mother in tow, to babysit so that he could whisk her away for an impromptu meal out. Either way it meant she was saved the trouble of extra cooking, which she appreciated hugely.

She had dropped Greg off at the nearby railway station earlier and he was on his way now to a conference in Birmingham, with a scheduled early start the next morning. She had the whole evening routine to contend with alone.

She went to the self-service check outs, glancing around before allowing her defence to slip and selecting two bars of chocolate from the display, just in case she needed to use bribery to get a few hours to herself. She allowed herself to relax as she placed the wine into her carrier bag, paid and made her way to the exit. Her car was parked outside as close as she could get to the doors. She glanced around the car park. Shoppers were coming and going to their cars but nothing appeared out of order. She just had to collect the kids from her parents and then she would be safely home.

She walked quickly to her car, pinging the boot open as she arrived and placed the bag in as quickly and carefully as she could. Once in the vehicle she locked all the doors and relaxed again. This was stupid, ridiculous even. Everything was fine. She would collect the kids, go home and chill out. There really was nothing to worry about.

She switched the engine on and edged out of her parking bay, concentrating on her manoeuvre. Her breathing was more normal now and the tightness in her chest had almost disappeared. She pulled forward slowly towards the gate, checking the car park one last time. A weary mother was battling to get her errant child strapped into a car seat. A street drinker leant against the supermarket railings swigging from a can of beer, deep in conversation with another drinker, their faces red and blotchy, their movements exaggerated and slow.

The traffic was spaced out now, a gap showing itself just before a double-decker bus full of commuters was about to lumber past. Annabel pulled out into the stream of traffic, quickly bringing her car up to the same speed as the queue. No other cars were tagging in behind her and nobody else seemed interested in her movements. She leant forward and switched the radio on, relaxing at the silky smooth voice of her favourite DJ. She was getting herself in too much of a state. After she'd put the kids to bed, she'd take a long, hot bath and get a good night's sleep. She obviously needed a rest.

*

Back in the car park, out of her sight now the man pulled his woollen hat further down over his ears and smiled to himself. She really was a piece and he wanted her now more than ever. He hoped she would like the flowers he'd left on her doorstep. Maybe he could go to her house and watch her reaction when she saw them there. He already knew the short cuts. She had a nice house; he'd taken a look when she was at work. In fact she had a really nice house and she didn't seem overly worried about security either. He'd got in very easily. Even the alarm hadn't been set. He'd walked from room to room, admiring the decor. She had taste, he could see that. Everything was perfectly matched and so very expensive. He'd loved the bedroom the most. He always did. The way her smell lingered on her pillow, her clothing, even in the air, that deep, intensely sexy scent she always wore; the scent that he had followed on numerous occasions, the scent that had brought him here. He had opened some of her drawers, looking for the one that contained her underwear, and there he had stayed for what seemed like ages.

He loved this drawer, what it said about the woman. How tidy, how ordered, how impulsive, how sexual, how practical she was. Whether the small lacy G-strings were on top of the pile or whether they were hidden below, tucked down at the back. Nearly every woman had them somewhere, either bought by themselves when wanting to impress, or selected by lovers for birthdays or Christmas or as random impulses. Sometimes they were just bought by the woman to feel sexy for a change. Annabel's drawer contained many small sexy pairs, dotted between the more practical day-to-day ones but even they were sexy, with lacy strips, black frills and small red bows. He'd taken his souvenir pair, breathing in the smell of her, spraying a little of her perfume on to the material to allow an even stronger scent.

He had them in his jacket now and even the thought of them excited him. He reached in to his pocket, his fingers brushing against the softness of the material, pressing the lacy panels into the palm of his hand. They were so soft, so sensual, so sexy. He could almost imagine his lips pressed against her flesh, his body writhing against hers, her scent deep inside his nostrils. His reaction was swift and strong and he revelled in it.

One day soon, when he was sure she was ready for him, he'd pay her a visit; one day, or one night when her husband was away on business again.

He'd look forward to that. He'd look forward to that very much.

*

The large bouquet of flowers lay within the confines of the small porch on the mat. She didn't see them straight away when she pulled up outside the house. It was only when her daughter let out an excited squeal that her attention was drawn to them.

'Mummy, look! Pretty flowers.'

They certainly were pretty. They were beautiful in fact. Upright in a small round oasis of water, the bunch sprayed out into a globe of colour. Predominantly blues and yellows with tiny, perfectly formed and sweetly scented freesias and a raft of bluebells that looked as if they had just been painstakingly selected and brought direct from the epicentre of a Kent bluebell wood. The bouquet was different from standard supermarket fare. Every flower seemed to have been selected for its fragrance and the collective smell filled the whole porch and took her breath away.

'Are they from Daddy?'

She didn't know. He didn't often buy flowers, but then he knew she was a bit stressed at the moment. Maybe he had arranged for them to be delivered for when she got back from running him to the station. How lovely!

She stuck her key into the lock and pushed the front door open. Jake and Jasmin bounded past her, Jasmin's interest in the flowers disappearing in a flash as she attempted to get to the TV first. Annabel bent down and looked at the bouquet. There was no obvious message attached, so she threw her briefcase inside and picked the flowers up, smiling indulgently as the fragrance hit her nostrils. She searched inside the cellophane for a card but there was none. That was strange, but then Greg was a man who found it hard to express his emotions. He always said that actions spoke louder than words. And in this case, they absolutely did: Greg was such a sweetie.

She didn't hear the twig snapping or the rustle of leaves from the bush by the alleyway at the side of the house as she entered the front door.

Once inside she walked through to the kitchen and placed the bouquet on to one of the surfaces. She never knew whether to leave these types of flowers in their cellophane wrap with the bulb of water underneath or take them out and try to cobble them into some type of sub-standard display in a mismatched vase. She'd leave them as they were, so Greg could see them still in their splendour on his return the next evening. She could hear the kids squabbling in the TV room now, same old argument. Jake would want his idol Fireman Sam on, Jasmin would want to watch anything other than Fireman Sam. Jake would scream the loudest and the longest and eventually they would both capitulate to his request. It wasn't the way to teach him to take turns, but after a long day and the evening routine still to come, it was the only course of action that brought peace to the house.

She sighed loudly and walked into the TV room, ready to at least start the process of dissuasion. Her iPhone vibrated in her pocket. Greg's smiling profile appeared.

'Look, Daddy's on the phone,' she started, pointing the phone towards Jake, whose scream just intensified. She pressed the phone to her ear.

'Hi, babe,' she shouted above the scream. 'How's it going?'

'Fine this end, though a little boring. Doesn't sound too good your end.'

'Just the normal Fireman Sam argument. No dramas.'

'Wish I could be there to help out.' His voice was quieter.

Annabel laughed. 'No you don't. You're probably breathing a sigh of relief that you're 200 miles away.'

Jake was trying to wrestle the TV remote from Jasmin's hand. Even though he was two years younger than his big sister, her size held no fear for him. He was equally as strong and twice as persistent.

'Look babe, can I call you back after I've got them settled.'

She shoved the phone between her ear and shoulder and took hold of each of her children's hands, trying to pull them apart.

'No problem. You sound as if you're up to your neck in it.'

'No more than usual. Oh, and thanks for the lovely flowers. What a nice surprise.'

There was a pause, in which Jake seemed to summon every last scrap of energy to let out the loudest scream yet.

'What flowers?' Greg's voice sounded surprised.

'The ones in the porch...'

The phone fell from her shoulder and clattered down on to the floor. She let go of both her children. Jasmin screamed back at Jake who succeeded in yanking the remote control from her hand and ran towards the TV. Jasmin lunged after him.

Annabel clutched her chest and breathed deeply, panic bubbling back up her throat. She ran to the front door and pushed the sliding latch into place before leaning with her back to the door and bursting into tears.

Not again. Please not again!

*

He heard the latch slide noisily into place and smiled. It didn't matter. He knew the best ways in, with or without an invite.

She was just playing hard to get.

He had seen her delight at the flowers and knew that she loved them. Who wouldn't? They were outdoors flowers, meant to be grown out in the countryside in quiet places. In just the sort of place he planned to take her. He imagined her naked, her body lying amongst the long grass, her mouth open slightly inviting his lips to cover hers.

He pulled the panties out of his pocket and held them to his face, stroking their softness around his cheeks and inhaling their smell.

It wouldn't be long. It couldn't be long. He wanted her now. He wanted her so fucking much it hurt.

Chapter 17

Meg was waiting at her flat when Charlie returned home that evening. She pulled herself forward on the settee as if to stand.

'Hi Mum. To what do I owe this pleasure?' Charlie leant over and kissed her mother.

'Hope you don't mind me letting myself in. Just checking you're not overdoing things now you're back at work. It's still not that long since you were out of hospital.' Meg paused. 'You look tired.'

'I'm fine, Mum, honest. Just an early start and busy on that missing person case. Stay there, I'll get myself a drink.' She decided it was definitely in her best interest not to mention the robbery incident from the night before. She knew what Meg was like. She'd worry even more, and she had enough on her plate dealing with her two sisters at the moment. Her mother followed her into the kitchen, watching as she poured herself a lager from the fridge. She saw her mother's shoulders stiffen slightly.

'Long day! Are you all right for a drink?'

Meg nodded. 'Yes thanks. Got myself a cup of tea while I waited for you.'

She caught the slight criticism. Her mother was extra-sensitive and overly protective about their well-being, always had been. Everything that went into their bodies had to be healthy: fresh food, natural products, no cigarettes or drugs and only small amounts of alcohol. It was as if their whole world would come crashing down if they dared to let their bodies be exposed to anything harmful; ever, even once.

Her attitude seemed overdramatic to Charlie but then she knew little of her mother's background and even less of her blood father's. Meg clammed up at any mention of her own childhood and early years. All she knew was that her mother had been born in Scotland, but after Charlie's arrival and the birth of a younger brother, Jamie, their father had abandoned them and Meg had moved to London. Apart from having the name Iain Frazer on her birth certificate, Charlie knew nothing else about her birth father. Meg refused point blank to go into any further detail. She'd even taken elocution classes to lessen the strength of her accent to nothing more than a slight Scottish burr in order to forget. Charlie and her sisters knew better than to ask these days. Their lives began at their mother's arrival in London.

Meg had eventually married Harry Stafford when Charlie was six years old and life had been comfortable. Harry earned good money as an insurance broker and Charlie, Jamie and Meg moved to their present family home in Surrey. Those years were the happiest, full of laughter and adventure, exploring the country-side, getting into scrapes. It was a Wednesday when she was eleven years old that it ended and they were all, her mother especially, plunged into chaos. Tragedy has a way of making people's lives shrink. If blame can be attached, then even that small world contracts. Meg's life narrowed to such an extent that she fixated on having more children to fill the void. Lucy and Beth were born within a few years, but even their arrival wasn't enough. Meg resorted to silence; Harry resorted to drink, and after a few years his remedy was to jump into the arms of another woman; loud, brash and also an alcoholic.

Meg coped. She would always cope, but she changed. Her three daughters became her life-blood. She was strong but silent, meeting every challenge head on, not afraid to fight. Barely concealed beneath the surface, however, Charlie recognized her mother's fear, genuine and raw. She had lost so much. She couldn't lose again. They both had. Charlie just wished they could talk about it.

She took a swig of the lager.

'Don't worry, Mum. I'm only having one.' One can was as much as she ever wanted, but she had the feeling that just because Harry had turned to booze Meg always feared that she would too. She decided to change the subject.

'How's Lucy getting on with revision? Organized as usual?' Lucy was, at seventeen years old, the elder of her two sisters. She was hoping to go into nursing, but unlike the olden days when you learned on the job, she now had to do a three-year degree. She had just started her A-level course and needed good grades.

'Lucy's always organized. You know that. She has her

schedule written down and never deviates from it. It's hard work though. If I don't have her meals ready within her allotted time slots she gets all stressed and won't eat. The weight's dropping off her and she hasn't any to lose in the first place.'

'You should make her cook her own then; she's going to have to anyway when she goes to uni next year.'

'Just like you do, Charlie?' Meg pulled open a cupboard door to reveal a couple of packets of dry pasta, three tins of baked beans and some Shreddies. She went towards the fridge, which Charlie knew contained little more than the remainder of a four-pack of lager and half a dozen ready meals.

'OK point taken. I really must go shopping. How's Beth with her GCSEs?'

Her mother stepped back.

'Oh the usual. The whole world is against her, especially me. She likes the idea of a revision schedule but spends more time creating and recreating the timetable rather than actually doing the revision. When I try to point this out gently, I just get a whole heap of hurt thrown at me.'

'Well you're welcome to escape up here if you need a break. I love them both to death, but I have to say it was as much as I could take listening to it all the time,, when I was just out of hospital. The nearer it gets to GCSEs and A levels, the worse it's likely to become.'

'Well I might just do that if it gets too bad, and I can check you're looking after yourself properly at the same time too.'

She knew how highly charged the family home was at the moment and she certainly didn't want to add to her mother's worries. If she looked tired, it was because she was tired but Meg didn't need to know.

'You don't need to worry about me. I'm a big girl now.' She pulled her stomach in and squeezed at the muffin top that would never quite shift. 'A bit too big!'

Meg cuffed her across the top of her head.

'Go on with you. You need to stop worrying about your shape. Just don't take on too much until you are completely fit again. I've made dinner, by the way.'

'Thanks, Mum. I noticed. It certainly smells good.'

Meg started busying herself by the cooker. She'd already prepared most of a coq au vin but was just adding the dressing to a mixed salad and sprinkling on some croutons.

'Did I tell you I asked for a new placement at work?' Meg lifted the top off a casserole dish and stirred the bubbling juices. Charlie leant forward, grabbed a spoon and lifted a piece of chicken out, for which she received a smart rap across her knuckles with a wooden spatula.

'Ow! No, what new placement?' She wasn't really listening. She was thinking about how she could get another spoonful without her mother noticing.

'I'm helping out at a school, most days at the moment, working with a couple of teenage boys with special needs. I thought I needed a challenge, so I phoned the school offering my services. Plus I'm enjoying being around loads of kids again, seeing as you've left home and your sisters spend most of their time in their room or plugged into Twitter or Facebook. It's difficult to get more than a few words out of them at the best of times, unless they're moaning.'

'You must be mad. I can't think of anything worse than working with teenagers.'

She grabbed a shallot and popped it straight into her mouth, wincing as the boiling juices burnt her tongue.

Meg turned, shaking her head at her as Charlie tried to suck some air into her mouth to cool down the onion.

'Serves you right!' Meg thrust a couple of plates into her hands. 'It won't be for too long. Just long enough to get the boys on the straight and narrow again. It makes a nice change for me. I was thinking I might even go back to my nursing at some point, now you girls are older, but I'd have to do a course to re-train.' Meg wiped the surface down where the spoon had dripped. 'Now. Best you start serving up while there's still some left.'

'Mum, thanks for this. It looks and tastes great. You're a lifesaver. I was thinking on my way home that I didn't know what to do for dinner tonight.'

Meg turned and held the bowl of salad towards her.

'Mum, I was hoping... did you want to come with me this Wednesday? I was thinking of taking some flowers...'

A look of panic shot across Meg's face. She stopped in her tracks for the briefest of seconds, her eyes closed tightly in silent agony, her hands balled into fists.

She unclenched her fingers and lifted some cutlery, studiously avoiding making eye contact with Charlie.

'Take that across to the table, love, and let's have dinner. I'm starving.'

Charlie took the cutlery from her mother's hands, immediately deflated. The answer was the same, as always.

Chapter 18

The Silver Merc swung precariously back and forth for a few minutes, its chassis creaking and groaning, and a small cascade of pebbles from the driveway showered down from the tyre treads. It slowed to almost a stop before coming to rest in the exact spot the crane operator wanted on the flatbed lorry.

'Incredible! I don't know how you aim it so accurately,' Charlie watched, quietly satisfied, as the operator jumped out of the cab and started to pull straps round the wheels.

It was only just gone 8 a.m. on Monday morning but the sun was shining brightly and birds flitted from branch to branch. All around, the neighbourhood was grinding into motion, parents chivvying bad-tempered children, still tired after the Easter break, into cars for school.

Justin Latchmere stood, flanked by two uniformed officers, watching his car, his jaw clenched in barely concealed rage. He said nothing, obviously knowing only too well that she, Hunter and the rest of the officers swarming around his house and gardens were there mainly because of his own arrogance and deceit. With Dana's information about his friendship with Julie, and Justin's lies about knowing her, they'd easily had enough to warrant arresting him on suspicion of her possible abduction.

'Are these really necessary, officer?' He raised his arms towards one of his guards, indicating the metal handcuffs clamped around his wrists.

Charlie sauntered over to him, biting her lip to stop herself smiling at his righteous overtures.

'Well. You have been arrested for a violent crime, one of the most violent in fact. I'm sure we have all the justification we need.'

Just to make a point, Charlie took hold of the handcuffs and pulled them up to her eye level, checking how close-fitting they were with her finger, while at the same time jiggling them round a bit. Justin winced in discomfort.

'They're not too tight, are they?'

He pursed his lips, his expression as dark as thunder.

Hunter joined her and they both walked away towards the house. She could feel his eyes boring into her back but she had no sympathy for him.

'How's it going inside?'

Hunter shrugged. 'It'll take most of the week to get it all done, but at least it's started.'

'I wouldn't like to see the place when the search team are all through with it.

'I'm sure the housekeeper will cope.'

'I do feel a little sorry for Dana and the kids being dragged into this.'

'Charlie! I never thought I'd hear you expressing sympathy for anyone connected with Justin Latchmere! You must be softening in your old age.' Hunter shrugged his shoulders. 'Dana knew exactly what she was getting into and has made her choice.'

Charlie glanced towards the house and raised her eyebrows. 'It's still a lot to give up. I don't blame Dana for sticking it out, especially when she knew she'd be in for a fight for every penny.'

'Her bed.'

She looked back at Justin who was still staring in their direction and shook her head.

'Well, all I can say is give her her due, I certainly wouldn't like to be sleeping in her bed, especially with that lying, cheating bastard.'

*

Having kept them waiting while he had a lengthy legal consultation, Justin Latchmere was at last ready.

He'd been booked in a Brixton police station and was sitting in the interview room, tapping his foot impatiently, his fingers drumming against the weave of his expensive trousers. Charlie read over the introductions and cautioned him.

There was nothing he was going to say.

A prepared statement was all they were to get.

He pushed it across the table towards them. She picked it up and knew they would get nothing more from him, although of course they would still have to try. The words were written in Justin's own handwriting. Each paragraph started and ended with a flourish, the first letter accentuated with a large flowing capital and the last with a long swirling tail. The rest of the writing was neat, with all the letters the same height and width apart, and Charlie couldn't help thinking how similar to his personality the handwriting seemed; very controlled and orderly but with the odd ostentatious gesture. She picked the statement up and held it so that both she and Hunter could read it together. It was short and to the point.

I, Justin Latchmere acknowledge that I did know Julie Hubbard and made an error of judgment in falsely saying I did not know her. She is the mother of one of the boys who attends my son's school and we met through the school and conducted a purely platonic friendship.

I have no knowledge of her disappearance or any of the circumstances pertaining to it. I have not harmed Julie or her son in any way.

I last saw her one evening at the end of March, about one week before her disappearance, when we met up in my car and went for a drive out into the country-side in Surrey. We stopped at a small pub called The Royal Oak, by the village green in Brockham, and had a couple of drinks and chatted. I dropped her home later that same evening. After that, we spoke several times on my mobile during the course of the week.

She was not happy at home and told me she had problems with her husband, who could become violent. She spoke of leaving him but was worried that he would cause trouble and she would have nowhere to live with the children. I was not aware of any imminent move but circumstances can change quickly.

I have not seen or heard from Julie since that last phone call, two days before her disappearance.

There is nothing more I wish to discuss about my relationship with Julie Hubbard and there is nothing more I can assist with in regards to her location now.

'So,' Charlie started forcefully. 'Why did you lie to us about whether you knew Julie Hubbard?'

'No comment.'

'Was it because your relationship with Julie was much more than simply platonic?'

'No comment.'

'Were you conducting a full-blown affair with Julie?'

'No comment.'

'We've spoken to your wife, Dana, as I'm sure she's told you and she seems to think you were?'

Justin narrowed his eyes slightly. 'No comment.'

'She says that you've had many affairs during your marriage, which she doesn't like but has come to accept, and this is another of your affairs.'

'No comment.'

'But this one had been going on for longer than most.'

'No comment.'

'Were you getting a bit too attached to Julie?'

'No comment.'

'Or was she getting too attached to you?'

'No comment.'

'Cramping your style?'

'No comment.'

'Causing problems?'

'No comment.'

'Did it cause an argument?'

'No comment.'

'Or a fight?'

'No comment.'

'Did it all go a bit too far?'

'No comment.'

'Something happen that you didn't mean to happen?'

'No comment.'

She could see Justin's composure beginning to slip. He was trying to seem blasé and unconcerned, sitting back, arms folded, that slight, smug smile glued to his face, but she could see the tell-tale signs that it was all beginning to get too much. His breath was becoming rapid, a slight tic was appearing at the corner of his mouth as the questions were getting more searching and his right leg twitched independently of the rest of his body. Hunter had obviously noticed too. He was waiting for her to come in for the kill.

'Was she threatening to expose you?'

'No comment.'

'And it all came on top?'

'No comment.'

'Justin, did you kill her?'

His face was getting redder and redder. He looked as if he was about to burst with rage. Instead he took a deep breath, closing his eyes briefly.

'No comment,' his voice was controlled and icy. She paused deliberately. Justin had sat up straight now, his chair pulled in to the table; his hands placed palms down on the surface in front of him.

'Well did you?' she said calmly, looking straight at him. 'You haven't answered my question.'

He stared back at her intently, but it was his eyes, rather than hers, that were the first to shift focus. He smiled then as if he suddenly understood, shaking his head almost imperceptibly.

'Read my statement,' he said calmly now.

'I did. You only mentioned you didn't know her location now, not what happened the day she disappeared. So I'm asking you if you know what happened at the time of her disappearance.'

'No comment.'

'We will be looking further into your relationship with Julie. You've lied to us once before already, are you sure you don't want to tell us all about it now before we can prove that you've lied again?'

'No comment.'

'Because I'm in no doubt that there is more to your relationship than you're telling us.'

'No comment.'

'And I'm sure you'll agree that if you're found to be *lying* again to us, we'd be totally within our right to assume that you're trying to hide something.' She accentuated the word lying. She'd managed to repeat it several times just to make the point.

Justin stayed quiet.

'So is there anything else you want to say before we conclude this interview?'

He didn't say a word.

'OK then. Interview terminated.'

Hunter reached over and pressed the switch to stop the recording. With a flourish, he pulled the tapes out from the machine and sealed them.

'Until the next time, Justin. I'm sure we'll be speaking again very soon.'

Chapter 19

The new pit was finished. It was ready and waiting and the trap was set. He couldn't wait to pick up his victims. It wouldn't be long. They were primed and ready. He'd known Helena a long while ago but recently he'd seen her and her daughter in the paper, smiling proudly, showing off the ballet medals the darling daughter had won in the national show. Spoilt little bitch! She was obviously the apple of her mother's eye, after all she'd been included in *The Times* cultural section.

So fucking what! Daisy McPherson could dance. She could spin around and stand on tiptoes. Why did that make her better than her sister? Why was her older sister, Abigail, forced to watch, time and time again, as her younger sibling got all the praise? No doubt she was told she should be proud: that Daisy was doing it for the family, that the family should support her. Bullshit, total and utter bullshit. Daisy was obviously Mummy's favourite and Abigail would know it. Deep, deep within her core, she would know she wasn't good enough, she never would be. She would always be in her younger sister's shadow.

He knew what it was like. He felt Abigail's pain. He hated Daisy McPherson and her snivelling, tedious, dreary mother, Helena, for what they were doing to Abigail. Very soon though Abi would be number one. Very soon!

He nudged the seat upright in his hired BMW and pulled his sunglasses into place. They were barely needed as the car already had tints. The fake driving licence which he had used to hire the car was safely in his pocket. Helena and Daisy McPherson would be climbing into his car soon to be driven to their deaths. He shuddered with the thrill of the chase. Didn't he love this bit the best? It was so fucking good!

Taking the side roads, he gradually made his way to the McPherson house. As he neared, he pulled on his chauffeur's cap, straightened his tie and adjusted his black leather gloves.

He was well disguised today, gold tooth, brown wig that was held in place by the cap, fake scar that ran from the centre of his left cheek down to the corner of his mouth, not too vivid but evident enough to be remembered, sunglasses. He'd thought carefully about the disguise and he was pleased. All of the additions were intended to be memorable, to divert attention away from his normal features but easily removable when the job was done. Even the chauffeur's uniform was a triumph; Helena McPherson and Daisy would be so stupidly pleased that he looked so official. It was so faultlessly simple. It would increase their feelings of self-importance, when really they were nothing.

They were standing on the door-step when he pulled up outside and he heard Daisy's squeal of pleasure and saw Abigail's sad, jealous face as she stood next to her. Both girls ran towards the car.

'You can't come with us today,' Daisy scoffed at her sister.

He hated her the moment she said those words.

'We've got time for a quick ride around the block,' he found himself saying to Abigail. 'Here, sit in the front next to me.'

Helena McPherson bustled towards them with a large bag before dropping it in the boot and squeezing in next to Daisy, who was slumped malevolently in the rear. Abigail sat up tall in her seat in the passenger side. He drove around the block slowly, carefully, taking sideways glances at Abigail, recognizing the conflict in her eyes. She loved her sister but she hated her too. She wanted her to do well, but not at her expense. Why couldn't she do well too? It wasn't fair. She couldn't hide her delight at this small gesture though and her eyes shone when she smiled at him. And he wondered whether that was how he had looked when he had made his own mummy smile, pleased and proud, happy for once in his life. He nearly missed the house, so carried away in his own memories was he, and if Daisy hadn't cried out he would have kept going.

'We're back now. She has to go in. She's not allowed to come with us today.'

He broke hard at those words, stopping suddenly, but the temptation to take Abigail with them nearly overcame him. Wouldn't it be nice to show her what he was about to do to snooty Daisy and her pathetic mummy? Maybe Abi would enjoy the show, just as he had enjoyed watching his own brother die; but what would he do with her then if she saw? He would have to kill her too or keep her locked away, and she was too nice to die or be caged. It was risky enough knowing that she had seen him. She'd seen the scar; he'd caught a glimpse of her staring at it through the corner of his eye. She'd no doubt remember his counterfeit features, but would she recall the face underneath? He had to hope she wouldn't. No! He'd accepted the risk. She deserved some time being indulged by her father. She deserved to live.

He got out and opened her door and she jumped out, leaning over spontaneously to kiss him quickly on the scar-free cheek and say 'thank you' and then she was gone, scampering back up the garden path into her house without a word to her mother or sister.

He missed her immediately. She was nice, ordinary, not spoiled like her little sister. What he was about to do would make things better for her. What he was about to do would make her number one.

Daisy was squealing again now, once more centre of attention. He glanced into the mirror and saw her pretty, doll-like face and it made him angry. He could see only ugliness and pride. He watched her crane her head up to see out of the window better and noted the way her neck stretched and twisted, so long, so graceful, so easy to slit open. It would be a pleasure after the way she'd treated Abigail.

Helena could not take her hands off Daisy; brushing her hair, adjusting her clothing, pampering and preening.

Mother and daughter were so wrapped up in their own world they didn't even realize they were going in entirely the wrong direction and he wouldn't say a word until he'd got them to the old deserted hospital. It didn't take long. As he turned into the site, Helena's head popped up, staring out the windscreen from the back seat. She had been so busy organizing her daughter she'd barely said a single word to him.

'Where are we?'

'Never you mind where we are. Just shut the fuck up and do what I say.' His voice was gruff and hard.

He saw the expression on her face change from mild interest at where they were, to sheer terror as it dawned on her what was happening. He loved watching that. He loved that look of terror so very fucking much. It was what made him come back day after day after day to see that same expression, to watch it change again from terror to hopelessness as their favourite offspring gradually decomposed next to them.

He watched her hand go to the door and slowly pull at the handle, but the door remained shut. Did she think he would be stupid enough not to put the child locks on? He was in control, after all. They would leave the car when he said they could; and not before.

He couldn't help the grin from spreading across his face.

'Give me your bags and your phones,' he said quietly but firmly. 'And no more messing.' He pulled out the hunting knife he'd placed carefully in his door pocket. The blade was so sharp that even the slightest brush against skin would cause the blood to flow.

'Where are you taking us?' her voice was shaking with fear. Even Daisy was silent now.

'You'll see. It's lovely. So quiet. No one will ever know we're here.'

He pulled the bags across to the passenger side and went through them, swiftly removing the mobile phones and switching them off. He didn't trust her though. He would be watching her every move. He lifted the knife up so that she could clearly see it.

'Don't do anything stupid now, will you? Or Daisy will pay.'

The message was simple and he could see she understood. What she didn't realize was that Daisy was going to pay, whether she behaved or not. In fact, he couldn't wait for the moment when he would shut her precious daughter up for good.

The entrance to the deserted hospital had long since fallen into disrepair, but he'd put his own padlock on the new security gates. It took only a few seconds to remove the padlock and open the gate, but even so, he took his knife and keys, locking them in as he did so and leaving the handle of the knife in full view. They always did as they were told. The threat was too great to ignore.

The small country hospital with just a few red-brick wards was surrounded by the most beautiful woodland. He had been born there, many years before when the hospital had been fully operational, serving the immediate community that was clustered around it. He had gone there alone as a boy for the broken wrist he'd sustained falling from a tree and the jagged cut across his chin where he'd been thrown from his bike. His mother had refused to accompany him, even though he'd wanted her there, more than anything. She had never been there for him; even when he was in pain. Never. His body had been mended, but his spirit further damaged; each absence a nail in her coffin.

He tore his thoughts away from his mother to the job in hand.

The trees were still, motionless, the calm before a storm. They hardly dared move, as if waiting for the impending slaughter. He grinned at the thought, navigating carefully through the secluded, overgrown avenues.

No one overlooked the hospital. No one cared about it anymore. It had been left for years now to deteriorate and die. Only he came back, wanting to relive his memories. Only he walked the woodland trails at the rear of the buildings. He had never seen anyone else within the confines of the grounds. Everyone else heeded the asbestos warning notices and security signs to keep out. Children, too, kept away, frightened by tales of ghosts of the dead. The only dead there now were his own; still he was glad of the tales to keep out prying eyes.

He was driving slowly through the grounds now. The small internal roads were still in reasonable repair, though weeds had forced weak spots in the concrete apart and congregated in clumps along the edges. The evening light was just beginning to fade, the sun casting long shadows as it eased itself from the sky. Helena and Daisy should have long since been settled in the theatre in which Daisy was just starting a background role three times a week. The producers would wonder where she was, debate whether her absence showed a lack of commitment. Little would they know that their new protégée would never be seen again. Little would Daisy know just how short her rise to fame was destined to be.

Glancing in the mirror, he saw Helena's protective arm around her favourite's shoulder, pulling her close. Daisy was crying, noiseless tears that spilt down both cheeks, leaving streaks in her theatrical foundation. She didn't look so doll-like and perfect now. She didn't deserve her mummy's love. But she still fucking got it! Whatever she did and however she looked, she would always know her mummy loved her, only her, exclusively her. Abigail would never know her mummy's love like Daisy would. He had never known his mummy's love, like Tommy had. It wasn't fair. It wasn't fucking fair. It was wrong.

The road was coming to an end now. It ran into the small building that had housed the laundry. Part of the roof had caved in, but a good part of the building was still intact. He drove the car into the courtyard and turned to face his prey.

Both were white with fear. He could see their limbs shaking, the way they huddled together for comfort.

'What are you going to do with us?' Helena whimpered; her eyes wide with fear. 'Please don't hurt us.'

He said nothing.

'If it's money you want I can get some for you. We haven't got much, but you can have everything that we've got if you'll just let us go, please.'

He didn't want her money and he didn't want her speeches. Her high, simpering voice was grating on him already. Ignoring her, he picked up the knife again and held it up so that its blade could be clearly seen, watching with pleasure as his captives shrunk as far away as they could possibly get from him.

He was acting out his own show now; the opening ceremony and Act One nearly concluded; the audience would be captivated at the next act. They would be open-mouthed with awe and expectation and he wouldn't disappoint. He would lead them through every twist and turn, every emotion until the finale, not grand and spectacular like the audience would be hoping, but final, full of pathos and angst until the light was finally snuffed out. He smiled at the thought. It fitted perfectly with Helena and Daisy fucking McPherson. Their first show would be their last; but now the show must go on. The stage was set for Act Two, the props prepared, the ending planned.

He looked at the knife, its blade so intensely sharp, and began.

Chapter 20

Charlie had one last visit she wanted to make before heading home. She cast her eyes round the small, scruffy yard, its paving slabs slightly askew and cracked at the corners. A small pile of fast-food containers and crisp packets, blown in by the wind, nestled near to the fence and a wheelie bin lay on its side to the rear, its lid flopped open, yawning against the concrete. A couple of small circular urns sat at either side of the pathway, completing the run-down appearance of the yard, with dried soil and the remnants of golden marigolds from at least two summers previous hanging out over the edges. Stairs led up to a small open porch at the front door, with a set of buzzers positioned halfway down on the right side of the frame. The one at the bottom was lit up with the name *B Jacobs*, in faded black print.

The house stood in a backstreet of Brixton, bought cheaply at a time when the Brixton riots had left the area unwanted and uncared for. Years of regeneration, however, had now made Brixton, with its easy transport links to Central London and eclectic population, highly sought after. Properties bought a few years earlier had rocketed in price, along with the rents, leaving local people, on low wages, struggling to survive. Ben Jacobs fell into this category.

The house itself was large, valued at a million pounds at least if it had been kept whole, but even more divided up into separate residences. It was split into four flats. Ben's was on the ground floor. The curtains were still open, a window ajar and a TV was on in the front room, its moving picture flickering across the walls and out across the front yard.

Charlie wondered again whether she should have come. It was getting late and she hadn't been able to phone ahead as there was no number shown for him as yet, his mobile having been stolen during the robbery. She wanted to check he was all right though, and was hoping that her slightly spontaneous decision would be appreciated. Anyway, this was how she rolled, she never really planned ahead, believing that what was meant to be would be.

She leant forward and pushed the bell.

'Who is it?' Ben's voice was loud in the quiet.

'Hi Ben, it's Charlie, your very own personal police officer, come to check on your welfare.' She tried to keep the lightness in her voice but then wished that she had made it a little more formal.

'Oh wow, Charlie, this is a nice surprise. Hang on! It might take a few minutes. I've got to retrieve my crutch that I managed to throw at the TV earlier.'

'No worries, take your time.' She heard Ben clattering around and the odd curse as he tried to get to the door and was immediately guilty that she hadn't given him advance warning. A few seconds later his head appeared at the window.

'Here, let yourself in! My crutch is wedged underneath the table. And don't disappear and go getting another key cut, though I'm sure you'd like to?'

She caught the keys that were lobbed out at her.

'You wish.'

She opened the external door and then the door to Ben's flat and was hit with the smell of cigarettes and beer. Taking a deep breath, she walked through, looking around sadly at the disarray. Clothes and dirty food plates lay on various surfaces and a pile of empty cans were stacked haphazardly next to the chair that was obviously Ben's favourite. A small wooden table stood in front of the chair with overflowing ashtrays, crushed, empty cigarette packets and a can of Special Brew.

'Excuse the state of the place.' Ben was yanking at the crutch which was stuck firm between the table and the TV unit while balancing on his good leg. The table was tilting precariously as he pulled at it. 'Had a bit of a weekend of it. If I'd known you were coming, I'd have been more prepared.'

Charlie lifted the table carefully, allowing him to free the crutch. He shoved it under his armpit and hobbled over to his armchair, falling into it heavily.

'Thanks. You seem to be making a habit of being around at the right time to rescue me.' He smiled at her a little sheepishly. 'Perhaps one day I'll be able to return the favour.'

'Yeah, I'm really sorry. I should have given you more notice but there wasn't a number to get you on and I was concerned.'

She stared a little too long at his face. It was still swollen around both eyes, with a small row of stitches holding together a jagged cut across the bridge of his nose. The swelling had gone down a little from the night of the robbery, although it still looked extremely painful.

'I have to say your face is still a right mess.'

'You say all the nicest things,' Ben gingerly ran his finger over his nose. 'It's broken but at least it's straight so I won't have to have it operated on. I think they've done me a favour actually because it's been broken before and it's straighter now than after the last time.'

She smiled. 'Always look on the bright side.'

Ben broke into song, '*Of life.*' He started to whistle the rest of the tune and she joined in the duet, finishing it together.

They started to laugh.

'Help yourself to a beer if you want one. Or are you still on duty?'

She moved across to the kitchen area, which was even dirtier up close than she had realized, and decided beer from a tin in the fridge was infinitely better than a cup of tea from one of the mugs left lying stained and dirty in the sink.

'Thanks,' she tugged on the ring-pull and took a large gulp of cool beer. 'I'm not on duty now, though really I'm here in my official capacity to see how you are. I probably shouldn't have come like this, especially on a weeknight but I've been rushed off my feet all day and I wanted to check how you were and, like I said, I couldn't phone.'

'I've got a new number' Ben fumbled with a small, basic phone. 'It's all I could afford, but at least I can be contacted now. You can have the number if you want? You could store it under the title "boyfriend".'

She shook her head at him in mock rebuke but, not for the first time, felt slightly uncomfortable. Ben liked to tease, but she wasn't sure whether there was an element of truth in what he was intimating. Maybe she shouldn't have come?

'I'll store it under "Ben".' She tapped the number into her phone. 'And I'll update the crime report.' She tried to get back to a more formal footing.

'OK, officer!' Ben took the hint. 'And now, what do you want to talk about?'

'I'll tell you what's happening with your case first,' She made herself comfortable on the sofa opposite Ben. 'And then, we can talk about anything you want to.'

After a few minutes chatting, her initial doubts disappeared. She was glad that she was there, although still a little worried about the ethics of visiting a victim when off duty. Ben was so easy to be with. She admired his tenacity and positivity.

Seeing Ben in his dirty flat though made her even more determined to be a support for him, but first she needed to catch the cowards who had targeted him.

She was painfully aware, however, that she had still to identify them.

Chapter 21

And so Act Two began. The walk through the woods had calmed him. Daisy and Helena were silent with fear. He could see it in their faces. The gags helped of course, not a word or scream able to pierce through the thick wadding. Their hands were bound too, not only individually but also to each other. They would never be able to run or fight, never mind escape.

They walked ahead of him so he could watch their every movement. Helena was slim, a bit too slim in fact, with a gracefulness in her movement that had obviously been inherited by Daisy. He liked a bit more weight on his women, a decent spread of fat across the top of the hips and buttocks, like his mummy in fact. She'd had that slight sagginess of skin across her stomach and hips from giving birth. He thought back to his childhood and what had made his mummy happy. He would try it on Helena.

The pits were almost in sight now. He would walk them right over the spot where Julie and Richard lay buried. How funny would that be? How fucking funny? They would have no idea that they would soon be facing the same fate.

He led them across the other pit, feeling the knife twitch between his fingers as they did so. He missed visiting them. There was still a faint smell of death in the air permeating up from the soil. Helena wrinkled her nose at the scent, a small gesture that brought a smile to his face. She would soon be surrounded by her own. And then they were there. He ordered them to stop and then walked past them into the small copse of trees. The fading light seemed to peter out completely within the hanging boughs. He could hear every step he took, every movement of theirs. Bending down, he lifted the branches to one side and swept the leaves from the surface of the pit. It was ready. He was ready.

He'd cleared a small area next to the pit, but within the copse of trees, to squat in. It was large enough for them all to huddle together, hidden from the outside. He pushed them forward into the space and removed the ligatures binding them together.

'Try anything and Daisy dies,' he mumbled towards Helena as he loosened the cord around her hands and mouth. 'Now strip.'

Panic swept across her face at the words and he felt himself instantly excited.

'Please no,' she whimpered, barely audible. 'Please, not in front of my daughter.'

He ignored her. It would do Daisy good to see her mother getting enjoyment from someone other than her.

'Do what I say.' He put the knife to his lips and let the tip of his tongue flick across its sharpened point.

Daisy was crying. Helena started to remove her clothing. She stopped at her underwear, crouching down on her knees and crossing her hands across her chest. The action made her breasts fuller.

'Take it off,' he commanded, watching as she shook her head and didn't move.

'I said, take it off.' He wanted to see her smile but she was crying. He would have to help her. Bending down, he hooked the blade of the knife behind the thin material of the bra. It was thin and lacy and easily split along the blade edge. She kept her arms folded.

'Let me see you.' He gestured with his knife towards Daisy, 'Or she gets it.'

Helena let her arms slip down to her sides. He gestured towards her groin, swinging the knife in Daisy's direction as he did so.

She did what she was told. She was totally naked now. She closed her eyes and he could see the tears squeezing out from the edges. He could see her shaking. She wanted him so much. She was trembling with pleasure, just like his mummy had. And now he would make her smile too. Leaning forward, he grasped her roughly, kissing her hard on the lips. She turned her head away so their lips separated, stiffening at his touch. He tried to kiss her again, but she kept moving away from him, whimpering quietly and begging him to stop. It angered him. All he wanted to do was give her pleasure. She should be smiling like his mummy had when he'd done this to her.

He tried again this time pulling his trousers down so that he too was exposed. This was where she was meant to say what a big boy he was, how good he was, how she wanted him. This was meant to be where she moaned with pleasure, like his mummy had, smiling and laughing with delight. But Helena wasn't smiling. She was crying and her eyes were full of fear.

He pushed her down on to the grass and climbed on top of her. She was too bony and lay motionless and stiff. He didn't like it. He didn't like it all. He could feel his temper rising as she failed to respond. The more he moved, the more she sobbed. He looked over at Daisy. She wasn't even facing in their direction. How could she know what pleasure he was giving unless she watched; the bitch, the conniving little bitch? She didn't want any other person making her mummy happy, except her.

He wanted to climax but he couldn't. Daisy was not watching and Helena was not enjoying it. They were both bitches and he hated them. He could feel the pleasure leaving him, draining away. He tried to keep going but it was useless. And the anger was rising in him; hot burning anger that was overwhelming him as it had done before. He knew what he had to do now. If he couldn't give pleasure, then he would give pain and it was all their fault. It wasn't his fault; he was trying to make them happy.

'Fuck you. Fuck you both.'

He pulled away from her and grabbed his knife. Helena immediately curled herself up into a ball. Daisy had her back to him. How dare she ignore him? He pulled his trousers back up and crawled across the grass to where Daisy sat. She didn't even turn her head to see him. Holding the knife between his teeth, he grabbed her around the neck and stood up. Her body arched out beneath him as she struggled to find her feet. She struck out with her arms trying to find something to hold on to, but the binding prevented her from getting her balance. Her neck lay bare, stretched out under his arm, and she was crying in discomfort. He pulled the knife from between his teeth and held it against her throat. His hands could feel the warmth of her flesh; his body craved the warmth and stickiness of her blood. It would calm his anger. He loved the blood.

Helena was on her knees now struggling to get up. He could see the terror in her eyes. He hated her for it. He hated Daisy for it too. How dare she love Daisy and not Abigail? How dare she turn him away when he was trying to make her happy? She was crawling towards him now but it was too late, way, way too late. She couldn't stop him. With a sweep of his arm, it was over. And as he looked at the shock and horror on Helena's face, he knew he had truly punished her.

Mummy's favourite was dead. The final Act was complete.

It was late by the time Charlie got to the family home. She hadn't meant to stay quite so long with Ben, having promised her mum she'd visit, in the hope that she might be able to inject some calm and civility into the house. She herself was not so sure. She did know, however, that she loved the general hubbub there, rather than her own empty flat. Empty places always bothered her.

True to form both Lucy and Beth threw themselves at her as she let herself in, full of what they were doing and who they were doing it with. She barely had a chance to get a word in.

They sat around the kitchen table swapping stories: Lucy confident in her unfolding ambitions, Beth avoiding having any. Meg kept them supplied with hot chocolate and joined in where she could. By the time they eventually wound their way up to their respective bedrooms, Charlie felt rejuvenated.

She could hear Meg in the kitchen unloading the dishwasher and noisily putting the saucepans and crockery back in the cupboards. The sound of the kettle was growing to a crescendo as it came to the boil for a final bedtime cuppa.

As she climbed into her bed in the still of her room, however, she thought of how quiet and empty it must be for Ryan Hubbard, without Julie or Richard to keep him company. Not knowing where they were even. How frightened and alone he must feel.

She thought of Dana Latchmere and Aiden, on their own, while Justin remained at the police station. What would Dana be thinking? Would she suspect him of abducting Julie and Richard, possibly even harming them? If she did, how on earth could she live with him under the same roof if he got bail?

She pulled the covers up around her neck and tried to relax.

Nothing had changed since she'd last slept here. The duvet and duvet cover still smelt of her mother's favourite fabric conditioner. It was comfortable and soothing and made the stresses of the day dwindle away.

She glanced up at the compilation of family photographs on her wall and the familiar feeling of loss ran through her. It was multiplying with each hour, as Wednesday got closer. She plugged in her iPod and allowed her favourite songs to drift into her head, gently nudging the ever-present nightmares away.

Her thoughts turned back to work.

Did they have the right suspects in Keith Hubbard and Justin Latchmere?

They still had no idea where Julie and Richard could be. Nothing had been heard from them since the day of their disappearance, just over two weeks ago, despite all the publicity and appeals. The priority must be to find them. After all, two people could not just disappear without trace.

Charlie concentrated on the knowledge that she at least had a family around her, that would always be there for her, and as the familiar smells and scents wrapped themselves around her she felt herself falling into a deep, comfortable sleep.

*

Helena McPherson did not sleep that night.

Locked deep under a heavy sheet of boarding, she lay, barely able to breathe, never mind move. Her body was wrapped in a thick layer of bedding, her clothes pulled back on in haste, but she was still cold, the memories of what she had witnessed filling her with freezing fear and unrelenting pain.

Daisy, the baby girl she'd sworn to protect with her life, lay next to her, her neck gaping wide, dead eyes staring straight upwards at the boarding. The man had lifted her into the pit, dumping her down roughly before moving her limbs into position so that she was laid straight. Helena had pleaded for him to shut her eyes, to let her sleep, but he wouldn't carry out even this small request. She'd failed her daughter even in this small way. The only small mercy was that Daisy hadn't been touched. She hadn't been raped. And for that Helena was irrationally but immensely grateful.

Her daughter's blood lay clotted around her. It was pooled on the leaves on which her body was positioned. Her Daisy, her beautiful, talented, special little girl was dead. The pain of knowing this was far greater than any pain he could deliver physically. She wanted to hold her daughter in her arms, cradle her, reverse things so that she could take Daisy's place, but she knew deep down he would never have allowed that. He had a plan. She could see it in his eyes. He was methodical and systematic, even though he allowed bursts of anger to sometimes overwhelm him. Now, as she lay bruised and bloodied, she wondered when it would all end; when his knife would slice through her flesh too. She wanted it to be over soon. She didn't want him to lay another finger on her. She wanted to wake from the nightmare and find it had all been a bad dream; that she was back at home with Daisy, Abigail and her husband and that nothing, and no-one could tear them apart .

Helena McPherson didn't sleep that night at all. Instead she lay, paralysed with fear and guilt staring into the blackness.

Chapter 22

The office was awash with senior officers when Charlie arrived the next morning.

One missing mother and son was bad enough; a second pair was catastrophic. Everyone was on their way in. The public would be frightened and the Commissioner, press and politicians would all want quick results now there were four missing persons. They would be desperate to know whether arrests were imminent. The signs were not looking good.

She made her way to the office to get the lowdown on what was happening. Most of the others were already in, their faces grim, silently interrogating the computer screens in front of them. She went over to Bet, who looked physically distressed.

'What's happening?'

'Hunter asked if we could start to go through the system and see if the new missing mother is known to us.'

'And is she?'

'I don't know yet, the poor woman; there's nothing obvious, but then we haven't had this system for that long. I think we're going to have to go back way further through the old paper records.'

'We may as well set up home here then,' Paul interjected. 'As far as I recall there wasn't a proper system for collating all that stuff until far more recently. You know as well as I do how bad coppers were if they were called to a domestic. They'd rather write it off than write it down and actually have to do something about it.'

Naz came in, throwing her coat over the back of her chair, breathless and agitated. 'Sorry I'm late. I heard on the news about the second missing pair, even before you called me. It's awful, isn't it? I would have been here half an hour ago but for Nathaniel playing up again. I could quite happily wring his neck. Wouldn't get up, wouldn't get dressed. And all because he'd got a Wagon Wheel rather than a Twix in his lunchbox!'

'That's kids' priorities for you.' Charlie shrugged. 'I know what our priority will be. And it'll be more about saving the Commissioner's skin than dealing with the real victims. Paul's right. Be prepared to forget any vestige of life out-side work until this is all over.'

'You haven't got one anyway, Charlie,' Paul chipped in. 'You spend far too much time at work already.'

'Dedication, that's what it's called. Besides, I have a vested interest in this case with that bastard Hubbard, as you well know.'

'Well I have a life outside this office and I'm not about to give it up.' Colin was busily scanning the newspaper as he did every day. He wouldn't start work any morning without first catching up on what was making the headlines.

'I've been there and done that in the past.' He pointed to a particularly critical headline. 'The trouble is, and it looks as if the papers are picking up on it, we don't have much of a clue about anything to do with this case at the moment.'

Charlie was irrationally annoyed; Colin might not be interested in putting in the hours, but they now had four potential victims. Surely that should provide the motivation, if nothing else did. She knew Colin was only stating the truth about the lack of progress on the case too, but somehow, verbalizing it just made it even more frustrating. She tried to ignore her irritation.

'Has anyone seen Hunter yet?'

'He's already at the briefing.' Bet looked up. 'We've all got to go in a few minutes, but he's been called in early to discuss the situation so far with the bosses.'

Charlie nodded her understanding and headed off. She wanted to be first into the room to show how much the case meant to her. Colin and Paul might not be dedicated, but she was. The briefing room was soon filled to capacity. Detectives in casual attire mingled with uniformed officers and senior officers in more formal suits. They lined the walls, leaning against every spare inch and sat on desks around the edges talking to one another. Tension crackled around the room as conversations were shared and thoughts aired.

Charlie was joined by Bet, Naz, Paul, Colin and Sabira and they all stood quietly to one side, their conversation restrained. Bet sighed heavily and shook her head.

121

'This is all just awful. We really need a bit of luck to get this madman stopped.'

The others all murmured their agreement, but no one seemed to have an answer.

The door opened and a contingent of senior officers walked in. The room became immediately silent.

Detective Chief Inspector Declan O'Connor was flanked by the Detective Superintendent and a couple of Detective Inspectors, Hunter included. The DCI was a strange mix of intelligence, aloofness and sheer bloody-mindedness, but it was his appearance that people remembered the most. He had the look of a scruffy Irish traveller, more at home at the side of a bare-knuckle boxing ring than the stuffiness of a senior managers briefing office.

He wore a cream linen suit that looked like it hadn't seen the inside of a dry-cleaners for several years. His hair was too long, with a natural kink that left half resting on his tattered collar and the other half swept off to one side of his neck. A tie hung loosely from the top of his unbuttoned shirt. He ran his hands through his hair constantly, either in an attempt to tame the abundant waves or to appear as if he was too busy to worry about such insignificant details like submitting to a haircut. His voice was authoritative and clear but with a distinct Irish drawl that left his companions unsure whether he meant what he said or was teasing. Today there would be no time for jokes. He took his place at the front of the room.

'Ladies and Gents,' he started. 'Last night Helena and Daisy McPherson were reported missing. That was at 22.37 hours. The last time they were seen was at 17.18 hours when they were picked up by a chauffeur-driven car to be taken to the Victoria theatre in London where Daisy was supposed to be taking over a new role in the opening night of *Billy Elliot*. They never arrived. Helena's husband was unable to contact either of them on their mobile phones but just presumed they had no reception inside the theatre. When they failed to answer his calls later on too, he phoned the stage manager who informed him that they had not turned up.

'I'm not going to bullshit. An initial search has failed to find any trace of them. Their mobile phones have been switched off, having last been tracked heading South. They have literally disappeared into thin air. We have to suspect they have been abducted, as there is no reason why they should choose to go. As far as we are aware there are no domestic issues. The last person they were seen with was the chauffeur. It appears that a male phoned Helena earlier in the day, purporting to be from the theatre, saying that they would be picked up in a chauffeur-driven car and taken straight into town. She obviously assumed this was all legit, however the theatre have denied making any such arrangement and we now believe that the call was likely to have come from the driver himself. Phone records are being checked as we speak.

'We have a good description of him and the vehicle he used from the other daughter, Abigail, who had a ride in it before they drove off. It was a Black BMW with a cherry-shaped air freshener hanging from the centre mirror. The chauffeur is described as a white male, mid-forties, medium build, with thick dark hair, a gold tooth on his front lower left side, and a large scar that ran from the centre of his left cheek to the corner of his mouth. Obviously with a scar as distinctive as that, we're hoping he will be known to us, either as a suspect or a victim in the past. We've started a search on this, but it's likely to throw up quite a few potentials. In any case, he must be viewed as our main suspect. We need to find him as a matter of urgency.

'You are, of course, aware that this is the second mother/child disappearance in the last few weeks. Julie and Richard Hubbard have not been seen nor heard from and there have been no positive sightings or financial transactions since they disappeared at the end of March. This is despite a concerted effort from police, social services, ports and the media. We have to fear the worst with every day there is no contact. Now we need to establish whether there is anything that links the two. There are suspects for the first case that need to be brought back in and questioned again. Keith Hubbard, Julie's husband, is a particularly nasty, violent individual, who seriously assaulted a police officer.'

Charlie swallowed hard at the reference to the incident. She could feel the colour draining from her face. Bet slipped her hand on to her shoulder and gave it a tweak. At least her colleagues recognized she had been assaulted, even if the CPS had failed to. It made the lack of justice ever so slightly easier. She looked up and caught the eye of Hunter standing to one side of the room and he nodded back at her.

'If we can't find a link then we are facing the prospect of a random, unknown person, or persons, who are still at large and capable of anything. We are also advised that this abductor may have struck before; psychologists don't believe he would be striking at this regularity without having abducted or killed previously.'

He paused and looked around the silent room. No one moved.

'I have briefed your DI's. All of you have been allocated jobs to do. I need you to put everything into your role however minor you think the task might be. Every tiny scrap of information must be checked; we can't afford to overlook a single clue. We need to find the missing McPhersons and Hubbards as a matter of urgency. The press and public are aware of their disappearances and the pressure is on. We need to locate them and get them back to their families. I'll expect a result at the earliest possible moment.'

He took a step back and everyone hesitated, waiting to see if any of the others senior officers would take the stand.

'Well! What are you waiting for?' He clapped his hands and the spell was broken. En masse, the room emptied. Each officer determined to be the one to solve the case. Charlie was swept along to the exit, with Paul and Bet on either side of her.

She was going to be the one to crack it. She was owed it.

Chapter 23

It was worse than the last time. Maybe the knowledge of how long it had taken to rid herself of the last stalker made this new one far, far worse. Sleep was spasmodic, interrupted by nightmarish scenes where she was running down dark alleyways followed by shadows whose faces she couldn't see or recognize. Her waking hours were spent watching for anyone who looked even remotely suspicious, whether standing aimlessly at the side of the road, sitting in parked vehicles, or anyone who she had seen more than once. Neighbours, workmen, itinerant teenagers, even the postman who had worked the same patch for years came under suspicion.

Annabel Leigh-Matthews was a haunted woman, pre-occupied now by memories of the past and fears for the future. The house had become her fortress, and her children, in her mind, potential kidnap targets, prevented from playing in the garden unless she was personally there to supervise them. All post was vetted by her husband, Greg, whenever he was there and she was putting constant pressure on him to avoid the regular two to three day business trips. Unless he was there, she was unable to function, the fears dominating her every waking moment.

She had told her colleagues and they knew to watch for any unusual post or irregular visitors. The security guard in the office block had been briefed to check the car park too at the time Annabel was due to leave or, if possible, to walk her to her car. Everything had been done that could be done, but still she felt on edge the whole time.

Now she had to travel to the police station for her client Keith Hubbard, who had been arrested yet again by police investigating the second pair of missing persons. It was getting beyond a joke. The police clearly had nothing on him but would no doubt keep harassing him simply because they believed he had assaulted one of their own. It was the way they worked.

The public would assume Hubbard was guilty – whatever the real truth – believing that there was no smoke without fire. He didn't help himself, to be honest. He wasn't a likeable character, and deep down she suspected that he probably had launched the police-woman down the stairs. He certainly had a thing about women in positions of authority. His attempts to be friendly did not really cover the underlying animosity with which he regarded her. He had denied any involvement and she was there to do what he instructed. So far, thankfully she had achieved that. God only knew what he was capable of doing should she fail; but so far so good. She would face his wrath if it came to it, safe in the knowledge that, if he stepped out of line, her firm would kick him off their books and refuse to do business with him ever again.

The security guard was waiting for her at the entrance to the building. He escorted her to her car and she got in, locked all the doors and nodded him her thanks. At least the first part of the journey was safe. It was only a short journey to the police station and the officers had said that Hubbard's arrest was a matter of routine; a quick interview to find out his movements at the time of this new couple's disappearance and to establish any alibis. They could, of course, just be saying this; trying to lull her into thinking they had nothing more than a similar victim type, but somehow she didn't think so. Hubbard was nothing more than a bully who took out his hatred of women with a dig in the ribs, a slap, a push, the language of intimidation. He was not a cold-blooded murderer, capable of masterminding the disappearance, without trace, of two women and their two respective children. He was just too Neanderthal.

She was only half a mile from the police station now. The street was packed with parents taking their children to school. Was it her imagination or were the mothers holding their offspring closer to them? Were there more fathers out doing the school run? The news had hit the press. It was written across the faces of each parent. Another mother and child missing, presumed abducted. Another family unit destroyed.

She looked across at the cluster of parents in the street next to the school, each face creased in earnest conversation; each child playing within the adult's reach, as if knowing that to misbehave that morning would illicit anger, born from pure panic. This was the fear of crime in its raw form, that which the politicians waxed on about, and for a moment it put her own fears and troubles into perspective.

The queue was clearing now and she edged forward, suddenly fearing her initial assessment of Hubbard was wrong. What if he was more than just Neanderthal? What if he was responsible for the disappearance of four individuals? She didn't usually doubt herself, but with everything else going on, she was worried that she couldn't trust her own judgement. If he was responsible, then she too would be culpable for assisting to facilitate his freedom. It didn't bear thinking about.

She turned into the road next to the police station. It was comprised of resident-only parking and pay-at-the-machine bays. There were spaces available as the residents had gone off on school runs or to work. She stopped parallel to a dark Mitsubishi and started to reverse, parking her car neatly in the gap behind it. A parking attendant stopped to watch, no doubt waiting to see whether she paid for a ticket or not. She glanced in his direction and the attendant stepped back into the shadows. He was the same one as she had seen on previous visits to the station.

She shivered as a fresh feeling of foreboding ran through her, catching her by surprise. Her hands started to shake and no matter how hard she tried to reason that the same attendant would no doubt regularly work the same patch, it didn't avert the trembling. She had to buy a ticket, but the man was still there. She was being irrational.

Taking a deep breath, she unlocked the car door and got out, walking unsteadily to the ticket machine. Her hands could barely feed the money into the slot. She placed the ticket into the windscreen of the car and pulled her briefcase out from the rear, her eyes flicking from side to side. She caught a slight movement from the area of shadows in which the attendant stood and took off, running as fast as she could towards the police station. Her breath was coming in short gasps at the effort.

When she turned back to check, the attendant was staring up the road after her. She watched as he looked away from her and sidled towards the driver's side, bending down to check the validity of the ticket. For a moment she thought it was a show, purely designed to allay her suspicions while he watched her.

But as he walked away without a glance back at her, she relaxed slightly. Maybe he hadn't been watching her after all? Cursing herself, she started to mount the steps to the police station. Damn Keith Hubbard for requiring her presence. Damn her own stupidity for suspecting everything and everyone. But more than anything, damn the bloody stalker, whoever he was, for making every minute of her day so tortuous.

*

The man was waiting for her when she left. He'd found her car easily in the nearby street. He knew what make and model it was. He'd memorized the registration plate. He knew where she parked it when at home, where it was left when at work, where her children went to school, where she normally did her shopping. He was learning something new about her almost every day when he got the chance. And what he knew, he liked.

She came to this police station regularly; it was the largest in the area and held up to thirty cells, so as a solicitor in one of the local offices, she was called in on an almost daily basis, to provide advice and service to an ever-changing clientele. She'd been there all day today, from early that morning when she'd arrived to deal with her first client until now, when the commuters were nearly gone and the streets were beginning to empty. He watched her as she walked, her heels clicking sexily on the pavement as she moved gracefully along. He liked the way her hips swung as she moved, the way her small waist emphasized the fullness of her arse and tits; the way her shirt was always closely fitted, showing the outline of her breasts and the small mound of each nipple. He'd seen them up close and had found it hard to take his eyes off them. Now they were covered by a close-fitting cotton jacket and he felt cheated. She was coming towards him now, passing several parked cars and a shoulder-high privet hedge. Her head was down as she advanced, no doubt concentrating on not catching her heels in the gaps between the paving slabs.

He slipped into the front garden of the large detached house she was about to pass and ducked down behind the red-brick outer wall. Slipping his hand into the inside pocket of his jacket, he pulled out the balaclava and gloves he'd stashed away.

She would recognize him if he wasn't wearing it and he couldn't have that just yet. He needed more time to win her over. He wanted to speak to her so much. He wanted to touch her even more. He pulled out the tiny pair of panties that he'd taken from her house and held them close to his cheeks, feeling the softness of the fabric against the roughness of his stubble. Oh God, how he wanted her.

A light came on in the house behind him. He pushed himself further against the wall and watched as a middle-aged woman came to the window and adjusted the curtains. He didn't dare move for fear of being seen. The last thing he wanted was for the coppers to be called. The station was so near they'd be on to him before he had a chance to escape.

He could hear the clicking of her shoes as she approached. She was so close now; he could almost reach out and grab her. Sweat was prickling on his brow and at the base of his back. The woman was still at the window and it wasn't yet dark enough to merge into the shadows. Carefully he pulled the balaclava over his face and put the gloves on, but he stayed still, undecided. All he wanted was to talk to her. Wasn't it? To talk to her and tell her what he felt, what he could offer her.

She didn't want her husband; that useless man was never there for her; but *he* would be there for her, every moment of the day, whenever she wanted him. He would never leave her side and she would never be out of his sight. He couldn't let her pass without speaking, could he? The sound of her shoes was right in front of him. He could hear the rustle of her clothing. He couldn't let her go. Pushing himself up from his hiding place, he emerged just as Annabel was about to pass and jumped over the wall in front of her. She screamed. He threw a gloved hand over her mouth to try to stop the noise coming out, but she pulled away and screamed even louder. He was trying to tell her to stop screaming, that he didn't want to hurt her, but she wouldn't listen. Her face was contorted with fear, her eyes wide and all he wanted to do was stroke her cheeks and tell her he would protect her, but she wouldn't stop screaming, she wouldn't listen.

He glanced round and saw the middle-aged woman still at the window but now she had a phone in her hand. She was staring straight at them and speaking. She was calling the cops and they would come and ruin everything when he just wanted to speak to her. He had to go before it was too late.

'I love you,' he shouted through the small gap in the woollen mask. 'I'll always love you. You'll see. You're my one and only.'

He could hear a siren now. He had to go. Annabel was still screaming. He reached out towards her one last time but she backed away. And then he was gone, running down the road, sprinting to make sure he wasn't caught. He couldn't be caught, they would throw him back in prison and then he would never get to see her. Vaulting over a fence, he ran through the front garden of a house opposite and out into the alleyway which bordered the rear of the house, through to the next road. He'd scoped out the area well before he'd come today, careful as always. He was nearly at his car now. The sirens sounded some distance away. He would be fine. He removed the balaclava and smoothed down his hair, glancing round in both directions before walking out from the alleyway confidently. It would draw attention to him and his car, if he was seen acting strangely. The less people who knew what car he drove the better, even if it wasn't registered to him. He was at the car now. He took his coat off and climbed in, firing up the engine and slipping it into gear. His legs were shaking but he took several deep breaths and pulled away slowly and carefully, up to the main road. A police car shot past the end of the road, turning left into the next side road, its sirens still blaring. He smiled to himself, knowing exactly where it would be going and knowing that he wouldn't be caught.

As a gap in the traffic appeared, he pulled out, turning right and accelerated away into the ether. It was a shame it hadn't worked out this time, but he lived to fight another day and he would be back; ready to try again, as soon as the opportunity arose. He would just have to plan it better next time and make sure there was no one else around to interrupt. She belonged to him and nobody else.

*

Annabel fell into the policeman's arms sobbing. She couldn't stop the tears from coursing down her cheeks and neck.

Why did it have to happen to her again? Why did she seem to attract all the nutters and madmen out there? She supposed it was her job that brought her into contact with them. Maybe she should change her line of work – go into the law around house purchases and conveyancing instead? At least there should be a better class of client in that field. She couldn't stop the events going through her head. Thank God that woman had seen and called the police. God only knows what would have happened if she hadn't.

The policeman was kind. He helped her into the car and calmed her. But she couldn't remember anything of use. The man's face was hidden and his clothing was dark. He had covered her face with a gloved hand so had left no DNA on her. She didn't recognize him. The policeman had tried to treat it as an attempted mugging at first but she knew differently. She told him about the flowers, the way she knew she was being followed. She'd already reported it. The policeman called up for confirmation before he'd started to treat it more seriously. It was part of an on-going problem, an allegation of harassment that was now escalating into a crime that was becoming more dangerous. The stalker had been lying in wait for her, gloved and hooded: who knew what his intentions were.

Annabel's mind was working in overdrive. There was something familiar about him.

He had told her that he loved her, that she was his one and only. *One and only.* She had heard that phrase a long time ago, but where from, who had said it? There was something almost pathetic in how he had said the words, as if he was pleading almost.

Her mind was spinning; the adrenalin turning to ice-cold fear now. She could have been killed or raped or anything. Her kids could have been left without a mother. She could be dead.

Somehow though, from somewhere at the back of her mind, a distant memory was beginning to bubble up to the surface. A blurry face was beginning to become clear. Hopefully soon she would remember a name, a case that she had dealt with in the past, a face to go with the voice. She just hoped it wouldn't be too late.

Chapter 24

'Bingo, I think I might have something here!'

Charlie watched as Bet pulled out a report from a huge pile and leafed through it.

'Look, it's Helena. Not her married name, but I'm sure it's her – same maiden name and same date of birth. Victim of a domestic assault in 1995.'

Only she, Bet and Hunter were still there, the others having packed up for the evening, tired and disillusioned from poring through boxes of old reports and getting nowhere. Charlie and Hunter clustered around Bet now wanting to share her excitement.

'Wow, that's a long time ago,' Charlie commented. 'Who's the suspect?'

'Not a name we've come across as yet. It's a partner from a different relationship, by the name of Gary Savage.'

She jotted the details down and immediately keyed it into her computer.

'I'll run some checks on him now. See what comes up.'

Hunter nodded. 'Good work, Bet, can you get this copied and then keep looking and see if there are any more reports. If it's happened once, it could have happened before, and if there's nothing that crops up on this report, there might be something on another. We need to see if there is any connection between Gary Savage and Julie Hubbard.'

Bet jumped up and almost ran to the photocopier. After hours of fruitless searching, her find had immediately injected a sense of urgency into proceedings. This was something they could actually get their teeth into.

'I've got him,' Charlie shouted excitedly. 'He's still shown living in Southwark, though not in the same house. He's been nicked a couple of times for theft of high-powered motorbikes and driving whilst disqualified. Last time was three years ago when he was done for death by dangerous driving and no insurance. Killed a pedestrian on a nicked bike then failed to stop for police.' She scanned through the report quickly. 'I'll check and see if I can confirm his current address.'

'I've got another report,' Bet almost screamed, returning to her computer and searching Helena's maiden name. She scrolled down to the details. 'For criminal damage. It says Helena had obtained an injunction against Savage but he returned and smashed a window. Both petty offences, but it sounds like he had a grudge against her when their relationship broke down if she had to take out an injunction?'

'Twenty years is a long time to bear a grudge.' Charlie typed Savage's name into the electoral register.

'Trust me, men can have long memories. I still get the odd abusive text from my first ex, and we split nearly thirty years ago. I've given up changing my number. If Savage is still living in Southwark, maybe they bumped into each other and it re-kindled old grievances? They don't live that far apart.'

'Right,' Charlie scribbled some more details down on a piece of paper and handed it to Hunter. 'He's confirmed on the electoral roll as living in a small estate just behind the Elephant and Castle shopping centre, with one female with a 1936 date of birth, probably his mother. Street View shows it as a ground-floor flat in a small block.'

She looked towards Hunter who was already shouting instructions down his radio.

'It's a ten-minute drive. Let's go and get him.'

*

The air in the pit was turning rancid already. He lifted up the boarding, watching with pleasure as Helena squinted at the light, screwing her face up against the glare.

Good she was still alive, and he wanted to keep it that way, for as long as possible.

He stared down at them now, Daisy stiff and lifeless, Helena, becoming pasty behind the gag, with smears of dirt across her forehead and cheeks. The insects had begun to arrive and the pit was filling with flies and maggots, writhing and squirming, and feasting on the blood and decomposition. A fly crawled over Helena's forehead. She didn't even flinch; she was obviously used to it by now. He liked the thought.

The tube from the water canister was still working well. Water filled it and the level in the tank was not too far down. He would top it up with the fresh water that he'd brought with him. Nice fresh, clean water to keep her alive longer, gradually starving to death.

He could see the look of pathos in her eyes now. Some of the terror had gone as she'd realized he wasn't going to kill her, at least not yet. She had a reprieve for the time being and he guessed she would be relieved that she had another day to live and attempt to plan her escape. Not that he would ever let her get away from him. She was his to do with as he liked. And he wanted her again now.

All those years when he was the forgotten one, pushed aside in lieu of his older, more favoured brother were a distant memory; he was in charge now and he was going to make the most of it. The buzz of the insects grew louder and the smell entered his nostrils as he climbed down into the pit next to Helena. She stiffened against him and he liked the feeling. She hated him but she also needed him. He reached across and pulled her head round so that she was staring straight up into his face. Her eyes were blank like his mummy's used to be after Tommy met his death so tragically in the accident.

He remembered how the life had gone out of her eyes forever, the second she'd heard the news. He briefly recalled Tommy's flailing arms, the cry of surprise, the look of panic as he'd felt the push, while edging closer to the sheer sides of the cliff to look at the seagulls. He'd been so convincing in the way he'd made himself cry when he'd recounted how Tommy had slipped, how he'd tried to grab hold of him but couldn't hold on, how Tommy had fallen to his death, his body broken and bloodied on the rocks below, the waves lapping over it as he'd stared down over the edge. It had been the first time he had killed, but he'd known even then that it would happen again. He loved the feeling of power as he shared the last seconds of his brother's life, the last fleeting glimpse of panic, fear, knowledge.

His mummy had known immediately that it had been no accident but she'd kept quiet. There had been no point saying something that could never be proved or disproved. But she knew, and he knew she knew, and the secret stayed between them, unspoken and unacknowledged. He would never replace

Tommy, as he'd hoped, but he'd enjoyed the thrill of the kill. Everything good in her life was gone. She had nothing to live for, just as Helena didn't now. The remaining child was nothing; the favourite was dead and all was lost, all was gone forever.

He took Helena now. She was going to get exactly what she deserved. He looked into her blank, lifeless, dead eyes and saw only darkness and desertion, just as his mummy had looked before she died, as she died, after she died.

He remembered now the second time he had killed; how he'd sat next to her with the knife poised at her neck while he instructed her to drink her vodka and swallow her tablets like a good mummy. Not a glimmer of emotion; Tommy was gone and he wasn't worth living for. He wasn't good enough, even when he'd done the things she used to like. She hadn't liked them in the end, but he had and he was stronger now and she did what he said. And he told her what words to write in her suicide note, words of love towards him that he wanted to see, however untrue, that he'd never heard from her lips. She'd written what she'd been told in between the tablets and vodka and before she died she'd smiled. She'd smiled and her eyes had lit up with hate for him. He'd wanted to kick her plain, vicious face in, wipe away her expression, stamp on that hateful smile, but he couldn't. She had to remain intact; no suspicious circumstances to make the death look anything more than the last desperate act of a bereaved mother, who couldn't bear to live without their precious favourite son, and as she breathed her last dying breaths he'd known he'd lost. She'd succeeded in making him feel useless even in his last act of contempt towards her.

He'd waited with her for several hours after she'd died, talking to her, shouting at her, but she didn't answer and it had further angered him. A thin smile played on her dead, blue lips and her eyes, black and empty, stared up at the ceiling.

When at last he'd phoned the ambulance, she was never coming back. Her skin was white, her cheeks were shrunken and her body was growing cold. The person who had caused him so much pain was gone, allowed to die quietly with a smile on her face. She had left victorious. It was unfair and yet her death had to be believable. It had to be that way. Two accidents in the same family within a short space of time might have raised suspicions, but one accident and a suicide from grief fitted the bill exactly. Nothing was ever suspected or said, other than in sympathy for the poor, lonely boy who had lost both his brother and mother in tragic circumstances within a year.

He was content for a while being the centre of attention. Even when life had gone back to normal, he was as happy as he'd ever felt in his life. Things remained like that for some time until he'd stumbled upon Mary Townsend and seen the way she treated her children. All the bad memories had come flooding back into his head; all the pain and bitterness and anger, and it had grown and grown inside his brain until it had exploded in violence.

And so it had begun.

He was nearly there now; he grunted in relief and pulled away, allowing himself to stare into those blank eyes as he did so. Helena McPherson would be dead soon, starved to death next to her favourite daughter, humiliated and abused until the moment of her last breath. The punishment would at least be fitting this time. Very soon he would start to dig another pit ready for the next pair. He punched the earth next to Helena's head and shouted in triumph.

Next time though, he would keep the favourite alive a little longer and punish them too for glorying in their favouritism.

Next time couldn't come quick enough.

*

Charlie pushed the doorbell several times before stepping back and listening. Hunter stood behind her, his radio in hand, having just alerted the officers at the rear of the flat they were about to go in.

She could hear the sound of movement from inside the hallway, a slow shuffle of slippers against wood flooring. The uniformed officers behind Hunter stood stock-still. She could feel her heartbeat quicken.

'Who is it?' the voice sounded crackly and high-pitched.

'Police!'

'What do you lot want?'

'Can you open the door?'

She heard a key turn in the lock and the door swung open.

The face that peered around the edge was an elderly female, with deep wrinkles creased into her forehead and only two remaining teeth left, on the lower jaw. The woman glared at them, her expression angry and contemptuous as Charlie held out her warrant card.

'Is Gary in? We need to speak to him.'

'Of course he's in. But I can tell you now, he ain't gonna want to speak to any of you lot.'

'Well he hasn't got a choice. We need to ask him about a missing person.'

She pushed on the front door and the old woman stepped back to let them through.

'We wondered when you would be knocking on our door about that bitch.' She let out a screech of laughter. 'We heard about it on the news. Well Gary ain't had nothing to do with her disappearance. And you lot should know why.'

She squeezed past them and pushed open a door into what appeared to be the lounge. The room was dimly lit, with just a small central ceiling light, and the curtains were closed. A TV flickered in the corner, directly in front of a navy-coloured armchair, its cushions so worn and compressed down as to be nearly flat. As Charlie entered the room, she saw a bed along the back wall with the figure of a man lying flat, his back and head propped up and supported by a number of large pillows. A drip fed into his arm through a tube running from a bag of fluids held up on a metal prop by the side of him. His hair was ginger and swept back off his face and his skin was pale from lack of sun.

'Gary, there's some police here want to speak to you about Helena.'

He turned towards them, a sneer plastered across his face.

'Well, well, well. If it's not the pigs! Sorry, officers. You're wasting your time. You see I've hardly been able to leave my bed, never mind abduct two women and their kids, since you lot made me come off that bike. If that is what you've come to ask me, yet again you've picked on the wrong man.'

He pulled the blanket to one side. His legs lay askew, misshapen and skinny from lack of muscle tone. He reached down and pulled at his left knee. It flopped across the bed when he released it, lying useless at an angle.

The woman moved over to the side of the bed and

straightened it, covering him over with the blanket again.

'Don't give them the satisfaction of seeing you like this, son.'

She turned towards Charlie and Hunter. 'He ain't left this bed for near on three years now, and I would happily tell a judge exactly that. So I suggest you lot piss off and leave us alone.'

Chapter 25

A lone crow perched on the corner of the church tower. Above it, the stone spire reached up towards the heavens, bathed, as they were, in the frail light of early morning. A metal weather-vane creaked gently on the point of the spire, its arrows barely moving in the light breeze. Below the decorative castellations at the top of the tower, a black and gold clock dominated the front aspect. Its hand pointed to exactly 7.05.

The crow ceased from preening its feathers as Charlie approached, casting a beady eye in her direction before stretching out its wings and swooping down to stand and watch instead from the top of a nearby gravestone. She picked up a twig and threw it in the direction of the crow. She didn't want it watching her. She didn't want anyone watching her. Bar, her mum being there, she wanted to be alone.

The crow did as it was bid and took flight, off out of the graveyard and away.

She waited for it to be completely out of her sight before setting foot through the gates and into the stillness of the graveyard. It was Wednesday, but not just any Wednesday. It was eighteen years to the day from the Wednesday when Jamie, her younger brother, had disappeared from her life. It was why she had always hated Wednesdays.

She could hardly bear to go to his grave. To do so was an acknowledgement that he was there, and even after all this time she still couldn't quite believe he was never coming back. In her hands she clutched his small teddy bear, the one with the sailor's hat and blue and white stripy scarf. She hated what it symbolized, the irony of the outfit, but she also knew it had been his favourite. She brought it with her every time she came here, just to show him she would always look after it; even though she had failed to do the same for him.

As she walked towards his gravestone, she could almost hear his excited voice the day he had decided that, just as his name ended in an 'ie' so should she become Charlie. 'Then we can go to-ie's, and fro-ie's'. He'd thought that so funny, repeating it time and time again, adding any word that ended in the same sound. Charlie, Jamie, happy, funny; laughing and laughing as he'd run up the beach at West Wittering, throwing himself on to the sand and burying himself up to his neck; pretending he was dead. How she wished it was pretend.

She rounded the edge of the building and trod the leafy path towards where his body was buried, in the shelter of a small cluster of conifers, whose colour remained solid and strong all year round, and whose height and thickness protected him from the winds and the worst of the rain. She liked that he was protected from the storm now.

As she arrived at the grave, she noticed the flowers, freshly planted, bright rainbow colours. She knew who they were from immediately and the knowledge only added to her loss. Closing her eyes, she stood silently remembering, trying to focus all her thoughts on the light, not the darkness, the happy not the sad. It was still so hard, even after all this time. Black was so much harder to erase than white, covering any brilliance in shadow. A raft of memories started to dance before her eyes. She concentrated on his face and felt tears spring up at the sight of his smile. She smiled back at him through the tears.

She didn't know how long she stood guard at the graveside. Nothing else mattered except clutching hold of all that remained of Jamie. Her reverie was broken at last by the screech of the crow. She opened her eyes and saw it land on top of the tallest conifer. The branch swayed and bent but held its weight. Her time with Jamie was over and she needed to return to work. It was, after all because of him that she had joined, to give others the justice that he had never had.

She glanced down at his name and age engraved in the headstone; ten years old. Way too young for his name to be etched in granite. She knew who the flowers were from, but like a wound that refused to heal, she decided to rub salt into it, pick at the scab further.

Bending down, she lifted the card and saw the neat, precise handwriting that she recognised so well.

To my dearest Jamie,

Always in my thoughts, my brave little man. Lots of love Mum xxxx

She placed it back in the same position, rubbing at the tears that were running freely down her cheeks. Why couldn't you have waited for me, Mum? Why turn me down and come by yourself. Why leave me alone when we both feel the same pain?

Touching her fingers to her lips, she blew a kiss towards the graveside before turning and marching smartly away.

'Goodbye, baby brother. Sleep tight.'

Chapter 26

A small, but steadily growing contingent of press were setting up outside the front of Lambeth HQ. Charlie noticed the group bustling for the best view as she approached the building and was immediately irritated. She was not in the mood today to deal with nosey reporters and pushy cameramen. Plus, after her earlier visit to the graveyard, she was now late.

Deciding she didn't want to elbow her way through the media scrum, she broke into a jog, before vaulting the car park barrier and waving her warrant card towards the attendant. It wasn't as if he didn't know her. But to her annoyance, he started to give chase.

'It's only me,' she shouted towards the pursuing man, who gave up running and shouted at her instead.

'For God's sake, Charlie! You're supposed to let me see your ID every time you come in or out. Especially at the moment, with that lot outside.'

'But you know me, so what's the problem?'

'Because we've got our orders and I'll get in trouble if they see me letting you in without checking.'

'If someone is sat watching CCTV just to make sure that *you're* doing your job right, then *they're* not doing their job right. There are far more important things to be doing.'

'I'd rather just see your warrant card next time, Charlie. It's much easier.'

'OK, Point taken. You have my word.'

She sprinted across the yard, before tapping in the security code and disappearing through the back door into the bowels of the building.

She could hear Hunter's voice as she walked towards the office, puffing slightly from the exertion of the sprint and the ensuing jog up the stairs. Everyone else was already gathered and working.

'Where have you been, Charlie? You're late and I've been

waiting for you!' Hunter looked tired; his skin was lacklustre, his cheeks blotchy and his eyes bloodshot. Deep frown lines were etched into his brow and he was squinting towards her, as if trying to focus properly, a clear indicator that he was stressed. He ran his hands up across his face and over his head. She felt the irritation from earlier lift. When the Commissioner of the Metropolitan Police was being made to squirm, everybody felt the heat. He was clearly under pressure.

'I'm sorry, guv. It's Wednesday. I had to go somewhere before I came in. You know how it is. Then I got caught in the extra security measures downstairs.'

Hunter knew she was often late on a Wednesday but he had never asked her why, perhaps guessing it was a personal matter he'd rather not have to discuss. He didn't mind talking job, or sport with her; but anything else was left for Bet and the others in the office.

'Be that as it may, we need to get on. Tidy yourself up quickly. You've missed the briefing, so we'll talk on the way.'

'Where are we off to?'

'They've found the car that was used in the abduction of Helena and Daisy.'

Hunter was already walking out of the office. He threw a set of car keys towards her and she caught them deftly, stopping briefly to run a brush through her hair, slip out of her trainers into her job shoes and grab a fresh jacket from the coat stand. She pulled a clipboard and several new pens from the top of Paul's desk, mouthing the words 'thanks' before sprinting out. As well as being his driver, Hunter also expected her to make any notes that were required. As she ran to catch up, she saw him talking briefly to the DCI. He motioned her to pass him, so she ran on ahead to get the car, picking him up as he waited by the back door.

'Where are we heading then, guv?'

'Pollards Hill Estate, Mitcham.'

She swung the car up to the barrier and waited for the attendant to open it before squeezing out through the waiting journalists, many of whom shouted questions as they passed.

Hunter ignored them.

'Good work by uniform in Merton. A member of the public rang to say a Black BMW had been left half across his driveway at some point, the night before last. He'd expected the owner to return, but by this morning they still hadn't, so he phoned in. Luckily the call centre staff recalled the circulation of the suspect's car as being the same model and colour and put two and two together. Got uniform straight there to check it out. It's almost certainly the right one; even has the cherry shaped air freshener. It's a hire car so I've had officers sent to the rental company. It was picked up by a man who fits the description of the abductor. The employee dealing with him recalls the same scar.'

'Excellent, have we got a name?'

'Yes, but so far it seems to be false. Hired with a fake driving licence and ID.'

'Any CCTV in the office?'

'Not working unfortunately. I've already had officers scanning CCTV for the nearby streets. He used the transport network to get to the car hire office but was careful to move around on it a lot, jumping from bus to underground so that we lost track quite quickly. Even when we can see him briefly he always wears a hat and keeps his head buried in a paper so we haven't any facial image for mapping.'

'He knows what he's doing then?'

'It doesn't take much thought these days to know how widespread CCTV is. Every other TV programme shows what people get up to on camera.'

They were travelling down Streatham High Road now, towards Streatham Common. As they got to the Common, they took a right, past the Greyhound Inn, the scene of the first big pub fight Charlie dealt with on arriving at Lambeth Borough.

'What about the car? Anything of use in it?'

'No, clean as a whistle as far as any possessions being left behind. No obvious blood or weapons either. The abductor must be confident that there's nothing for us to find, or else he wouldn't have left the car in such a conspicuous place. I think he's playing games with us. We don't really need to attend as it's just about to be taken off for a full forensic examination but the bosses wanted no stone left unturned. It'll be good to see exactly where it is though, especially in relation to the rental office and the McPherson house.'

She nodded. She too was visual. When she'd been there and seen for herself, she would remember. If she was told the details, they would not necessarily stick.

Mitcham was situated in the most southerly part of London, only a few miles before the borders with Surrey. The estate was a large sprawling council development, made up mainly of blocks of flats set at right angles to each other and serviced by its own shops and community centre. It didn't take long for Charlie to spot the flashing blue lights and the small crowd of hecklers. The car itself was cordoned off with a length of blue and white tape and a flatbed lorry was waiting to take it away.

Hunter climbed out of their car, ignoring comments thrown by a particularly vocal, spotty-faced youth who looked like he'd just been sniffing the interior of a bag of glue. Charlie joined Hunter and they were met by two uniformed colleagues from Merton: a detective from the investigation team and a Scene of Crime Officer, dressed in a white overall, gloves and overshoes. Introductions over, Hunter came straight to the point.

'Anything interesting?'

The SOCO was the one to speak first, directing his comments straight to Hunter.

'I've taken preliminary lifts from fresh prints I found in the rear of the car and these have been sent straight up to the lab. They've been positively matched as Helena and Daisy McPherson from control samples taken at the McPherson House. So, unless they make a habit of going out in hired BMW's we can pretty much say for definite that this is the car that was used in their abduction. I've also taken some swabs for their DNA, which should confirm that in due course.'

'Excellent. Anything from the driver?'

'There are no obvious fingerprints in the driver's area. I would say your man was almost certainly wearing gloves and probably also wiped around before leaving. There are a few hairs on the driver's side, which I've already sent up for DNA profiling. One was looser on the seat than the others and looks the most recent, but there are others, slightly more ingrained in the fabric, that I've also sent up. As it's a rental though, there are likely to be a good few profiles in here. I'll get an ID on the newest to you as soon as I can, but any others may take a little longer. The lorry driver's just waiting for your say-so to start getting it lifted. You should have an ID for the newest hair by the end of the day, if our man is known.'

Hunter nodded. She could see he was disappointed not to

145

have a name for the suspect already, but it was never going to be that easy. At least they had the right car. They'd just have to keep their fingers crossed. They deserved a bit of luck, especially after the previous evening.

'OK thanks. Let me know as soon as you have anything; the sooner the better.'

'Will do boss.' They started to walk away when the SOCO called them back.

'Oh and just before you go. You should also know that the vehicle looks to have been somewhere muddy, maybe a yard or wooded area, or somewhere similar. There are small stones and pebbles caught within the tyre treads. We'll make sure we get them analysed to see if we can get an idea of the area it's been in, chalky or clay. Might help to confirm a scene for you.'

'Thanks. We'll bear that in mind.'

They climbed back into the car, Charlie throwing the clipboard on to the back seat. Their next stop was the McPhersons' house, where a reconstruction was to be filmed during the afternoon for a *Crimewatch* appeal. There were no charges as yet and they all knew that a slot on *Crimewatch* meant admitting the investigation was stalled and they needed to beg the public for more assistance.

'Well at least, we know we have the right car, with the right people in it and we know what sort of place it's been driven through.' She was trying to be positive. 'And Bet called back to say that she'd found another report of a similar assault between Helena and Gary Savage.'

'Yes, so I heard.'

'She's still checking to see if there are any links between any of the three McPherson reports and the Hubbards', but there's nothing obvious at the moment.'

'And, after seeing him last night, we know that Savage is not our man.' Hunter snorted. 'Though how that ignorant bastard has the nerve to blame us, when he's mown down an innocent woman on a stolen bike and then made his choice to ride on, rather than stopping. He should have been done for murder.'

They came to a standstill at a set of red traffic lights positioned at a large, noisy crossroads. A cycle was chained to the railings at the junction, painted white; a symbol of another cyclist killed on London's busy roads. She stared at the bike.

'Well, at least there's a bit of summary justice this time:

Savage won't be able to destroy anyone else's life and I wouldn't like his now.'

The lights changed to green and she pulled away. She changed the subject.

'How did it go with Hubbard and Latchmere?'

'How do you think? Both made no comment to everything that was asked.'

'I don't understand why they always make no comment. Why don't they just say if they had nothing to do with it? I would.'

'Because they both have too much knowledge of the legal system. If they say no comment, they give us nothing. Nothing that we can research. If they don't give us an alibi, we can't break it. They leave everything to us.'

'Well we can prove Latchmere has lied throughout the whole enquiry. Hopefully he might be looking at a charge of hindering an investigation, if he wants to carry on insisting his relationship with Julie was purely platonic. And Hubbard is up to his neck in it and is probably the reason why Julie and Richard disappeared. They both have the motivation and the means.'

'But,' Hunter picked up a pen from the centre console and shoved the end of it in his mouth, 'and this is the problem. Neither appears to be linked to the disappearance of Helena and Daisy, and at the moment we can't even prove in what way they were involved in the disappearance of Julie and Richard. Which leaves us with the worst possible scenario.'

He chewed the pen top, crushing the end into a flat, misshapen lump.

'That we have a random unknown abductor who, according to the DCI is almost certainly going to strike again. He's got away with it twice in quick succession and we're reliably informed by our psychological profilers that it is highly likely he will continue at the same pace or even quicker. He's on a roll and he's enjoying it. There has been no contact from the abductor, no ransom notes and no blackmail attempts. He has them for his own reasons, and they don't appear to be financial.

'He's likely to be a loner who has all the time in the world to plan and execute his next move and he seems to be continually one step ahead of us. We just have to hope that he'll slip up in his haste to capture his next victims.

'And to make matters worse we are about to lay our investigation open to the public on *Crimewatch*. He'll see that we're desperate and know that he's winning. It might even make him worse. Let's just hope that the appeal throws up a suspect quickly and not too many red herrings or else it might end up hindering us, more than helping. We'll have to wait and see.'

They were nearing the McPherson house now, both fully aware that they had no answers to any of the family's questions. Charlie checked the number and pulled up outside the address. There was no mistaking the fact they had the right one. A group of journalists were camped directly at the end of the driveway. As she turned to reach for her clipboard, she saw several of the reporters turn cameras towards them.

'Vultures! Can't they leave the poor family alone? It's bad enough having them outside our building, just waiting for one of us to make a mistake, or say something out of place.'

Hunter placed the chewed up pen back in the centre console.

'That reminds me, Charlie, after we discussed the case, the DCI gave me a pull. He wanted me to reiterate to you that at the moment we have no choice but to use the Press. We need them on our side.'

'OK guv.' She didn't understand what Hunter was on about.

'In other words! Seeing as you're clearly not getting it. Use the correct procedure for entering the building, rather than vaulting the barrier in front of them all.'

Chapter 27

The wall was covered with her images. There were photos from Google; with clippings and cuttings from newspapers, reporting on her high-profile court cases. There were photos from more personal moments taken from her Facebook page and there were his own photos of her coming and going from her house. He even had some of her inside her bathroom naked, taken after he'd placed a tiny, hidden camera within a picture frame, on one of his visits. How he loved those especially, following each inch of her body down from her breasts, around her tiny waist and broadening again over her curvaceous hips. He traced a finger down over one of the larger pictures, following the shape of her body back up to her mouth and full lips.

And then it was time to hear her again. He did it every morning, following the same ritual; sight, sound, smell; sight, sound, smell. Pushing the button on his laptop, he watched as the screen flickered into life. He waited impatiently until it had loaded then logged on to Facebook. It had been easy to invent a name, upload a few photos, make himself out to be a friend of a friend that she had met through law school. People didn't really care who they added as friends these days, they weren't scrupulous; the more the better, to share their lives with.

He waited as her profile loaded, watching as the close-up photo of her dressed in shorts and T-shirt, relaxed on a beach holiday in Egypt, took form. He had that photo on his wall too; it was one of his favourites. Scrolling through her pictures and videos, he found the best one, the one that showed her emerging from the swimming pool, laughing and giggling as one of her kids splashed her with water. He loved her in this one, truly loved her, with all his heart and soul. She was laughing and smiling towards him, she really was. He watched the video again, and again, and again, taking in that moment when her face broke into a huge grin and she giggled with pleasure. She really was beautiful, utterly beautiful, and completely perfect. If only he could have her now.

He pulled the bedside cabinet drawer open and took out her panties, holding them to his face to catch her aroma while he watched her on various videos as she laughed and frolicked and giggled. It was intoxicating. He could feel his whole body filling with her sight, sound and smell. Now he wanted to touch and taste, but he couldn't have that, not yet, couldn't kiss or lick her yet as he wanted to. He wanted her so badly.

He paced across the room and stared at himself in the cracked mirror. He wasn't so bad for his age, his features slightly more rugged then before but still relatively taut skin around his cheeks and jowls and only a smattering of grey in his hair. He liked to keep himself looking good for when he would get the chance to be with her. He ran and worked out on the weights bench and free weights he'd picked up cheap on the Internet. He checked out his biceps and shoulders, all nicely toned and defined, and his chest covered with a thin layer of dark hair. He'd had plenty of time to work on his body, get himself looking fit, biding his time; always biding his time. Yes, he was ready now, but how was he to do it?

He turned away from the mirror, scowling at the sight of the small, poky room; his belongings all arranged neat and tidy in the dismal, poorly furnished bedsit that had been provided by the council begrudgingly. He had taken it begrudgingly too. It was way less than he had expected. A single bed with a stained mattress that looked as if it had been slept on by at least a dozen others in the last three months stood to one side, next to a mid-brown wooden wardrobe with wonky doors that had obviously been reclaimed from the back of a charity shop. A small chest of drawers that didn't match the wardrobe and a bedside table that was white melanin and looked totally out of place was the sum total of his accommodation.

If it weren't for the weights and his display of colourful photos of her covering the broken patches of plaster on the walls, the room would be just too depressing to return to day after day. What would she think when she joined him? She wouldn't be impressed, coming from a house like hers; still, hopefully she wouldn't notice those things when she felt the same for him as he felt for her. Love would blur the surroundings.

He went back to the computer and scrolled through some

more of her posts. Sometimes when he did this it made him happy; happy just to be able to watch and occasionally add the odd message, like, comment. She never really replied, but he knew she had read his comments. She knew he was there. Sometimes there would be a 'like' against his comment and that would make him feel really special. She liked what he had to say, therefore she must like him. More recently, however, he had become restless, he wanted more. She needed to come to him now, be part of his life properly, not just a face and voice on a screen.

When he'd tried the other day it had all gone wrong. He'd wanted the chance for her to get to know him properly, not make judgements based on a distant memory; that's why he'd worn the balaclava. She was the only one for him; the only one he wanted, always had been and always would be, but she hadn't been prepared to give him even a few minutes. Next time maybe he should take the mask off, show himself to her, smile and be friendly and hope that she wouldn't remember him. Yes, he'd done it all wrong, he realized that now. It was no wonder she'd been scared, a masked man jumping out on her. Her screams still went through him and he was ashamed he'd made her scared when all he'd wanted to do was show her his love. But now he wasn't sure what to do: mask or no mask, hope for a second chance or resign himself to failure?

He looked back at her photo; the way her eyes lit up at the sight of him.

There was no choice. He couldn't stop now.

He made a decision, there and then, while staring into her eyes: he would go to her very soon and wait in her house for when she returned. He would have to be careful that it was only her though; he didn't want to bump into her lying, cheating husband, Greg. He didn't look after her properly; he was always going away on business. He was probably sleeping with other women, like all the other business-men did, boasting about their prowess behind their wives' backs; boasting and bragging and shagging and fucking, while Annabel stayed at home and looked after his children. The man didn't know how to treat a lady like her. He didn't buy her flowers or appreciate what he had. Maybe it would be good if he did actually bump into the man; maybe he could show him the error of his ways, tell him how wrong he was to leave her alone, treat her like he did. But then what would happen? Maybe the bastard would change and she would grow to love him more, and then where would he be? Left out in the cold.

No, that would not do; that would never do. He would go prepared to teach the bastard a lesson, but not a verbal lesson because that wouldn't help. He paced across the room and opened the kitchen drawer, rifling through the utensils until he found the vegetable knife. It wasn't large, but it was sharp, four inches of razor-sharp metal that could teach her cheating husband a lesson, make him undesirable to all women, disfigure, distort, mutilate, maybe kill; but he didn't really want to do that, not unless he had to.

He wrapped the knife in a tea towel and put it on the table next to his computer. Her face smiled up at him still; she was pleased that he was going to show her wayward husband that he should treat her better. He could tell.

He was getting excited now, very excited and very aroused at the thought. If Greg was there alone he would teach him a lesson; if she was there alone he would show her how much he cared. If they were both there or the kids were there, he would sneak back out and wait for another opportunity. He had her door key, he'd found the spare hanging in the little cupboard in the hallway when he'd broken in the first time, got another cut the same day and returned the spare. It had been easy. Since then he'd come and gone as he pleased, making sure to leave everything as he'd found it, nothing disturbed, every cushion back in place, every piece of furniture or bedding smoothed down and unruffled; pristine like it always was.

He put the key next to the knife and checked her status one last time. A new post had just pinged up on the screen.

Looking forward to a glass of vino and lunch with my lovely hubbie for our anniversary. Roll on tomorrow. Counting every minute.

So they would be around tomorrow at lunchtime, both of them. Would they be going home first or meeting straight out? He wondered idly which anniversary it was. It didn't really matter though. Their marriage was a sham and her "lovely hubbie" didn't give a shit about her. It made him fucking angry.

Grabbing his towel, he busied himself in the communal bathroom. The shower was fitted to the taps of the bath and the previous resident had left a mixture of soap and dirt to dry on the bottom of the bath. He swore out loud. He aimed the shower head at the dirt and scrubbed it away before climbing in and standing under the water. The pressure was good and he soon felt clean and exhilarated. He was buzzing now. It wouldn't be long before he was there, waiting for her, waiting for him.

He would soon be giving them an anniversary to remember.

Chapter 28

The evening rush hour was almost over as Dana Latchmere pulled her Mercedes convertible out of the driveway.

Gemma, their daughter, was back from West Sussex University for a long weekend and they were having a mother daughter outing to indulge in some retail therapy at one of the out of London factory outlet complexes that were springing up all over the place. It was late-night shopping on a Thursday, and as Gemma had not had any particular lectures that she needed to attend on the Friday, she'd come up a day earlier, very happy to comply with her mother's wish to lavish new clothes, jewellery and handbags on her.

They were heading out towards the Valley Park Retail centre in Purley, a drive of between half an hour to an hour, but she knew a few short-cuts through the industrial estate leading to the main shops, so hopefully it wouldn't take too long. They were a little later than anticipated. Time had run away from them, chatting over an initial cup of tea, but they'd still have the evening. Valley Park was one of their favourite destinations; there was a good spread of stores stocking well-known brands and a variety of restaurants in which to sit and discuss their purchases afterwards.

The gates swung open as she aimed the remote at them. She pulled out and then waited stationary as they clicked back into position, glancing around the bushes and dark spots of their driveway for any sign of that Keith Hubbard. There hadn't been any incidents recently and she was at last beginning to feel cautiously optimistic that he had decided to leave her alone, but then that could all change with a moment's notice if there were any further developments in the case. The police had still not found any sign of Julie and Richard, and until they did, it was hard dealing with her husband's rants at the injustice of still being on bail after his recent arrest, as well as Keith Hubbard's rather alternative methods for abstracting revenge on the man he obviously held responsible for making him look a fool.

Dana didn't know what to make of it herself. She had to believe that Justin was not involved, even though he had definitely had the affair. Could he have orchestrated something? She didn't know and she didn't like to think about it too much. He did have another side to him that she tried to overlook; the side that could ignore her and their two children, while picking up other women to guiltlessly use and discard when he'd had enough. When some of his past conquests had sought more than just a little physical pleasure, he had been quite ruthless in the way he had dispatched them, but it had only amounted to dumping them, as far as she knew. Nothing stood in his way, whether in love or at work, and he would go to whatever lengths necessary to put a lovelorn woman or a prosecution barrister in their place. Justin was a force to be reckoned with, as well she knew.

Gemma was obviously excited about being back, chatting and laughing as she shared with her mother the stories of her latest adventures at university. Dana wondered whether her daughter and her mates ever did a minute's worth of work or whether she and Justin were, in fact, paying for a three year sojourn into the pubs, clubs and nightlife of Brighton.

'So, have you actually done any work this term or has it just been one long social?'

'Mum.' Gemma's voice was slightly petulant. 'You know I work hard.' Her mouth turned up into a wide grin. 'We just play hard too. You wouldn't have it any other way.' She paused as if for effect. 'Remember I take after you.'

Dana laughed at the last comment.

'Cheeky! You might be right though.'

'You know I'm right.'

'You have no respect.' She tutted out loud and slapped her daughter playfully on the knee. She loved having Gemma around. Now the teenage angst was over and done with, they actually got on as much as friends, as mother and daughter. They fell into a companionable silence. She loved this too; the fact that they could talk until the cows came home, or sit silently in each other's company without a moment's self-consciousness or awkwardness.

'So how's Aiden at the moment?' Gemma suddenly asked, as if she too was thinking about her relationship with her mother. 'Still giving you and Dad a hard time?'

Dana sighed. She didn't really want to think about him at that precise moment. He was fifteen going on thirty and full of outspoken advice on how she and Justin should conduct their marriage, in the light of the revelations of his father's infidelities. She had to feel sorry for him really. He was obviously getting a rough ride from the kids at school, notably Hubbard's other son, Ryan. Rumours and gossip about who was to blame for the disappearance of Julie and Richard were rife, and were no doubt being fuelled by both boys, who were obviously trying to accuse each other's fathers. Aiden did, however, have to deal with the fact that it was now common knowledge that his father had been shagging Julie, as all the kids were putting it, and Aiden was therefore on the back foot, trying to stand up for a man who, as her son said regularly to her during his marriage guidance lectures, 'couldn't keep it in his trousers'.

'He's having a hard time – and I suppose he has to vent on someone.'

'Yeah, but it's not your fault. He should be aiming it at Dad, not you.'

She paused, not wanting to agree and therefore look to be criticizing her husband.

'Gemma, your father's not a bad man. He just has...' She looked across at her daughter's face that was set hard in anticipation of what was to come. 'Needs.'

She waited. Three, two, one.

'What do you mean he has *needs*?' Gemma nearly exploded. 'What about your needs.'

'Gem, let's not get into this again.' She pulled to a stop a little too quickly at the set of lights just on the outskirts of town. 'You know I love your father and I don't want to discuss our marriage yet again. I've done enough of that with Aiden in the last week. It's a strong marriage and we will get through it. Everyone has to turn a blind eye sometimes to their partner's failings. I'm no different.'

'Yeah, other women have to turn a blind eye to their husband failing to put the toilet seat down or squeezing the toothpaste the wrong way, not to them shagging other women whenever they get the urge.'

'Gem, don't speak to me like that.'

'Mum! That was tame. You know I could have put it in a much cruder way.'

'I'm sure you could, but shall we just leave it now?'

Gemma shook her head in obvious disgust. 'Well I will never let my husband get away with what you're letting Dad get away with. He'd be straight out the door.'

She smiled at her daughter's naivety. She was too young to know the complexities of relationships, how one party nearly always had to compromise more than the other, how marriage was a trade-off between what you could put up with and what you could gain as a result. However, her daughter did have a point.

They were nearly there now. She turned into an access road in an industrial estate, behind a large coach park, following it round towards the rear exit, where Justin, months ago had shown her a fantastic cut-through to a small leafy lane. The lane skirted round the back of the local council's municipal dump, before eventually weaving out into the end of a small cul-de-sac in which a rival law firm was situated. The offices were a stone's throw from the main road leading into Valley Park. The short-cut was about half a mile in length but shaved off the last busy two-mile section of the journey. Very few people seemed to know about it, apart from those working in the nearby buildings, and as they were shut up for the night now it was even quieter than usual. A car horn brought her out of her reverie. The car behind was hooting at her and flashing their lights. She looked in her mirror and saw the driver gesticulating for her to pull over. She braked without thinking, stopping at the nearside kerb. What could be wrong? The car behind pulled up next to her. The window opened and the man driving leaned across into her line of vision and motioned for her to also open her window.

She did as instructed, wondering in that instant, as the chillier air pushed past the stuffy warmth of the interior and hit her in the face, why on earth she had stopped for a total stranger. Still, it was broad day-light and there was something vaguely familiar about him that she couldn't put her finger on.

'Sorry to disturb you, but you've got a flat tyre.'

'I haven't, have I?'

She hadn't even noticed, but then she'd been more intent on speaking to Gemma than concerning herself with the tyre pressures of her car.

'Yeah, sorry, rear off-side one's as flat as a pancake.'

'Oh dear.'

Gemma joined in the conversation. 'What are we going to do, Mum?'

'If you want, I could help you change it. I'm a bit of a dab hand at roadside wheel changes? I presume you've got a spare?'

Dana was suddenly unsure. She'd heard about scams where drivers were pulled over and robbed. Maybe this man was about to do the same. But then why had he pulled up next to her, as opposed to in front or behind? Surely he would have blocked her in or straight away asked her to get out of her vehicle if he was thinking about getting her into a vulnerable position. He was too casual and relaxed. If he had been planning anything, he surely wouldn't be having a chat first. Plus, he didn't look the sort. He wasn't your normal, young thug; he was smartly dressed and well spoken. And there was definitely something familiar about him.

She looked around her, quickly assessing where she was. It was doubtful anyone else would come past. If she didn't take him up on his offer, there would be no alternative other than to try and change the wheel herself. She didn't even know if she could. Or she could give Justin a ring for help, but by the time he got to them, the shops would all be shut and their evening would be over. She made a quick decision.

'Thank you! That would be great. I haven't changed a wheel for over twenty years… and then only with the help of a bus driver who came to my rescue. I would really appreciate a hand, if you don't mind?'

'No problem. Stay there and I'll park up and get things sorted.'

She watched as the man pulled over in front of her and reversed back so his car was close to the front of hers. She saw him glance into the mirror and caught his eye looking back at her, and for the briefest of moments a slight shiver of apprehension ran down her spine.

'That's nice of him.' Gemma's voice broke through her thoughts.

She turned towards her daughter. 'Yes it is. Let's hope it doesn't take too long. I don't want to run out of time for our shopping.'

She relaxed again. What had it come to when you got suspicious of every Good Samaritan? There were still honest people out there who wanted to help for the right reasons. You didn't have to question everyone's motives or fear the worst in every good deed.

The man opened the door and appeared next to her. He bent down, so his face was level with hers and nodded towards her and Gemma.

'Right,' he said quietly calm. 'Let's get started… I want you both to keep your mouths shut, get out of the car and walk towards mine. I want you to get into the rear of my car without saying a word. If either of you speak or scream or attempt anything stupid, I will kill you both.'

He smiled as he finished.

Dana was taken aback, confused even. What was he talking about? Why was he saying those words to them? It didn't fit. She opened her mouth as if to remonstrate but shut it again quickly as she saw the flash of the blade in the interior light.

The man moved the knife up into their line of vision, twisting it in his hands as if to emphasize his willingness to use it.

He held it against Dana's leg, pushing at it slightly so that the tip of the blade slipped through the thin material of her trousers and into her skin.

She turned and looked at Gemma, whose expression was frozen in fear, her eyes wide and frightened and her mouth slightly open as if gasping for air.

In that second, Dana realized that it was her error of judgement that had got them into this position. Not only her life, but that of her daughter, was now well and truly in the hands of this so-called Samaritan.

Chapter 29

The studio at the BBC Broadcasting House, Cardiff, was pulsing with nervous energy as Charlie sat waiting, excited and nervous, at the prospect of being part of Crimewatch. It wasn't every day you were chosen to take part in such an iconic programme, and it wasn't every day that an investigation in which you were involved, was of such national interest. Although initially feeling a sense of failure at having to use the programme, any negativity had turned to enthusiastic positivity. Tonight could be the night to provide the luck, and the answers, they so badly needed. Hunter sat opposite, leafing through a few sheets of A4, obviously trying to memorize a last few details to make his appeal more fluid. He was to be the one interviewed at the conclusion of the appeal.

Crimewatch was going out live and she was honoured to be part of the small team in the background taking the calls. She'd watched the programme as a young child. Since its first broadcast in 1984, its appeal to viewers and members of the public had not diminished. People still switched on, in their millions to help solve the latest crimes, hoping to be able to recognize a face that appeared on the screen, or assist with a situation played out in the reconstructions. Some tuned in simply out of morbid fascination with the high-profile murders and yet more tuned in to ensure it was not their mug-shot being shown on national TV. Whatever the appeal, *Crimewatch* reaped results and Charlie hoped it would for them too.

The reconstruction footage had taken most of the previous afternoon to film; actors taking the place of the two missing pairs. She had hardly been able to watch; each minute that the cameras shot, taking them steadily towards the moment when the actresses playing Helena and Daisy had waved goodbye. She had never had that chance. Jamie had just disappeared, no opportunity to take a final glance, to record for ever in her memory his final expression, the last few seconds of his life.

Maybe it had been better that way.

The whole team had been deeply moved by the time filming was concluded. It was awful watching the sequences being filmed, knowing that the persons portrayed were, in all probability, dead now, but having no certainty that this was the case. Anything, absolutely anything, was better than not knowing. Even if to know meant relinquishing all hope.

With that in mind, the journey to Wales had been a sombre affair. It was personal to all of them now and they wanted to get a result. They had been silent in the studio, the tension mounting as they got closer and awaited their turn to be broadcast.

Some of the relatives were sitting in the waiting area; their pain still raw for all to see. Keith Hubbard was the only exception, refusing to take part; his remaining son, Ryan, having tried, without success to persuade him. Julie's parents were standing in for him. They had wanted to bring Ryan so he could feel as if he had contributed, but again Hubbard had stubbornly refused. Poor Ryan! Charlie could well imagine how dreadful it must be for him, sat at home, feeling useless and alone, prevented from doing anything to help bring back his brother and mother. She knew what it was like.

The broadcast was nearly ready to start. Charlie was seated, nervously eying her phone and checking once again that she had enough paper and pens to cope with the expected rush of calls. Reconstructions of this sort of crime historically brought a huge number of leads. The team would be sifting through the essential, the useful, the not so useful and the downright useless pieces of information for weeks to come if no early arrests were made. They needed names more than anything; anyone who had been acting differently to normal, whose movements were a little haphazard, whose manner had changed; names of anyone fitting the psychological profile; names of people fitting the physical description of the suspect caught on CCTV. Names of anyone that might be linked to the suspects they had. Not having a clear facial image would mean more information being thrown into the pot, but it was better to have too much, than too little.

The most recent profile from the hair in the rental car had not yielded a DNA profile matching anyone currently on the DNA database, another huge bit of bad luck. It was not a certainty, by any means, that it did belong to their man, and Latchmere and Hubbard were still suspects for that very reason. However, if a new subject was named as a result of *Crimewatch* and that subject's DNA matched the hair, it would at least provide a good basis on which to base the ongoing enquiries. They would have something to explain.

Theirs was to be the second main appeal. Its inclusion in the programme had been widely publicized, so the team were hoping that, with the huge public interest in the case, even more people than normal would tune in.

The first appeal was just concluding and Kirsty Young was getting ready to introduce their case. Charlie nodded towards Hunter who was sitting opposite her and mouthed the words 'Good luck'. He nodded back his thanks then made his way over to the interview stand. The introductions were being made and the sequences were being run now.

The camera zoomed in as the presenter started to speak to Hunter. What were they hoping for specifically, was there any information in particular that would assist in the investigation? Hunter was cool and clear. He always presented himself well during interview and this was no different. Anything would help; any tiny piece of information, even if the viewer thought it to be irrelevant. The abductor had struck twice now within a fairly short spell of time and it was paramount that he be identified and stopped before he struck again. Police had been advised that this could well happen imminently, as the cycle of his offending was increasing and he would know that it was only a matter of time before he was caught. He may well be riding a wave of adrenaline at the moment, at having escaped capture so far. He finished with a direct plea for viewers to provide names of any suspects, even if only a hunch.

Kirsty Young was thanking him now and walking towards the relatives. John McPherson sat next to Abigail, her face blurred out. It was thought that the presence of Abi, the family's remaining child, would provoke more viewers to ring in.

She spoke to Dan Grayson, Julie Hubbard's father, first.

'I know this must be extremely hard, not knowing where your daughter and grandson are, but is there anything you would like to say to the viewers out there who might be worried about picking up their phones?'

Dan Grayson sat up in his chair, shuffling slightly, and

cleared his throat. His wife gripped his arm tightly as he spoke. He looked old beyond his years.

'If there's anything that you know, however small, please call in. We've heard nothing from Julie and Richard since they disappeared at the end of March. Our other grandson is missing his brother and mum and we are desperate for their safe return.'

Charlie swallowed hard at the speech. It was interesting how Julie's father had not mentioned Keith at all. Her mind spun back to their first meeting, remembering the smell of disinfectant in her throat and the power of his boot on her shoulder. Maybe they disliked him as much as she did.

A cry stirred her from her thoughts. Abigail was sobbing unashamedly. Her father put his arm around her shoulder, pulling her close as he spoke. There was nothing false or forced about his voice. He looked and sounded like a broken man.

'Please we just want Helena and Daisy back...'

Another loud sob escaped from Abi's lips. He gave up trying to speak altogether and pulled her head towards his shoulder, burying her face into his clothing. His other hand lay impotently on his knee. Actions spoke louder than words. The camera panned back up to Kirsty Young who was herself trying to maintain control.

'My thanks to Dan Grayson and John McPherson for coming in to speak to us at this distressing time. Please; if there's anything you can help us with, contact *Crimewatch* now. We have a large group of detectives just waiting to take your calls. You can see what it would mean to the families to locate their loved ones. So please call.'

The numbers came up on the screen. Charlie checked her paper and pens one last time. The 'most wanted' file had started. Kirsty Young thanked the relatives and Hunter for their efforts. Julie's parents were crying quietly. John and Abi were still clinging to each other. Hunter looked visibly relieved that it was all over.

She tore her eyes away from them, her thoughts running haywire. A shiver of determination ran down her spine. They were going to crack this case; they just needed their luck to change. As her phone burst into life, she had a gut feeling that it was going to start tonight.

Nearly an hour of phone calls had passed and they were beginning to send in results for the *Crimewatch* update programme to be held shortly. Charlie had fielded quite a large number of calls, taking a very brief précis of the information given and collating the details of all callers to be contacted back at a later stage. The information was graded, depending on whether the caller themselves knew the information to be true, or whether they had heard it from a separate source. Several had given the names of potential suspects and these were being researched straight away. As far as she knew the names she had been given hadn't been corroborated by any other callers, which was a shame; it was always good to get several independent sources coming up with the same suspect. All they needed was one name to be right and they'd have their result. She hoped it would come from one of hers.

She glanced across at Hunter whose head was down speaking on the phone. It had been hectic from the moment the phone numbers were given out and it was likely to remain so for some time to come. She watched as he put the studio phone down and took a call on his personal mobile, pulling it from his pocket and putting it to his ear. He frowned immediately and shook his head. She could see it wasn't good news.

The light was blinking on her phone again. She reached over and picked it up.

'Hello, you're through to *Crimewatch*. DC Stafford speaking. How can I help?'

A woman came on the line. She had a slight accent that Charlie placed as from somewhere in Eastern Europe. She sounded nervous.

'Hello.'

'Hello can I take your name and contact number, just in case we get cut off.'

'Will I get in trouble?' the woman's voice was quiet, almost a whisper.

'Well, I will do my best to sort out whatever problem you have. I can promise you that.'

'My name is Olga Kaplinski and I can be contacted at my father's address at 23 Farthing Way, York.'

'And what do you want to tell me about the case?'

'I didn't know whether to call or not. It happened a long time ago.'

Charlie waited. She was hoping for something a little more up to date and relevant. Her eye was drawn back to Hunter, still speaking seriously on his mobile. He was on his feet now, beckoning towards Kirsty Young and one of the producers. Whatever he needed them for was clearly important.

'So what happened and why do you think it's relevant to this case?' She was a little shorter than she meant to be. It was getting late and she wanted to know about the conversation that was unfolding in front of her.

'Well,' the woman's voice got even quieter, 'a long time ago when I wasn't supposed to be here, I was given false documents and forced to pretend that I was leaving this country as another woman, with a child.'

She jotted the details down automatically. Hunter was walking towards the team now, obviously waiting for a chance to announce something to them all.

'Thank you for your phone call, Olga,' she said. 'We'll be in touch soon for further details.'

She put the phone down, just catching the caller's last words before it disconnected.

'The woman and child had been reported missing.'

Hunter was standing directly in front of them all. He looked around to see if he had the full attention of all the detectives. Most had finished their calls, cutting them short as she had, in response to the urgency of his expression.

'Ladies and gentlemen, sorry to disrupt you in the middle of your conversations but we've had a further incident that you all need to know about. It isn't to be divulged at this stage to the public but you all need to know that about half an hour ago the incident room had a call from Justin Latchmere. It appears that his wife Dana and their daughter Gemma have gone missing and it's feared that they too have been abducted.

Chapter 30

The lights from the ambulance lit up the whole street, casting an eerie blue tinge across everything they touched. The road was otherwise quiet. It was the early hours of the morning and the moon was still casting a pale glow in the sky. The boughs of the trees lay still with hardly a breath of wind to stir them into movement. A black and white cat perched on a fence nearby, watching carefully, with green eyes glinting turquoise, as the paramedics pulled up outside the house.

Ryan Hubbard was standing at the door and ran towards them as they climbed out of the cab.

'Quick, my dad's been beaten up,' he shouted as he jumped over the wall by the front door and sprinted across the lawn. 'It's bad.'

The paramedics nodded in his direction and split, one making his way towards the front door, while the other collected the kit.

Keith Hubbard was lying in the hallway. His head rested on the flooring and a thin steady stream of blood trickled from the corner of his mouth and his nose, which was obviously broken. Both eyes were red and swollen so that neither opened more than a slit, showing bloodshot pupils which failed to focus. His torso lay at a strange angle to the wall, one leg splayed out in front of him while the other was curled up underneath his body. At least two fingers were distorted and bent. He moaned quietly as he shifted his body weight off his bent leg, attempting to open his eyes and mouth.

'What's his name?' The paramedic glanced towards Ryan who was staring down at his father.

'Dad,' he replied without thinking. 'No sorry, it's Keith. Keith Hubbard.'

'Keith!' the paramedic spoke loudly next to Keith's head. 'Can you hear me?'

Hubbard appeared to hear the man but his body didn't want

to move when he tried to shift. He managed to nod.

'Do you know if your dad's been unconscious at all?'

Ryan shook his head in panic. 'I don't know. I think he has. I couldn't get him to talk to me at all when the men who did it first went, and he wouldn't move. I was calling his name, but he just lay there.'

'Do you know what happened?'

'Not really. I got woken up by shouting. I came downstairs and there were two men laying into him. They were dressed all in black with their faces covered. When they saw me, they legged it. Dad was just lying there. I tried to get him up but he wouldn't move.' Ryan stared down at his father. 'He was bleeding and couldn't talk to me. He was just groaning; then he went all quiet. I called for the ambulance.' He looked at the paramedic as if checking to see that he'd done the right thing.

'You've done very well, looking after your dad like this.'

The other medic came in, carrying some kitbags and a bright red blanket. Ryan stood back and watched as they checked his father's blood pressures and pulse, inserted a line for fluids and generally looked for other injuries. There were bruises and wheals all over his arms and legs and torso, livid red and purple, with swelling distorting the skin. He'd certainly been given a good hiding. They brought in a trolley and got ready to lift him, stabilizing his neck carefully, all the time explaining what they were doing to both Ryan and his father.

Hubbard was getting more alert as the paramedics spoke but he didn't appear to want to give much in the way of explanation. He remained tight-lipped if any questions were asked about what had happened.

Ryan stood to one side watching, his mouth open as if he was only now taking in the full shock of what had happened.

'One of the men said his name if you want to know that,' he said quietly as they were nearly finished. His dad glared at him and lifted his hand to his mouth, pinching together his thumb and index finger and moving them over his lips as if to zip them. Ryan nodded his understanding. He wouldn't say a word, but what on earth had his dad done to justify this?

As Hubbard was being lifted on to the stretcher, a police van pulled up, its blue lights revolving at odds with the ambulance's so that the whole road was lit up alternately. Bill Morley was one of the officers attending. He watched as Hubbard was made comfortable on the metal stretcher and tucked up tightly in the blanket. One of the paramedics briefly described what wounds were obvious and the fact that he may have head, neck or spinal injuries due to the severity of the attack. Bill concentrated as they spoke. This was the same man who had attacked his friend Charlie. He wanted to commit everything he was being told to memory. His colleague brought tape to secure the house as a crime scene. Bill knew that they still had to treat the case professionally, but what a sweet turn-up for the books.

'Give us a minute, son,' he said to Ryan, indicating for him to wait outside the ambulance. He climbed on board and edged up next to the casualty.

'So, do you want to tell me what's happened?' He couldn't help his slight smile as he asked the question.

Hubbard went to shake his head but he couldn't move it. Bill knew he'd caught his expression.

'Any idea why someone would want to do this to you?'

Hubbard remained quiet.

'Have you got any enemies? Anyone who holds a grudge against you? You know? Is there anyone that you've recently had issues with, whose friends or relatives might wish to have a word with you?'

Hubbard squinted towards him, his eyes tiny slits. Bill checked that the paramedics were still busy preparing the ambulance for leaving. He winked at the man and tilted his head slightly. 'I'm sure there must be someone? After all you've got a bit of recent history, haven't you? Now, let me think. There was that police-woman who you kicked down the stairs, wasn't there? You know, the one that you stood in court and lied about? Got away with that one, so I heard?'

Hubbard turned his eyes away. Bill Morley exhaled through his nose noisily.

'Oh yes, and then your wife and son have gone missing, haven't they? And people think you've got something to do with that too, don't they? You know? No smoke without fire and all that. Too guilty to even appear on *Crimewatch* last night. Or was that because you've heard that shrinks might be watching you for tell-tale signs of guilt? Maybe you thought you might give the game away?'

He raised his eyebrows towards Hubbard knowingly. Hubbard's eyes held a glimmer of fear now. He clenched his fists tightly but couldn't move any further.

'Then there's your solicitor who's been reporting a stalker? Attacked in the street by a masked man just a few minutes after you'd been released from the police station? Coincidence? Maybe, but the picture's coming together, don't you think? A bit of a woman-hater eh?'

Bill Morley bent down so that his mouth was close to Hubbard's ear.

'Or now, could it be the fact that you've been spying on Dana Latchmere and turning up at her home address, so her husband thinks? He was telling us about it a few hours ago, at the same time as he reported her and his daughter missing. You're stalking his wife and then she goes missing. He has represented some very nasty people and got them off all sorts of stuff. I'm sure he could call in a few favours, don't you think?'

He pulled back and winked at Hubbard again, and he knew that Hubbard knew that he had the measure of him.

'And that's just to name a few cases that I know about. I'm sure you will have pissed off a lot more people, especially women, in the past than I've just mentioned.'

The rear door to the ambulance opened and a couple of plain-clothes officers stepped up into the warm, stuffy interior. Bill Morley looked at them with amusement. He knew what was coming. Hubbard's eyes flicked from him to the new officers and back again.

'Well you seem to have lots of people who want to speak to you, Keith. I'm sure there'll be even more who would love to hear the truth instead of the lies you tell.'

He beckoned towards the officers and one moved across towards them. 'Keith Hubbard, I'm arresting you on suspicion of involvement in the abduction of Dana and Gemma Latchmere last night. You do not have to say anything. But it may harm your defence if you do not mention when questioned, something that you later rely on in court. Anything you do say will be written down and given in evidence.'

'Piss off the lot of you.' Hubbard spat out, wincing in pain as he moved his mouth. 'And leave me alone.'

Bill bent down low and put his mouth close to the injured man.

'Now, I don't think we'll be doing that for a long time, do you? Actually, I personally will make it my mission not to leave

you alone until you pay for what you did to my mate. And...'
he paused as if to accentuate the meaning. 'I think I may well
be at the front of a very long queue.'

*

Two hours later, Keith Hubbard was lying within the
disinfected walls of the local accident and emergency
department debating who had done this to him. He had two
names, Bear and Ratman, but didn't know who they were, or
more importantly who had sent them. It was clear they were
just paid thugs. His body ached all over and his face in
particular hurt like hell, but he knew the damage wasn't lasting.
The X-rays hadn't revealed any major damage to his neck or
spine, though he did have a fractured finger and nose and a
displaced eye socket. A splint had been applied to his finger,
and his nose was to be looked at later to see whether it would
need to be reset, but at the moment all the signs were that he
would make a full recovery. The facial fractures would be left to
mend on their own and the swelling and bruising would
disappear.

Whoever the bastards were who did this would pay though!
He, Keith Hubbard, did not take kindly to being set upon in his
own house, without returning the compliment.

He thought back to what had happened. He was an idiot. He
should never have opened the door, but then no one usually
took him on without expecting a taste of their own medicine.
But the contest had been uneven; he was no match on his own
for two hooded thugs armed with iron bars, and with Ryan in
the house, he dare not try to escape. It was too late when he'd
tried to shut the door. He had known then that he was fucked.
Barely had he opened his mouth to remonstrate when a fist had
hit him squarely in the face, sending him reeling back against
the small chest of drawers in the hallway. From then on the rest
was history; blows and kicks had rained in on him relentlessly
and he'd barely managed to reply with any punches of his own.
He had been knocked to the floor and kicked senseless.

The two thugs had said little until the end, letting their
actions do the talking. At each blow, however, he heard the
abuse. 'Bastard, bastard, bastard.' And when they'd planted their

last few blows, the larger of the two bent down towards him and sneered at his crumpled body.

'So! Where are they?'

He'd said nothing.

'Do you still think you're a big man now, attacking women and kids? Well this is for them. You'd better release them immediately or we'll be back, you understand? My name is Bear and this here is Ratman, remember those names. We're not to be messed with, so don't even think about it, or the next time you won't be getting back up. Do you understand?'

He'd sneered back, but the thug had hit him again across his swollen face and then he'd heard the footsteps and was aware Ryan was running down the stairs towards them. He didn't want him involved or, worse still, in danger.

'I said, do you understand? I'm talking to you?'

He nodded. He understood. Violence was a language he knew only too well.

When he found out who they were and who was behind this though, he would get his revenge; and it wouldn't be verbal. It would be in a language they all understood. No one disrespected him in his own house, in front of his own kid, and got away with it.

Chapter 31

It was 4.05 a.m. precisely when the coach pulled up at the scene of Dana and Gemma's abduction, having been diverted from the direct route back to Lambeth from Cardiff. Hunter had been seated next to Charlie for the journey, but both had been deep in thought for most of the way. She had tried to sleep a little, knowing that once they arrived, most of their day would be taken up with the new investigation. Sleep had come fitfully, but she had managed to drift off a few times and was grateful for even the couple of hours she'd managed.

Hunter tried and failed to stifle a yawn.

'Think that's all the shut eye we'll be getting for a good long time,' he said sleepily. 'Come on then.'

The coach was finishing its manoeuvre now. Most of the occupants were staying on board, but she and Hunter wanted to take a look around the latest crime scene.

They shuffled down the gangway and out of the door, the freshness of the early morning hitting them immediately. She pulled her jacket collar up around her neck and folded her arms into her body, trying to keep the warmth of the coach trapped within the fabric next to her skin. A street lamp at each corner of a large parking area lit up row upon row of coaches, standing mutely shoulder to shoulder, their headlights, like eyes; huge, silent witnesses to everything around them.

The rear exit of the coach park led them through width restrictions into a narrow back street cordoned off with blue and white incident tape. They stopped briefly to give their details to the uniformed officer on guard before heading towards the inner cordon lit up with arc lights.

Hunter nodded and continued walking toward the lights. It was quite a distance. To the side of them, huge, stinking mounds of rubbish lay piled high, with JCB's abandoned, their cabs tilting over precariously, their buckets empty and lifeless.

There was no sound of traffic, in fact there was barely any

sound at all, just the slight movement of rubbish shifting in the breeze and the odd rustle of animals and birds in the shrubs to the side.

The road was made from tarmac, cracked and broken at the edges but wide enough for two bin lorries to pass. A small stony verge on either side was dotted with rubbish blown from the nearby landfill. The dump was situated to the right-hand side of the road and a small area of thin trees and scrub was on the left. Plastic bags clung defiantly to some of the branches.

A telegraph wire ran along the length of the roadway, with the poles set at uniform distances. There were no other pathways or kerbs on which to walk.

As they approached the inner cordon, the floodlights appeared even brighter against the darkness of their surroundings. More cordon tape marked out the immediate area of the car.

'It looks kind of spooky, doesn't it?' she whispered. 'Freaks me out a bit, to be honest.'

Hunter nodded.

It looked to be quite a straightforward crime scene. Dana's car was silhouetted against the roadway, the backlighting making the outline of the vehicle cast long shadows that reached out towards where Charlie walked. She stepped back involuntarily away from the shadow, as if somehow the shape might suck her into its darkness. Looking down at it, she wondered whether it might hide the identity of the killer; if she would be privy to the truth should she step back into it.

The vehicle would remain in situ until daylight when the specialist search teams would arrive. Only when the area inside the cordon had been examined would the car be taken away to be forensically scrutinised; every panel and every surface dusted for fingerprints, DNA, hair or fibres; any tiny scrap of evidence that might help connect a suspect with a scene, or a scene with a suspect. It would remain to be seen whether, this time, the abductor had left any clues.

Hunter spoke first.

'What on earth would make Dana stop on a road like this? It's so quiet and remote. You'd have thought she would have kept going to somewhere a bit livelier, with people around?'

She nodded. 'Who knows, but she must have stopped voluntarily by the look of it. The car's well parked and there are no skid marks. It doesn't look as if she's been forced off the road.'

The Mercedes had been found by Justin Latchmere himself. When Dana and Gemma had failed to arrive home or answer his calls, he'd retraced the special route he'd shown Dana and found the car abandoned, unlit, unlocked, with the key still in the ignition. When the engine had purred straight into life, he'd known something was badly wrong. The police were contacted, but not before his solicitor, a fact that had not been lost on Hunter and the team. All the facts had then been duly reported, under the strict control of his adviser who had not allowed him to elaborate on any details other than the bare minimum.

Details of the shopping trip were not forthcoming, nor too was any information on the current state of the Latchmere's marriage since Justin's release on bail. He was remaining tight-lipped, despite the best efforts of the first uniform police and detectives alike to obtain the fullest account of what might have happened and why. Justin and his solicitor knew that he would again be a suspect, as would Keith Hubbard, who would no doubt rue his decision not to take part in *Crimewatch* and therefore have the perfect alibi.

They wandered round the edge of the inner cordon looking at the car. There was no damage to the vehicle; it didn't appear to have been involved in any sort of accident or to have been attacked in any way. The bonnet was down, the tyres were intact and it appeared to be in full working order.

'What the hell has happened?' Hunter was shaking his head again.

'Who knows? Who knows anything, actually? There's no CCTV. There's nothing here. It's sterile. I don't know how the fuck we're going to get any further forward, unless someone just happens to have driven past this god-forsaken place at the precise moment that Dana pulled over and has seen the suspect.'

'And recognizes him.'

'It's not going to happen is it? We've lost them too. That's three pairs now and we haven't a clue where any of them are.'

*

174

Dana Latchmere lay under the wooden trapdoor. She was alive. Gemma was alive. But she knew it was only a matter of time.

Beside her, her daughter slept. She could hear her breathing slow and shallow through her nose, her mouth being covered with wadding. She'd only just fallen asleep and Dana was glad she had.

She couldn't bear the knowledge that she had allowed this to happen.

The man had seemed so frantic when he'd waved and hooted initially but, looking back, her response was hasty and ill-considered. Just a kneejerk reaction to what appeared to be an emergency. Why hadn't she thought it through? Why pull over in such a quiet place? Why listen to the man's lies and then, worst of all, wait while he walked towards them, even though she'd had reservations. Why hadn't she locked the doors and escaped? Momentary indecision had stopped her bolting and it was, crucially, this hesitancy that meant her beautiful daughter was lying next to her, so frozen with fear that she had barely been able to speak.

She tried to move again, but the cord was bound tight around her feet and hands. There was no way, at least for the time being, she would be able to escape. She was impotent and it was not a feeling she had ever been accustomed to. Even when Justin had become too involved with his affairs, she'd always maintained a degree of control and been able to find out who they were and warn them off. Now though there was nothing she could do but lie and wait for whatever it was the man wanted from them. And that was the worst thing! She had no idea what he wanted. He had barely uttered a word, other than warnings to follow his instructions and get into the car, keep quiet and pass over their phones. She had watched as he had switched them off and thrown them on to the seat next to him, their only real means of escape lying out of arm's reach.

He had driven along side roads, around estates, always seeking to avoid the main roads where the cameras might be. He wasn't stupid; he was smart, very smart, and she had recognized that in him straight away. It was a well-practised drill and one that she had imagined in her head night after night as she had worried about Justin's involvement in Julie's disappearance. At least she now knew that it wasn't him. What had happened to her and Gemma was likely to be a carbon copy of what had happened to Julie and her son, and the other mother and daughter, whose names she couldn't remember. She was now under the control of this same man, with no idea what he had prepared for them or what their fate would be. If only she could remember why he seemed familiar, where she had seen him before. Perhaps then she could determine what was driving him and what might persuade him to change his plan. It was driving her mad that she couldn't recall.

She knew it was still night outside. The blackness was near total. Darkness had always scared her; it was the loneliness of it, the knowledge she could be surrounded by all or nothing and she would never know. She could at least hear Gemma and sense her body close. She wasn't alone, although she wished that she was, and that Gemma was safe and secure back at their house. How she wished that was the case.

He had brought them to this hidden place. They had walked through woods and undergrowth. Twice he had made them stop and look at small areas of woodland; one piled high with twigs and leaves and the other trodden down around a small area, with a couple of larger logs. In between the logs she had seen the slightest glint of metal, but she couldn't tell what it had been until later, when she'd realized it was a padlock, just like the one she'd heard being fixed to the doors above where they lay. The man had laughed and muttered to himself as they stopped, but it had only been later when the awful realization hit her that this was where the other victims lay. The knowledge caused an icy chill to run down her spine. The area piled with leaves looked undisturbed, unattended, forgotten; the other looked to still be in use. Maybe the others were still alive? How long would it be though before that area too was forgotten?

She shivered at the thought.

How long too, before her own area was forgotten?

*

Helena McPherson lay under the wooden trap-door and wished she was dead. Her body was weak with hunger and her mind had long since gone. She was insane with the smell of decomposition and the movement of the insects. Still he came, night after night, to check she had water and lie next to her and abuse her. What made him tick? What the hell did he get out of this? What did she care now anyway? She knew she was going to die; she'd long since given up any hope, and now she just wanted to get it over with.

Tonight she'd heard him, but he hadn't come straight away. Tonight there had been more footsteps, and for a few minutes she'd allowed herself to dream of seeing John and holding Abigail one last time and tasting freedom instead of the rancid coffin she was in. Just for a few seconds she'd thought she might be able to bury Daisy in a clean comfortable place where she could rest in peace, be remembered as she'd been and not how she was now.

She'd heard him laugh though and then the footsteps had moved away and she'd recognized immediately what was happening. His next victims had been shown where she was buried, just as she'd been shown the graves of her predecessors.

Salty tears started to run down her cheeks as she remembered the way the knife had sliced through Daisy's neck. Now it was happening again to another innocent child, and she was powerless to stop it happening. It made her feel physically sick to think about what these latest victims had yet to go through. A vision of Daisy's head dropping backwards came rushing into her psyche and the bile rose up her throat. She tried to swallow it back but it kept coming, acidic and burning, filling her mouth. She tried to spit it out, but the wadding prevented her and she was too weak to care any longer. She started to choke and her head swam as her brain tried to force her malnourished body to find the oxygen that it craved, but it wasn't happening; she was losing consciousness.

Thankfully, at last, the torture was at an end.

Chapter 32

Charlie was exhausted by the time she eventually left Lambeth HQ early Friday evening: mentally and physically shattered, having barely slept the night before and continued without a break throughout the day. It looked like another long weekend stretched out before them all. Her head was pounding.

Now, as she walked away from the building, she inwardly groaned as she saw Ben's figure propped up on his crutches, tucked under the railway bridge in Lambeth Road. Although pleased to see him, she could really do without this now. She desperately needed sleep. She walked under the lamp post on the corner of the junction just as it flickered into life, spotlighting her. He smiled as he spotted her and she couldn't help noticing how smart he looked, with a fresh haircut and clean new clothes. The bruises on his face had faded, the swelling had almost disappeared, and she had to admit he looked pretty handsome in the glow of the lamp.

'Hello stranger.' He leant towards her, kissing her on the cheek and she noticed at once the waft of after-shave. He'd obviously really made an effort and she was immediately guilty for having been ambivalent about seeing him.

'Hmm you smell nice. What have I done to deserve this?'

'Are you saying I don't normally?' His smile widened into a grin. 'Actually, don't answer that. You haven't seen me at my best the last few times. See I can scrub up well if I get the chance. I thought I'd treat you to a cup of coffee? Unless you fancy something a little stronger?'

'Let's start with a coffee,' she yawned. 'Sorry. Hopefully a strong dose of caffeine will perk me up. I'm knackered.' She clapped a hand to her mouth to stifle another yawn.

'I must be losing my touch. I don't normally have this effect on women.'

'Sorry. Just lack of sleep and needing my bed.'

'Well maybe I can help with the second one?' Ben's

expression was mischievous.

She shook her head at him. 'Cheeky! Right come on then, Mr Jacobs. I can see that you have some excess energy to burn off.' She set off at a fast pace, heading towards Lambeth Bridge, with Ben swinging along on his crutches behind. The air was cool.

'This should clear away the cobwebs.'

He was next to her now, keeping pace. 'So… why haven't you been round to see me again?'

'I honestly haven't had time. This investigation is driving us all crazy. We're all working every hour, and so far – nothing except frustration. We really need a break.'

'So I've gathered.'

'Oh, are the papers that negative?' She sighed heavily. 'Well, they're right really. To be honest, we don't have much at all, considering we now have six missing persons.'

'Six?'

'Yes, as of last night. I'm surprised you hadn't heard. It's all over the papers today and on TV.'

'Talking about TV. Was that you in the background of *Crimewatch* last night?'

'Yes, it was me. Did you see Hunter too?'

He nodded. 'He was good.'

'We're getting desperate; especially with this latest two having gone missing. And the only real evidence we have is a DNA profile from a hair off the seat of a rental car that could be our suspect's… but might not be. And we don't have a match with it anyway. Our main two suspects' DNA is different from the sample, but we haven't got enough on them to be able to discount it. It's so frustrating. We have lots of circumstantial evidence but nothing direct and our kidnapper doesn't leave any clues. He's too good.'

'But he's got to slip up soon? And when he does, Charlie, you'll be there.'

Ben looked so serious. He had total faith in her, even if she didn't have the same confidence in herself.

'Well, I would absolutely love it if that were the case, to nail my first really major enquiry, but at the moment I can't even put a name to the face of the person who attacked you. Sorry Ben, I did mean to update you. I've looked through a few profiles, but as yet haven't found your man. At least we still have the spit sample, but I was hoping to name your attacker myself first before that came back. Professional pride and all that!'

She slowed down, staring up at the sight that was opening up in front of them. It always took her breath away. The London Eye shone brightly, in the afterglow of the day's end, each pod lit up against the grey of the sky. Small wisps of white cloud, edged with light reflected from the street-lamps, floated across the upper echelons of the atmosphere, the wind carrying them slowly on a light breeze. She loved to walk along the South Bank and people-watch. It was quietening down as the day drew to a close but a few children ran along backwards and forwards, their parents looking stressed as they tried to keep watch over them. Tourists still lined up to take selfies standing in front of the huge wheel.

They walked on past the wheel to where the street artists were beginning to pack up; life-size statues in gold and silver moving wearily from the positions they'd held for hours at a time, their limbs creaking as they stretched and bent their bodies back into action. They stopped to watch as one man removed his outer golden clothing to walk away in jeans and jacket, a hat pulled over his yellow hair, his face and hands still glistening gold.

They stayed still, watching silently for several minutes, Charlie running the last few days' developments through her head. Something was pricking her memory that she suddenly thought was important but she couldn't think what, and it was driving her mad.

'Don't worry.' Ben squeezed her hand. 'You'll crack both cases. Honestly, I think you will. Now shall we have a glass of wine, instead of a coffee?' He pointed towards a bar at the side of the walkway. It was busy but there were still a few empty tables dotted about. 'You look as if you deserve it after the last few days.'

'Why not!'

She couldn't argue with that. Besides, they were heading in the direction of the skateboard park where Ben had been robbed. It probably wasn't a good idea as yet.

Ben steered them to a table on the periphery of the bar and waited for the barman to come over.

'You know wine will go straight to my head?' she felt

suddenly nervous as Ben sent the waiter scurrying off to get a bottle of Pinot Grigio.

'That's what I was hoping. But... don't worry, I'll order some food too. Wouldn't want to take advantage.'

He buried his head in the menu.

She watched as he concentrated, deep frown lines accentuating his conscientiousness in ensuring she was at ease. She liked him even more for it. He was already a good friend, but she wasn't sure whether she wanted any more.

'Thanks Ben. I'm not sure I'm quite ready to be taken advantage of at the moment, but it's nice to have someone who's trying.'

She looked across to where some of London's iconic buildings stood, lit up against the night sky: the Gherkin, the Shard and Canary Wharf all spiralling upwards.

London was at its best at this time of day. People were relaxed and chilling after a day's work and the buzz in the bars and cafes along the riverside grew louder as the wine took effect. This part of the city changed on a Friday evening from the business heart of England to the cultural nucleus of the capital. It was a great place to live and work.

The waiter returned with their wine and poured a good-sized glass.

She took a long sip. It was cold and refreshing and went straight to the right spot. She speared an olive with a cocktail stick and popped it into her mouth. In spite of her fatigue, she suddenly felt alive.

They chatted for what seemed like hours over several courses, each taking it in turn to tell the other some of their life experiences, hopes and dreams. She was completely honest, speaking about her relationship with her mother and sisters, her work and her recent experience with Hubbard. When she struggled to find the right words, Ben waited, not making a fuss; instead allowing her emotions to ebb and flow unquestioned.

He in turn spoke about his time in the army and the subsequent decline of his relationship with his family as his drinking increasingly became his solace. She listened, at times stirred to tears by the way his voice faltered as he described some of the things he'd witnessed and shared the same emotions as she herself had felt.

She had no idea their lives had so many parallels. Ben spoke easily, seemingly not worried about laying himself bare to her and she appreciated his honesty. It was rare to find someone who could allow themselves to open up without fear of humiliation.

The city was completely bathed in illuminations when they eventually moved to leave. Ben wandered across the walkway to stare down at the Thames. The bridges appeared as glowing tracks across the dark footpath of the river. Cruisers left trails of fluorescent light along the water, like comets across space. Charlie joined him, shuddering visibly at the sight of the muddy, black water, lapping lustily at the bank. She turned away as a chill ran through her body.

'What's the matter?' Ben shifted alongside her. 'Don't you like the river?'

'My little brother Jamie drowned.' She closed her eyes and was hurtling back in time like a roller coaster ride, out of control and unable to stop. 'We were on holiday. We went to the same seaside town every year. Harry, my step-father, knew some of the locals at the harbour. He would go out drinking with them. One of them in particular was friendly. His name was Arthur. He had a little boat. I saw him bringing in some fish he'd caught one evening and I asked if Jamie and I could go out fishing with him. My mum didn't want us to go, but Harry said he'd go with us, if Arthur said we could.

'Harry and Arthur were drinking beer and laughing together. We went out a long way and it was getting dark. It began to rain and the waves were getting bigger. We began heading back, but the boat started taking in water. Arthur went to put the bilge pump on but it wouldn't work. And there was more weight in the boat than normal. It was taking in more and more water. Me and Jamie were trying to scoop it out with buckets but it was coming in quicker than we could get rid of it. Jamie was so frightened. I'll never forget the look in his eyes. The boat was getting lower and lower. A large wave hit us and knocked us all to one side. The sea just flooded in.

'The boat went down within seconds. I never saw where Jamie went. One second he was there beside me, clinging on to me, the next he was gone. The coast-guard found me and Harry. My mum called them when we didn't return. Jamie was missing for thirteen hours before they found his body. I will never, ever forget a minute of that time.'

She spoke in a staccato monologue, her voice faltering. She couldn't trust herself to speak at any greater length. She rarely, if ever, talked about this and didn't really quite know why she was telling Ben, a relative stranger but now, just days after the anniversary of her brother's death, somehow it just felt right.

'I'm so sorry.' Ben took her hand. She was glad that he said nothing more.

'My brother and Arthur died that Wednesday. There were so many things wrong that Harry and Arthur ignored. We should never have gone out to sea that evening. Maybe if they hadn't been drinking they would have seen the storm clouds coming and got us back quicker. The boat was unseaworthy. Arthur only had the one life jacket, which they gave to me because I was a girl. If there were flares they were out of reach. Even the radio didn't work properly.'

Charlie pulled her hand away from Ben's gently and put both arms up behind her head.

'At the inquest the responsibility for Jamie's death was pinned firmly on Arthur and the faulty boat, but he was dead so no one was ever prosecuted. My mother blamed Harry too. They tried to make a go of it for a few years. They had my two sisters but after Jamie there was always a void that would never go away. In the end they split up. For years I hated Arthur. I hated Harry too. I went off the rails for a long time. In the end I knew I would have to do something to make up for letting my brother down. I joined the police because of Jamie, to fight for victims; so that no one would ever lose someone they loved and not get justice.

Her voice was dull with pain.

'And do you know who I hate the most? And what the worst bit is?'

Ben was staring straight into her eyes, concentrating on every word she said. 'Only if you want to tell me.'

She suddenly did. He looked so serious. She knew without doubt he would understand. It was the one recurring thought that came to her every time she saw water. It was what came to her every night, if she forgot to put the nightlight on or plug her headphones in take away the silent screams.

She turned towards the river and opened her eyes, shivering at the sight of the fast-flowing water, imagining in an instant Jamie's fear.

'I hate myself the most. Jamie was my little brother. We did everything together. He was my best friend. He came with me just because I wanted to go out on the boat that evening. He would always come with me, everywhere. It was all my fault. I took him to his death.'

She paused letting the words rest back down on her shoulders.

'And the worst bit was. I couldn't save him. I saw his little face, so frightened, clinging on to me and I let him down. I didn't even see him go. I never got the chance to say goodbye.'

She stopped talking then, keeping the rest of the pain inside. There were some things that she would never be able to verbalize. She would always, always, blame herself for his death. And, deep down, she knew her mother blamed her too; even though she would never say it; even though she had told her time and time again that it wasn't her fault, she was only eleven years old. How could she have known? It was why now they couldn't speak about Jamie. It was why they went to his graveside separately. She would never be free from her guilt.

'I watched friends die, knowing I couldn't save them,' Ben said quietly, moving off from the riverside. 'So I know what it's like. But it really wasn't your fault.'

Charlie watched Ben's eyes cloud over with his own memories. She appreciated his attempts to make her feel better but deep down, she knew that it was her fault Jamie had died. Nothing would ever convince her otherwise.

They meandered slowly back towards the Tube station, both lost in their own thoughts, comfortable in the silence between them. Maybe that was the reason she had been able to speak. Because she had known that Ben would understand.

They moved unhurriedly, neither wanting to leave. As they neared the station her focus was drawn to a tattily dressed woman sitting on the footpath nearest to the entrance. She had a scarf tied around her head and sat on a pile of newspapers, with a toddler wrapped in a grubby blanket held tightly in her arms. In front of her was a piece of brown cardboard on which a message was written imploring passers-by for money.

Charlie checked her watch. It was nearly eleven p.m. and the child was still being dragged around the streets. As if thinking the same, Ben stopped directly in front of the woman, who immediately raised her hand towards them, palms outwards begging for cash.

'Do you have a home?' Ben asked gently.

The woman nodded.

'Listen to me, then,' he continued, his voice becoming firmer. 'You need to get yourself and your child home.'

Charlie pulled her warrant card out and held it towards the woman, as if to emphasize what Ben had said. 'I agree. It's far too late for this little girl to be out on the streets.'

The woman looked panic-stricken. She struggled to her feet, gathering up her meagre belongings, nearly losing grip of the sleeping child, whose eyes blinked open in shock.

'Will I get in trouble?' she asked in a clipped Romanian accent.

Charlie shook her head. 'No, not this time, but you shouldn't involve your child. Take her home now and go down to your local council if you need further help in the morning.'

The woman nodded and pulled the little girl close. The child was whimpering quietly now, having been woken. She shuffled off quickly into the distance.

Ben accompanied Charlie to the platform and waited until her train was pulling in.

'Thanks for a lovely evening. We'll have to do it again soon.'

'Yes, we will. Thank you too.'

He stood on the platform as her train left, waving at her until she could see him no longer. She thought about the evening and how they had spoken about anything and everything with no fear or pressure. He was a lovely guy. She was impressed with how he had dealt with the Romanian beggar and her child with care and compassion, when many others would have berated her.

But most of all she remembered the words of the woman herself - 'Will I get in trouble?'

She'd heard the very same phrase recently. Now she needed to follow it up.

Chapter 33

He was excited now.

Her house was quiet and still. He'd seen, smelt and heard her already that morning and now it was his turn to touch and taste.

Thank God the kids were at private school and weren't around on a Saturday. He'd never have been able to wait until next week. He needed her now.

He wandered into the kitchen and opened the fridge, reaching in and taking out a can. Pulling the tag, he almost laughed as a fine spray of lager shot upwards. He lifted it to his mouth and drank down the whole of the contents, crushing the can in his hand when he finished and tossing it towards the bin. It missed and clattered across the floor, spilling the last few droplets as it skidded across the tiles. He stared at it hard, debating whether he needed to pick it up. Today was the day when she would become his, so surely she wouldn't care about such things, but then he remembered how house-proud she was. He bent down and scooped it up, placing it carefully into the top of the bin. He wanted things to be perfect for her.

He loved being in her house. It made him feel part of her life. He could move around from room to room, sit on the sofa, watch TV, even lie on her bed with her scent all around him without being out of place. He was at home here and he knew without doubt that she would feel the same. They were meant to be together.

He walked into the lounge. On the wall hung a large photo of Annabel on her wedding day; her dress exquisitely clinging to her body, her face beaming with joy, her husband Greg standing beside her. He was tall and toned with blonde hair, teased into spikes, clean-shaven and clean-looking. He hated the man. It should be him there next to her. Reaching up, he turned the frame round so that the photo faced the wall. He couldn't bear to see her with another man. It wasn't right. It should be him and only him. She was his one and only.

Pulling up his sleeve, he took hold of his small kitchen knife. The blade was like a razor; he'd sharpened it carefully. He took it out and made slashing movements through the air, pretending he was a martial arts expert about to defend himself against an unknown foe. He caught sight of himself in the gilt-framed mirror above the mantelpiece and turned towards it aiming the knife at the reflection of his own face and body.

The sound of a car pulling up outside brought him out of his daydream and he ran to the window, peering round the edge of the curtain. It was Greg's car, but he couldn't see who was in it. Could it be his beautiful Annabel or her bastard husband? Or both of them together? All he knew was that his heart was pumping wildly now at the thought of being with her or dealing with him. Either way, he was so excited he could barely move. He inched away from the window and crouched down behind the back of the sofa. It wouldn't do for her to see the curtains twitch or any movement in the shadows. He didn't want to scare her off now he was so close.

A single car door slammed and a key turn in the lock. He could hear the blood pumping through his ears so loudly that he could almost imagine that his quarry could hear it too. He squatted on his haunches, holding on to the sofa with one hand and pushing the knife back up his sleeve with the other, daring not to move a muscle for fear of being heard. The front door closed and the residual sound of the traffic disappeared as quickly as it had come. The house was silent and the man held his breath.

Footsteps sounded across the tiled flooring in the kitchen. There was no conversation. He wondered whether the occupant would notice the lager missing from the fridge, the slight spillage, the crushed empty can in the bin. He didn't really want the element of surprise taken away. The footsteps came out of the kitchen and he didn't know where they went, moving across the carpeted hallway. A man walked into the lounge and threw a newspaper down on the sofa. It was the man he hated, Gregory Leigh-Matthews, the bastard who possessed his Annabel.

He twitched with the desire to jump straight out and thrust the knife into the bastard's back, but he waited, holding his breath so that he didn't give his position away.

Greg stretched and eased himself down on the sofa, just a

few feet from the man, and picked up the paper. He opened it up so that it was spread wide and looked as though he was about to start reading it when his eyes peered upwards and he focussed on the photo frame. Placing the paper down, he stood, frowning, and walked towards it, glancing around him as he did so. He reached up and turned the frame back around concentrating on getting it positioned absolutely horizontally. The man watched, seething with anger at the sight. How could the bastard spend all his time worrying that the frame was straight when all he should be doing was concentrating on the beautiful woman, in the beautiful dress, with the beautiful smile on their wedding day? He stepped out from behind the sofa and stayed silently watching as Greg stood back to check the photo was not askew. He didn't move, save for the up and down of his chest as he inhaled and exhaled.

'It's perfectly straight,' he said at last, his voice cold.

Greg started, spinning round to face the man.

'What the fuck! Who are you?'

He stared hard at Greg but said nothing.

'What are you doing in my house?' Greg tried to pull himself up to his full height but he could see the fear in his face. 'Get out!'

'You get out. It's my house now and Annabel will soon be my wife. You don't want her like I do.'

Greg stood staring at him open-mouthed, obviously trying to make sense of what he'd said.

He took a step towards him, smiling as his foe recoiled against the wall.

'What do you want?'

'I want Annabel. She belongs to me. Not you. You never wanted her. You didn't even look at her just then in her beautiful dress. You were more interested in making sure the photo frame was straight. Look at you now. Not the big man like in the photo on your wedding day, are you? You're pathetic. So get out.'

Greg still looked perplexed. 'Don't tell me to get out of my own house,' he said eventually. 'You'd better go now before I call the police.'

'You think that will scare me?' he laughed. 'I don't think so. I've done time in prison. The police are nothing compared with what I've faced?'

He wasn't frightened in any way. He was in his element.

'Annabel loves me,' Greg said simply. 'It's our anniversary today. We're going out for lunch.'

'She's not going with you now. She's coming with me. I'm going to look after her properly, not like you, going away all the time and leaving her to bring up *your* children on her own. You don't care about her like I do.'

'How do you know what I...?' Greg stopped mid-sentence. 'Are you the guy that's been stalking Annabel?'

'I wouldn't say stalking her. I've been looking out for her in your absence. She loves me.'

'What do you mean she loves you? She doesn't love you! She hates you. She's frightened of you. She loves me.'

The bastard was mocking him. His anger surged. The blade of the knife up his sleeve burnt against his skin. He pulled it out. It felt good grasped in the palm of his hand; it gave him power. He was right. The bastard was wrong and yet he could only hear those last few words.

'She won't love you like this,' he screamed, lunging forward and aiming the razor-sharp metal at the bastard's face. The point made contact, slicing deep into his cheek. Gregory Leigh-Matthews froze, putting his hands up to stop the attack, but the knife slashed at his hands and wrists. He dropped his guard, powerless to respond. Blood spurted out as the man lunged again and again, slicing at his face and neck until the bastard was unrecognizable. He slumped to the floor, his blood soaking into the carpet, bright red and frothy. He tried to speak but his words were lost in the gurgle of more blood filling his throat. He coughed and a red stream sprang from his mouth, out on to the carpet spreading out slowly; the patch getting larger and larger. His expression was pure fear. His eyes focussed momentarily; then they grew glassy and still.

He wiped the blade of the knife on the shoulder of his dead foe and threaded it back up his sleeve. Annabel would be his now. There was no one to prevent her coming to him and he knew without doubt she would be happy about it.

As if on cue, her red BMW pulled up on the driveway. He watched from behind the curtains as she climbed out from the driver's seat, her lithe body, long legs and short skirt an open invitation. She really was sexy and he longed to touch her. He moved away from the window towards the door of the lounge. It wouldn't do for her to be scared at the sight of her husband, although she might also be glad to see his handiwork. Not yet though; only when he was ready to show her. He pulled the door shut and slipped into the kitchen just as he heard the key turn in the lock.

The door opened and she entered.

'Greg I'm home,' she called, peering up the stairs. 'Are you nearly ready to go? Or have you got a surprise for me upstairs?' She waited for an answer but none came. He tried to forgive her for her words. She had no choice, so she'd had to make the best of it. He was looking forward to showing her his surprise, laid out in the lounge. Then she would be happy! She ran lightly up the stairs, calling out Greg's name but all was silent. After a minute or so she walked back down the stairs.

He could hear her getting nearer.

'Greg?' her voice this time was low and questioning.

He couldn't wait any longer. She was so close. He stepped out from the kitchen.

'Greg's not here. He's gone.'

She jumped backwards, her eyes wide with fear.

'Who are you? What do you want?'

'I want you.' His reply was simple and clear. He said what he'd been thinking for a long time. He stepped towards her waiting for her to fall into his arms. She shrunk away from him against the wall, throwing her arms up in front of her to hold him off. He was taken aback, shocked even, but then he suddenly realized why she had responded like she had. She must be frightened that her husband would see them together.

He moved back again, giving her space, and tried to look friendly.

'Don't worry. You don't have to worry about Greg finding out.' He was keeping it nice and personal for her, so she wasn't afraid. He reached towards the lounge door and threw it open. 'Look, Greg's gone. He won't bother us anymore.'

She turned her head towards the open door and screamed, loud and long, clasping her hands to her mouth so that the scream was muffled.

'Oh my God, Oh my God. What have you done to him?'

Lurching forward, she ran the few steps to her husband's body and threw herself down next to him.

'Greg, Greg. Talk to me.'

Her hands were against his bloodied face now, trying to rouse him. She stroked his hair but he didn't respond.

'Quick, Call an ambulance.' She pulled a phone from her pocket and started to dial 999 but he stepped forward, twisting it from her hands. Why was she doing this? He didn't like it. He put the phone in his pocket and stood watching her, his frown deepening.

'What have you done to him? I said "Call an ambulance". She was crying and her voice was accusatory. He didn't like how she was speaking to him.

It's too late. He's dead. I've got rid of him so that we can be together. He won't bother us now.' He paused, watching to see if the words had taken effect. 'You should be pleased?'

'Pleased?' her tone was incredulous. 'That you've killed my husband!' She glared up at him and then buried her face against Greg's chest, sobbing.

He stood and watched her, not understanding what was happening. He loved her. He loved her so much he'd killed for her. She needed to start appreciating what he'd done.

*

Her husband's body was unnaturally still. Normally when she rested her ear against his chest she could hear the rhythmic beat of his heart, pumping loud and strong. Normally her head would rise and fall with the movement of his rib-cage and she would see the muscles in his abdomen flex and tighten, with the extra pressure required to lift the weight of her body. Normally he would hold her close, as if he never wanted to let her go.

Now though his chest was motionless, his arms limp, his heart unmoving. She knew he was dead. And she also knew she was trapped in a room, with his killer.

She glanced at the man through her fingers. She'd seen him before and his voice was familiar. He was staring down at her, his face stern. She needed time to think, to work out what he wanted with her. He was obviously mad, to have done what he had, but he was calmer now. Her training was starting to kick in. She had to keep him talking. She had to keep him sweet. She had to survive for the sake of her children. But first she needed an answer.

'You're the man who attacked me the other evening, aren't you?'

'I was trying to speak to you.' He sounded almost apologetic.

'You jumped out at me in dark clothes and a face mask?'

'I thought you would recognize me.'

She stared at him. She did recognise him. She just hadn't really had time to realize that she knew him. His voice had been familiar then and it was familiar now and now she remembered his face too, but she couldn't quite place where from.

'You acted for me years ago,' he started to explain. 'You didn't get me off but I know you did what you could. You told me that. I knew you did your best and that you were upset to see me convicted. I don't blame you for it. It wasn't your fault. It was the policeman lying in court. He set me up. Who would they believe? Him or me? I didn't stand a chance. But you were there for me when it mattered. You believed me. You were the only one. You still are the only one.'

He tailed off and then she remembered. It was those last words; the way that he said them. He'd said them to her then, the last time that they had spoken in the cells at the court before he was taken away. He'd told her then that she was the only one and that he would always remember her. She'd ignored it. Lots of cons said similar. They were desperate, clutching on to anyone or anything that seemed to be on their side before they were taken away to be locked up for years.

He'd said the same words the other night when he'd jumped out on her. She'd remembered the words and the voice then too, but what was his name and what was his crime? And how many years ago was it? How long must he have been harbouring these feelings; thinking about them, feeding on them, allowing them to grow and fester until he was able to act on them. How long?

She looked back down at her dead husband. Greg had not been involved in any of this. He was the innocent victim, even more so than she was. He had never met the man, never spoken to him and yet the man had murdered him for no other reason than he existed as a barrier between him and his delusions.

'Do you remember me?' the man seemed desperate.

She did remember him but not his name.

'Yes I do remember you,' she suddenly knew instinctively that she had to be careful. 'I remember you well. I spoke to you in your cell before you got taken away. I did do what I could for you.'

The man seemed to relax. He smiled. 'I knew you did. If it hadn't been for that lying policeman planting the sweet wrapper with my DNA all over it at the crime scene you would have got me off.'

And now she remembered the case. It had been a particularly nasty stranger rape. The suspect had climbed into the woman's ground-floor flat through an insecure bathroom window and raped her in her bed at knifepoint. It turned out that she worked at the local authority housing department and had helped him with a housing application some months before. He had obviously fixated on her afterwards and stalked her for some time. The suspect had been arrested as one of several known rapists on the Sexual Offenders register living in the nearby vicinity. A Twix wrapper that the suspect had torn open with his mouth and which was found later during the two-day forensic examination of the crime scene appeared to verify that he was indeed the correct suspect. The man had insisted, however, that he had been picked upon simply because he was known and that the Twix wrapper had really been found at his home address when he was arrested and planted by the police officer afterwards at the crime scene.

She had fought his case hard, wanting to believe that the personable man sat in front of her at the police station when she'd first met him, pleading his innocence, could not be guilty of such a crime and although there was a fair amount of circumstantial evidence that pointed to him being involved, it was really this single sample of DNA that had convicted him.

'I remember your case well!' she volunteered, realizing with a jolt that the previous case was almost a carbon copy of what he was now doing, with the exception that he had committed murder instead of rape, so far. 'But just remind me of your name? I deal with so many people it's slipped my mind at the moment.'

He obviously wasn't happy and she knew straight away she had said the wrong thing. She tried to recover the conversation. 'I tried to get an appeal on the basis the police officer had lied, but it was turned down. They said I had no new evidence and the court had already found in the police officer's favour.'

'You don't remember my name?'

'I didn't give up straight away but they wouldn't change their minds.'

'You don't remember my name?'

'I'm really sorry.'

'All this time I've been thinking about you, wanting to be with you. I thought you felt the same after how you spoke to me that last time. You seemed so upset that I'd been convicted...'

'I was upset. I believed you.' She knew she had to persuade him, regardless of whether she had believed him or not. At this point possibly even her life depended on it.

'But you don't remember my name?' He focussed on her and she was suddenly more frightened than she ever had been in her life. He stared at her long and hard, appearing to be weighing up what to do. She knew she had mere moments to make the right decision or it might be too late. Pulling herself away from her dead husband, she stood up and took a step towards him, her hands outstretched.

'I still believe you now. I might not remember names very well, but I do know that I believed you then and I still do. I've thought about your case many times over the years and wondered how you were getting on.'

'Have you? Have you really?' he was suddenly animated. 'My name is Brad. Bradley Conroy. I'm glad you've thought about me.'

He stopped again just as quickly, staring at her with obvious suspicion. 'I hope you're telling me the truth. I don't like liars.'

He took hold of her arm and walked her to the hallway, picking up her car key from the table. 'We can't stay here. The police will come and I don't want to speak to them yet. You can come to my flat and I'll show you how much you mean to me. I have pictures and video clips to show you that I've collected. You'll be pleased. Now come.'

She considered fighting him but knew instantly that he would win. Her brain seemed to be scrambled. Fight or flight kept running through her mind, but neither was a viable option. Her job was discussion, debate, manipulation even, and it was the only way that she could win. She needed to use her skills. They would be the only way to get out of this alive.

He seemed to sense her reluctance and his expression darkened.

'Tell Brad you're happy to come with him,' he instructed,

stepping towards her and taking her by the arm roughly. 'You're not lying to me are you Annabel? Tell Brad!'

'I'm happy to come with you, Brad.' She did what she was told, walking with him out to her car and climbing in the passenger seat. She heard the locks go on as he slid into the driver's seat next to her. There was no escape, at least for the time being.

Chapter 34

She was fucking dead. Another one! He couldn't believe it. What was it with these women that they just seemed to give up without a fight? Kill their favourite and they don't fight for their other child. Is that how it was?

Helena had given up. There was no reason. She still had water; she hadn't been there long enough really to starve to death; she had just chosen to die. True, she was getting more emaciated and her face was caked in dirt and insect excrement, but that was no excuse to give up. He stamped down on her face in anger. The bitch, the cheating bitch. He hated her.

Mummy, why did you die so easily too. You shouldn't have swallowed those pills I gave you. You didn't have to. You could have refused.

He slammed the boarding down, blocking the vision of Helena and Daisy away. He didn't want to see Helena, especially her, ever again. She was a bitch. She too had denied him his chance to teach her a proper lesson.

Mummy, Mummy. You were a bitch too. You couldn't even write me a letter telling me you loved me. You couldn't even pretend for even a few minutes of my life. You fucking bitch. You fucking, fucking bitch.

He wrenched the padlock off. He didn't need it for this one now. He would use it for the next one. He would need to get digging again soon, maybe even straight away. He could feel the anger rising up from his belly. It was getting uncontrollable. He was energized, animated, invigorated. He liked it, the urge, the desperate need; he loved the planning and he loved the fact that they were no closer to catching him.

He'd watched their pointless appeal on *Crimewatch*. They were grasping at straws, clueless. He was too good; too fucking good. He grinned to himself at the thought of the six he had surrounding him now. The execution of each individual plan had been perfect, the way that everything had fallen into place, but Helena had now dis-respected him, just like Julie had, just like the others. They had died when they, not he, had chosen. Why did women not respect him? The bitches! Not even his own mother had respected him.

Mummy, Mummy. What was wrong with me? I loved you. Why did you love Tommy more? Why? Why? Why was I never good enough? Tell me, you bitch. Tell me, you fucking bitch. I hate you!

He would do it now. He would dig another pit, then another, then another. They would never get him because he was too clever for them. He might not have been the best little boy then but he was the best man now. He ran back to his car and pulled the shovel and fork from the boot, jogging back quickly. He had so much fucking energy; so much anger, rage, fury.

Before he started, he removed the water tank and tubing. He could use this for the next one, so it would be ready straight away. He yanked the bedding out from around Helena, watching as her body spun round and landed face down in the dirt. Then he pulled the boarding away too and shovelled the spare earth over their bodies, finally covering their grave with leaves and foliage; camouflaging it to the naked eye.

Moving a short distance away, he started the next one, working hard and fast, shovelling the earth from the hole into a pile. He stood back when he'd finished admiring his handiwork. It wasn't quite so perfect around the edges as the others had been, but it was good enough. He got down inside it, lying in the dirt and earth, and pulled the boarding over him, allowing the smell of the woodland to seep up his nostrils as he always liked to do. He let his fingers run through the soil, picking some up between his fingers and bringing it to his nose so he could inhale the earthy scent further. It was fucking good, so fucking good. He needed to get his next subjects as soon as he could, to fill the pit with living, breathing people for his experiments. He knew who the next ones would be already. He'd been waiting and watching and listening.

And then he remembered Dana and Gemma, captive just a few metres from where he lay now, waiting for him to visit, waiting for him to decide their destiny. His pulse quickened at the thought. They were still so new and virginal and they were desperate for him to return, to free them; but he wouldn't be doing that. No, he would never let them go. They were his to do with what he wanted until death. And he wanted them badly now. This time she would do what he wanted and die when he wanted. This time it would be right.

He climbed back out and covered over the new pit with the boarding, pushing the leaves with his feet until the woodland carpet was smooth. His pulse was quickening already at the thought of Dana Latchmere, *the* Dana Latchmere, exquisite and demure, an excellent prize, and her spoilt brat of a daughter. It seemed that Justin Latchmere's recent behaviour had made Dana tar her own son, Aiden with the same brush. Like father, like son? She was lavishing all her affections and her money on her daughter, but poor Aiden! What of him? Punished for the sins of the father. It had made him boil with rage to hear the rumours, however true or untrue. Just the fact that the stories were being mooted was enough for him to know there would be some truth behind them. Dana needed to be punished and now he would start the punishment.

Dana would want him, just as his mummy had wanted him, and he would oblige and Gemma would see how happy he made her, again and again.

He was at the side of their pit now. He undid the padlock and pulled open the doors, watching with a smirk as the two females inside screwed up their faces against the light. Dana still looked demure even though her cheeks had smears of dirt across them and her hair lay flat against her forehead. And he wanted her now. He wanted her to love him just as his mummy had wanted him to love her and touch her and make her smile and groan with pleasure.

He climbed down into the pit. Gemma was wide-eyed with fear but he didn't want her, not yet: he just wanted Dana. He peeled back the bedding and undid her jacket. The top that she was wearing was delicate and slightly see-through. He ripped it open, exposing her flesh, burying his head against her stomach, her neck, her breasts. He needed her now and she needed him; he could feel it. But did she love him? He didn't know as yet. He didn't really care though at that moment as he felt the attraction rising in him.

Mummy, mummy, I love you really. You know I love you. But I still don't understand why you didn't love me. Mummy, mummy, love me. Please love me. Love me! Fucking love me.

Chapter 35

All the phones were going to answerphone or ringing out and Miss Saunders didn't quite know what to do. Jasmin and Jake Leigh-Matthews were still awaiting collection, playing on gym equipment in the school hall. It was highly unusual. Ms Leigh-Matthews was always prompt to collect them, or if she was unable to, her replacement would be arranged and waiting at the school gates. She had never failed to arrive before. On weekdays, on the very rare occasions that she had been held at court and was running late from her busy schedule, she had always, always phoned to warn them and they had held on to the children for as long as it took. On Saturdays she was never late.

Today, however, over an hour after school had finished there was still no sign of either parent or a stand-in, no phone calls from Ms Leigh-Matthews and, to make matters worse, neither parent was answering their phone. She was the last one there and the caretaker was waiting to lock up and go home. Miss Saunders didn't know quite what to do!

She dialled 999. The kids seemed quite happy still. She made sure their belongings were all ready and sat and watched them for a while. They were totally unaware of the problem and didn't seem in any way upset. Miss Saunders had carefully questioned them earlier about any potential problems but, listening to their answers and watching them playing together now, she was quite satisfied that there weren't any problems at home with their parents that they were aware of.

It wasn't long before the police car arrived and she explained the situation to the female police officer and her male companion who were first on scene. She watched as the children were led away, climbing excitedly into the marked police car and waving happily towards her as they were driven from her sight.

Slowly she gathered her things together and walked from the building. Something was badly wrong.

PC Karen Baxter was tired. It was nearing the end of a very long shift and she just wanted to be finished. The day had started at 7 a.m. standing at a crime scene, then progressed through various allegations of criminal damage, a dog bite, a burglary, a minor traffic accident and a complicated landlord/tenant dispute and was now set to end with two forgotten children. She had a nasty feeling that she would be late off, and although she had nothing particularly planned, she just wanted to grab a takeaway and veg in front of the TV. Twelve hours at work was hard enough without having to stay on dealing with this shit just because another set of feckless parents had failed in their duty of childcare.

She checked her rear-view mirror and saw the children's excited faces and felt guilty at the thought.

'Has this happened before?' She already knew the answer. This was obviously the first time; the teacher had said as much and she could tell by the children's exuberance.

'No, but this is fun,' Jake said, with no obvious worry. 'I can't wait to tell my friends I went in a police car.'

She smiled at the words even though she was beginning to feel a sense of dread at the outcome of this situation. She was heading for their home address now. It was not too far away. Maybe the mother had thought she'd got a message through but the message had failed and she was waiting for them to turn up at home. Maybe she had arranged for someone else to come, while she was otherwise engaged at work and that person had let her down. Whatever the case, she was hoping that a visit to the address, and if necessary a chat with neighbours, might throw some light on what had happened.

She pulled up outside, noting the car directly in front of the house. Maybe one of the parents was here all along, too busy with their own affairs to realize what time it was.

She told her colleague to wait with the children and eased herself out of the driver's seat. Her back ached from the weight of the kit-belt around her waist and the stab-proof vest dug into her shoulders. With any luck it could all be resolved quickly, with a lecture to the errant adults and a report to the local social services letting them know how irresponsible the parents were, then home to fish and chips and a dose of *Britain's got Talent*.

She rang the doorbell and waited, listening for footsteps from within. Nothing came. She rang again and then knocked, bending down to peer through the letter box. Everything was silent. She swore out loud. Her nice relaxing evening was looking to be in jeopardy. Pulling herself upright, she squeezed behind the wisteria to stare through the window into the lounge. Her eyes scanned the room. Everything seemed in place. Her radio blared into action, making her start slightly. She shifted position ready to move on to the next window and it was then that she saw the body lying on the red, bloody carpet. It wasn't moving. She could see it was a man, though she couldn't be sure whether he was dead or alive. She needed to act fast. She considered the front door; it seemed quite substantial. She didn't think she'd be able to shift that, but time was of the essence. She ran round the back of the house but that was all secure. Returning to the front she signalled to her colleague to stay where he was. The last thing she wanted were the kids wandering up to the house and seeing the bloody scene.

That done, she radioed for more assistance before drawing out her asp and smashing the lounge window, carefully knocking any large jagged pieces out of the frame, before hoisting herself up on to the window ledge. Her heart was pounding with fear and adrenaline as she climbed through. Every sense was heightened, as she listened for any sign that could point to the killer still being present. The man was clearly dead when she reached him. His body was cool and his eyes fixed and glassy. Most of the blood had drained out of him through the mass of open wheals around his face and neck. Christ! He was a bloody mess, quite literally.

She stood up, realizing she needed to check the rest of the house. Her eyes darted about watching for any movement. Apart from the man's body, the room looked relatively untouched, with little sign of a struggle. There was no obvious forced entry either, as the house had still been secure. Whoever had done this appeared to either have had keys, or been granted entry by the dead man, in all probabilities, the children's father. Vaguely she wondered whether her colleague would give in to temptation and come to join her, but she hoped he would stay where he was. She needed to know that the children would be safe from whoever had done this. For a second she thought of their little faces, so excited at the ride in the police car. Who would tell them their father was dead?

She realized with a jolt that their mother was nowhere to be seen, possibly lying dead, or dying in another room. Grabbing her asp and CS spray, she started to move around the house, stopping, after every few steps to listen for any slight sound, any tiny noise, that would alert her to the fact that she was not alone. She moved carefully and swiftly through each room, checking each crevice, each wardrobe, under each bed, anywhere big enough for a person to hide. The silence crowded in on her and all she could hear was the rush of blood pumping around her brain, but, thankfully, there was nothing more to be found.

She was just returning to the lounge when she heard the first sirens exploding in on the air. Her colleague came running up the path towards the house, having grabbed the first arrival, to take his place with the kids so he could join her.

He took one look at the body and swore.

'Christ, Kazza. Are you all right? I didn't know what the fuck to do. I wanted to leave the children but was worried in case they followed me. Anyone else in the house?'

She shook her head; anxious to reassure him that he had done exactly the right thing staying with the children. If he'd left them alone and something had happened, she'd never have forgiven herself.

'No, I've had a look and there's no trace.'

'I presume that's the father? What about the mother? Any sign of her?'

She shook her head.

'Well, I think we have our suspect then,' her colleague stared down at the cuts inflicted on Greg Leigh-Matthew's face. 'Fifty quid says those are the actions of a jealous woman. She's caught him out and now he's paid the price. He certainly won't be looking at any other women again!'

A tide of uniforms was arriving outside now. She had to stop them all from coming in and trampling over the murder scene. She went to the front door and waited for the Inspector to arrive, barring the way from the curiosities of the ensuing constables.

'Well, what do you say then?' Her colleague repeated the bet, offering his hand to shake.

Karen raised her eyebrows as she took in the offer.

'I hope to God you're wrong,' she said slowly. 'Because, if you're right, and she is his killer, those poor kids out there will grow up without either parent.'

Chapter 36

Bear sat in the cells at Charing Cross and chuckled quietly to himself. Information had been received that he was involved in the assault on Keith Hubbard. Information? Most probably from Hubbard himself then, the snivelling grass. Well he would be paying the dirty snitch another visit when he got out and next time the man wouldn't be able to go running to the filth with his tales of woe. He'd have no tongue.

They were out getting Ratman now or so they'd said; as if that was going to bother him. Ratman would never grass on him. They were, like the saying went, as thick as thieves. He trusted him like he would trust his own brother; more so even. They went back a long way; back to when they were kids in the middle of one of the largest estates in Peckham, glamorized amusingly on TV in *Only Fools and Horses*. There had been nothing glamorous in their existence though. Alcoholic crack-head mothers, non-existent fathers; the two of them had lived next door to each other back in the day when you could rely on your neighbours to help out, if they weren't nicking from you! They had grown up together, scraping what little food and cash they could lay their hands on, thieving from the back of restaurants, pilfering from shops, anything to fill their growing bellies and frames.

Bear was built in the likeness of his street name: huge, muscular, powerful and covered in a layer of thick, black hair across his chest and back. He barely needed to work out; he was naturally powerful.

Ratman was built in the likeness of his street name too: skinny, thin-faced with a way of moving that resembled a rodent, twitching and darting one way and another as if always scared of being spotted. He was, however, fearless and Bear loved him for his courage and bravery in the face of adversaries much larger than he. No, the filth could bring his mate in and they wouldn't get a squeak out of him. He laughed at his own joke.

Lying down on the thin mattress of his cell, he folded his arms up above his head. It would only be a matter of time before they were released on bail or with no further action. Hubbard was a fool to pursue them this way. It wasn't worth his while; in fact it would be more than his life was worth. Bear was amazed he'd gone this far, but he must have. If they were bailed out pending statements and advice, it wouldn't take long before Hubbard was eating his words. He'd make sure of that. He knew from previous experience that bail conditions not to contact the victim weren't worth the paper they were written on.

He peered across as the cell wicket opened and the gaoler, young, naive and fearful, glanced in.

'Just checking I'm still alive, are you?' he swung his legs round and ran at the door, pushing his face towards the small open square. The gaoler jumped backwards and slammed the wicket shut with shaky fingers. Bear threw his head back and let out a roar of laughter. He loved putting the fear of God into the youngsters; particularly the ones who thought they were it just because they were wearing a uniform. They were nothing; nor were the jumped-up detectives who had treated him with surly arrogance. They would never keep him caged. Nothing would keep him or Ratman caged. It never had and it never would.

He ambled back to the bench and lay down again. They were Teflon, him and his mate; nothing stuck to them – and if something was causing them a little more trouble, then there was always Justin, wasn't there; the slippery snake of a legal rep who Bear hated but admired at the same time. He'd literally got them off murder in the past, and robbery and the odd GBH. The arrangement worked well. Justin Latchmere would use every trick in the book, every technicality he could find, to get them off a charge. In return, they would do his dirty work, settle a few scores, in such a way that he didn't get those precious, manicured hands of his soiled with blood or scandal.

Justin said little of his private life when he gave them a job, even though his reputation for affairs was well known all around the legal and criminal fraternities One day very soon the great Justin Latchmere would be a prime target for blackmail and if things didn't change, he and Ratman would be up there among the list of prime suspects; after all they knew exactly who was organizing all the paybacks and Bear was always careful to keep the proof.

Hubbard had obviously pissed Justin off big time and it didn't take too much imagination to work out why. Bear had watched *Crimewatch* and had recognized Hubbard's case and besides, everyone was talking. Justin had supposedly had an affair with Hubbard's missing wife. Hubbard was apparently stalking Justin's wife. And now Justin's wife and daughter were missing. It wasn't difficult to see why they had been hired.

He could hear a commotion now outside the cell. He wandered back to the door and pressed his ear to it, chuckling quietly to himself as he recognized his mate's high-pitched voice. Ratman liked to argue for the sake of arguing, to question every comment the custody officer or arresting officer made. He revelled in being difficult.

Bear couldn't be bothered. He just took it all in, said nothing and sat the time out until he was released. Still, it amused him to listen to how his little mate made the filth squirm; how he pissed them off without giving anything away.

If they were lucky, he'd be put in an adjacent cell and they'd be able to shout to each other. If not, whoever was released first would wait outside the nick for the other to be released and go out for a few drinks to celebrate their escape from justice again.

And if the worst came to the worst and they were charged, well they'd just go and see their mate Justin and he would get them off their charges.

And they in turn would reward him with their services… again.

Chapter 37

'Charlie, I need you in my office now.'

The phone summons was clear. Hunter was not to be argued with and she abandoned the idea of a quick bite to eat in answer to his command. The whole of Lambeth HQ was in a frenzy of activity. The buzz was almost palpable. Something big was kicking off, but cocooned within the custody suite conducting interviews, she had no idea what.

She climbed the stairs two at a time and almost bumped headlong into Hunter as she threw open the door to their corridor.

'Charlie,' he shouted excitedly.

'What's going on?'

'Well you know Hubbard's slippery solicitor. Her husband, Greg Leigh-Matthews, has been found dead at the family home, and it looks like Annabel has been abducted.'

Charlie fought the urge to be pleased. That woman had helped Hubbard get off assaulting her. She deserved everything she got.

'And what's more, we've only got a bloody suspect this time.'

'Who?'

'Turns out to be some saddo called Bradley Conroy. He was a client of Annabel's some years ago but got sent down for a nasty stranger rape. She and a barrister defended him at court and it seems he developed some sort of crush on her when he was inside, and has waited until now to follow it up. She's reported a stalker recently and we think it may well be this guy. Forensics got hold of a few items from the house to look at straight away. One was a can of beer in the top of the bin which was still wet and appeared to be recent. We didn't know whether it would be Greg's or the suspects but they thought it was worth a try. They got a good enough set of fingerprints off the metal to send them up for a match; which came back to Conroy. There's no legitimate reason for his prints to be in Annabel's house.

We're doing some checks with probation and the prison service to find his most recent addresses. We'll be ready to go and look for him shortly.'

*

She felt immediately guilty for her earlier thought. Whether she agreed with Ms Leigh-Matthew's ethics or not, she was, after all only doing her job. She really didn't deserve this.

'Count me in. Might he be the suspect for all of them?'

'We don't know yet but the MO's too similar to discount. We won't know for sure until we've got him.'

'He could be anywhere by now.'

'Yes, he could be, but we've checked with our psychological profiler who thinks Conroy will have been preparing a place for a while to take her to; a cosy little love nest somewhere. Let's hope it's an address we can identify. We also know Annabel's red BMW is missing, so we might be able to get a lead on that, presuming he's taken it. I've already had the registration number circulated in case it comes to notice.'

'Wow, I disappear down to the cells for a couple of hours to interview Hubbard's assailants, though I just wanted to congratulate them really, and when I come out, not only do we have a murder on our hands, but you also have the case solved! Do *you* think this Conroy's our main man?'

Hunter shrugged his shoulders.

'I don't know. To be honest, this guy sounds more like a nutter that gets off on stalking women. I'm not sure that he's sophisticated enough to be our main suspect; leaving a beer can on the bin et cetera, and then there's the fact he didn't take the kids.'

'It's still a very similar MO though. Maybe he was targeting Annabel and the kids, but her husband came in too early and the guy just panicked, killed him and took Annabel before she had the chance to collect the kids. You never know? Let's hope he is and let's hope we get him quickly.'

'Well, fingers crossed.'

She crossed the fingers on both hands and held them up towards Hunter. He looked one hundred per cent better than he had even a few hours before. The worry lines had gone for the time being. His eyes were alive, his whole face animated with the adrenaline. It was what he stayed in the job for.

'Charlie can you find out what addresses have been identified and who is going to each one? Bet and Paul are searching for me. I need to be able to speak to the officers directly to let them know what's happening.'

'Will do, guv. I'll get back to you shortly.'

Hunter's enthusiasm had injected a new sense of urgency into them all. She turned sharply and almost ran to the main office.

Bet's fingers were on fire, busily tapping search enquiries into the computer. She looked up as Charlie ran over and got straight to the point.

'I identified four addresses that he's been connected with previously. One is his mother's and one is his sister's. There's also a council bedsit he was temporarily housed in before he was sent to prison, but that was obviously a few years ago now. I also spoke to the Integrated Offender Management team and got the details of his prison discharge address.'

'Thanks Bet, you're a star. Do we know yet if cars have been dispatched and who is going where?'

'A car has been sent to each of the four addresses and we've already heard back from them all. The council bedsit looks uninhabited so that has been discounted and the sister's house appears all quiet. The other two; the mum's and the discharge address look occupied and the officers there have seen movement, but so far the occupants have not been verified.'

Charlie started to jot down the two live locations and the names of the officers at each address when her phone rang. It was Dick Talbot, an officer she'd worked with on a team previously. She pressed the on button and immediately caught the excitement in his voice.

'Hi, Charlie? Hunter said you were in charge.'

'Yep, I don't know about being in charge but what have you got?' Hunter was a bugger sometimes.

'We're at the release address and we've just found the victim's car. It's parked in the next street. We can see the house clearly and have done a little recce, and presuming that Flat One is on the ground floor it certainly looks as if there are people inside.'

'Excellent.' She mouthed the word *yes* to Bet and anyone

else listening. 'Stay watching the front of the house. I'll get another unit to come and watch the rear of the premises and I'll get you a photo of the suspect from before he was in prison, although bear in mind he's been inside a good few years and we don't know how much he will have changed. Let me know if you hear or see anything else. I'll let Hunter know. He's already sorting out troops to do the doors.'

She took a quick screenshot of the most recent police custody image of Bradley Conroy and pinged it down the phone to Talbot. Then she confirmed the address, got another car on the way to them and hurried to inform Hunter.

Within thirty minutes, there were half a dozen carriers of police lined up outside Lambeth HQ bursting with uniformed officers in full riot gear, equipped with batons, shields and Tasers, ready for action. Two armed response vehicles and their crews joined them and two had been sent direct to the address to be on standby around the corner should the occupants of the house leave the premises. Tension crackled through the air, almost as sharply as if one of the Tasers had let off its 50,000 volts.

She phoned Talbot for a situation report. Nothing had changed. There were lights on inside the premises but the occupants could not be seen as the curtains were closed. No one had left the building.

As she entered Hunter's office she could hear him talking on the phone, briefing his bosses. A specialist firearms squad were being deployed to do an armed dig out and a hostage negotiator had been called. They were obviously keen to deploy every squad available. This had to be done properly; the reputation of the Met was on the line. Charlie groaned inwardly. It was good that the resources were there, but it would almost certainly delay any action and nobody knew what the hell was going on in Conroy's flat.

Hunter appeared to feel the same; frustration manifest in every visible crease of his brow. Gone was the look of excitement; replaced now by ruddy cheeks, frown lines and a tone of petulance in his voice. He shook his head and raised his eyebrows as she stood to one side. When he finished on the phone, he turned towards her.

'Bloody hell! Talk about Operation Overkill! If Annabel's in there, we need to get her out quick. The longer we wait...' He left the sentence unfinished 'Though I suppose there're some fairly senior arses to cover if anything goes wrong!'

They caught each other's eye.

'Let's go. I've discussed tactics as much as I'm going to. If I have to come back when the hostage negotiator arrives then I will. Never mind the Commissioner. What's left of my career could rest on what happens tonight.'

*

It was getting increasingly difficult for Bradley Conroy. Annabel wasn't responding as he'd hoped. Yes, she was talking to him, but he didn't believe what she was saying. She kept her face tilted away from him and sometimes he saw tears glistening, sometimes he saw fear. She wasn't happy and he wasn't stupid. He could see that, in every facial expression, every time she shifted her body or glanced in his direction to check out where he was.

He didn't know what more he could do. He'd cooked for her and watched as she'd tasted a tiny bit and pushed the rest around her plate. He'd tried to give her wine to relax her, but she'd insisted on only drinking water she herself got from the tap. Did she think he was going to poison her or dope her? He loved her.

It made him slightly angry, but then it was early days. He had to be patient and let her grow to love him, as he had grown to love her, but at the same time he wanted her now. Now! Hadn't he dispensed with her lazy, uncaring husband? Hadn't he put his neck on the line to do so? And for what?

He gazed across the room at her. She was just as lovely close up as all her photos and videos. There were no imperfections. She was the one for him; had been for years, and now she actually was his, he didn't quite know what was going wrong.

He caught her glance towards his wall of photos; that should show her how much he cared, how much he adored her, but instead all he could see was her alarm. Maybe he should just grab the moment and show her how much he loved her, hold her in his arms so she could feel his strength and longing. He let his eyes wander all over her body. Her top was low-cut, revealing a slight cleavage. He stared down at the gap between her breasts, watching as each soft mound of flesh rose and fell. He wanted to feel them, touch them, nuzzle against them and taste them. His body was already responding to the sight; now his head was impatient. He'd waited all these years, and now here she was, in his room, sitting on his sofa, just waiting for him to make his move.

He moved across the room and sat down beside her, allowing his leg to rest against hers and his arm to fall around her shoulders. She didn't pull away, but she didn't move towards him either. She sat still as a statue, unmoving, unresponsive, her body rigid. Her heat was against his leg and he moved his own closer, allowing their hips to meet, pulling her body into his. His head started to swim. Fuck! He wanted her now!

He stroked her cheek with his hand, pulling her head round so that she was facing him. Her eyes looked wide and wild. Maybe she wanted him as much as he wanted her. Maybe it wasn't fear, maybe it was lust, like he himself was experiencing.

He kissed her on the lips, his tongue rough with longing. She wasn't responding, so he probed deeper, his body urgent now. He manoeuvred her down along the sofa, climbing on top of her, holding her firm. She squirmed beneath him. Maybe she was starting to want him after all. He kissed her again. Nothing. He opened his eyes to look at her. Her eyes were still wide, still wild.

'What was that?' she said suddenly.

'What?'

'That noise. I heard something.'

He hadn't heard or seen anything. He didn't know whether to believe her.

'There was something. I definitely heard a noise. From outside.' She nodded towards the window.

He wanted to ignore her, but he couldn't just disregard what she said. He'd known that time might be short, but he'd wanted so much to show her his wall of photos. Besides, it was only a few hours since he'd left her house. They surely couldn't have identified him and tracked them down that quick? They were never that quick? His passion was ebbing. Her face was close to his and he wanted so much to continue, but he daren't. Climbing off her, he moved across to the window, pulled the curtain back slightly and peered out from the edge of the glass.

A movement caught his eye. He focussed on the movement and saw the figure of a man lurking behind the fence at the bottom of the garden. His hair was blonde and showed up clearly in the fading light. The man was looking directly towards his window. He pulled his head back maintaining his view without being seen. The man moved slightly to one side before talking into a telephone, a light glinting off the small screen. Another man moved into his view and they both turned to stare towards the house. They were obviously cops.

Shit! So Annabel had been right, even though she had obviously made the story up. There was no way she could have seen or heard them from where she was. He would deal with her later.

He didn't bother to gather up any belongings. All he needed was the car keys, a couple of knives and something to keep her hands tied together. He looked around his meagre belongings and found one of the headbands he used when he was lifting his weights. He obviously couldn't trust her as yet, much as he'd liked to have. He'd have to be firmer. She was still resisting him.

Taking her by the arm, he pulled her to her feet.

'Where are we going?'

'Never you mind. I've got somewhere else sorted, where no one will find us. But until then, you do exactly what I say, when I say. Or else…' He brandished the knives in front of her. 'I'm getting increasingly pissed off with you and your lack of appreciation for me, so don't let me have to use them. Because I will.'

He opened the door to the flat and peered around the frame, listening and watching for the slightest movement or sound. It was all quiet and still. Slipping the knives up his sleeve, he took Annabel by the arm and led her towards the back door.

'They won't see us from here. Quick, keep up with me.'

He held Annabel by the hand and walked quickly across the lawn into an area of bushes at the rear. There were some holes in the fencing that he'd found earlier, obviously made by one of the previous residents to allow an easy escape route. He pushed Annabel through the gap, into an alleyway and followed her out. He knew the maze of walkways in all the adjacent roads. He'd made it his business since coming out of prison to learn every minute detail of the area. Left, right and left again and the path would come out opposite their vehicle. He relaxed a little, allowing his gaze to fall on the back of Annabel's neck and the way it remained still even when she walked. The car was directly across the road from them now. It didn't look as if it had moved. He pushed the key fob and the lights flashed on and off and the locks clicked open. Quickly, he bound her wrists tightly together with the headband. It wouldn't do for her to try and escape while he was at the wheel.

There was no one following them, no copper in sight. Maybe they weren't there for him after all.

'Follow me and get in the car as quick as you can. Do you hear me?'

Annabel nodded mutely.

'And don't try anything.' He pulled one of the kitchen knives out from his sleeve. 'Or this little beauty will slice through that beautiful neck of yours before you even have a chance to cry out for help.'

*

'The target vehicle is on the move, just pulling away heading towards the High Street.'

Hunter could barely conceal his anger.

'How the hell did that happen? Someone should have seen the suspects leaving the flat or at least getting into the motor. Get behind it,' he barked down the radio.

'All received. On way now. It's not going fast.'

'Thank fuck for that.' Hunter's face was white.

They watched as two marked police BMWs accelerated past the end of the road in which they were sitting, their blue lights flashing and sirens activated. Charlie pulled away too, following in the wake of the marked vehicles.

'Are you with the target vehicle yet?' Hunter called into the radio. 'They'd better be,' he mumbled under his breath.

'They won't get far, guv.'

Hunter opened his mouth to ask what she meant when the radio crackled into life again.

'We're behind them now, two occupants; one male driving, female in the passenger side. Looks like they've got a flat tyre on the rear nearside.'

'Bunch of wasters!' she laughed. 'Lucky you dropped me off

by the flat en route to check things out. I stuck a nail in the tyre as I was making my way back to you. Not that any of the officers supposedly watching the vehicle noticed. It's no wonder it pulled away without them seeing anyone getting in.'

'Christ, Charlie, lucky our subjects didn't see you.'

'All done in the blink of an eye, guv. Well you should know. You're the one who taught me that trick after we lost that nicked Range Rover. Don't you remember? It disappeared before anyone was seen getting into it. Well worth the risk of being seen, I think.'

'It is this time.'

The radio burst into life.

'The vehicle's speeding up. Now heading towards Park Avenue. It's doing a left, left, left. Looks like the tyre is coming away. Speeding up again, now up to forty-five mph. There's sparks coming from the rear wheel. We're right behind it.'

She was enjoying herself now. Throwing the car round the corner, she quickly caught up with them. She could see the blue lights on the marked cars just a short way ahead of them.

'Charlie, go careful. I want to live to see him caught.' Hunter was smiling this time though. Pulling out his radio, he pressed the transmit button.

'Be ready to put in a hard stop when you get the chance.'

*

Bradley Conroy picked up the larger of the two knives that he'd slipped into the door pocket and pointed it towards her. He was angry and confused. This wasn't supposed to happen.

'If I'm going down, we're both going down.'

The car lurched to the left. He could see blue lights ahead of him now too. He mounted the kerb and shot through a wooden gate into a park area, watching as shards of wood burst across his path. The car pitched to the left again as the metal of the wheel dug down into the soft grass. He yanked the wheel to the right, but nothing happened, looking up just as a huge tree loomed up in view. The sound of glass and metal exploded all around him. Tiny, sharp fragments were flying into his face from the smashed windscreen, hitting his cheeks and forehead. He could feel the blood springing up, trickling into his eyes.

The steering wheel had shunted forward towards his chest, the airbag cushioning the impact slightly, but his feet and legs were squashed into a space that was far too small for them. Pain ricocheted up and down his spine and body and the side of his head crunched against the door window.

Everything was happening in slow motion now. He could see a wall of smoke and steam in front of him, seeping into the body of the car through the smashed windscreen. Annabel was crying loudly. Oh God, she was in pain. He could see blood all over her face too. The airbag on the passenger seat had activated, pushing her back against the seat. It was smoking but had deflated enough for her to squirm slightly towards the door. She was reaching towards the handle. He couldn't let her go. He wanted her so much.

The larger knife had spun off from him during the crash. He reached down for the other one, but all he got was a handful of glass which cut into his palm. The passenger door was opening now and he could see the back of Annabel's head as she kicked the door fully open and launched herself forward out of the car, her hands still bound. He reached out and tried to take hold of her clothing, but he lost his grip as she pulled away. She was slipping through his fingers, literally. She was all he could think of.

'Don't go Annabel,' he screamed through the noise. 'I love you.'

She was rolling away from the car now, trying to stand. He had to stop her. Punching desperately at the door, he managed to force it open enough for him to squeeze out from between the seat and the steering wheel. His whole body was screaming out in agony. He could barely stand and he could feel the blood flowing down his cheeks and neck from the glass wounds. Reaching down, he managed to locate the knife and pulled it out into the open, holding it up in his right hand as he struggled to get to Annabel who had stopped moving and was now lying immobile on the grass on the other side of the car. Maybe if he could get to her, he could force the cops to pull back, take her away with him.

He staggered a few steps forward, his arms raised to try to get his balance. The blue lights and noise were preventing him from thinking. He heard a shout but didn't recognize the word that was being said.

Two tiny wires shot towards him. He was just aware of them through his peripheral vision as they hit him on the chest and leg. A pain like nothing he had experienced before shot through him and his legs buckled as his whole body tensed and went into spasm. He hit the grass and lay unable to move, his arms and legs twitching. He had no control of his body and as the agony gradually subsided he felt a warm sensation around his groin and realized with horror that he'd pissed himself. He heard more shouting and saw several burly men running towards him. The knife was lying nearby, out of his reach, and he automatically reached towards it. Pain shot through him again as 50,000 volts of electricity were released for a second time. He screamed out in agony as his body arched with the shock. He saw the knife being picked up, as he lay helpless on the grass, all his energy spent.

He was doing what he was told now. There was no point in fighting. He'd lost against the Old Bill and he'd lost Annabel. As he felt the metal of the handcuffs tighten round his wrists, he started to cry and he didn't stop sobbing until eventually he was hauled up into an ambulance to be taken to hospital.

Chapter 38

It hadn't been hard to get this one. In fact it had been far too easy.

She'd trusted him and it had made him laugh. She had even walked to the woodland with him and her young son, totally oblivious to any danger, laughing and playing around. They'd chatted as they'd walked, speaking about her aspirations, her career, her family. She'd even been talking about how naughty her youngest son was being and how she could cheerfully wring his neck. They'd just dropped him off, the naughty one, at her gran's, and now they had her other son, the good one, the perfect child who could do no wrong, the one who was being taken out for the day as a special treat for being so good.

It had been he who had suggested it. Her good son deserved her undivided attention. She obviously loved him the most because he wasn't naughty; he did what she said, whatever she asked, without question. And she had agreed to do it, even though she was busy at work; a few hours off to spend time with her precious son.

It had been priceless when he'd unsheathed his knife. She clearly had not understood what was going on; had even laughed and told him to stop messing around. But he wasn't messing around. He never messed around. He was fucking serious. Deadly fucking serious.

She still hadn't understood though, even when he'd told her to put her arms behind her back. Little Dean wasn't sure what was happening either; his face was a mix of excitement and confusion. He obviously thought it was a game, until the moment his mother had been grabbed round the neck, pushed up against a tree and held at knifepoint, the blade pressing into her jugular. How it had pulsed under the pressure of his arm. How he loved the sight of it, squeezing up against the tender skin, throbbing sweetly. Dean's little face had grown more and more alarmed. She'd wriggled then, breaking the stranglehold slightly, and screamed at Dean to run and he'd done what he'd been told. The boy always did what he was told; and at that moment he'd panicked slightly, unable to let go of the mother for fear of losing her, but then he'd called out to the boy.

'Dean, you can't leave your mummy now. Dean, she needs you.'

And Dean had faltered then because he couldn't leave her; because she was his perfect mother, the mum that he adored, who favoured him over all others. Wasn't she? The bitch! The fucking bitch!

So he'd watched as Dean ran behind a tree and out of sight inside a small copse, but he could see behind the copse to the clear grass beyond and it was easy to watch if the boy tried to slip away, but he wouldn't because he couldn't leave her. He didn't have it in him to leave his mum. It had only taken a few minutes to bind her arms tightly behind her back, tie a gag around her mouth so she couldn't scream out again and throw her down into the newest pit. And now he was back out hunting. Fuck, it was exhilarating stuff. He could see where the boy was hiding. He slipped around the trees so that he came up behind the small copse and watched Dean as he laid shaking in the grass and fallen foliage; watching, just watching. The young boy was tearful, craning his neck towards the area where his mother had disappeared, obviously not knowing what to do next. He was rooted to the spot, yet clearly desperate to leave.

He would be easy to catch, lying on his belly as he was; stranded like a baby seal at the approach of a polar bear, ensnared with barely a whimper. And so he was moving slowly now on the grass area behind the trees and it was so exciting, thrilling even, creeping ever so slowly up behind his prey. Just as he took the final few steps, Dean spun round and saw him, but it was too late. He pounced, holding him down while the boy tried to wriggle and squirm from underneath, pinning him down by the neck.

'Keep still, you little bastard, or I'll kill you.'

He was enjoying himself now, watching as Dean's eyes widened, further and further, and the whites bulged and tiny blood vessels burst. He was enjoying this too much. So he pressed a little harder against the soft skin, watching from just a few inches above as the boy's lips started to turn blue. Maybe he should have done this before, rather than with a knife. Skin to skin, feeling the last moments of his victim's life slipping away as the pulse weakened, instead of watching their blood drain.

Both ways were good though. Both ways were fucking good.

But now his bare strength was killing the boy and he liked it. It was him that had the power, not his knife, not tablets or alcohol; it was his decision to give life or take it away. He had the control literally in his hands. It was just what he had wanted. He released his grip, staring as the redness came back into Dean's lips and he choked out loud, gulping in huge mouthfuls of air.

The boy started to cry. It took him by surprise; his mother was made of sterner stuff. But Dean was crying like a baby and he wouldn't, or couldn't, stop; sobbing and choking and coughing and sniffing. It was beginning to irritate him.

'Where's my mum? What have you done with her?'

'I'm just about to show you.'

He pulled the boy up and dragged him across to where the pit was, binding him tightly before opening the trapdoor and throwing him down next to his mother. The boy squirmed against her, squeezing himself into her body as close as he could.

'Aah, how sweet, you're with your mummy again. I don't think you're going to be much help though, do you, Dean?'

He emphasized the last question, his voice mocking. The woman glared at him with angry, accusing eyes.

'And I don't think you're going to be much help to Dean either. Mummy and Mummy's favourite are going to die right here, together.' He laughed. 'Well actually, not together. I didn't tell you what I was going to do, did I?'

She glared at him again, her brows pulled down into a deep, angry frown. It made him want to laugh.

'Ooh, come now, you look cross. Got a bit of attitude, have you? Well you won't have soon, when I slowly squeeze the last drop of breath from little Dean's body, while you watch, unable to stop me; unable to save your precious, precious favourite son.'

He pulled the knife out from up his sleeve and ran his finger slowly along the sharp, serrated edge. 'Or shall I slit his throat, like I did to the others? So that you can lie there next to him and feel his warm blood seeping all around you; so that you can wait for it to go cold, just like his body will, and you won't be able to do anything to warm him back up again. And you'll have to lie there while the insects come and feed on him and they'll grow fat on his stinking remains while slowly, very slowly, you die of hunger.'

She was still glaring at him, her anger almost palpable. He was enjoying himself now as he spoke with her. She was like his own mother, strong and angry and in control of her own emotions. He was looking forward to gradually breaking her and it would start later when she wouldn't be able to collect her naughty son from his gran. He would feel abandoned and she would know that he was on his own with just an old woman to look after him. And he wouldn't be able to do a thing to help himself, but at least he wouldn't be victimized by a mother who only doted on one son, just like his own mother had.

'So, what's it to be then? Maybe I should let you choose how little Dean here dies. Strangled or bled to death? Hmm now that's an idea. Yes, I think this time you can choose. Or maybe you might prefer another way? Tie a bag around his head so you can watch his eyes pop, feed him tablets until he falls asleep forever, watch while I remove parts of his body bit by bit, his ears, fingers, tongue, and he bleeds out. There are so many ways to choose.' He spoke slowly and precisely, enunciating every word, feeling himself getting aroused more and more at the thought.

He checked his watch. Dammit, he needed to go, but he couldn't wait to come back. The game was getting better each time.

'Think about how you want him to die then. Think carefully because it is your choice and if you don't want to choose, then I will pick the slowest, cruellest way, just to punish you further. You will choose the way that I will murder your favourite boy.'

Closing the trapdoor, he plunged them into darkness, pulling some branches over the top to cover every little chink of light. He still had to sort out Dana and Gemma, but he didn't have time today. Maybe he would kill Gemma later tonight or tomorrow so he could get the process started. He wanted time with these two.

He walked away, a smile flickering on his lips.

Yes, he had picked well with these new ones. He would enjoy playing with them very much.

Chapter 39

St Pancras railway station stood tall against the brightness of the midday sun, its Victorian architecture magnificent in all its faded glory. It now boasted high-speed links to Europe via the Channel Tunnel as well as routes to the North and South-east of England from fifteen platforms.

Charlie waited on the concourse. She'd wanted to pay the Eastern European lady from *Crimewatch* a visit since her encounter with the beggar woman on Friday night, but with so much happening she'd barely had enough time to make a phone call, never mind travel up to York herself. Luckily, Olga Kaplinski had been willing to travel to her.

It was good to have the DI keeping you thoroughly involved in the investigation, particularly with the pace that things were changing, but this time she really wanted to be able to follow up her own hunch. She had an itch, which needed to be scratched!

The events of the night before had been adrenaline-filled, but one look at Bradley Conroy crying as he was detained and she'd known he wasn't their man. He was certainly a dangerous individual, but he was not a cold, calculating and highly organized abductor, meticulous in both the preparation and execution of his crimes. Conroy's was a crime of passion, albeit misplaced passion. He was just a sad, infatuated, pathetic man who was now destined to spend the rest of his life back in prison. Charlie had no doubt it was where he belonged, but this was not the monster they were after.

She had slept fitfully for a few hours in the office from about six a.m. when Conroy was finally bedded down, but now she was back on a mission. Hunter had given her his blessing to leave HQ. She had good instincts and he knew it; and that instinct was now leading her back to Olga Kaplinski, and the story of an illegal immigrant forced to take the identity of a missing woman leaving the country. It hadn't made sense then but the more she'd tried to concentrate on other jobs, the more it kept coming back into her consciousness.

The train was just pulling in now. She strained to see if she could pick out Olga from all the passengers disembarking. She saw her immediately, singling her out by the hesitancy in her step and the way she held back from striding off the carriage. Olga was a well-built woman, with wrinkled cheeks, a ruddy complexion and a shock of blonde hair wound round and pinned on the top of her head in a rather severe bun. She was in her late forties, but could well have been younger, if life hadn't dealt her the hand it obviously had, but her bearing was still one of a proud, hard-working woman. She was the last person to the exit gates when Charlie stepped forward. Their eyes locked briefly.

Olga's expression was one of anxiety. Charlie held out her hand and Olga took it, shaking it carefully, her head still bowed.

'Will I get into trouble?' Olga repeated the last words that Charlie recalled from *Crimewatch*.

'No, I think I can pretty much guarantee that you won't. We're going to talk through what you remember over coffee then we'll go to the police station where someone can write it down if we need.' She smiled, trying to put the older lady at ease. By the time they were seated, Olga was chatting animatedly about her journey.

Charlie came straight to the point. 'You said that you were made to take the part of a missing woman with a child, when you spoke to me on *Crimewatch*? I know we've spoken briefly on the phone but can you tell me exactly what happened?'

Olga looked panicky for an instant but quickly calmed.

'It was about twenty years ago when I was still a young woman. My parents had left me in the care of an auntie and uncle in Poland for some years when they first came to England until they got things sorted out. I missed them and I know they missed me too. Things were hard for them at first. Poland wasn't part of the EU then and they were initially refused permission to stay.'

Olga glanced up and Charlie nodded her encouragement.

'The authorities wanted to send them back but my father was convinced that this country was where he wanted to settle and it offered more stability and opportunities than Poland did. He and my mother went on the run, with my father taking work where he could. At the same time, they were desperate to bring me over to join them. My mother in particular missed me and they both thought that I would have a better life here. They arranged for a Polish friend to stow me in the back of his truck and bring me across the Channel from France to Dover. It was risky, but there weren't so many people making the trip in those days, so border controls were not so tight.'

She took a sip of her tea and looked nervous again.

'I was here illegally for quite a few years. We lived in Dover at that point, moving from one backstreet lodging to another. I took work where I could, but it was hard. I would get paid pennies to work for hours in launderettes or kitchens or pubs, anything I could find really. Sometimes I had bad experiences and now, looking back, I think I am lucky to have come out of that time without being seriously hurt or raped even.'

Charlie shook her head. 'Go on,' she prompted gently.

'It was the December, I think around 1993 when I got myself in trouble. Christmas was coming and I wanted to get my parents small gifts to brighten the day. They missed their brothers and sisters. I was working in a bar down by the docks, doing long hours for just a few pounds. One of the customers, a man in his sixties, started making lewd comments towards me. He was dirty in body and had a dirty mind too. He worked on the sea and smelt of fish and stale tobacco. I didn't want to talk to him but he was a regular and my boss told me I had to humour him or I would be out of a job. So I did what I was told and played with him, flirting a bit and letting him think I liked him, to keep him buying. He ordered a drink and my boss told me to take it over to him. When I got there he patted his lap and told me to sit with him. The boss was looking across and laughing. I think they were friends. I needed the job, so I did what he said. As I sat down, he put his hand up my skirt and grabbed me. He was disgusting. I knew I shouldn't have to put up with this, so I slapped him hard around the face.'

'He pushed me on to the floor and threw his drink on me as I lay there. I was all wet and was shaking and crying, but he was still very angry. The boss was angry too. They were both shouting at me. Then this other man came over. He seemed to know the others and said he would deal with me. The boss seemed happy because he didn't have to pay me for that week's work and the man was calm. I was glad to get away from the place. So this man took hold of my arm and made me walk with him to a small room in a nearby street. He said he was a policeman.'

'Did he ever show you any identification?'

'Not proper ID, no, but there were things around the room. There was a uniform and handcuffs. I thought he was a policeman and he spoke like a police-man. He said that he could arrest me for assaulting the customer and get me sent back to Poland. I believed him. He asked me who I was with and I said I was here with my parents. He said he would track them down and get them sent back too. I was terrified that he would do what he said. Then he changed a bit and became friendlier. He said that if I did a favour for him he would forget all about what had happened. He said that all he needed me to do was take a young boy over to France and return later the same day. We were to go as foot passengers on the Dover to Calais ferry. He would have documents for me in another woman's name. He said that she had run away from her husband who treated her badly and that she wanted to move to a different part of the country and start a new life in a different name, but she wanted her husband to think that she had gone to the continent with her son, rather than staying in this country.

'I knew how easy it was to set up a new identity. People I met in those days were doing it all the time. There was always someone that could make up false passports, bank cards, anything you needed if you wanted to disappear and start again as a new person. I thought I would be doing this woman a favour, helping her escape from her violent husband.

'And the police-man offered me fifty pounds to do it and I needed the money. It was a lot for me and meant I could buy my parents the presents I wanted to and we could all have a good Christmas. And, of course, it got me out of the trouble I was in and stopped me getting deported back to Poland. I couldn't refuse.

'I didn't tell my parents what had happened. I didn't tell anyone. On the day it was to be done, the port was busy with people going over to France for the Christmas markets and cheap alcohol. The policeman said I was to meet him at his rented room at four p.m. I went there like I was told and he was there. He made me wear a dark wig and glasses so I looked like the other woman, and some clothes that he had brought with him, including a long coat with a hood. He had the little boy with him too. He must have only been about five years old. He got him all dressed up, with a hooded Batman top and batman face- mask.

'I did exactly as I was told. It was easy. It was dark and rainy. They barely checked the passport in the terminal. I kept my head down on the boat, staying in the same area for the whole journey. When I got to France I pretty much went straight through. We caught a train straight out of Calais before getting off at a country stop, taking our disguises off and throwing them away. We then came straight back. The policeman had got me a different passport to come back because I didn't have one of my own.

'When I got back he gave me my fifty pounds, took the young child and I never saw the man or the boy again.'

'So what made you call *Crimewatch*?' Charlie was fascinated by the whole story.

'Well over the years I have learned better how things work and how the story does not seem right. The local papers at the time, and some of the National newspapers, were showing pictures of a young woman and child who had been reported missing. The woman looked like I had and the child was the same age as the young boy I had taken.

'After a few weeks there was an anonymous tip-off that the woman and her child had fled the country. I even saw CCTV on the television supposedly of the woman and her child going over to France, although the film was grainy and dark. It was me on the footage. They checked and the tickets were booked in the missing woman's name and the passport verified it, but it was me all along. The plan had worked: everyone thought the woman and her child had left the country but she hadn't. I knew that. As far as I know, her and her little boy were never seen again. They just disappeared.'

'And you never said anything about what had happened?'

'How could I? I would have got into trouble and been thrown out of the country. I couldn't risk it. But over the years I have worried about what could have really happened to them. Maybe the policeman had done something to them? Maybe the husband had killed them and the policeman was his friend and was trying to help? I don't know. It seemed to me they disappeared here in England and my trip to France was to make people think they were still alive and abroad somewhere else.'

Olga pulled a tissue from her pocket and dabbed at her eyes which were moist with tears.

'What happens if they were murdered and I helped the police think they were still alive? I have had sleepless nights worrying over the years whether I might have helped their murderer. When I saw that *Crimewatch* programme with those other mothers with their children who have gone missing it brought it all back to me. My life is good now. Both my parents and I got leave to remain and now Poland is part of the European community there are no problems. We moved away from Dover when the opportunity arose and live in York. It is a very beautiful part of this country. We have worked hard over the years to get what we have. It may not be much, but it is ours and we are proud of it. I never told my mother what I did that day, but I have told my father recently. There seemed no reason to go into a police station and tell them what happened because it was only my suspicions, but now, with this…' She paused, her head lowered again. 'Will I get into trouble now you know what I did?'

She looked so fragile but Charlie could hardly contain herself. In her mind, her hunch was almost certainly right. There had to be something in the story. It was mind-blowing.

She took a deep breath and looked directly into the woman's eyes.

'Olga, what you did was well intentioned. You thought you were helping the woman and her child get away from an abusive husband. Plus, you were pretty much forced to take part. You were threatened with arrest, deportation and the deportation of your parents if you didn't do what you were told. At the time you knew no better. Maybe you could have said something later, but, like you said, you only had suspicions. It is all credit to you that you have come forward now to tell us what happened all those years ago. You could have remained silent. It might be that if we can find the missing persons report relating to this mother and child, there might be something there that will link it to our cases and potentially be exactly what we need. I will need to try to track down the television news reports with the CCTV footage and we'll need you to help us with further details. Are you happy to have this all written down in a statement?'

She already knew what the answer would be from Olga's

obvious relief at finally being able to share her story.

'Of course I will. The mother's name was Mary Townsend and her son was Cain. I remember it to this day. I will do anything I can to help you. I wish I had spoken out before, but at least now I might be able to do something to help stop another mother and child going missing.'

*

Charlie rang Hunter straight away. He spoke first at the sound of her voice.

'Charlie, it's not Bradley Conroy. He's given an alibi for the time when Dana and Gemma went missing. Funnily enough he was stalking Annabel, CCTV captures him in several places and there're quite a few other bits and pieces that don't add up.'

'Well, you didn't really think it was him anyway, did you?'

'No, but I was hoping. Would have been a real touch if we'd got the right man and could find out where the victims are.'

She couldn't contain her excitement any longer. 'Guv, look I think I might be on to something. We need to get in touch with someone in Dover, Kent Constabulary as soon as we can. Get them to search the records for a missing person report in the name of Mary Townsend and her son Cain, reported missing around the end of 1993. I've just met up with the woman I spoke to on *Crimewatch* and she says she was paid by a policeman to pretend to be Mary Townsend and leave the country with her young child to make it look as if she'd run away. She saw all the reports about the case on TV, even saw herself on BBC news. She says that the policeman told her that the woman had run away from her abusive husband and wanted him to think that she had left England to start a new life abroad.'

'So why didn't she report it at the time?'

'Because she was an illegal and was threatened with deportation by the policeman. She was too scared and she needed the money. He paid her fifty quid.'

'Sounds far-fetched enough to be true.'

'Guv, I have a good feeling about this. I'll give Bet and Naz a ring so they can start making phone calls, just the girls. I don't want anyone else to know. We need to find who the husband was and the names of all the police officers connected with the missing person enquiry.'

'That could take a while.'

'Not if you can get someone started on it straight away. I'll be back soon with Olga Kaplinski and someone can get a full statement from her, maybe even show her some photos if we get any names. Guv, the psychologist said that our killer has almost certainly abducted or killed before; especially with the recent escalation. This could be the break that we've been waiting for.'

Chapter 40

It was mid-afternoon when Charlie arrived back at Lambeth HQ. She was going to ask Naz to take Olga's statement as she thought the two of them would have experiences in common.

She brought Olga up through the back staircase to her office. There they had a small, comfortably furnished room that they used for taking statements from domestic violence victims. It was equipped with a kettle and a small cupboard of provisions, as well as a children's play area with a few toys that had been donated by previous thankful victims. Bet was in the office when they walked in, having tucked herself away behind her work-station to concentrate on the phone calls that were beginning to arrive from Dover. Sabira, Paul and Colin were tapping away at their computers too.

'Where's Naz?' Charlie stopped to speak briefly with Bet. Olga stood waiting quietly.

'She's not in as yet. Texted earlier to say that she had some sort of problem with her kids and she'd be late in, or not in at all. Looking at the time now, I'm guessing she won't be coming in at all.'

'In that case, Sabira could you get Olga's story down for me please.'

Sabira and Colin both looked up towards her and she nodded.

'Yep, no problem, Charlie. Not got too much on at the moment anyway.'

'Thanks Sabira. I'll get Olga settled and then I need to speak to Hunter.'

She started to show Olga towards the interview room.

'Anything yet?' she turned quickly, whispering to Bet.

'A few interesting snippets and I think we've found the report. I'll speak to you in a few minutes when you're free.'

She nodded her approval and disappeared into the room, settling Olga down in a comfortable chair before leaving her.

She needed to find Hunter asap.

'What's all the secret squirrel stuff?' Paul said with a conspiratorial wink as she came back out.

'Nothing for you to worry about,' she winked back, as she dialled Hunter's number. Paul was such a gossip.

'Go on Bet,' he insisted. 'You can tell us.'

Bet shook her head and glanced towards her. She nodded her approval. If her own colleagues couldn't be trusted, who could? Plus, then they could all help and get the job done quicker. It was a shame Naz wasn't there too, especially if her hunch proved to be right. They could all share the glory.

'Well, it's just a Polish woman called Olga who Charlie spoke to on *Crimewatch*. Came up with a story from twenty years ago that seems to mirror what is happening now. Might have nothing to do with it, but it's an interesting line of enquiry.'

Charlie put her finger to her lips and turned to Paul. 'Don't say a word to anyone out of our office. I want to keep this just between us lot until I know more. I don't want to look an idiot in front of the whole station if it turns out to be nothing.'

Paul put his finger up to his lips too and smiled back at them both.

'Don't worry, Charlie. Your secret is safe with me.'

*

Charlie was in Hunter's office when Bet called her on her personal mobile. She sounded worried.

'I need you to double-check something for me. Can you come quickly. I don't want to explain over the phone.'

'Bet, I'm in with Hunter. Can you come to his office? It's a bit quieter here.' She ended the call. Bet was on her way.

'Bet's got something. It sounds important'. Bet looked on the verge of tears when she came in, clutching a wad of papers.

'I need to show you something on the computer,' she said, placing the papers on the desk. Hunter stepped to one side and she quickly sat down and navigated to the right report.

'Look!' she said, pointing towards the screen. 'I was sent the missing persons record by Dover a while ago. They scanned it for us and sent it on. Look at who was assisting with the investigation.'

She pointed to a name on the screen. Charlie looked, recognizing the name instantly. 'Now look at this.' Bet spread the domestic violence reports from Helena McPherson out across the desk.

'When I saw that name on the Dover report I knew there had to be a connection between the Hubbard and McPherson cases that we'd missed, so I've searched through it again. Helena's ex, Gary Savage, was arrested and interviewed by PC Kate Rossler, but I knew that there must have been another officer present, so I checked out the custody record. Look who's shown as booking Savage out for interview.'

Charlie peered over at the small print. Clearly written was the name PC C Butler. Instantly, she knew what Bet was getting at.

'Shit. And he dealt with Julie Hubbard's domestic issues. And he knows Dana and Gemma Latchmere. Shit, shit, shit!'

'Butler? Colin Butler?' Hunter mouthed.

Bet nodded.

'I wonder if Olga would recognise him, or more importantly whether he would recognise her.'

'Does he know she's here?' Hunter was animated again.

'Oh, my God!' Charlie looked horrified! 'He was in the office just now when she came in with me, he must have seen her.'

'But he surely wouldn't recognize her from all those years ago. She could be any domestic violence victim that we're dealing with.'

'Yes, she could have. But we mentioned she was the Polish woman from Dover who spoke to me on *Crimewatch* about a similar incident twenty years ago. I think I even mentioned her first name when I brought her through. Shit!'

She turned to Hunter. She could feel her legs beginning to shake slightly. Without another word, both burst through the door into the main office.

Paul looked up surprised. 'What on earth's the matter?'

'Where's Colin?' she almost shouted.

Paul stared from one to the other of them, their shock registering on his face too.

'He's gone out. About ten minutes ago. Said he had to make some urgent enquiries.'

She sprinted out of the office, taking the stairs three at a time, closely followed by Hunter. They ran through to the back of the building and straight to the car park, but Colin's car was missing.

'Where could he have gone to?'

Hunter shrugged. 'I think I could hazard a guess.'

They turned and ran back up the stairs to the office. Maybe Colin had left some clue as to where he might be heading but as she climbed the steps, she realised they were clutching at straws. He was too clever for that. It was too late. He knew.

Things were falling into place. How could they have missed the connection? Julie Hubbard's disappearance had been the first case they'd known about and he had dealt with her previous domestic issues, but who would have suspected him, especially with the likes of Keith, her violent husband, and Justin Latchmere, her lover?

He knew Dana and Gemma from the Hubbard enquiries.

Olga Kaplinski's information about the circumstances surrounding the case of Mary and Cain Townsend, flagged up the role of a police officer in their disappearance and indeed named Colin.

That in turn had provided the link to Colin's role as a witnessing officer in Helena MccPherson's domestic assault allegations.

It was so simple.

But what the hell had he done with them all? Could they still be alive? If they were and he knew they were on to him, he would more than likely be looking to silence them properly now. His victims were in more danger now than ever before.

They ran back into the main office where Bet was now sitting, white-faced and crying, her phone lying on the desk in front of her.

'Are you OK? You've done brilliantly, even though it is a shock. None of us would ever have dreamed it could be Colin?'

She ran across and threw an arm around the older woman who was shaking.

'It's not that. I've just had a call from Nathaniel's gran. She has me down as a contact if there're any problems. Apparently Naz hasn't turned up to collect Nathaniel as they'd arranged and she was supposed to be going out. Naz is nearly two hours late and she's had to cancel her outing. Nathaniel's still there, but Naz and Dean are missing. And I heard her and Colin talking the other day about places to go for day's out. Colin was offering to take her.'

Chapter 41

'We need to find out every little thing we can about Colin Butler.'

Hunter's voice was authoritative and urgent. 'Where he lives, any places in the vicinity of his house that could be worth looking at. We know that the vehicle that was used when Helena and Daisy were abducted had mud on the wheels, so it's likely to be somewhere in woodlands, countryside, parkland. I'll get the helicopter scrambled straight away with its heat-seeking capabilities to search areas near to where both Dana's and the rental car were abandoned. We know what car he owns and that's been circulated as a matter of urgency to all units, although he'll no doubt know that.

We also need to find out what hobbies he has now? Gardening perhaps? There might be small-holdings, allotments that he could be using? Those of you that know him; sit down and go through everything that you can think of that he might have told you.'

'He doesn't say much about his personal life,' Bet's face told the story. It was what they were all thinking. How could the abductor literally have been under their noses all this time, pretending to help when really he was revelling in his access to the investigation?

'He must have said something. Any little thing, wrack your brains. Naz's life might depend on it.'

Charlie was listening to Hunter intently. Where would they get this information from quickly? Her mind was working fast. She vaguely remembered a conversation. Hadn't he recently worked with informants? He would have had to be given extra vetting for that job to make sure there was nothing that could make him open to bribes. His whole history would be on that vetting form, every family member, past and present, old addresses, place of birth, even old partners. It would be a few years old. He'd been working in their unit for a couple of years now, but it would still be relevant up until then.

She shouted across to Hunter.

'I'm going to the Yard for his vetting forms. I'll give you a shout if I find anything.'

Hunter gave her the thumbs up and she was gone, running back down the stairs and out into the car park.

New Scotland Yard wasn't far; across Westminster Bridge, around Parliament Square and straight into Victoria Street. She was soon passing Big Ben, standing tall, peering down on to the roof of the Houses of Parliament and Westminster Abbey. The car in front moved across into her lane. She hooted at the driver irritably, swinging her vehicle around it and accelerating away towards Victoria. The Yard was about halfway down, set back into Broadway, its triangular rotating sign synonymous with reliability and history.

She guided the car into the underground car park, cursing the attendant who seemed to be working in slow motion. Then she was flying up the stairs, running and running towards the records department. Hopefully she would locate Colin's vetting form easily and it would point them in the right direction. Time was of the essence.

She found it quickly, her hands shaking as she scanned through the twenty pages of personal information that only a handful of people would ever have seen. Shit, he'd had a hard time when he was younger. A brother shown as deceased at a young age in a tragic fall from cliffs, a mother who had committed suicide, no trace of a father. She'd had no idea. None of them had. Colin only ever spoke politics: judgments in favour of ex-wives, laws against paternal rights, the rights of local communities and individuals who he believed had been overlooked. Now it seemed there was a whole hidden life of tragedy that had formed his beliefs, maybe turned him into the monster he had become. She was reading as she walked towards the car again. She had to get the form back, so they could dissect every entry.

She read down through the first couple of pages. Nothing, then a name registered; what was it she remembered, something from a recent conversation with Colin. The local news headlines talked about a nearby hospital that was being closed and he had become animated by the political issues surrounding its closure. The news story mirrored what had happened to a hospital linked to his childhood. She read it again and strained to recollect the anger in his words. His hospital had been shut down forever, years ago, even after the local council had promised to keep it running as a downgraded non-emergency unit. It was the hospital where he had been born, into a busy thriving maternity wing. It was the hospital where he had gone alone, as a child, to be stitched up in an accident and emergency unit that no longer existed and hadn't for some time. She recalled Colin's words and his disbelief. How could they shut it down after all their promises to keep it running as a cottage hospital? How could cost-cutting come before the needs of the community? He had been incensed, particularly after a large petition from all the people in the neighbourhood had been ignored. The government was full of broken promises. They were then and they still were now.

She wondered.

She read it again. Place of birth, The War Memorial Hospital, Carshalton. It wasn't too far to check it out personally before going back to the office and it was in the right direction to fit with Purley where Dana's car had been found and Mitcham where the hire car was abandoned. She gave Hunter a quick ring to let him know where she was heading, leaving a message when he failed to answer, then she slapped the magnetic blue light on top of their nondescript Mondeo, put the sirens on and set out. If her hunch was right, Hunter would know where to come. If it was wrong, she could be back to the office within an hour or two. She had to try.

Thirty minutes later, with all the lights and sirens switched off, she was climbing a small hill at the side of a park. Through the boughs of a large horse chestnut tree, the landscape of London stretched out as far as the eye could see; the sky-scrapers of Canary Wharf bunched together in their own mini metropolis. The gates to the deserted hospital were set back to her right, out of view from the road, heavy and covered in a reddish hue of rust. A raft of notices warned trespassers of the presence of asbestos and instructed them to keep out. She parked her car up and walked across. A large padlock swung from the centre of the gates, holding them secure. She peered through a gap in the metal-work and looked into the hospital grounds. The grass all around seemed long but she could see a path worn down by vehicle tread through the centre of the

237

overgrown interior roadway. She lifted the padlock up and examined it. It wasn't rusty like the gates; it had obviously been opened and shut frequently. The metal was smooth and worn. Somebody had been going in and out.

Her heart beat was starting to race now. She had to find a way in. Barbed wire wound round the whole of the perimeter in several razor-sharp circuits. The walls were high and secure. Circling the exterior wall she came to a large oak with one of its branches extending out towards the wire. It was precarious but she had spent her childhood with Jamie climbing trees and running through mud, moors and forests; and there was no other way. She clambered along the branch, pulling the wire back just enough to balance on the top of the wall, and thudded down on to the long grass. Nothing had been trodden down here. She inched forward using the trees as cover, trying to find her way back towards the small roadway where the grass had been squashed down.

The sun was setting and the whole place seemed dark and threatening. Trees overhung the grounds and low clouds prevented any light from the full moon getting through. Ivy had taken control, covering the walls of the buildings, hanging down off drainpipes and intertwining with weeds and thistles. She dare not use the light from her phone to show her the way, she had to let her eyes acclimatize and watch in the gloom for any movement. She moved slowly, straining to hear over the soft swishing of the grass. The roadway and buildings all led to the main entrance of the hospital, its door covered in thick metal security bars. The entrance was in darkness and there appeared to be no way in. She moved round the corner of the nearest block, to where the roadway spidered off to a separate building, it's roof partially missing. The gates to this building were pulled to one side, leaving the entrance opening into a small yard. The roadway led into this courtyard, the trampled weeds pointing into a far corner out of sight of the gate.

She tiptoed forward, holding her breath as she crossed the gap between the two buildings. She thought she could hear the sound of a man's low guttural laugh carried across in the breeze, but when she stopped moving all she could hear was the sound of a wood pigeon cooing in the silence.

She stepped into the courtyard of what appeared to be a laundry block and saw the car immediately, standing in the far corner with only the slight glimmer of the moon reflecting off its headlights and grill. It was Colin's all right; but the engine, when she touched it was stone cold. He'd obviously been here for some time. She checked the interior and was relieved not to find the body of Naz or little Dean lying across the back seat.

She was right: he was here, somewhere in the grounds of the hospital where he had sat alone and in pain as a child without the care of his mother.

Charlie shivered as a shudder of pure fear ran through her. This whole place was sinister, malevolent even; filled with Colin's evil. She could almost feel his breath on the back of her neck. She needed to get away from this building and out into the open where she could summon more help and where she wouldn't be trapped if he were to return. Sliding back away from the car, she inched out into the fresh air and round to the side of the building. She squatted down against the wall and pulled out her phone, tapping a text to Hunter explaining what she had found. She dare not speak out loud. He would know what was needed and would be straight on his way. The light from the display on the front of the phone shone bright in the darkness but she hid it behind her jacket. Standing up when she finished, she gazed out past the back of the building.

The grounds seemed to spread out behind the main blocks. She had no idea how far they went or how many other small outbuildings were tucked away. All she knew was Colin Butler was somewhere out there and he was the only one who knew the fate of his victims and whether they were alive or dead.

Chapter 42

The darkness was just what he needed now. He revelled in the cloak of invisibility it gave him. He knew this place like the back of his hand, every tiny outbuilding, every pathway through the trees; he even knew drains where the lids came off and he could access the corridor of sewers that lay beneath the hospital. He'd spent his life coming back and forth, back and forth, both as a child when it had been open and now, in the last few years, since it had been closed. It was here where he loved to be with his memories.

He'd checked on both his latest pairs when he returned; Naz and Dean safely tucked away, Naz's eyes shooting pure hate at him as he'd looked down at her. She was more like his mother than even he had realized. Fuck, it turned him on at just the thought.

Dana lay silently, so demure, so afraid; her eyes blank with pain. He had shown her no pity; she was a bitch who had chosen her favourite daughter over poor Aiden. Gemma lay cold beside her now. He had enjoyed killing her, her long neck slit from ear to ear within the last few hours. Dana's eyes had screamed at the awful sight she was witnessing. The temptation to finish her off too was strong but she, more than the others, deserved to lie next to her dead daughter for as long as it took for them to find her. She deserved to live long in the knowledge that she had caused this by her overt favouritism. Hopefully they wouldn't find her straight away, but he knew that his time was limited. Charlie was already here.

She was squatting just within his sight now and she would no doubt have told the others where they were. They would know he was the person they were hunting, he Colin Butler, innocuous, hard-working, oh so hard-working, keeping up with the investigation down to every last enquiry; meek and mild Colin, who everyone talked down to, who everyone ignored and disrespected, who nobody listened to. Well they would be listening to him now, wouldn't they? They would have to, if they wanted to see Dana and Naz and Dean and Charlie alive again? He intended to make the most of every second.

His eyes and ears were so attuned to the atmosphere that he'd felt her presence immediately. It had only taken a few minutes to find the freshly trodden grass; he knew every inch of the hospital grounds and then he'd just followed the track, like a predator following a scent. Now he had her in his sight. Charlie's phone had given her position away, when it had suddenly blinked into action and she'd taken it from her pocket to read the incoming message. He guessed that she'd have sent a message out first, probably being careful not to show its light, but when a message had come through to her she hadn't been so careful in her hurry to read it. If she was here she'd obviously worked out the last piece of the jigsaw.

He'd known the game was over when Olga from Dover had been walked through the office. Even though she'd obviously aged, she still bore a remarkable resemblance to the woman he had bribed to help him all those years ago. The bitch had ruined his plans. It was all her fault. Another bitch was here now, spoiling things for him, but he wouldn't let her stop his fun. No, the fun was about to start.

He shrunk back behind a tree and pulled out his own phone. She was obviously confident that he wouldn't know she was there. What a fright she'd have, in a few seconds. He chuckled to himself.

Pressing her number, Colin waited for the phone to show that it was ringing then he shoved it down deep in his pocket and started to creep through the grass towards where she was wedged against the wall. He grinned to himself as she glanced down into her pocket, the thin chink of light illuminating the shock on her face. She was stock still, clearly not daring to move while she decided what to do, her whole body tense and rigid. He wasn't expecting her to answer; she wouldn't risk her voice being heard but he guessed that she would be itching to.

She was still staring down into her pocket at her phone when he pounced, pulling his knife out as he did so. By the time she realized he was there it was too late. He had the blade pressed up to her cheek while his arm pinned her against the brickwork.

Deftly he pulled her hands up behind her back and wrapped twine round both wrists, pulling it tight.

'Well, fancy seeing you here, Charlie. Have you come to rescue Naz?'

He sneered towards her, his teeth yellow in the moonlight.

'Doesn't look like you've done very well now, does it? And there was I thinking you were a bit stronger than most of the others; the great Charlie fucking Stafford who single-handedly tackled a handful of robbers and nearly lost her life at the hands of that vicious arsehole, Keith Hubbard. Yet now you've walked straight into my arms. Do you think you're better than us men? That you don't have to take care? You can do it all on your own?'

'I'm not on my own.'

'Well it certainly looks like it to me. Only one set of tracks and you hiding here scared to death while you wait for the cavalry to arrive. I'm sure you must have called them by now. But it's going to arrive too late for you all. I've got nothing to lose now.'

'You mean the others are still alive?'

'Only the ones that need to be punished.'

'And who are they?'

'The mothers.'

'But why are you punishing them, Colin?

She didn't understand. Nobody ever understood him. He could feel his temper rising.

'They deserve to be punished for having a favourite. They shouldn't have a favourite. They need to know that it is because of their favouritism that their child has been killed. Their punishment is to live while "Mummy's favourite" dies.'

He laughed suddenly, enjoying the sound of his voice in the silence.

'Do you want to know why, Charlie?'

She nodded.

He would have told her anyway because he would soon be dead himself.

'My mother had to live after my brother died but she hated life without him. She always loved Tommy more than me. He was her favourite. Always. Even when I did everything for her. I even had to fuck her when she wanted me too.'

He laughed again at the flash of revulsion that crossed her face. 'She beat me so many times when I was little. I thought that when Tommy was gone she might love me, but she hated me even more. It killed her to know that he had died so tragically. She despised me even more for taking him away.'

'What happened to Tommy?'

'He slipped from the top of a cliff when we were playing. I'll always remember the look on his face when I pushed him. Shock and horror, just like you now.' He stared straight at her. 'I love that expression.'

'But surely it wasn't his fault that he was your mother's favourite?'

'He revelled in it, like they all do. Mummy this, mummy that. He loved it when he saw me getting beaten. He never tried to stop it. None of them do. They feed off it and grow stronger while their poor siblings remain downtrodden. All of them are the same.'

'What have you done with the kids, Colin?'

He could hear the fear in her voice now, fear and disbelief at what she already knew.

'What do you think I've done?'

He pulled the knife out and made a cutting action across the front of her neck with it.

'I've slit all their pretty little throats.'

'Oh my God, Colin. How could you do such a thing?'

'Oh I've done much worse than that, Charlie. It's easy for them because it's so quick. One slice and within a few seconds they're unconscious, bleeding out all over the place. No, they're the lucky ones. Really I should have made it harder for them.'

'So what have you done with their mothers?'

'What the bitches deserve. What my mother deserved. To watch their favourites die right in front of their eyes while they're powerless to stop it happening. To lie next to them as their children's bodies decompose and the insects feed on them, for as long as they can last before they starve to death. Oh, I give them water. I'm not that heartless. I don't want them dying too quickly. They need to suffer, just like I did.'

'And your mother? What happened to her in the end?'

'She took an overdose. I gave her the choice, even though I had a knife: "tell me you love me or keep swallowing." She kept on washing the tablets down with vodka until she died. She refused to tell me she loved me, even right to the end. She knew that I had killed Tommy because I wanted her to love me, like she'd loved Tommy, but she chose to die rather than tell me so.

She wouldn't even pretend to love me to save her own skin.'

'I'm sure she must have loved you too.'

'No, no, no, she didn't. She hated me. All I wanted was her love.' He turned away from her, his teeth and fists clenched. Tears stung at his eyes but he brushed them away angrily with the back of his hand. 'She won't make me cry, the bitch! She won't ever upset me again because I have the power now. She's gone and it is my destiny to make these women pay for their choices.'

'You don't have to do that, Colin.'

'Oh, but I do, and you need to shut up now and stop trying to tell me what I should or shouldn't do. My mother was a bitch. All these women were bitches who chose one child over another. They deserve to be punished for what they have done. Do you have any idea what that makes the abandoned child feel like? Do you? So shut the fuck up now.'

His voice was getting louder as he spoke but he didn't care. There was no one there to hear him or her for that matter. They were still on their own. He wanted to shut her up; to shut them all up; all the women who had let him down.

Angrily he grabbed her, pulling her with him as he started to walk. It was pitch-black under the canopy of trees but he knew exactly where he was going. Charlie stumbled in the darkness but he dragged her with him. He'd show her his handiwork before killing Dean in front of them both.

Then it would be his turn to die. It wouldn't be long before the back-up arrived; trained firearms officers, their fingers on the trigger, itching to be the one to take out the infamous serial killer; the bad apple hidden right under their noses, one of their own. He smiled at the thought, wondering what name the media would give him. He'd go down in history, another madman who psychologists would write about, scrutinize; whose brain and motives would be dissected and analysed until they had worked out just what sort of mental illness he had. But he wasn't ill. He was far, far too clever to be mad. He'd enjoyed every minute of it.

They were at Naz's copse now. Quickly, he bound Charlie to the nearest tree so she could see everything. He left her without a gag, let the bitch plead for the boy's life. Let them both see what happens when you have a favourite. Hadn't they all listened while Naz complained about poor Nathaniel's misdemeanours, how she was at the end of her tether with him. The poor kid was only trying to win his mother's attention.

He pulled out his torch and aimed the beam at the wooden trapdoor, lifting it wide open so Charlie would be able to see the figures of Naz and Dean lying in their grave. He shone it directly at Naz's face so that she squinted away from the brightness, closing her eyes against the brilliance.

'Look who's come to rescue you, Naz?' he scoffed, pointing the torch-light in Charlie's face. 'Unfortunately she didn't see me coming.'

He bent down and removed Naz's gag, laughing again as she licked her dry lips before spitting towards him.

'Ah, what's the matter, Naz? Can't believe that you two women could be so stupid?'

'Get me out of here, Colin.'

'Now why would I do that? Especially since you're trying to tell me what to do.' He pulled the two knives out and scraped them together. The metallic sound reverberated through the still air. 'Nobody is going to tell me what to do. Especially not you two.'

'Naz,' Charlie called across to her, 'are you OK?'

'As OK as I can be, tied up and kept hostage in a fucking pit by this prick.'

'Shut up, both of you. You speak only when you're spoken to. Understand?'

'Is that what your mother used to say to you, eh, Colin?' Naz's expression was sarcastic.

'Shut the fuck up, Naz.' He stamped down on her chest hard. 'I've had enough of you being disrespectful. You do what I say, or I put the gag back on you and then you won't be able to even try to talk me out of killing little Dean here. Do you understand me?'

Naz closed her mouth, her eyes flashing with fear now. He loved that look.

Roughly, he grabbed Dean by the arm, pulling him up on to the grassy area in the centre of the trees. He removed the boy's gag. Dean started to whimper and cry.

'Dean, don't worry. You'll be all right.' Charlie's sentiments made him laugh.

'No Dean, you won't be all right. In a few minutes time I'm going to slit your lovely long neck from one side to the other, unless, that is, your mother here has chosen for you to die an easier way.'

He turned towards Naz.

'Well, how shall I kill him?'

'You don't have to kill him. Kill me instead.'

'But that's not part of the game,, Naz. It doesn't work that way. I kill mummy's favourite and then mummy has to live as long as she can without them. It's a good game. So what's it to be, Naz?'

Naz said nothing. He walked over to the pit and pulled her up out of it, throwing her forcefully on to the grass next to Dean.

'So what's it to be? If you don't give me an answer I'll choose.'

'Leave her alone, Colin.' Charlie was angry now. 'She's not going to choose.'

He rounded on her, lashing out with the back of his hand across her face. Blood sprung immediately from her nose, dripping unabated into her mouth and down her chin. It looked good. He smiled, flashing the torch from one to the other.

'I know then,' he said animatedly, untying the twine that held Charlie to the tree. 'You decide. You decide how your friend's favourite son is going to die, right now in front of us all. Maybe you can even help me do it.'

He pushed Charlie down on the grass and dragged Naz up, tying her instead to the tree so that she faced into the centre.

'There now, mummy can watch. Perfect view for you. Prime position.'

Pulling his knife out again, he untied Charlie's hands and placed the cord around her knees instead.

'There we go. Now you can help me without being tempted to run, and if you do try anything, they both die, understand?'

Charlie nodded, wiping her nose so the blood smeared across her arms and hands too.

'Nice! I love the sight of blood.'

In the distance a low rumble vibrated through the air, getting louder every second. His time was nearly up. He needed to get started. He dragged Dean to his feet, waving the knife with one hand before pointing it towards his neck. 'So what's it to be then, Charlie?'

A spot-light suddenly lit up the copse as the air filled with noise and turbulence. The trees started to bend and the branches were thrown around wildly as a helicopter circulated directly above them. He stared up into the light, his eyes wild with excitement.

'The final act. Lit up and filmed for all to see.' He was laughing manically now.

'So choose, now Charlie, or I'll slit his throat anyway.'

Dean was sobbing. He grabbed hold of the boy's hair, pulling his head back and clasping him across the chest so that his neck was exposed. He pushed the knife against the boy's soft skin.

All around them he could see movement as Charlie's backup arrived; glints of metal from the barrels of MP5s. He shuddered with pleasure. It was all playing out as he'd hoped. Suicide by cop, going down in a blaze of glory and gunfire, destined to provoke discussion for many years to come.

He was in control now. Everyone would do what he wanted because it was him who had the power to make the decisions; he was the one with the life of a child in his hands.

'So what's it to be then?' he screamed over the sound of the chopper. 'Sliced or strangled?'

Charlie held her hands to her ears. He beckoned her closer and shouted the question again. She moved towards them, shuffling slowly with her knees tightly bound. He stepped across the grass towards Naz, pulling Dean with him, the knife fixed squarely to the boy's neck. The four of them were close together now.

'Last chance to decide or I cut his neck from ear to ear. I don't care what happens to me now. I want them to kill me.'

'You can't kill him,' Charlie screamed.

'You watch me.' Colin's eyes blazed.

'You can't kill Dean because he's not Naz's favourite. Nathaniel is, isn't he, Naz?'

Naz stared hard at Charlie.

'He's the one you love the best, isn't he Naz? It's Nathaniel?' She nodded slightly. Naz stared back, their eyes locking momentarily.

'It's always been Nathaniel. You know that, Charlie.' Naz nodded in return. 'He might be naughty. He might be cheeky and do my head in, but he's my special boy.'

'And Dean? He's just second best, isn't he?'

Naz nodded.

'So you see, Colin. Kill him and you'll be doing Naz a favour. She won't have to put up with Dean anymore. She can just have Nathaniel; just the two of them. Bet your mum wished she could have got rid of you and just had Tommy. Bet she would have loved it if it had been you falling down that cliff face. Watching you scream.'

'Shut up, shut up. She loved me really.'

'No she didn't, Colin, she just put up with you because she had to. It was Tommy she loved, just like it's Nathaniel that Naz loves, not Dean. Your mother hated you. She even chose death rather than you, what does that say, Colin?'

He couldn't listen to her anymore. He had to stop her screaming at him. Clasping his hands over his ears, he tried to block the voices out. He had to stop the noise. He was in the cupboard again and she was screaming at him, telling him he wasn't good enough, that she loved Tommy more; that she'd always loved Tommy more. And she was downing vodka now and pills and her face was nasty and sneering at him and she didn't love him, she'd never loved him.

And he was falling down. She was pushing him and he was grasping at the air to stop him from falling and he had nothing in his hands, nothing to grab hold of as he fell off the cliff. And then he opened his eyes and there was a strange woman that he half recognized pushing him downwards into the grass and she was shouting and other people were running out of the bushes and he wanted to die, but he wasn't dead and he knew that this woman who was lying across him was in control and he could do nothing to stop everything happening around him.

Metal cuffs were being clamped around his wrists now as he was pushed face down into the mud. Hands were all over him, pressing against his arms, his legs, going through his pockets, round his waistband, pushing his face further down into the soil. His other knife was pulled from up his sleeve and taken away. He could smell the soil and he wanted to be down inside it, like all the favourites were, buried and decomposing next to their mummies. He wanted to be like Tommy, dead and lying next to his mother in the earth, but as he was lifted up on to his feet, he looked into the woman's eyes and he knew he'd been beaten again. He could hear the words now, 'Colin Butler I'm arresting you for murder', but the words were fading again and he could see his mother's mouth chewing up tablets and swigging from a bottle, and bits of tablets were dripping from the sides of her mouth and vodka was dribbling out the corners and down her chin and she was laughing at him while she chewed and swallowed and chewed and spat and he couldn't watch anymore, and as he felt himself being dragged away from the copse he threw his head back and screamed as long and as loud as he could scream.

Chapter 43

Dana wailed in agony as her gag was removed. She clung to her daughter's lifeless body, refusing to be lifted out of the pit, cradling Gemma's head against her breast while she sobbed unashamedly. Charlie watched appalled as the spotlights were turned on the grisly scene, knowing that a man she had until that day worked and socialized with was responsible. If only they had realized sooner, she could have saved Gemma. If only they'd had a bit more luck. If only Colin hadn't had been there when she'd brought Olga in.

If only...

Naz stood next to her, staring blankly down into the pit at the two women, her eyes filled with tears. It had been Naz that had led them so quickly to this copse and she was ready to point out the other pits. Colin had made her and Dean stop over various sites, but she too had only realized the significance when shown her own. 'That could have been me and Dean if Colin had done what he was planning. Thank God you got to us when you did.'

Charlie put an arm around her shoulder and squeezed her gently, watching as the tears fell unabated down her friend's cheeks.

'I only wish we'd worked it out sooner. Gemma might still have been alive.'

'He had us all fooled, Charlie.' It was Naz's turn to offer comfort now. 'I can't believe I didn't suspect it was him when he was arranging to meet Dean and me. He was going to take us out for a special day, just the two of us he said, with free tickets he'd got. He even insisted I bring Dean this time, not Nathaniel. Said Nathaniel was too small for the rides and anyway Dean deserved it more because he never gave me any trouble. Why didn't I see it?'

'Because nobody suspected him. Why would we? He was part of the team and we were all working together supposedly.'

Hunter wandered across to Charlie, patting her on the back.

'I'm proud of you. Well done, Charlie. You're a star.'

Naz looked across at Hunter, curiously.

'It was Charlie here who worked it out. We were still chasing around after the wrong man. She was the one with the hunch.'

She shook her head, embarrassed.

'We all did it together. The guvnor backed me all the way. It was just a stroke of luck that it was me who spoke to Olga Kaplinski on *Crimewatch*. She told me about being involved in a similar case, years ago in Dover where a policeman had been involved.'

'But other officers might not have made the connection. You did.'

'Unfortunately he realized we were on to him, but again I was lucky in remembering a conversation I had with him when he had been angry about the hospital where he had been born being closed down.'

Naz still looked puzzled.

'So how did you know he went for *favourite* children?'

'Because he told me, after I'd stupidly let him capture me using my phone. He loved the fact that he'd caught me out. He told me everything about his childhood. How his mother had abused him, but favoured his brother, Tommy. How he had pushed Tommy off the top of a cliff and threatened his mother with a knife. How she had chosen to kill herself rather than tell him she loved him. He was killing who he deemed to be the favourites, to punish the mothers.'

'Shit.'

'That's how I came up with the idea of persuading him he'd picked the wrong son. I just had to hope that it would throw him, thinking he had let the favourite escape and was about to kill the wrong one. Thank God you backed me up on it, otherwise I've got no doubt he would have killed Dean in front of us and there would have been nothing we could have done. The armed lot would have taken him out, but that's what he wanted; to be killed in a blaze of glory. He wanted the recognition at last.'

'Rather than being the forgotten son.'

'He's been side-lined all through his life; by his mother, by his ex-wife leaving him and taking his kids, even at work, sitting in the background. He was born here originally, but after his mother died, he moved all around the country, working in Kent and Surrey constabularies, never being picked for promotion, never really being included properly because he just comes across as a sad, bitter little man.'

'Which he was.'

'Except that no one had a clue how dangerous he also was and what he was capable of. So don't blame yourself for being fooled by him. We all were.'

They fell into silence at the thought. Charlie watched as Dana was gently prised apart from her daughter's dead body, wrapped in a blanket and taken from the pit. She was still sobbing hysterically, but at least she was alive, though Charlie could hardly begin to imagine how difficult it would be for her to come to terms with Gemma's death. She knew how much her own mother had struggled to cope with Jamie's.

Thank God her plan had worked and Colin had paused in confusion, just long enough for her to launch herself at him, knocking the knife from his hand and giving the surrounding officers a chance to reach him before he could pick it up again or get to his other one. It had been difficult with her legs bound together but she'd got close enough as he'd forced her to decide on how he should kill Dean. She'd been lucky, so lucky. He could have turned the knife on her just as easily.

Fortunately too the armed officers had held their fire. Hunter had obviously realized what she was doing. When she had dived at Colin, Hunter had thrown himself towards the melee and the others had followed suit. Colin was captured alive; his plans of being pumped full of police bullets foiled. The public would be horrified and repulsed at his evil, warped world, almost as much as they all were, looking at the sights in front of them now.

With Colin taken from the scene and Dana on her way to hospital they now needed to search the whole site and track down all the other pits. God knows what they would find. Hunter had suggested Charlie and Naz go to the hospital to be checked out but Charlie was having none of it. She was determined to stay and see it through.

Naz too was refusing to leave, even though she was still in shock and desperate to comfort Dean. Charlie knew exactly why she needed to stay. They all felt responsible for allowing Colin to thrive and kill under their very noses. Of course, she knew it wasn't really their fault. He knew all the pitfalls to avoid; checking the progress of the investigation daily and using his knowledge of forensics, CCTV, phone work, to keep one step ahead the whole time.

How he must have loved the whole stalker business with Annabel that had muddied the waters and given him time to claim his last few victims. No, they had just needed luck to be on their side and in the end it had, thankfully, come from a middle-aged Eastern European lady watching *Crimewatch*. Who would have guessed that?

The whole team was now anxious to help, in any way they could. Bet and Paul had just arrived, with Bet immediately volunteering to look after Dean for Naz, her vast experience coming to good use to soothe the petrified boy. Paul was to co-ordinate the seizure of exhibits. Sabira had remained at Lambeth HQ but was obtaining the full story and statements from Olga. Hunter was in charge. And so it was with hope that Naz, with Charlie by her side, started to retrace her footsteps through the woods. Overhead, the clouds had disappeared, allowing the light from the moon and stars to cast what little light they could down on to the scene. Any other time the sky would have been stunning, a small, remote corner of London where the absence of neon lights allowed a glimpse of the firmament above in all its glory. Tonight, however, as each dark, brooding copse of trees revealed its secret, any possible beauty in the heavens was eclipsed by the pure evil of what had lay hidden beneath the soil.

Chapter 44

The sights Charlie saw that night would remain with her forever. Every last scrap of hope at finding any of their victims still alive was soon extinguished. Helena and Daisy's grave was located first, shortly followed by the decomposing remains of Julie and Richard in their copse; five bodies of women and children, whose only misfortune was to have come across the wrong man at the wrong time.

By the time she arrived back at Lambeth headquarters, it was nearly noon the following day and she was exhausted; mentally and physically. More of Colin's victims were still to be traced; Mary and Cain Townsend for a start, not to mention his own mother and brother. There could be more over the years that he had dispatched but whose disappearance he had concealed. The investigation was just beginning.

She tried to concentrate her mind on having saved Dana, Naz and Dean, but over-riding any positive thoughts were the images of those woodland graves. She would never forget them.

Other officers and colleagues were clustering around her, congratulating her on her work. They seemed overjoyed that they had at last got the killer. But they hadn't seen what she had seen.

Making her excuses, she pushed through the group and headed towards the custody area just in time to bump into Justin Latchmere being showed through to the exit by Hunter.

'What's he doing here?' she blurted out. He obviously wasn't involved in the abductions because they had Colin now. 'He's not trying to get Butler off is he?'

An image of Dana and Gemma in the pit flicked back into her memory. 'I'm sorry for your loss though.'

Justin was unusually silent, turning his head away, rather than looking her in the eye.

'Maybe if Justin here had been more honest with us in the beginning, we would have had more time to concentrate on the real suspect, rather than trying to untangle his web of lies. Anyway. He's just been bailed pending further enquiries. The custody officer took pity on him because of the circumstances and got him dealt with quickly.' Hunter said, 'I'm showing him out.'

Justin twisted back towards them. 'No charges though.'

'Even if you're not eventually charged, your career is shot to pieces. You'll never work again.' Hunter was blunt and caught Charlie's attention with his directness. 'By all accounts he was the driving force behind the assault on Keith Hubbard, not that that was a bad thing. A little bird told us that when Keith was being assaulted, his bully boys named Justin here. I think you met them, Charlie? Called themselves Bear and Ratman 'cause they thought that made them sound really tough.'

She nodded.

'Anyway the officer in the case does a bit of digging and it seems like Justin has represented them on a few occasions and got them off. Had them in his pocket, so to speak. One good deed deserves another and all that. So the officer carries on digging and then guess what he finds?'

Hunter was in his element now.

'Only that Justin here had phoned old Bear's mobile, several times in the few hours before they burst through Keith's door and beat the shit out of him. So, cutting a very long story short, Justin got nicked for conspiracy to assault. Seems like he can never say the right things these days.'

He turned to Latchmere. 'You must be losing your touch, old boy?'

Justin scowled back at Hunter.

'I haven't been charged.'

Hunter ignored him.

'That's the least of his worries, Charlie. By all accounts, the officer who's looking after Dana now, says that she wants nothing to do with him. She blames him and his womanising for everything that has happened to them. I'm very sorry for your loss too, Mr Latchmere,,, but can't say I blame Dana, can you?'

Justin was waiting for him to open the door. Hunter had his hand on the handle but was looking towards Charlie. She could still hear Dana's wail of anguish as she clung on to her daughter's body.

'Can't say I do either, Mr Latchmere,' she said eventually. 'I bet she wishes that she'd never set eyes on you.'

*

Colin Butler had been settled into a sleep period when Charlie walked through into the custody office. Although everybody who worked at Lambeth just wanted to see him given a taste of his own medicine, he was in fact getting the reverse.

He was a criminal celebrity now; another twisted serial killer to be probed and analysed and he had to be treated as such. It made her feel physically sick, especially when she thought of what he had done. She longed to be able to tell him exactly what she thought of him; how incomprehensible his crimes were; how being a police officer made what he'd done a hundred times worse; how he was supposed to be the one fighting for justice, not dispensing his own warped reality. Everything in the custody office was recorded these days though and nothing was worth risking his possible acquittal. She knew how the system worked only too well. So did Colin.

She was checking the board to make sure all the correct procedures had been followed when the door to custody was thrown open and Keith Hubbard was launched into the custody cage. He turned round as he came through, spitting and swearing towards the officer behind him who just happened to be Bill Morley. For that, he was grabbed round the shoulders and held against the railing, his head pressed flat against the metal, his face pointing away from him.

'Don't you spit at me you animal,' he murmured under his breath.

Hubbard reared up, as if to fight and then changed his mind, defeated.

'There that's better. Don't start anything you can't win.'

She watched as Bill frogmarched him over to stand in front of the custody sergeant. To his rear a whiteboard flagged the names of each person arrested and in custody and their offences. Bill turned towards her and winked.

'Great job, Charlie. Heard all about you getting Butler in. Who'd have thought, eh? The evil bastard.' He nodded towards the board. 'And I'm glad you're here now, 'cause I think you might be interested to hear what I've got to say.'

She had no idea why Hubbard was here this time. He still bore the marks of his assault. A dark mauve bruise extended all around both eyes, his nose was still slightly swollen and out of shape and his fingers bandaged and splinted. She could still hardly bear to look at him.

'You'd think he'd have given up fighting by now, wouldn't you,' Bill said, obviously reading her mind. 'Unless his opponent is a woman, of course. Those are the only fights he wins. Maybe if he'd kept his fists, and feet to himself in the first place, he wouldn't have got his whole family into this. Not that he cares.'

'If you lot had been doing your fuckin' job properly , none of this would have happened.'

Hubbard laughed suddenly, his lip curling at the side. Nodding towards the white-board above the sergeant's head, he took a step towards Charlie.

'Nice to see you've got the right man at long last. Maybe if you'd got him in the beginning you wouldn't have had to come hassling me and had that nasty fall, if you get what I mean.'

He leered towards her, looking her up and down as he spoke the last words.

Bill Morley was having none of it. Grabbing Hubbard by the arm, he pushed him up against the sergeant's desk, lifting his handcuffed wrists up slightly at the rear so that Hubbard was forced up on to his toes, whimpering out in pain.

'Sarge, I have arrested this man for GBH on DC Charlie Stafford here.'

He looked across and winked at her again. 'Further evidence has come to light and the CPS has advised that he should be arrested and charged with her GBH. I have all the statements and paperwork to show you.'

He turned to her, this time grinning broadly. 'I've been looking forward to saying that for a long time. You might want to go to the first interview room. Everything will be explained there.'

Charlie was amazed. She'd had no idea this was about to happen or what the new evidence was. Surely they'd got everything they could have got the first time. Still, the news was just the tonic she needed. Hubbard was quiet now, brooding on the details. She rubbed her fingers carefully against the scar on her head. It was still tender to the touch. As she walked towards the interview room, she turned one last time to look at the man who could so easily have killed her. She still hated every molecule of the man.

'Looks like we did get the right man after all, doesn't it?' she put her finger to her lips as Hubbard went to speak. 'Now shut it, and don't open them again unless it's to say "Guilty" in court.'

*

Meg was sitting in the interview room when Charlie walked in. She got up immediately and opened her arms towards her. Although, curious to know why she was there Charlie couldn't have been more delighted. She almost fell into her mother's arms, feeling the tiredness wash over her as she rested her head against her shoulder. They didn't need to say anything. Perhaps it was better that way. They'd only muck it up.

'What are you doing here?' she asked eventually, confused. Today was throwing more surprises at her than she could ever have imagined.

Meg ignored her, her face full of concern. 'You look shattered, love.'

'I am, Mum. It's been a long time since I slept.'

'It sounds like you've been busy. I've been hearing all about how my daughter saved the day.' She hugged her close. 'I'm very proud of you.'

'Thanks mum, but it wasn't just down to me. Anyway, what are you doing here?'

Meg pulled a chair up for Charlie, sitting down on the one next to it and patted the seat for her sit down. She did as she was told, smiling at the realization that she always did as her mother instructed.

'Well?'

'Well,' Meg took hold of her hand. 'You're not the only one who has been busy. Do you remember me telling you recently I'd taken on two new boys that were special needs in a new school?'

She nodded, vaguely remembering the conversation.

'Well it wasn't any old school. It was Ryan Hubbard's

school. I had to do something, so I persuaded my boss to let me go on a placement. I phoned the school direct and offered my services as a child and adolescence mental health service counsellor. I said I was doing work on the mental health of young adolescents who had been traumatized by recent events. Did they have any children that might fit this category? Luckily they came back to me with two, one of whom was Ryan, as I'd hoped. They didn't have a clue you and I were connected, otherwise I doubt they would have ever let me work with him. I know it was a bit unethical, but I couldn't bear what that man, Keith, had done to you and how he'd got away with it.'

Meg shuffled in her seat, looking uncomfortable. She ran her fingers through her hair, trying to flatten out a stubborn wave, and tilted her head to one side. Charlie suddenly realized how alike they both were.

'You know me. I can't just let these things go. I thought that if I worked with Ryan and befriended him I might be able to find out what really happened that night and whether Ryan had witnessed anything.'

'But Hubbard said Ryan was in a room downstairs and didn't see anything.'

'Yeah, well it turns out that Ryan has managed to see an awful lot more than his dad thought he had. He's a sweet kid really, always eager to please. Even in the short period of time that I worked with him, he got quite attached to me and I to him. I gave him lots of attention, something he apparently hadn't had from either parent, and he responded straight away. I would read with him and was there to give him any extra support he needed. Even though it's only been a few weeks he started to talk very openly about what's been happening recently.

'The other day he came in with a load of bruises on his arms and a cut at the side of his mouth. He wouldn't tell me where they came from to start with. Anyway, as luck would have it, we had a visit from the local schools police officer that day. He was only doing a talk about road safety but it seemed to get Ryan on edge. I had a session with him straight afterwards and we started chatting. He said he wanted to tell the police officer something but last time he'd spoken to one, his dad had beaten him up. I asked him what he meant. He said that he had seen his dad beaten up the other night by two men who had forced their way into the house. He'd heard exactly what they had said to his dad. He even heard their names, Bear and Ratman.

'He didn't tell the paramedics or police at the time what they had said because Keith had told him not to, but afterwards the police had come and spoken to him again and he thought he should tell them, because his dad's injuries looked so bad. He thought he was doing the right thing. The two attackers got arrested a few days ago, as has the main guy Ryan said they'd mentioned. Keith was asked again if he wanted to press charges but he still didn't want to know. Of course he found out that it had been Ryan who had spilled the beans. That's how Ryan got the bruises. Apparently Keith gave him a backhand across the face and threw him about a bit.'

'Poor kid,' Charlie was horrified. 'I know what it's like to be on the receiving end of that man's fury. I thought he stooped low enough beating up women, without taking it out on kids too. So what happened then?'

'Well… Ryan was in a right state. He was upset and angry. He told me he hated his father and didn't want to live with him anymore and that he wished his mother had taken him away too when she disappeared with Richard. He kept punching his fist down on the table. I told him he should tell the police what his father had done to him, but he said it was no use, because his mum had tried that in the past and nothing had happened. Keith would just take it out on him even more. I tried to say that wouldn't happen, but it's sad really; even at his young age he's realized that victims don't get the help they need.

'Then he went all quiet. I asked him if he was OK. He said that he knew something that his father had done that would mean he would get sent to prison for a long time. I think I guessed what he was about to say, but it was still a shock when he told me. He said he'd been there that day when you and Hunter had come round. He said how his dad was in a foul mood thinking his mum had walked out on them. He had been swearing and shouting and going round the house taking down all the photos of the family and scrubbing and cleaning every little thing that reminded him of them. He was calling her a bitch and saying how he hated women. Ryan had pretty much hidden himself in the lounge with the Play-station. Anyway, he remembered you arriving and talking to his dad and how he was worried when his dad followed you up the stairs. I think he kind of knew what might happen. He left the Play-station on so that it sounded as if he was still playing and went into the hallway to see what his dad was doing. Charlie, he saw his father kick you down the stairs and laugh at you lying crumpled at the bottom.'

'And he didn't say anything…?'

'He wanted to, but he was too scared. His mum and brother were gone and he was frightened that he'd lose his dad too. At that point, having a father like that was better than not having a father at all. Since Keith has turned on him though, he knows that it will never end. His dad will do this again and again, just like he did to his mum.

'I told him he was a brave boy to have told me and that I was very proud of him for having the courage to speak to me about it. But in the back of my mind I knew I needed to get him to tell someone else. If I went to the police with what he'd said, they could just say I'd made it up. Certainly any defence would. So I persuaded him to tell his teacher. Once his teacher knew it was easier to then go to the police.

'So that's what I've been doing. Ryan came with me and his teacher and made a statement about what he'd seen that night and also what Keith had done to him more recently. I didn't tell you or Hunter because I didn't want to get your hopes up if the CPS refused to charge, and anyway you were too busy. Luckily the new investigating officer in the case has done a great job. I even got to speak to the same CPS lawyer that was at court with us. He remembered the case and how he felt that we'd been badly let down by the system. He wrote the advice for Keith Hubbard to be further arrested and charged, Charlie. He thinks we should have no problem now we have an actual witness, albeit the defendant's son. Hopefully Hubbard will plead guilty, rather than drag his son into the witness box, but even if he does, Ryan is adamant he will do whatever he needs to this time. He's living with his grandparents at the moment. I'd like to stay in touch with him, if he wants me to. As I say, he's a good kid who just wants to do the right thing.'

Charlie was amazed. Meg had not said a word about what she was up to, but all this time she had been quietly working towards this moment. After being failed by the justice system after Jamie's death, the family were at least being allowed the chance to obtain justice for her this time.

'Thanks Mum.' No other words were needed.

Wordlessly, Meg put an arm around her and gently pulled her head down on to her shoulder. She tensed but then relaxed and allowed herself to rest, though it did feel strange. Meg was more practical, than demonstrative. The sights and sounds of the last day all seemed to blur.

There was a knock on the door and Hunter poked his head in, grinning from ear to ear.

'I've just been told the news, Charlie. I'm so pleased. Meg, now I know where she gets it from.' He threw an arm around each of them and kissed Meg enthusiastically on the cheek. 'Oh, and look who else I just found, skulking about by the gates.'

He pushed the door ajar and she could just see Ben propped up on his crutches against the wall. He looked freshly showered and smart.

'Sorry,' he sounded a little embarrassed. 'I heard how well you'd done getting that madman and I thought I'd try and catch you by the gate. I just wanted to say congratulations. Your boss here saw me and literally frogmarched me in. I didn't mean to intrude.'

She lifted her head off Meg's shoulder and smiled towards him.

'You're not intruding at all, Ben. It's lovely to see you. Hunter is just about to take us home and, if you'd like to join us, Mum here will make us all brunch, won't you Mum?' She turned towards Meg who shrugged.

'Do I have a choice?'

'No, of course not. Not when it comes to home-cooking. Ben, she's the best.'

A few minutes later, Charlie, Ben and Meg were sat in Hunter's Jag as he pulled slowly out on to the main road. A dozen or so journalists parted to let them through and within minutes Hunter was away from them and heading homeward.

'Thank God they moved quickly?' she breathed a sigh of relief. 'I had a sudden vision of a bowling ball hurtling towards ten pins.'

'Strike one,' Ben shouted and they all laughed. A sudden surge of relief swept through her at the knowledge she would soon be back in the safety of her family home, with food and sleep awaiting. Having Ben there was a bonus.

She was just starting to drift off slightly when Hunter slowed at some pedestrian lights by a small parade of shops. A small group of youths sat on the back of a bench under a nearby tree. Her eyes scanned over them hazily, taking in the nonchalant way the tallest of them threw an empty beer can on to the ground next to the tree and stamped down on it. He obviously couldn't care less and it annoyed her. She peered at him again, concentrating on his posture and the way his chin jutted out arrogantly as he moved. Suddenly she remembered why she recognised him.

'Stop the car,' she shouted, opening the door and running towards the rear of the bench before the others knew what was going on. Deftly, she grabbed hold of the youth, dragging him down on to the ground, where she pinned him to the concrete, kneeling on his arms so that he couldn't move. He barely had time to shout out or struggle before she had him detained. The other youths jumped off the bench and stared at their friend.

'Police! Get back,' she roared, worried for a brief moment that they would try to free him.

She could hear the sound of footsteps running towards them as Hunter came into view, red faced and panting at even this small exertion. The other youths turned and sprinted off and then Hunter was with her, kneeling down to help keep her captive restrained.

The youth was still now after a brief struggle.

'What's going on?' Hunter raised his eyebrows towards her questioningly.

She could see Ben swinging himself towards them on his crutches. Meg hurried alongside.

'Wait a sec.'

'What's going on?' Ben repeated Hunter's question as he joined them. The youth turned his head to look at who was talking and a look of recognition crossed his face.

'It's you!' Ben's look was stern. 'I should give you the same pasting as you gave me when I was down on the floor, you cowardly bastard.' He stopped a foot away from the youth's face and lifted one of the crutches in line with his head.

'Well, if it's not our fallen hero,' the boy sneered, trying and failing to raise his head further as Charlie leant down on his shoulders. He spat impotently towards Ben. 'Go on then, hit me, if you've got the bottle. Oh wait, you can't, can you, you've probably drunk it and chucked it away.'

She saw Ben tense as the youth sniggered. He stood stock-still staring at him for what seemed like ages then lowered the crutch and shook his head, a brief glimpse of sadness replacing the anger.

'You're not worth it. I'm better than you and I always will be. I wouldn't kick a man when he was down, like you did, because you have no honour.'

'Oh yeah prove it.'

'You've just done that for us,' she pointed towards the spittle. 'We'll compare that against the spit you left last time. I recognized you as soon as I saw you, but if they don't believe our identifications they'll believe the DNA. Cheers.'

'Strike two,' Ben added, raising his hands and clapping them against Charlie's.

*

The blue lights were fading from view when Meg turned towards Charlie.

'How on earth did you know it was him?'

'I'm not a super-recognizer for nothing, you know!' She laughed, yawned and rested her head back down on her mother's shoulder.

'I never forget a face.'

We hope you enjoyed this book!

Sarah Flint's next book is coming in spring 2017

More addictive fiction from Aria:

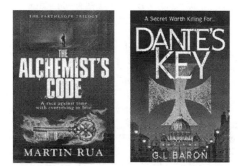

Find out more
http://headofzeus.com/books/isbn/9781784977474

Find out more
http://headofzeus.com/books/isbn/9781784977511

Acknowledgements

My agent Judith Murdoch once said to me that it often took many years of trying before getting to where you wanted to be – I have to say she wasn't wrong; even though at the time I hoped she would be.

Judith has had the utmost patience over the years when I was producing little – and not even that often. She has been my mentor and friendly counsellor and has never put any pressure on me and for all of this, I am immensely grateful.

My appreciation too, to Caroline Ridding at Aria who has already proved to be welcoming and encouraging and seems willing to take a chance on me – I hope I meet your expectations.

After small successes with a couple of early novels it has taken many years in the wilderness trying to find a central character I loved. In the end experience always seems to be best. Charlie (and Hunter) are therefore based very loosely on people I worked with. Some of you may recognise them. I hope you will all love them. The Metropolitan Police Service is full of great characters, from all walks of life, the great majority of whom just want to do the best they can for the public and serve their communities, sometimes at great personal cost. I can honestly say I have loved the Job and the many colleagues I have had the pleasure to work with. My thanks to all of them for great memories past and present.

My gratitude also goes to all my friends, who have listened to my woes over the years and encouraged me to keep trying.

I would also like to say a huge thank you to my three gorgeous daughters, all of whom I am extremely proud and who have supported me unfailingly through a difficult few years. Every year they are displaying more and more of the family spirit.

Big thanks to my inspirational family, particularly to all my brothers and sisters for their continued belief and support and the way they have actively canvassed their friends to read my earlier efforts. I have to especially mention Dee Yates, my eldest sister who was the inspiration for me to start writing, having written several books herself. She, above all, has provided the encouragement, positivity and proof reading skills to keep me going. Thank you, Dee.

Last but by no means least, lots of thanks to my lovely partner for putting up with my ups and downs and who is always there to pour oil on troubled waters – and red wine in my glass.

Cheers and many thanks to you all.

About Sarah Flint

With a Metropolitan Police career spanning 35 years Sarah has spent her adulthood surrounded by victims, criminals and police officers. She continues to work and lives in London with her partner and has three older daughters.

Become an Aria Addict

Aria is the new digital-first fiction imprint from Head of Zeus.

It's Aria's ambition to discover and publish tomorrow's superstars, targeting fiction addicts and readers keen to discover new and exciting authors.

Aria will publish a variety of genres under the commercial fiction umbrella such as women's fiction, crime, thrillers, historical fiction, saga and erotica.

So, whether you're a budding writer looking for a publisher or an avid reader looking for something to escape with – Aria will have something for you.

Get in touch: aria@headofzeus.com

Become an Aria Addict
http://www.ariafiction.com

Find us on Twitter
https://twitter.com/Aria_Fiction

Find us on Facebook
http://www.facebook.com/ariafiction

Find us on BookGrail
http://www.bookgrail.com/store/aria/

Addictive Fiction

First published in the UK in 2016 by Aria, an imprint of Head of Zeus Ltd

9 7 5 3 1 2 4 6 8

A CIP catalogue record for this book is available from the British Library.

Cover design: stuartpolsondesign.com

ISBN (E) 9781786690692

Aria
Clerkenwell House
45-47 Clerkenwell Green
London EC1R 0HT

www.ariafiction.com

45575705R00155

Made in the USA
Middletown, DE
07 July 2017